Extraordinary Praise for

A Fine Summer's Day

and the Inspector Ian Rutledge Mysteries

"An excellent tale. As always when it comes to Charles Todd, this mother/son team of authors are in-depth, refined, and offer up a true thriller of a story."   —*Suspense* magazine on *A Fine Summer's Day*

"A very welcome addition to, and expansion of, a much-loved series."
—*Booklist* on *A Fine Summer's Day*

"The books are Charles Todd recounting the cases of Scotland Yard Inspector Ian Rutledge in the days following WWI are as quintessentially English as anything by Ruth Rendell, P. D. James or John Harvey. . . . These are some of the finest historical mystery novels in print. . . . Todd [is] in top form again."
—*BookPage* on *A Fine Summer's Day*

"Readers familiar with the series can't imagine a Rutledge who doesn't hear the voice of MacLeod in his head, and this novel adds poignancy to the Rutledge we avidly follow. Grade: A"
—*Cleveland Plain Dealer* on *A Fine Summer's Day*

"A tight plot keeps readers on the edge until the stunning final pages."
—*Library Journal* on *A Fine Summer's Day*

"*A Fine Summer's Day* is a high point in this evocative series that has never disappointed."   —*South Florida Sun Sentinel*

"Pure fun for fans."   —*Charlotte Observer* on *A Fine Summer's Day*

"A bittersweet gift to longtime readers of this wonderful series."
—Marilyn Stasio, *New York Times Book Review* on *A Fine Summer's Day*

"*A Fine Summer's Day* is an absolute pleasure to read and a true treat for faithful readers of this series."
—Bookreporter.com

"Tricky plotting and rich atmospherics distinguish bestseller Todd's 16th novel featuring Scotland Yard's Insp. Ian Rutledge. . . . Todd (the pen name of a mother-son writing team) has rarely been better."
—*Publishers Weekly* (starred review) on *Hunting Shadows*

"Another well-written, well-plotted entry in this always engaging mystery series."
—*Booklist* on *Hunting Shadows*

"Another winner. . . . Strong atmosphere and a complicated mystery make this book one that readers won't be able to put down."
—*Romantic Times* (4.5 stars) on *Hunting Shadows*

"As always, the North Carolina-based mother and son who write under the pseudonym Charles Todd do a beautiful job with the period detail, making these books a nostalgic outing to England between the world wars."
—*News & Observer* (Raleigh, NC) on *Hunting Shadows*

"Readers who stick with the chase, though, should be enthralled, as Rutledge sorts through a fascinating portrait gallery of witnesses and suspects, most of whom aren't telling him the whole truth."
—*Wilmington News Journal* on *Hunting Shadows*

"Of all the places where Inspector Ian Rutledge's Scotland Yard assignments have taken him, the desolate Fen country must surely be the eeriest. [This is an] excellent historical series."
—*New York Times Book Review* on *Hunting Shadows*

"Elusive clues, suspense and excellent writing make for reading pleasure." —*Oklahoma City Oklahoman* on *Hunting Shadows*

"You're going to love Todd."
—Stephen King, *Entertainment Weekly* on *A Question of Honor*

"As with any good mystery, the tension ramps up as the story progresses, pulling more and more characters into the fray, weaving three murders flawlessly into a tight tale. Mr. Todd's characterization is his strength." —NewYorkJournalofBooks.com on *The Confession*

"Another excellent Inspector Ian Rutledge mystery. . . . You follow a twisting road when you read this book. You won't soon forget your trip to Furnham and the people who may not be who they seem to be." —*Suspense* magazine on *The Confession*

"A gripping whodunit." —*Publishers Weekly* on *Proof of Guilt*

"Another dark and gripping saga."
—*Washington Times* on *Proof of Guilt*

"With its typically intricate plotting, detailed characterizations, and red herrings, this is a compelling addition to the popular Ian Rutledge series." —*Library Journal* on *A Duty to the Dead*

"[A] complex British-style police procedural that explores the intersection of justice and vengeance served up cold. It's especially recommended for readers who relish P. D. James's Adam Dalgliesh mysteries." —*Boston Globe* on *A Matter of Justice*

A FINE SUMMER'S DAY

Also by Charles Todd

The Ian Rutledge Mysteries

A Test of Wills

Wings of Fire

Search the Dark

Legacy of the Dead

Watchers of Time

A Fearsome Doubt

A Cold Treachery

A Long Shadow

A False Mirror

A Pale Horse

A Matter of Justice

The Red Door

A Lonely Death

The Confession

Proof of Guilt

Hunting Shadows

The Bess Crawford Mysteries

A Duty to the Dead

An Impartial Witness

A Bitter Truth

An Unmarked Grave

A Question of Honor

An Unwilling Accomplice

Other Fiction

The Murder Stone

The Walnut Tree

A FINE SUMMER'S DAY

An Inspector Ian Rutledge Mystery

Charles Todd

wm WILLIAM MORROW
An Imprint of HarperCollins*Publishers*

P.S.™ is a trademark of HarperCollins Publishers.

A FINE SUMMER'S DAY. Copyright © 2015 by Charles Todd. All rights reserved. Printed in the United States of America. No part of this book may be used or reproduced in any manner whatsoever without written permission except in the case of brief quotations embodied in critical articles and reviews. For information address HarperCollins Publishers, 195 Broadway, New York, NY 10007.

HarperCollins books may be purchased for educational, business, or sales promotional use. For information please e-mail the Special Markets Department at SPsales@harpercollins.com.

A hardcover edition of this book was published in 2015 by William Morrow, an imprint of HarperCollins Publishers.

FIRST WILLIAM MORROW PAPERBACK EDITION PUBLISHED 2015.

Map by Nick Springer, copyright © 2014 Springer Cartographics LLC

Library of Congress Cataloging-in-Publication Data has been applied for.

ISBN 978-0-06-223713-2

19   OV/LSC   10 9 8 7 6 5

1914—1918

To the men and women who served and died in the Great War. And to
those who waited at home for the knock on the door and the telegram
that informed them their loved ones had made the ultimate sacrifice.
And not least to the wounded and the survivors, who ever afterward
carried the mark of that war on their flesh and in their minds.

And to John, whose war was different.

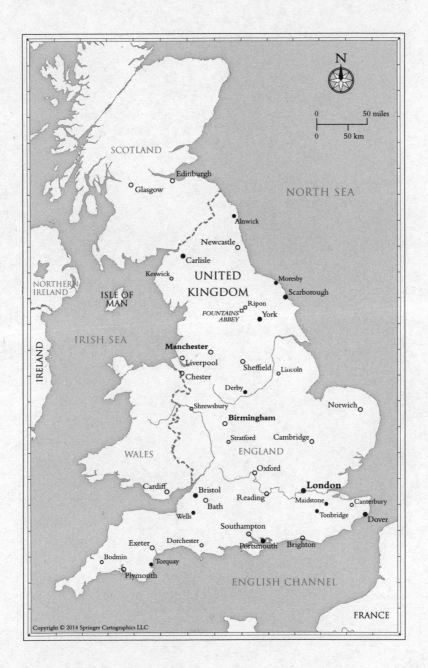

I

I t was a fine summer's day in England.

In fact, one of a string of bright days, languid and unhurried, full of promise. As if the weeks to come stretched out in an endless spool of long, leisurely afternoons on the lawn, croquet mallets and tea trays, men in summer white, women in frothy wide-brimmed hats, and girls with blue ribbon sashes. Peaceful, measured, and like the Empire, destined to go on forever.

The distant sound of gunfire was too faint to hear. It disturbed no dreams, it marred no plans, it stirred no fears.

Nevertheless, before the sun set on this fine summer day, the lives of a handful of people would have been changed by murder.

I an Rutledge drove down to Kent on Friday morning, having been given leave from his duties at Scotland Yard after a fortnight of hunting a suspect through Derbyshire. With him was Jean Gordon, whom he'd been seeing for some time.

Melinda Crawford had invited a number of people for a house party, taking advantage of the fine weather. She was an excellent hostess, and everyone had a very pleasant weekend.

By Sunday afternoon the party had begun to break up. Frances Rutledge had said good-bye to her brother and Melinda shortly after the alfresco luncheon, traveling back to London with the Kerrs, who had brought her down. Ross Trevor, Rutledge's close friend, had gone off to the tennis court with another guest, demanding revenge for a disastrous defeat on Saturday afternoon. And Ian had strolled in the direction of the lake with Miss Gordon.

Melinda sat in her favorite wicker chair on the terrace, shaded by a white lace parasol trimmed with pale green ribbons. With half her mind she listened to the shouts and laughter from the tennis players, easily picking out Ross Trevor's baritone. Despite his high spirits, she thought he was unhappy about something. Or someone. She had tried to speak to Ian about that, but the Gordon woman clung to him like a limpet. If she got no satisfaction from Ian before the weekend was over, she'd say something to David Trevor, Ross's father and Ian's godfather, when next she saw him.

But much as she cared for him, it wasn't Ross Trevor who had occupied her thoughts most of this weekend. It was Ian and the girl he'd apparently become rather serious about. Frances had mentioned Jean Gordon in a few of her letters, which in itself was a sign. Melinda had noted it and acted accordingly. She made a point of traveling to London several times, but Ian had been busy at the Yard, and she'd had only a few opportunities to meet Jean.

The girl was lovely, there was no doubt of that. Small and delicate-boned, bright and charming, from an excellent family. A perfect choice, in many ways, and together they did make quite a handsome pair. But Melinda had found Jean shallow. That was when she had decided to arrange a house party. It was important, she told herself, to be fair, to give the girl a chance. Jean could have been overawed by the attentions of Ian's formidable, elderly family connection. And so Melinda had drawn up a list of young people, arranged for caterers and a small orchestra for Saturday evening, and then invited Ian first, to be absolutely certain he could come down.

And the more time she'd spent in Miss Gordon's company, the more she dreaded the thought that Ian might marry her.

Melinda, old enough to be Ian Rutledge's grandmother, had been friends with his parents before he was born. And of all the young people she was close to, this was the one she loved the most. Frances, attractive and bright, had inherited her mother's grace and steadiness. She would do very well. And Ross too, in the end, whatever was worrying him at the moment. Melinda's young cousin Bess had her mother's spirit and her father's clear mind. There was nothing to worry about there. She'd been invited for the weekend as well, of course, but she and her parents were in the south of France visiting with friends from India.

In spite of her careful planning, the weekend had not gone precisely as Melinda Crawford had expected. Jean had seized the chance to spend more time in Ian's company, and rather than sharing him with the other guests, she had often contrived to separate him from his sister and his friend Ross.

Now, trying to tell herself that a walk through the wood to the lake was cooler than the tennis court, and that it was the only reason Ian and Jean had gone off on their own, Melinda waited for them to return. They had set out after lunch, talking companionably as they disappeared into the trees. They had also disappeared for a while after dinner the night before, and she'd found them in the gardens. Their voices low, their laughter intimate, their chairs drawn close. She had been fearful that he might propose then, but nothing had been said at breakfast, and Melinda had felt almost faint with relief.

Perhaps Ian *had* planned to speak to Jean last evening, she thought, and for some reason changed his mind. Perhaps seeing so much of the girl had given him pause. He was an Inspector now at the Yard—well thought of, his career assured. Melinda had friends in high places, and when she met them in London for a luncheon or a dinner, they'd begun to mention Rutledge's prospects in their conversations. Of course it wouldn't be surprising if he had begun to think of marriage. After all, he would soon be twenty-five, and he could afford to keep a wife. But pray God, not Jean!

Ian was a strong-minded man. He'd chosen to become a police-man rather than join the family firm of solicitors, which had set the cat amongst the pigeons. His father had not been happy with the decision. This was his only son, and he'd seen to his education with an eye to a future in law. But Ian had eventually won him over and joined the Metropolitan Police as a constable on the street. To no one's surprise in the family, he'd earned promotion after promotion on his own merit. Intelligent, with a quick wit and a sense of humor, he would have succeeded in whatever he'd wanted to do with his life.

But Jean, who was noticeably ambitious, had astonished Melinda by commenting that she thought it rather fun to be acquainted with a policeman. As if this were a hobby that Rutledge would soon tire of and come to his senses.

Melinda, knowing the man, knowing how he thought and felt, had nearly snapped that it was as unlikely to happen as it was to snow in London in July. But she'd bit her tongue in time.

What was keeping them? Impatient, worried, she sat there facing the wood, watching for them, sending up a silent prayer that it would *not* be now. That there would still be time to introduce him to other more suitable young women before he made his choice . . .

Melinda would have worried a great deal more if she'd known what was in his pocket. The small green velvet box he'd carried around with him for a fortnight. Rutledge was very conscious of it now as he walked beside Jean. He'd debated with himself for days about proposing this weekend. It had seemed a romantic thing to do, here in Kent, at Melinda's house, which he'd always known nearly as well as his own home. After his parents' deaths, he'd come here as often as he could, bringing his sister with him. She was younger, and the loss had hit her particularly hard.

Last night, in the dark garden, the stars wonderfully bright and close, he'd been sorely tempted to go down on one knee. He couldn't have said afterward why he hadn't. It wasn't a matter of courage. Or doubt. He was in love with Jean. And he was fairly certain she loved him. That she would accept him.

She was sweet, vivacious, amazingly pretty, and amusing. He could imagine the years stretching out before them, growing old together, loving and being loved.

Frances hadn't been particularly keen when he'd told her what he was thinking.

"Are you quite sure, Ian? Look at Mama and Papa. They had the most wonderful marriage. To the very end. Won't you grow tired of Jean? Won't you find that over the years she's more than a little—narrow?"

But he'd laughed and told Frances that she would find that having a sister would make it easier for her to fill the void of their parents' deaths. The last thing he wanted was for her to feel shut out of his life, left behind with the past.

But Melinda had said much the same thing to him on one of her visits to London, and he hadn't been able to smile and reassure her in quite the same way. Melinda was no fool, and he valued her opinion. He told himself she hardly knew Jean, that for his sake, in time she'd come to love the woman he married. Still, he'd waited. When the invitation to the house party in Kent had arrived in the post, he took it as a peace offering from Melinda, and was grateful.

As they stepped out of the shadows of the wood, sunlight was dancing across the lake. White swans moved serenely over the surface, their half-grown cygnets trailing behind.

"How beautiful it is," Jean said softly, as if afraid to break the spell.

And how beautiful she looked, he thought, watching her as her gaze followed the swans, her hair like spun gold in the light.

"A penny for your thoughts," he said.

"I was thinking that they have not a care in the world," she replied. "The swans. I should like to have a lake and swans one day. It would be lovely to stand by it and watch them for hours at a time."

Hardly the right beginning for a proposal, he thought wryly. On an Inspector's pay at Scotland Yard, there was no likelihood of such a lake in the near future. He hadn't touched the trust his parents had left him, and he had his eye on a flat convenient to the Yard. The Rutledge house, where he lived presently, was to be Frances's when she turned twenty-one. Less than six months from now . . .

They strolled on toward the gazebo, set by the water's edge. Jean was saying, "Are you happy, Ian? There's something on your mind. Is it Frances?"

Rutledge was saved from answering as the heel of Jean's shoe mired down in the soft earth by the gazebo. Laughing, she reached for his arm, and he bent down to retrieve her shoe. Holding on to him, she limped on one foot as far as the gazebo, and he helped her up the steps to one of the cushioned seats overlooking the softly lapping water.

"Perhaps a lake isn't the best feature for a garden after all," she said archly as she sat down, reluctantly letting go of his arm.

He knelt to help her put the shoe on again, and as she bent her own head to watch, he said, "Jean."

Something in his voice warned her. She caught her breath, and didn't answer.

"My dear," he began, and then with a smile, he added simply, "will you marry me, Jean?"

She put her hand to her throat. For an instant he thought she was going to say no. Or ask if she could have a few days to think about her answer.

In the silence, all he could hear was the murmur of bees busy among the flowers by the steps and the soft movement of water among the reeds.

And then she whispered, "Yes."

Sarajevo was a Serbian town in the Balkans, a place of no particular importance to the rest of the world. A part of the Ottoman Empire for generations, it had been annexed to the Austrian Empire through the Treaty of Berlin in 1878. Not everyone was happy about that. There had been more than a little trouble over it, and the Serbs had been behind a number of bloody assassinations.

Archduke Ferdinand, the heir to the Austro-Hungarian Empire, had come to Sarajevo on a state visit to review troops and open a museum, for God's sake, a duty hardly worthy of the honor of having a Habsburg present for the occasion. But he loved his wife, Sophie, and only in these lackluster outposts of Empire was she given the status of an equal with him. In Vienna, in the eyes of the court, a Czech countess had no standing, and so she walked well behind him, sat far from him at table, and would never be crowned Empress when he succeeded to the throne of his uncle. He'd been forced to accept a galling morganatic marriage, which branded her as unworthy of his high estate. It was only on those terms that the Emperor would permit him to choose Sophie.

And so they were together here in Sarajevo, she in an elegant hat and gown, he in uniform, feathers in his helmet blowing in the soft breeze, to be honored and feted side by side. Only it didn't quite work out as planned.

On the way into the city from the railway station, a bomb had been thrown under the motorcar they should have been riding in, wounding a number of the Archduke's staff. That had upset the Archduke and his wife, and the welcoming speech at City Hall had not gone well. The Mayor's hospitable words to a man who'd just narrowly missed being blown up fell on deaf ears.

The Archduke was eager to visit the wounded in hospital, and it was arranged that they would be driven there. Again, they took the third motorcar, open so that they could be seen, and set out.

There was some confusion about the route, and close by the Latin Bridge, the driver made a wrong turn.

The crowds had thinned noticeably. The Archduke frowned but said nothing. Beside him his wife stirred anxiously. It wasn't the most direct route. But perhaps it was the safer one?

A handful of assassins had set out that morning, determined to kill their high-ranking guest. A blow for the freedom of the Serbian people. But most of them had got cold feet and failed to act. Only one man had actually thrown his bomb, but at the wrong motorcar. He'd been captured almost at once. However, the youngest, most zealous assassin had continued to shadow the royal couple. And now he saw his chance. Unfortunately he was armed not with a bomb but with a pistol.

The Archduke, a smile pinned to his face despite the lack of interest along the street in this part of town, froze as someone darted out toward the carriage, a dark young man in dark clothes. Almost in slow motion he saw the raised pistol in the assassin's hand, the scowl on his face. In the same instant he realized that no one was trying to stop the fool. His first thought was of his wife, but before he could move to shield her, the man fired at almost point-blank range. Sophie cried out as the bullet struck her in the stomach—she was several months' pregnant with their next child—and her blood began to spread across her white gown in an ugly red stain. The Archduke, his attention on his wife, still saw the barrel of the pistol swing up sharply again, and the second shot tore through his neck even as he reared back.

It would not be an easy death for either of them.

The driver, shocked, sped off. Not to the hospital, where something might have been done, but toward the Governor's Palace a little distance away. Sophie lay slumped against her husband, and he tried to hold her, begging her to live for his sake, for the sake of the children. But by the time they reached the Palace, she was dead, and he was nearly so.

Their killer was caught, a Serb and a member of one of the outlawed nationalist groups—aided and abetted, it turned out, by Serbian intelligence officers.

The news shocked Vienna. Archduke Ferdinand and Sophie were given a hasty, slapdash funeral, their children shunned, even as the aged Emperor demanded that something be done. For God's sake, the heir to the *throne* had been murdered, examples would have to be made, and Serbia punished for harboring assassins.

No one in Vienna reckoned on Russia's reaction.

And in Scotland that sunny afternoon, a man Ian Rutledge had never met proposed to his own sweetheart.

Hamish MacLeod had taken Fiona MacDonald to Glen Coe, to see the land his grandmother had left him. Where he intended to build a house and one day bring a wife.

They'd carried a picnic basket with them, spreading a rug across the dusty ground and laughing together as they sat down. Not quite touching, but close enough that Hamish could smell the lavender scent she wore and feel the rustle of her blue trimmed skirts against his knee as she reached inside the basket to draw out the packet of sandwiches.

It had taken some doing to persuade her family to trust her with him this day. They were strict Presbyterians, and besides it was a Sunday. He'd prayed for fine weather, and when it had dawned fair, he'd watched the sun rise with a sharp sense of elation. Fiona knew how he felt about her. She must have known that one day he intended to propose to her. But he was a patient man, giving her time to make up her own mind about *him*.

There was all the time in the world.

He had known her all his life. And then in the early spring, he'd been a guest at the wedding of a cousin, and she had been in the bridal party. With a shock, he realized, watching her, that he'd been in love with her for a very long time. And he'd sought her out the very next week, carefully crafting a chance encounter. It had, slowly, led to this moment.

Smiling at the memory, he took the sandwich she was holding out to him, then the handful of fresh strawberries.

"The house will stand just there, where the land flattens a wee bit. See the stakes driven into the ground?" he asked, pointing them out with his sandwich. "No' a grand house, ye ken, but a comfortable one. I can see it a' in my heid."

"Will it have a verandah? I've read about them in books, with chairs to sit in and ferns hanging in baskets above the white railings." She was lightly teasing, and yet he thought she was telling him that she would like to have a say in his plans.

"Ach, it will no' be any trouble to add a verandah. It will take two months to put up the house, I'm thinking. If we begin in August or September, the inside will be finished by Christmas. I'd start this week if I could, but I'm told the builders willna' have the time until well into August."

"It will be a verra' fine house," she said, and reached out to touch his hand, a spontaneous gesture.

He froze. "Lass, don't do that," he said huskily. "I'll be asking you to marry me now, this day." He tried to keep his voice level. "And I havena' asked your uncle if I could speak to you."

"And you should," she said quietly. "It's the proper thing to do. Still, it would do no harm to inquire of the lady in question if she cares for you. That's to say, before you add yon verandah."

Rising quickly, he walked a little distance from her. "Fiona. I'll no' be rich. But you'll want for nothing. You ken that. I'll take care of you as long as there's breath in my body."

She rose as well, shading her eyes as she looked toward him. "I've never doubted you, Hamish MacLeod." She hesitated. "Is it a proposal, then?"

"Aye," he said, holding out his hands. "It's a proposal. Lass, will ye have me?"

"I will," she said softly. "Yes, I will."

"Ye're verra' young, Fiona. I didna' want to rush you, I do na' want you to regret saying yes. Are ye sure?"

"I'm sure. I've been sure for weeks, now."

She came to him, taking his hands, leaning close for his kiss. He bent his head but kissed her on the cheek, gently.

He would speak to her uncle tomorrow. He had a feeling the man might make him wait until her next birthday, in September. But that was fair enough. He could wait forever for Fiona if he had to.

A nd on this same day, a man sat at the table in his mother's kitchen and listened for the undertaker's carriage. The doctor had just gone, and the silence in the house was almost more than he could bear. The ticking of the clock on the mantelpiece seemed overly loud, and after a moment, to drown it out, he got up and began to make himself a cup of tea.

She'd died of a broken heart. No matter what the doctor had given as a cause of death, Henry knew better. It had taken years to kill her, that broken heart. She'd had a son to raise, a duty to his dead father to see him right before she could give in to her grief. And yet grief had been a presence in the house for as long as he could remember.

Perhaps it was fitting that she had died on this day of all others. The anniversary of the day his father had been hanged for murder. He'd been five, and he'd sat beside his mother in this very kitchen as they watched the hands of the clock creep toward noon. And when it had chimed the hour, she had thrown the bowl of sugar at it, as if to stop it. To stop time. But the bowl had crashed harmlessly against the stone surround of the hearth, and he had knelt to sweep up the spilled sugar and the blue china bits that had been the bowl while she sat there and cried.

He hadn't understood then. Murder and hanging were incomprehensible to him. But he remembered his father being taken away by two burly constables, his mother's fists beating against their backs as she cried out and begged for a moment to say a proper good-bye.

He'd never seen his father again. He'd been left with his granny while his mother went to the Bristol Assizes and watched her husband convicted and then condemned to hang. She'd come home tight-lipped, her face nearly gray from sleepless nights and the strain of traveling to and from the trial.

"He didn't do it. I know Evan, he didn't. He couldn't have," she'd said, her voice harsh and bone dry.

He hadn't been allowed to say good-bye to the condemned man. But on each anniversary of his father's death, they had sat here together, he and his mother, his father's photograph in her worn hands, and watched the clock.

"They killed him," she'd said once. "They took him from us and *killed* him. It wasn't right. He had a family, but no one in the village cared about that. No one in Bristol gave us a thought. Cold and black-hearted all of them, and they didn't *care*."

She had never told him what his father had done. But people seldom came to the house after his father had been carried off to gaol. And his mother had had to take in mending and then washing to make ends meet. It had taken every penny they could scrape together to keep food on their table, clothes on their backs. He himself had gone to work as early as he could, to help provide for the two of them. And it was then he'd learned why his father had been hanged.

"Killed Mr. Atkins," they said. "That's what he done. In cold blood. He claimed that Mr. Atkins's son had cheated him, but it was all a lie. Young Mr. Atkins was upstanding, a good husband, a member of the church. And your father was ne'er-do-well, a nobody who liked his drink. You're no better than he is, so keep your place if you want to work here."

Henry had tried to ask his mother about what they had said, and she told him his father had been falsely accused, that Mr. Atkins's friends had refused to believe that the man could be both cruel and mean.

They hadn't cared. His mother had been right about that. When she was unable to wash the clothes of her betters, he'd done it himself, and never told a soul. Working in the back of the greengrocer's shop all day and staying up to wash the linens and the bedding and the tea towels and the stockings and overalls and God knew what. Pressing them dry, folding them neatly, and carrying them back to the people who owned them, before going on to work another day in the shop.

Taking a deep breath he tried to think what to do, now that his mother was gone. He hated this village, he hated the people in it, and he only wanted to get away. He'd stayed this long for her sake. He couldn't have left her. He could never have been that selfish.

The clock on the mantelpiece showed nearly noon. He stared at it now, waiting for the hands to reach twelve, and the little chimes to ring out. He got up and went to his mother's room, to find the photograph of his father that she'd kept by her bed. Stopping only for a moment to look down at her worn, peaceful face.

And then he went back to the kitchen, held his father's photograph in his hands as she had done and waited.

By the time the undertaker had come to fetch his mother's body, he'd made up his mind. As soon as the funeral was over, he'd go away where he wasn't known and could live a decent life.

But sitting there in the silent house, the memory of his mother's voice and her presence filled the room. He could almost hear her telling him not to leave with his tail between his legs, not to slip away in the night like a thief.

He hadn't slept the night before. He hadn't rested all through the long, lonely day. He was nearly drunk with fatigue, he hadn't eaten since noon on Friday. He couldn't think clearly. As the long rays of the summer sun faded into sunset and then into darkness, he got up finally and began to pack. Taking only what he needed, only what meant something to him or to his mother, he would be ready to set out as soon as the service ended. When he had the money, he'd send to have a stone placed on his mother's grave. A large stone. He'd see to it, if he had to starve to do it.

He debated about the clock, then took the weight off and padded the pendulum with rags, wrapping the clock and the weights in an old blanket before adding them to his bundle.

It was while searching through the house to find everything that he should take, that he found two things. In a drawer in his mother's room, yellowed cuttings of his father's trial, which his mother had never shown him. And something unexpected in the tiny room behind the kitchen.

Squatting, he stared at it. Found himself thinking about the contents of the pail. He wasn't quite sure where it had come from, or why his mother had bothered to bring it here, or hide it behind a barrel of rags. Opening the pail, he peered inside, then put the lid back in place.

Later, after he'd read through all the cuttings, studying the notes she'd scrawled in the margins, the idea seemed to come out of nowhere. As if his mother had spoken in his ear. He listened, considered the possible repercussions, and decided he didn't care.

She must have had something like it in mind herself, for the feeling to be so very strong.

2

On the Monday morning, Rutledge called on Major George Gordon, and found him in his study, working on accounts. He looked up as Rutledge was announced, and smiled.

A broad-shouldered man with blue eyes and dark hair streaked with gray, he'd been a soldier all his life. In the spring, he'd retired to take over the management of the family estates from his younger brother, who had fallen ill. Even as he smiled, lines of worry bracketed his mouth. According to the doctors, it was not certain that Kenneth would live past the summer. And the brothers were close.

"Come to make it official, have you?" Gordon asked. "Jean's feet hardly touched the ground last evening."

She had promised Ian she wouldn't say anything to her parents until he'd asked her father's permission to speak to her. And perhaps she hadn't, but she had made it clear that something had happened. The Gordons hadn't found it hard to guess what that was.

"I'm sorry I spoke to Jean out of turn," he said, taking the chair that Gordon had indicated. "If you wish me to withdraw my proposal, I shall."

"Nonsense. It's a good match. And she's pleased. That's what matters most to me. If you've come for my blessing, I give it freely."

Relieved, Rutledge said, "Thank you, sir. I'll do my best to make her happy."

"I know you will. I've been friends with your godfather, David Trevor, for some time. He tells me you have a strong interest in architecture. Any thoughts about joining his firm?"

Trevor had asked him, once it was certain that Rutledge wasn't following in his father's footsteps, if architecture held more interest than the law. "The door's always open, Ian. Ross already has the makings of a fine draftsman, and he has an eye for detail. I'd be content to have both of you there, with a view to a partnership down the road. What do you say?"

But Rutledge had had to say no. With some regret. He was close to David and knew his future would be certain with the Scotsman.

Now, facing Gordon, Rutledge said carefully, "I've considered his offer, sir. Perhaps one day."

"Yes, yes, best to keep an open mind." Gordon nodded. But Rutledge noted the slight frown in his eyes.

If Gordon had had a choice, he would gladly have seen his daughter marrying a career Army officer. But a solicitor with a noted firm, or an architect, would have done very well. He could hardly tell Rutledge to leave the police. But it was clear that he hoped as this man's responsibilities grew, he'd come to his senses.

Rutledge, on the brink of answering the thought, wisely held his tongue.

Gordon offered him a celebratory drink, early as it was, and then toasted the future, saying, "She's my only daughter. This day was bound to come, but every father has his concerns about the man his child will choose. You'll understand this better, once you have children of your own. Meanwhile, I can say that Jean's mother and I are both delighted and wish you every joy."

Rutledge couldn't stop himself from grinning. "Thank you, sir. Jean has made me very happy." He finished his whisky and set the glass down on the tray.

"Her mother and I would like to arrange a party, once the announcement has been sent to the *Times*. Friday evening in two weeks' time? Will that suit?"

They had already discussed the party, the Major and his wife. That was clear.

"Yes, of course." And then, remembering what he did for a living, Rutledge added, "I shall put in at once for leave that evening."

Gordon nodded, and then walked with Rutledge to the door, clapping him on the shoulder as he said, "Have the two of you considered a date for the wedding?"

"Jean has said she would like it to be at Christmas."

"Not surprising. Elizabeth and I were wed at Christmastime. Quite a pretty affair it was. I was a young lieutenant at the time, and I can remember being terrified of her father, the Colonel. He had mustaches that were as fearsome as he was. But as I got to know him, I grew quite fond of him. I hope you and I go on as comfortably together."

"I'd like that." Rutledge took his leave and walked out to where he'd left his motorcar. The wash of relief he felt left him almost euphoric. Gordon had been welcoming and gracious. He'd had a far more formidable reputation with his men, although unlike the Colonel, his own father-in-law, he didn't favor mustaches.

He smiled to himself at the thought. Gordon didn't need them.

Arriving at the Yard, Rutledge found Chief Superintendent Bowles fuming, waiting for him to appear. There was a murder in Dorchester, the county seat of Dorset, and Rutledge was to leave at once to support the local man on the scene.

"The dead man had connections," Bowles pointed out as he went over the file. "And it won't do to ignore that fact. I depend upon you to act with discretion and to take great care in conducting your interviews, so as not to upset anyone. I don't wish to hear complaints from the family or the Chief Constable."

Rutledge had received similar instructions before, and he accepted them with a wry understanding of their source.

For Bowles, Rutledge was a useful tool. Even as he resented the man's social presence and his education, he had profited from both. Cases such as this one required finesse, and he knew all too well that he and more of the Yard than he'd cared to count still had the rough edges of someone who'd come up through the ranks from lower-middle-class origins, and however high he rose, he would never shake those roots nor the occasional slip in accent that exposed them for all the world to see. It galled him to admit that Rutledge could move easily in circles closed to him. Still, what made Rutledge palatable was his ability to collect sound evidence that saw to it a case stood up in a courtroom. The reflected glory that accrued to the Chief Superintendent when Rutledge successfully closed an inquiry was recompense enough. For the moment.

As Rutledge packed his valise, his mind already occupied by the details forwarded by the Chief Constable, he found himself distracted by the thought that in less than six months' time, he would be a married man. That brought a smile to his face as he walked out the door.

He was halfway down the walk when he found himself thinking that he had smiled often in the past four and twenty hours. It was, in a way, the measure of his happiness.

Despite the distance to Dorchester, southwest of London almost to the coast, he had taken the time before he left the Yard to write to Melinda Crawford, to David Trevor, and to Ross, giving them his news. He owed it to them to see that they learned of the engagement from him rather than the *Times*. It occurred to him as he put stamps on the envelopes that he would like to ask Ross to stand up with him. There would be an opportunity for that later.

He was glad to find Frances at home, and when he came into her sitting room, he told her, quite simply, "There's an inquiry in Dorset. I have to leave straightaway. But before I go, I wanted to tell you. I spoke to Jean and to her father. She's accepted me, with his blessing."

Later, on the road to the West Country, he still wasn't sure how she'd taken it. She had turned away for a moment. "I thought perhaps you'd say something to me first. To let me know what was in your mind."

"I thought I had," he'd replied.

"In general terms." She'd turned to face him. "Well. I want you to be happy, Ian. More than anything. You know that." And she had come forward to kiss him on the cheek.

He had put his arms around her, saying lightly, "I can't tell you how much that means to me."

It would have been better, he thought now, if he could have spent the evening with his sister, perhaps taking her out to dine, giving her a chance to talk to him about the future. But he was expected in Dorset as soon as possible. There was no time for such consideration.

Ten days later, Rutledge walked into the Yard and encountered Chief Inspector Cummins on the stairs.

"Just in from Dorchester?" Cummins asked. "I've been reading the early reports. Well done."

"Thank you," Rutledge answered. "I can't say I'm particularly happy with the outcome, but there you are. The evidence was overwhelming."

Cummins smiled. "Even nice people kill, Ian."

"Sadly, yes. It will be up to a jury now, of course, but I rather think in the circumstances I might have done the same as Mrs. Butler. He was a right bastard, that man. He made everyone's life wretched. I daresay most people were relieved rather than shaken by his demise."

Changing the subject as they reached the top of the stairs, Cummins said, "I saw the notice of your engagement in the *Times*. I wish you both every happiness."

"Thank you, sir. I hope you'll have an opportunity to meet Jean sooner rather than later."

"Set a date, have you?"

"Christmas, I think."

Cummins nodded. They had reached his door. "By the bye. A warning. The Chief Superintendent is in a foul mood. That case in Northumberland blew up in Penvellyn's face. Three witnesses, and they've recanted, to a man."

Both Rutledge and Cummins had been aware from the start that Inspector Penvellyn had not been the best choice to take on Northumberland. A Cornishman, he'd never been north of Birmingham. He knew very little about the border counties. And that business in Alnwick had needed delicate handling.

"Bowles isn't thinking of sending me there in his place?" Rutledge asked, realizing that the word *warning* might mean just that. He'd been given leave on Friday for the Gordons' party, but Bowles could rescind that as quickly as he'd granted it.

"No, I think Martin is going to be the unlucky man. But on a lighter note," Cummins continued, "Davies has run into an odd case. In Somerset actually, a village outside Bristol. In the night someone crept into a churchyard and blackened several graves. Sludge more than paint, according to his report, and the very devil to clean. I doubt they'll have it removed in six months' time. Nothing else touched. And the graves weren't even in the same part of the churchyard. Random vandalism, apparently."

"Whose graves were they? Men, women, children?" Rutledge was intrigued.

"Men, every one of them. The vicar couldn't think of any connection among them. Which is not to say there isn't one. Various occupations, various ages. Farmers, shopkeepers, a doctor. Davies combed through their lives and came up with nothing of note."

"How long has the vicar been in that parish?"

"A good point. Ten years. But Davies asked living relatives, and they couldn't provide an answer either."

"Did he find the culprit?"

"Davies did his best, but no, he came up empty-handed. The vicar is quite upset. He seemed to think the villain's next target might be the church itself. It's old, there could be serious damage done there."

"Did the victims die at the same time? A calamity of some sort?"

"Davies and the vicar looked for a pattern, but there was none. Had they died in the same month—odd years—consecutive years—murdered? Any variation he could think of failed to hold up. And there were no witnesses, if you don't count the churchyard owl. A constable made his rounds at ten, then again at midnight, and went away home." He shrugged. "Whoever it was had a clear field for some hours. Well, needless to say, Davies isn't in the best of moods either." Cummins tossed his hat to the top of a file cabinet and said, "I thought you'd be interested. So was I. If you think of anything Davies hasn't tried, tell me."

Rutledge stood in the doorway. "Why was the Yard involved in the first place? It appears from what you've said to have been a petty crime."

Cummins nodded. "Apparently the vicar has a few connections of his own. He complained to his bishop, and someone at the Home Office listened. It was a shocking scene, of course, and it unsettled the entire village."

Rutledge smiled. "Too bad Davies failed to uphold the honor of the Yard."

"I'll wager it was nothing more than a prank or a dare by local youths. They may still come forward, if their consciences are guilty enough. Or if their fathers find out. What connects these graves may simply be high spirits."

"I expect Davies would rather have discovered some diabolical plot."

Cummins laughed.

Rutledge walked on to his own room, where he found Sergeant Gibson with a file in his hand.

"More grave stones?" he asked.

Gibson glared at him. "Hardly, sir. It's a murder. In Moresby. Yorkshire."

His spirits plummeted. He hadn't seen Jean since the weekend in Kent. What's more, Frances was away visiting friends. Her note gave no indication that she expected to return before Friday evening's party.

Somehow Melinda had discovered that he was in Dorchester and replied almost immediately to his news, asking him if he was sure of his heart. By return post, he'd told her that he'd never been as sure of anything before, not even his decision to join the Metropolitan Police. That he'd lost sleep over that because he'd known it would disappoint those he loved.

A second letter assured him that she was happy for him, and that she looked forward to seeing Jean again. And she had suggested a year's engagement, to give them both a chance to know each other better.

A spring wedding is always so lovely, she'd written. *Your parents were wed in May, and so was I. Of course it is Jean's choice, but you might suggest the possibility to her.*

He had found a way to bring the date up when next he wrote Jean, but he already knew what her answer would be. She had her heart set on Christmas, because of her own parents.

David's letter, waiting for him at the London house, had been more wholeheartedly happy for him. He'd never met Jean, David had written, but he was looking forward to it.

Frances's note had troubled him.

I'm not certain when you'll arrive at home. I'm visiting the Haldanes for a few days. I'm happy for you, of course. It's just that I'm not sure I'm ready to share you, Ian. That's terribly selfish, I know, but I've only just begun to recover from the loss of our parents, and while I've leaned on you more than I should, perhaps, there has been no one else but Melinda I could talk to about Mama and Papa. I hope Jean will understand. But as you say, I have until Christmas to grow accustomed to the idea, and I'll not let you down. I promise.

He'd already decided that it might be best to continue to live in the house on the square, if Frances had no objections. Nothing, he knew, would ever change the fact that he was her brother. And perhaps that decision would reassure her. In time, he hoped she would find someone of her own, and be as happy as he was. Even as he thought it, he realized that he'd have to learn to accept *her* choice, if she'd accepted his. That brought a wry smile.

As for Moresby, it was a long way from London, up on the northeast coast of Yorkshire. He'd hardly arrive there before he would have to leave, if he intended to be in London on Friday evening. And *that* he had no intention of missing. For a moment he was almost willing to wager that Bowles had remembered the date and deliberately scuttled his leave.

He sat at his desk, reading through the file, then he sent a message round to Jean to tell her that he was on his way to Yorkshire, but she mustn't worry, he hadn't forgot the party. She would be worried all the same, and he damned Bowles for being callous about the lives of the men under him. After all, he'd gone to Dorset with no complaint. It would behoove him, he thought sardonically, to bring the Yorkshire inquiry to a swift conclusion.

3

With that intention firm in his mind, Rutledge took the afternoon train to Yorkshire instead of driving. It was a day more suitable to lawn parties than murder, he thought, settling himself in his carriage. Jean would be on her way to town from the country, to do last-minute shopping while her mother attended to all the arrangements for Friday evening, the caterers and florists, the small orchestra and the wines. He tried to concentrate on that, but he found that the case in Dorset was still troubling him, and he turned instead to the newspapers he'd bought before boarding.

They offered little cheer.

Europe was aflame with charges and countercharges after that business in Sarajevo. Austria was in the mood to blame all of Serbia and punish its people accordingly. As the investigation into the appalling events dragged on, Russia was taking a hand in the matter, declaring that she spoke for all Slavs and would stand by the Slavic Serbs, in the event

that Austria decided on military action. There had been other assassinations, long before the bombing of the motorcade in the Archduke's procession, but killing the heir to the throne was not simply murder, it was
an act of treason, and Vienna's position was that the troublesome Serbs
deserved to be taught a sharp lesson. The fact that they were Slavs had
nothing to do with it, and Austria told Russia to mind her own business.

Rutledge shook his head. He didn't envy the policemen, Austrian
or Serbian, who had to get to the bottom of this business and keep
a lid on the powder keg of emotions that threatened the peace of the
Balkans. Franz Josef, Emperor of Austria and King of Hungary, was
well into his sixties. His wife, the Empress Elisabeth, had been as-
sassinated years before by an anarchist, his only son had died in a
murder-suicide pact, and now the Archduke, his heir, was dead. The
fate of Europe might well depend on what a bitter old man decided.

The clergyman across from him, seeing him set aside the newspapers, asked if he might read them. Rutledge passed them to him.
Sometime later, he too set them aside.

"Nasty business," the clergyman said, gesturing to the headlines.
"I hope we don't find ourselves drawn into it. Although I don't quite
see how. Still. You never know."

"Hotheads," the third man in the compartment agreed. "For one
thing the Emperor may be past controlling his own people. For another, Tsar Nicholas is too foolish to see where this claim to be the
savior of the Slavs could lead him. There's the German treaty with
Austria. If she goes to war with Russia, Germany easily could find
itself involved."

"Well," the clergyman said, "my wife's sister lives in Vienna. Married a banker there. For her sake, I hope this comes to nothing."

I t was late when the train pulled into Moresby. There had been
some trouble on the line after York, and they had waited an hour or
more for it to be resolved.

The town was dark and quiet, the stillness broken only by the soft whisper of the sea from the harbor. No one was waiting to meet him, and so Rutledge went directly to the Abbey Hotel, recommended to the Yard by the local Inspector. There he ordered a light dinner sent up to his room and then went to bed.

At first light he rose and looked out his window. The town curved around a pretty harbor, where pleasure craft bobbed on the incoming tide. The fishing fleet was just visible on the horizon, sails turned red by a distant sunrise. On either side of the harbor mouth, the land rose sharply to headlands that jutted into the sea, protective arms securing the anchorage. On the higher eastern headland stood the magnificent ruins of Moresby Abbey. Only a shell, the roofless walls soared into the sky, and where the great stained glass windows had once hung, only the frames were left, a tracery against the blue above. The western headland, on the other hand, was wild country given over to nesting seabirds.

In winter storms, a dark and angry sea would pound those cliffs and roll unhindered into the center of the town, lapping at storefronts, and sometimes tearing vessels from their moorings and leaving them stranded on shore as the waters receded.

But on this day as the sun climbed higher, bright and warm, the sea a deep and blinding blue as far as the eye could see, only a light breeze touched his face as Rutledge walked out of the hotel and went to find the local police station.

Inspector Farraday was in, sitting at his desk in a back room, poring over the statements his constables had collected, when Rutledge walked in.

"And who are you?" Farraday demanded, looking him up and down.

"Scotland Yard," Rutledge replied, and gave his name.

"Are you indeed?" Farraday frowned. "We've had a dozen or more strangers in Moresby these past few days. I've tracked most of them down. I was hoping you were another of them, and I could tick you off my list."

"A stranger, nevertheless," Rutledge said pleasantly and took the chair in front of the desk. "Tell me what's happened here. Could it have been suicide?"

"He couldn't have managed it himself. Not just there. Didn't the Yard show you the report sent in by the Chief Constable?"

"It did. But I usually find that what the local people tell me is more helpful."

Farraday grunted. "We don't have much in the way of trouble. The occasional drunken seaman from one of the ships that put in. The occasional drunken landsman, celebrating something or drowning his sorrows. Fisticuffs on market day, petty theft, the random wife-beating, and sometimes housebreaking. Occasionally visitors come to see the abbey ruins are set upon and robbed. The last murder was four years ago. A wife killed her husband for philandering, then she marched into my office and turned herself in."

"How likely is that in the present case?" Rutledge asked, striving for patience.

"Damned unlikely, sad to say. Ben Clayton was an unremarkable man. Fifty-six years old. A widower. Minded his own business. No enemies that anyone knew about. As a rule, ordinary people seldom have them. Not the sort that resort to killing them, at any rate. He's owned a prosperous shop on Abbey Street for many years. Survived by two sons and a daughter. They can account for their whereabouts, all three of them, and there are witnesses as well who verify their stories. But *someone* came into the house late in the evening and hanged Clayton from the turning at the top of the stairs."

"What manner of shop? How successful is it? Did he owe anyone money?"

"Furniture making. The older son, Peter, says not. The firm is on a sound footing. Has been for years. We spoke to the staff. They are all respectable, respected men, employed there for a long time. What's more, they can prove they were at home when the murder took place. If they held any grudge against their employer, they were careful never to let it show, but the consensus is that he was a fair and generous man to work for. I myself never heard any complaint against him."

"Wives do lie for their husbands, sometimes. Clayton was a widower, you say? Any other women in his life?"

"Not that the daughter knows of. Annie. She was her father's housekeeper, and says he kept regular hours. That's not to say that a few women in the town didn't wish it otherwise. Miss Sanderson and Mrs. Albertson among them."

"Where was the daughter when the murder occurred?"

"She spent the night at Peter's house. His wife is expecting and wasn't feeling well. She served her father's dinner, turned down his bed, put the cat out, and left him sitting in the parlor reading a Dickens novel. He was fond of Dickens. As a young man, *his* father had heard the writer speak. Made quite an impression apparently. There was a glass of warm milk at his elbow, Annie Clayton says, and it was still sitting on the table, half full. His spectacles were beside it, and the book, closed, lay on the floor by the chair. No sign of a struggle. Nothing stolen, the house wasn't searched. Apparently Clayton hadn't gone up to bed. It hadn't been slept in."

"Did the neighbors hear anything useful?"

"Nothing at all."

"What sort of man was Clayton?" Rutledge asked.

"Not tall. He'd put on a stone or two in the last few years. I don't think his daughter could have strung him up like that. I can't see why Peter would. Besides, he was at home with his wife and sister. They played a board game or two, then went to bed."

"And the younger son? Where was he?"

"Michael and three friends had traveled down to York to visit a fourth friend who'd just become engaged. I've spoken to the York police, they were there, in a pub, celebrating the occasion. Nor could any of them come up to Moresby, do the deed, and return to York without being missed."

"Michael's friends wouldn't cover for him if he asked them to lie?"

Inspector Farraday took a deep breath. "It's possible, of course, but I doubt it. The groom's parents put them up. Responsible people, they'd have kept an eye on their son and his friends."

"Mistaken identity, then? Did someone kill the wrong man?"

"As to that, I can't say. See for yourself."

Farraday handed over the statements he'd been reviewing. Rutledge scanned them. The Moresby police had been thorough, speaking to each of the suspects several times, and the interviews had been carefully documented.

"Who were the other strangers that you mentioned?" Rutledge asked, still reading through the statements. Someone had taken the time to type them out neatly, but the original handwritten copies were there as well.

"One came here to write an article about the abbey ruins for a London magazine doing a series on monastic sites. So he says. I've telegraphed the magazine, but there's been no reply. Two came in with the *Lillian,* a sailing yacht up from Sandwich in Kent. Cousins on holiday. They took rooms at The Anchor Inn. The landlord vouched for them. Four others have come up from London on a holiday. To go fishing. They hired Danny Craven's boat to take them out each morning. The other four were women, on their way to York, stopping off to visit a sister who lives just outside Moresby. The one we haven't tracked down is an artist, I'm told. He does paintings of local beauty spots. Apparently they sell well in Harrogate, to those who come to take the waters. I've spoken to the Swan Hotel, where he sometimes displays his work. They call him harmless. But I haven't clapped eyes on him yet. He's staying at your hotel."

Turning to another interview, Rutledge looked up. "Four women, working together, could hang a man."

Inspector Farraday stared. "Could, possibly. Yes. But did they? I think not. I've seen them."

Rutledge studied Farraday to see if he were serious. And it appeared that he was. "I'll begin with the neighbor." He shuffled through the statements again. "Mrs. Calder."

"Good luck to you," Farraday said, leaning back in his chair.

Rutledge made a note of the address and set out on foot. The house was back in the direction he'd come into Moresby, on a side street that ran a little way up the western headland before ending in a cul-de-sac. A turn-of-the-century bungalow with a door painted a dark green. He studied the Calder residence for a moment, then looked at number 17, where the murder must have occurred. That door was painted black. He realized that along this street the range of colors included a dark blue, an egg yolk yellow, and even a brick red. There might have been difficulty deciding which color was which in the dark . . .

The houses weren't cheek by jowl, but they were close enough for a struggle in one to be heard in another. The house on the far side of number 17 had a TO LET sign in the window. As far as he could tell, it was empty. Rutledge turned back to the Calder house and walked up the short path to the dark green door and knocked. The front garden was trim, well kept, like that of number 17. If Mr. Clayton did the gardening himself, then there must have been an occasional chat between neighbors, if only about the plantings.

There was no answer. Although he tried a second time, the house *felt* empty, as if no one were at home.

He walked back down the path just as a woman stepped out of number 12 with a market basket over her arm.

Rutledge caught her up, and, removing his hat, politely asked if she knew where he could find Mrs. Calder.

She examined him with a mixture of curiosity and wariness, as if uncertain whether to reply.

"I'm from London," he said in explanation. "Here on a matter of business."

That whetted her curiosity. She turned to stare at the Calder house, then turned back to Rutledge. "She's often in the tea shop by the harbor at this time of day. The Tea Cozy. Her sister owns it, and she helps out if they're busy."

Rutledge thanked her, and as she was going in the same direction down the hill, he said, "I've been told there was an unpleasantness on this street several days ago. I'm surprised you spoke to a stranger from London."

"It was shocking," she agreed. "Poor Mr. Clayton. Hanged, he was." She shivered. "I didn't sleep a wink for the next two nights. I told Mrs. Calder she was welcome to come and stay with me. For the company, you understand. Her husband is away, taking their son to Thirsk to visit a cousin on Mr. Calder's side of the family."

"She was alone, then, in her house?"

"Indeed she was. And in the morning she heard such a scream as would curdle milk. It was Miss Clayton coming home and finding her father like that. She fainted, and it was several minutes before she came to herself and fled to Mrs. Calder, who had come to her door and was looking to see what the screaming was about. Miss Clayton begged her to find someone to help cut the poor man down. Together they went to find a constable, and the police came. They saw to everything. And Miss Clayton went back to her brother's house, I'm told, refusing to stay in number seventeen alone."

"How old is Miss Clayton?"

"Eighteen last May, poor love."

He nodded, agreeing with the unspoken thought that she was too young to have suffered such a shock. "Why was she out? Had she gone to market?"

"She'd spent the previous two nights at her brother's house. His wife is expecting their first child and it's been a difficult time for her. I told my husband that it was a lucky thing too, or Annie might have been killed as well."

"I can't think who could have done such a thing to Mr. Clayton," Rutledge said as they came to the junction with the main road down to the harbor.

"None of us can. He's never been one for the drink, and he wasn't a betting man. Since his wife's death, he's never so much as looked at another woman," she added approvingly, as if this were a measure of his regard for his late wife.

"How long has she been dead?"

"Six years. She died of a tumor."

They walked in silence for a time, and then Rutledge said, "Did Mr. Clayton have any enemies? Anyone who was jealous of him? Or who had a grudge against him, or perhaps against his shop?"

"I can't think of anyone," she said, "and that makes it worse, doesn't it?" She sighed. "We never locked our doors. It took me over an hour to find the old key, but we lock them now, Tom and I. I expect Mrs. Calder does as well."

They had reached the greengrocer's shop, and his companion stopped. "You can't miss The Tea Cozy. At the end of this street."

He thanked her, and walked on.

The shop was a woman's domain. In the large window was a collection of handmade tea cozies, apparently for sale, and behind them were displayed a half dozen teapots of various sizes and shapes. He turned to look up at the eastern headland, where the ruins of the abbey stood out against the sky. What, he wondered, must it have looked like before it had been destroyed? A dark, elegant church soaring above its outbuildings, and strong enough to withstand the winds and storms that blew in from the sea.

Beyond the tea shop he could see the lighthouse, shorter than many but marking whatever rocks guarded the harbor. The tide was turning, and the boats at anchor bobbed and swayed, as if eager to escape their moorings and move out to sea on their own.

He opened the door of the shop and stepped inside. A counter to his left held trays that must have been laden with pastries and cakes earlier in the day. Even now there seemed to be a wide sampling. French-style tarts, traditional buns, a variety of biscuits, and even a few scones. Three cakes, slices missing, sat on tall, stemmed glass plates, and there were three small pies inside a glass box, wedges already cut.

Rutledge nodded to the fair-haired woman behind the counter and took one of the empty tables. There were only a few people in the shop now, an older couple sitting to one side, finishing their morning tea, and a younger woman with a baby in a pram awaiting her order.

A second woman came out from the back, bearing a tray with teapot, cup, and saucer, a small round bowl of sugar and a smaller jug of milk. Setting it down in front of the younger woman, she said, "There you go, Maggie, love." On a floral plate there was a fruit tart, strawberry, he thought, or possibly rhubarb. The younger woman thanked her and with a glance at the sleeping baby, turned eagerly to the treat before her.

The woman crossed to Rutledge's table and said, "And what would you like, love?" She looked to be in her early thirties, pretty and all-business, despite the warmth of her greeting.

Rutledge ordered tea and a lemon tart, then said, "I wonder if I've missed Mrs. Calder. I was told by a neighbor that I could find her here?"

"And who shall I say is wanting her?" the woman asked, her face changing from friendly to cold.

"My name is Rutledge, I'm from London. Inspector Farraday can vouch for me, if you like."

She glanced over her shoulder to where Maggie was pouring her tea, then pulled out the chair from the far side of his table and said in a low voice, "I'm Mrs. Calder. Is this about poor Mr. Clayton? We'd heard someone was coming up from London and might wish to speak to us."

He took out his identification and held it out to her. She studied it before handing it back to him.

"Let me fetch your tea, then."

She disappeared for several minutes and returned with another tray, setting it before him and then sitting down again.

"It was the most terrible thing," she said, keeping her voice low. "I never went into that house, you understand. Constable Blaine did what needed to be done. Annie Clayton was in such a state, and I didn't want to see for myself . . ." Her voice trailed off. "She told me she feared he was dead," she went on after a moment. "And I didn't doubt her. Later, I called myself a coward for not being sure."

He poured his tea and added sugar, then the milk. "The doctor's report says the victim had been dead for some time. That he'd been— er—killed around two or three in the morning. There was nothing you could have done. But your house is next to the Claytons. You must have heard something in the night? Raised voices, a struggle?"

"But I didn't," she said earnestly. "Not a peep. Our bedroom is on the far side of the house, of course. Still, if there had been a fight or the like, I'd have heard it. I don't sleep as deeply when my husband isn't here."

"Where is he?"

"In Thirsk. His aunt hasn't been well, and he took our son down to visit her." She cast him a wry look. "Auntie and I never saw eye to eye on anything. And so I seldom go down. Just as well, for poor Annie's sake. I was glad I was there when she needed a woman to turn to."

"Had you seen anyone in the area, before this? A stranger, some- one watching the house, or someone you recognized, appearing to be looking for Mr. Clayton?"

Mrs. Calder shook her head. "There's no one been about. It's a quiet street. Someone would have noticed."

"Did Mr. Clayton have any problems? Anyone who disliked him? Or perhaps someone he owed money to?"

"Mr. Clayton? He was a respectable man, never in any trouble that I know of. He was the sort who'd be right there when you needed help. Caring, he was. My husband liked him. And Annie, Miss Clayton, is the sweetest girl. She kept house for her father after her mother's death. Peter was already helping out in the shop, Michael was off to school. She's never been a minute's worry to her parents. I told Mr. Clayton not a fortnight ago that he'd have to think what he'd do when she found a young man and was wed, but he said he had told her that when the time came he'd manage just fine."

"And are there young men coming to call?"

"A few. I know them all. For heaven's sake, they grew up in Moresby, I knew their parents, sometimes even their grandparents. But there was no particular one. She was a sensible lass, you know, she wasn't the sort to be swept off her feet by pretty words. She enjoyed the attention but wasn't ready to settle."

A man without enemies, no bad habits, a good friend to his neighbors . . .

Rutledge said, "I saw that the house next to his is for let."

"Yes, old Mr. Talmadge died of his heart not six months ago, and the family put the sign up not two months' gone, when they'd finished clearing it out. It needs a little work inside, Mr. Talmadge was in his eighties, but it's a solid house, nevertheless. I told Mr. Clayton he ought to buy it for Annie and let it until she made up her mind."

"Could someone have mistaken the Clayton house for the Talmadge house? Clayton was alone, he might have been taken for his neighbor."

She shook her head. "Anyone in his right mind could see the difference in age. And Mr. Talmadge was bald as a plate."

He finished his tea, thanked her, and walked with her to the counter to pay for it.

Mrs. Calder stopped him as he was about to leave the tea shop. The warm July sun spilled through the doorway, a shaft of gold across the wood floor.

"I've been thinking," she said, her eyes on the ruins above them on the headland. "He must have known this person. Mr. Clayton. If I never heard any noise, it was because he wasn't afraid of his killer and so he didn't cry out. No struggle. Until it was too late." She shivered. "Not a very pleasant thought, is it?"

Rutledge had already considered that possibility, but here was the first proof. He thanked her and walked back the way he'd come.

It was time to speak to Clayton's daughter, and his sons.

P eter Clayton lived above the family's shop on Abbey Street, just off the High. He was a cabinetmaker by trade, like his father, and the samples of workmanship on display indicated a prosperous business. Bookshelves, bedsteads, tables and chairs were spaced neatly to show them at their best angles. The turnings on table legs and bedposts were smartly done. The woods were of good quality as well, suggesting that the shop served prosperous townspeople in addition to the carriage trade. Chests and armoires stood against the far wall, many of them miniature samples of what the larger piece might look like. Even the miniatures were elegantly made, with the pride of a craftsman. Rutledge studied them with interest, thinking that it wouldn't be long before he'd be looking at furnishings for his own house or flat. Once Frances was engaged . . .

A thin young man came out of the back room and said, "I'm sorry. The shop is closed today. There has been a death in the family. I was just coming to put crepe on the door."

"Inspector Rutledge, Scotland Yard. I'm sorry to intrude, but it would be helpful to speak to Miss Clayton as soon as possible, and her brothers as well."

The young man hesitated. "I'm not sure—and they've already spoken to Inspector Farraday."

"Yes, I know. But the inquiry has been turned over to the Yard. May I ask who you are?"

He flushed a little. "Joseph Minton. I help out in the shop when Mr. Clayton and his son are making these pieces." He gestured vaguely around.

"Would you ask if the family will see me?" Rutledge persisted. This was one aspect of his work that he disliked, speaking to members of the family before the shock had fully worn off. "If too much time is lost, the chances of apprehending their father's murderer are slim at best."

Minton hesitated and then went back the way he'd come. Rutledge could hear his diffident footsteps on stairs, and a tentative knock at a door at the top of the flight. Voices followed, and after a moment Minton clattered back down the stairs, as if relieved.

"Mr. Clayton asks that you not disturb his wife. She's in a delicate condition."

"I understand."

But when Minton had led him to the door on the landing and stepped aside for him to enter, the first person Rutledge saw was Mrs. Clayton, just sitting down with the awkwardness of late pregnancy, in a chair by the window. A man—clearly her husband—and a younger woman were trying to persuade her to lie down again.

They turned as one to stare at Rutledge. Then Clayton came forward, introducing himself, his wife, and sister.

"I'm grateful you're here," he said, "although I was surprised that Farraday has sent for the Yard."

"Usually an inquiry such as this can be closed in the first few days. But there appear to be no leads in your father's death, and Inspector Farraday rightly saw that the sooner the Yard was brought in, the better."

He was invited to sit, and as he came fully into the room, he could see how pale Mrs. Clayton was. She was wrapped in shawls in spite of the heat, and he thought she must be suffering from nausea still.

Miss Clayton, dark haired and pretty, was nearly as pale herself, and as Rutledge smiled at her, she said quickly, "Please—don't ask me to go back over that morning."

"I've read the report, Miss Clayton. I've come to ask about your father and anyone who might have wanted to harm him."

"There was no one," she declared. "I can't think of anyone with a grudge against Papa."

"Nothing was stolen? You haven't discovered anything missing since Tuesday last?"

"Even my mother's jewelry is still in the little case where she kept it. Inspector Farraday asked me to look. And Papa's purse was on the table by the bed, next to his pocket watch. Where he puts—put them every night before going to bed."

"You said his watch and purse were where they should be if he'd gone to bed. Then why hadn't he retired for the night himself? Why would he stay up and open the door to a stranger at such an hour? Was he expecting someone to call?"

Peter Clayton answered for her. "We've talked about that. It's possible that he fell asleep in his chair. And when the knock came, his first thought must have been that we'd come for him because something had happened—that Claire was taken ill."

And that was very likely, Rutledge thought. The question was, how had the intruder kept his victim from raising the alarm once Clayton discovered that his daughter-in-law was safe. What had been said between killer and victim, that had made it possible to hang the man without a hand raised to protect himself?

Rutledge studied Peter Clayton. While he was strong enough to overpower the older man, there were no scratches on his face, hands, or arms. Surely the older man would have fought his son, especially if he thought Peter had run mad?

Annie Clayton said, "I wondered if perhaps he must have gone upstairs, taken out his watch and purse, then decided he wasn't really sleepy. And so he went back to his reading. Peter thought he might have been worried about Claire. This baby is—would have been—his first grandchild, and he was excited about that." Her voice caught on a sob.

"Did he do that often? Change his mind about going to bed?"

Again Peter spoke for her. "After my mother died, he seemed to miss her most at night, and he had some trouble sleeping. The warm milk was to help him with that."

"Were there financial problems with the shop downstairs?"

"No, we've been very fortunate. My father's doing, he worked hard to make it succeed. And I have a gift of sorts. I'd been able to introduce a few new designs that've been quite popular."

"No arguments between you over any aspect of working together?"

It was Mrs. Clayton who answered, her voice hardly more than a thread. "My father-in-law was proud of the new designs. He told me so himself. I don't think he'd have lied about that."

Annie Clayton nodded. "It's quite true. Papa was pleased. He said the shop would be his grandson's inheritance. He was certain Claire would have a son."

Mrs. Clayton smiled wanly. "I promised I wouldn't disappoint him."

"Your staff is trustworthy? No problems with you, sir, or Mr. Clayton?"

Peter shook his head. "They've been with us for years. Minton, downstairs, is the second generation working for us. Annie can tell you—anyone can tell you—my father was a good employer. I don't think we've ever had to dismiss an employee."

"There's a younger brother, I understand?"

"Yes, he was in York, but he came home at once."

"Where is he now?"

A look passed between brother and sister, standing by the window.

"Drunk," said Peter Clayton shortly. "He hasn't been sober since he arrived. He took it hard. They were close, Papa and Michael."

"And what part of the cabinetry business will he share? Your brother?"

Peter Clayton frowned. "He doesn't want to work with me. In September he's going to university. He wants to be a doctor." Taking a deep breath, he said, "Papa was proud of that too. Although I've had my reservations."

"Why?"

"We've done well, of course. But university isn't cheap. Michael will need the proper clothes and books and digs. I wasn't sure he had a calling. I thought it was more likely the fact that he doesn't want to stay in Moresby. Dr. Sutton is getting on in years. I asked my brother if he intended to come back here and perhaps take up Dr. Sutton's practice. He said he'd rather live in York. He goes there every chance he has."

It was the first ripple of trouble in what had seemed an extraordinarily close family.

"And now, with your father dead, will Michael go to university?"

"There will be his inheritance, of course. And I'll help him all I can. But I have my wife and sister to see to, I can't do for Michael what my father would have managed to do."

"I'd like to speak to Michael."

Peter said, "Come see for yourself." He led Rutledge down a passage and stopped at a door near the far end. "You needn't knock. He won't hear you."

Rutledge opened the door. The odor of stale beer and wine seemed to leap out at him. Sprawled on the bed was a younger version of Peter Clayton, fair hair and wide shoulders and the same hooked nose. He was snoring raucously, and it was no pretense, although Rutledge crossed to the bed to be sure.

From the doorway, Peter said, "Claire insists if he keeps drinking he'll have to go back to the house, like it or not. It upsets her to see him like this. He doesn't handle being drunk very well."

Rutledge came back to the doorway. "I can understand your sister's grief. She found your father, after all. But isn't this a little excessive? This heavy drinking?"

"My father hadn't wanted him to go to York. He thought it a foolish trip, but Michael insisted on having his own way. I think that's bothering my brother more than anything else. He believes if he'd been in Moresby, in the house that night, he'd have saved Papa's life."

4

Rutledge spent another quarter of an hour interviewing the Clayton family, and when he left he'd discovered very little more that would help him understand why Ben Clayton had been murdered.

He sought out Doctor Sutton, who lived on one of the lanes that ran up the hillside below the abbey cliff. Sutton was nearing seventy, a spry man with thick white hair and a bristling mustache that was more salt than pepper.

He was just seeing a patient out of his office when Rutledge arrived, and he glanced at the others waiting, then nodded to the man from London.

"Come in, I can spare you a moment. Gossip tells me you're Scotland Yard."

Rutledge smiled, but he was thinking to himself that if the rumor mill had already named him, why hadn't it also whispered the name of a suspect? It wasn't as if Moresby was a large city, where a man didn't know his neighbor's business. "Yes, I've come about the Clayton murder."

Sutton shut the door to his office and gestured to a chair. "Nasty business, that. I haven't seen a hanging death in some fifteen years. And then it was a man who'd lost his wife and couldn't face life without her." He crossed the room and sat down at his desk. "Nearly botched the job for that matter."

"And in Clayton's case? Was it a professional knot or a makeshift one? I assume you must have seen it in place."

Sutton frowned. "It was quite professional. I doubt a hangman could have done any better."

"Any hangmen living in Moresby?"

"Not to my knowledge. But you can't be serious. You aren't looking for such a man?"

"I'm not sure who I'm looking for. I'll know when I take him into custody." He glanced at the shelves of medical books behind the doctor's desk. "Tell me how a man could walk into that house at two in the morning, and hang Clayton without a struggle? No one appears to have heard anything—the house wasn't in disarray. I'm told there were no marks on Clayton's body indicating that he'd fought for his life. Why would a man simply let himself be hanged? It's not a pleasant death."

"I've asked myself that as well. The answer is, I think, that Clayton was not awake enough to offer much resistance. Occasionally he takes a powder I give him to help him sleep. Lumbago, you see. And when it's particularly bad, he uses the powder. It's perfectly safe, of course. But if he took it at ten or eleven, his usual bedtime, by one or two o'clock he'd still be feeling the effects of it. Groggy, at best. And young Peter suggested that when someone came to the door, his father thought Claire might have been in difficulty. There were two previous miscarriages, you see, and although this pregnancy has been trying for her, so far it appears she'll carry it to term. Still, the family is worried. You can understand why."

"Which makes me wonder if the killer was someone Clayton knew. A member of his family. A neighbor. A customer. After all, he stayed, whoever he was, long enough to hang the man."

"Hardly his family. Ben and Peter worked very well together. Different temperaments, but they respected each other, and I think Ben was pleased that his son has a true talent. He needn't copy furniture he'd seen, he could create his own designs. As for Michael, I don't believe he'd have the strength of character to murder anyone. Even if he walked into that house with every intention of doing murder, he'd fail."

"I'm told he wishes to be a doctor."

"He says he thinks it would suit him. But he's never cut open a living body and watched the warm blood pouring over his fingers. It's the best way you could wish for, to thin out applicants." Sutton smiled. "First time I had to pick up a scalpel, I nearly fainted from sheer fright. But I managed, and there's the difference. Still. You never know, do you? It might be the making of that young man."

"The powders Clayton had for sleeping. How did he take them?"

"Usually with a little water in a glass. He had a glass of milk in the evening, generally read for a time, and then if need be, before retiring he swallowed his powder. He didn't care for them. If he used them I knew his back was painful."

"Did anyone think to test the half glass of milk on the table by his chair?"

Sutton frowned. "I sniffed it. It had turned. I poured it out."

"It smelled only of sour milk?"

"Yes, that's right. What are you thinking, that there was something in the milk?" The frown deepened. "Are you asking if there was *poison* in that milk? It didn't show up in the postmortem."

"But were you looking for it? I'm suggesting that if more than one of his powders was put into that milk, he would have been so deeply asleep that he wouldn't have struggled."

"I see. If that's true, it changes nothing. He died of a hanging."

"Who would have known that he took these powders?"

"Myself. My nurse. His family—Annie, certainly, because she would ask every evening if he wished to have one. I'm sure his sons knew. It was no secret. His back could be quite painful. There was nothing to be done for it, but the powders allowed him to sleep when it was at its worst. But surely you don't believe it was Annie or Peter? When Peter has looked forward to this child to the point of nearly driving his wife mad, cosseting her, I hardly see him setting himself up to be charged with murder. If he wanted to kill his father—and I don't believe that for a moment—he'd have waited until the child was safely born. What's more, I can't imagine Annie getting her father as far as the top of the stairs, if he were heavily drugged. As for Michael, he *was* in York. Farraday has already confirmed that. And as I've poured out the milk, there's no way to test your theory."

"There isn't," Rutledge agreed. "But *someone* has murdered Benjamin Clayton. He couldn't hang himself. And it was done quietly. That speaks of a murderer with no fear of being caught in the act. He must therefore have known that the house was empty. Did the postmortem indicate any medical problems that you weren't aware of?"

"He was in good health. He was mentally sound. There was no reason for him to consider suicide. Besides, he was in here nearly every week, using some excuse or other to ask me if I was certain Claire was all right. I've never seen any man happier to welcome a grandchild." Dr. Sutton took out his watch, opened the case, and glanced at the time, snapped the case shut again and looked up. "I don't know who is to blame, but I'd stake my reputation that it wasn't one of the family."

"Nor a neighbor, nor a competitor, nor a thief in the night."

The doctor grimaced. "Clayton didn't live all his life in Moresby. Perhaps there was something in his past that eventually caught up with him."

"What do you know of his past?"

"He met a Moresby girl who was away studying to become a teacher. They were married here, of course, and he found he liked Moresby. His own parents were dead, he had no ties holding him in the south, and for some time he'd wanted to strike out on his own as a furniture maker. He and his father had owned a shop selling ready-made furnishings, and with the money from selling that, he set up in business here. It wasn't long before he moved to larger premises on Abbey Street, and he never looked back. I must say, Beatrice's parents were amazingly perceptive. They never doubted him, and he didn't disappoint them."

That tallied with what Clayton's children had told Rutledge. He said, "But where did he live before his marriage?"

"Damned if I remember. Dorset, I think? Or perhaps it was Somerset. Peter might be able to tell you."

But when Rutledge went back to speak to Peter, he was no more sure than the doctor.

"His parents were dead. It wasn't as if we visited them from time to time," he said apologetically. "Somewhere in Gloucestershire or Somerset? The West Country."

"Where did your mother go to school?"

"In Somerset, I believe. She never really wanted to teach, but it was a proper profession for a young woman." Peter Clayton smiled a little. "She lived more in the day and didn't dwell on the past. She did say once that leaving home even for her training was the hardest thing she'd ever had to do. I expect that's why she never talked about it. And why Papa was willing to live here in Moresby."

"Did she make any friendships at the school that she might have kept?"

"There was a Mary something or other," he said vaguely. "But she died of cholera out in India where she'd gone to marry an officer in Delhi. I only remember that because it was one of the few times I saw my mother cry. She kept repeating 'How sad, how sad,' and 'Poor

Mary,' as she read the letter, and then she saw me in the doorway and told me she'd just received unhappy news from her dear friend's brother. Afterward she let me have the stamp."

"Was there anything in your father's past that might have caught up with him? An old quarrel, an old jealousy?" Rutledge asked. "If he was content to live here in Moresby, perhaps he was glad to put the past behind him."

Clayton shook his head. "You didn't know my father. He was even tempered, a man who did his duty and took pride in his work and his family. I can't imagine any wild youthful indiscretions coming back to haunt him."

Annie came into the room just then, nodding to Rutledge and asking if there was any news.

"None, I'm afraid." He put to her much the same questions as he'd put to Peter, and she agreed with her brother.

"I think the death of Papa's father was hard for him. He lost heart. He said to me once that the shop held too many reminders, but I doubt he'd have sold it, if he hadn't met my mother. She was his salvation, she gave him back love and hope. He said as much at her funeral."

But someone had killed the man. Michael? There appeared to be no motive, for if he did wish to be a doctor, his father was the best chance of seeing that through. Certainly he'd have had better luck persuading his father to pay for his education than trying to convince his brother he was serious about his future.

There were footsteps on the stairs, and as if conjured up by Rutledge's thoughts, Michael came through the door. Annie exclaimed, and hurried to embrace him.

He looked ill. He'd shaved, but he'd missed patches of beard at the jawline and under his chin. His clothes were rumpled and his hair lank.

"I went to the house," he said to his sister. "But no one was there. I couldn't bear to go in."

Peter Clayton frowned. "Surely you didn't come through the shop looking like that?" he asked his brother.

"There's no one in the show room. After all, the shop is closed, isn't it?" Michael answered. He stared at Rutledge. "You aren't Papa's solicitor."

"Were you expecting him?" Rutledge asked.

"We can't bury my father until the police give us permission. And so Mr. Adams suggested that the will be read before he's interred," Peter Clayton explained. "I doubt there's anything new in it. Papa drew it up after Mama's death." To his brother, he said, "This is Inspector Rutledge. We told you—he was here earlier."

"Except that now I have no place to live," Michael said morosely, ignoring the introduction. "I expect Annie must feel the same way." He appeared to be sober now, although his skin was sallow. From a monumental hangover?

"How is the estate likely to be divided?" Rutledge asked.

"The house goes to Annie for as long as she cares to live there. Then it will be sold with equal shares going to each of us," the younger brother answered.

"Michael is right. I'm not sure I can bear to live there now," Annie said in a low voice, shivering.

"In time, perhaps," Peter said, reaching out to rest a hand on her arm. "We're in no hurry, love."

"And the business?" Rutledge persisted.

Peter glanced at his brother. "My father saw to it that it was equal shares there as well. And I shall carry out his wishes, of course. I've worked downstairs from the time I was fourteen. By rights the business should be mine to go on with, I expect. But Annie will have a share in the profits until she marries, and then a dowry. Michael will have a share in the profits for as long as he works with me. If he chooses not to, he'll be given a lump sum. The only problem is, I can't afford a lump sum just now, but I can pay him monthly until I'm able to do more. We didn't expect Papa to die so young. He'd been putting money back into the business to build it. As our bank manager can tell you, we are debt free, but there aren't a lot of pounds on hand."

Rutledge had been watching Michael's face. His lips twisted in a sour grimace, and it occurred to Rutledge that if Michael were to kill one of his family, it might well be his brother, not his father.

He turned to the younger brother. "Did your father ever tell you stories about his childhood or his parents?"

Michael shrugged. "The usual stories of growing up. He lost his mother when he was six, and he went to work in the shop with his father because there was no one to look after him. He liked it, he said, but his heart wasn't in it, even when his father made him a partner. He wanted to build furniture, not wait on elderly ladies who couldn't make up their minds."

Shortly after that, Rutledge thanked them, and walked down to the harbor. The water was a sparkling dark blue, and the boats riding at anchor bobbed a little as the tide ran. Overhead, gulls shrieked with interest, flying closer to inspect him, then moving on when they saw he had nothing to offer them. The steep-sided valley, carved out by the River More, lay basking in the sun.

Who killed Benjamin Clayton? he asked himself, staring out to sea. He had to agree with Dr. Sutton that even if Michael had been tempted, he wasn't likely to have the fortitude to see the attack through. Certainly not a hanging. And as Rutledge had seen for himself, there was more reason to kill his brother than murder his father. Peter would be fair, Rutledge thought, splitting the inheritance in equal shares as his father had wished, but he wasn't as easily cajoled. Even if he were angry with his father, Michael would have been stupid not to think of that before acting. He was younger than his brother by a number of years, and perhaps he'd been spoiled by his mother. He might kill if the opportunity, the temptation, presented itself, but he wasn't one to lose sight of his best interests even in the grip of anger.

Rutledge walked back to the police station and found Inspector Farraday filling out forms.

"Don't tell me you've finished your work and can give me the murderer's name?" he asked with a grin that was more sly than humorous.

"Not yet. It's a shame the doctor poured out the sour milk before it could be tested. I wonder if Clayton had been given something to sedate him."

"The odd thing is, he hadn't gone to bed. Instead, he'd fallen asleep in his chair, in his shirtsleeves but still fully clothed. That would tend to make you think he hadn't got around to taking his powders. The milk was gone before I got there, I can't tell you what was in it. I know it existed, but at the time I was more concerned with what was hanging there above my head. The doctor tells me Clayton died from hanging. Not an overdose of anything he'd swallowed, although he appeared to have taken his powders. That brings us around to the fact that it was the daughter who set out the milk on the tray. Do you think Annie Clayton drugged her father?"

"It's hard to believe, but stranger things have happened."

"Or Michael Clayton, more likely. Although I have sworn statements that place him in York. I can't think he'd find that many people prepared to lie for him. Not in a case of patricide."

Rutledge sat down in the chair across from Farraday's desk. "If it isn't his family, and there were no known enemies, then we're back to the outsiders visiting Moresby. You've been interviewing them. Is there any reason to question them again?"

Farraday reached for a writing tablet, then tossed it across the desk to Rutledge. "You're the man from Scotland Yard."

Ignoring the sarcasm, he read the list, then nodded.

"All right, I'll have another look at them."

Farraday opened his mouth to say something, then shrugged. "Suit yourself."

Rutledge returned to the flat above the furniture maker's shop. But Peter Clayton was in the shop itself, sitting at a desk in the back of the show room, head in hands. He looked up as Rutledge walked in, hope flaring in his face.

"You've found out who it is?"

"We're pursuing our inquiries," Rutledge said, and handed him the list. "Know any of these people? Have any of them come to the shop?"

The man read through it, frowning as he came to each new name, then shook his head. "I don't recognize any of them. If my father knew one of them, then he kept it to himself."

"Which once more brings us around to his past."

"I can't think he was running from anything he'd done. You didn't know my father—he was upright and good."

"Even upright and good men can do things they've regretted."

"I refuse to believe it. And my mother was a good judge of character. Come to that my grandfather—her father—wouldn't have trusted his only daughter to a stranger. He'd have made inquiries, he'd have been certain that my father was the man he claimed to be. It wouldn't surprise me if he himself made it his business to travel to the village where my father had lived." He passed the list of names back to Rutledge.

He realized that Clayton's children, Annie, Peter, and Michael, were young, and the young dwelled in the present. They weren't of an age yet to ask their parent about his own youth, or for that matter, even think of him as having been young. The possibility that the father might have been an escaped murderer or had enjoyed a dissolute year or two in his twenties was as foreign to them as the West Country.

He thanked Clayton, and set out to find the men and women whose names were on the list.

That took him nearly three hours, but he managed to find all but one of them. They had been questioned before by Farraday and knew why he had come to speak to them, but they had nothing to add to what they'd told the local man. Only one of them had been to Moresby before, and that was seven years ago. None of them had roots in the West Country. On the whole, Rutledge thought they were telling him the truth, that they'd never heard of a man named Clayton until Farraday had appeared to interview them. Even the elusive artist, a man in his late fifties, was appalled that anyone could consider him guilty of murder. As he was a short, slim man, unlikely to have managed a hanging, Rutledge tended to agree.

No one seemed to know where to find the name at the top of the list—it wasn't familiar to anyone Rutledge spoke to, and the man didn't seem to frequent any of the usual restaurants or tearooms that catered to visitors. And so Rutledge went back to Farraday.

"That's the only one of that lot I didn't like," the Inspector told him. "This is the man who came to view the ruins. There's something rather odd about him. Anxious, couldn't look me in the eye. A writer, he says. Amateur archaeologist. But when I talked to him about the abbey, he only seemed to know what had been drummed into our heads in school. You'd think, wouldn't you, that he'd have learned something new about the monks or the building, if he was going to write about them? Or how Moresby compared with the other well-known Yorkshire monastic ruins at Ripon or Fountains?"

"I thought you told me earlier that it was possible he was telling the truth? That you were waiting for a response from the magazine that intended to print his article?"

"The magazine hasn't got back to me. Look, his story about where he was all evening appeared to check out. But I ran into him a quarter of an hour ago up on the path to the abbey, and we talked again. I hadn't sought him out, mind you. He'd have stayed in the clear if he'd kept his mouth shut. I'd have believed him if he'd said he couldn't discuss his work."

"Interesting. If he isn't writing for a magazine, then why is he here?"

"A German spy? There's a good harbor here."

"You can't be serious?" Rutledge asked.

"Who's to say? Like everyone else in the country, I've been follow-ing the news. If the Russians attack Austria and the Germans come to Austria's aid, where will we be? I can't believe it's a question of if, but of when. I tell you, if Russia has her wits about her, she'll leave those assassins to stand trial for what they did. She won't interfere. But who knows what the Tsar will decide to do? And how steady is the German Kaiser? Then there's France," he added darkly. "France has a treaty with Russia, just as Germany has an alliance with Austria."

"You've been following events very closely."

"I'm of an age where I might find myself in uniform, if worse comes to worst. But more to the point, my younger brother most certainly will, if we're drawn into this business. And I'd not like to see that. I could fend for myself. I'm not sure he has the bottom to last it through. He's a theology student. He failed at everything else he tried, but he seems to like this."

Rather like Michael, Rutledge thought. What would the Army do for someone like Michael? Make a man of him? Or turn him bitter?

Farraday was saying, "You're of an age, yourself."

"So far, Britain's stayed out of it." In truth, Rutledge hadn't given much thought to the chances of war. For one thing, he was a police-man, not an Army officer. For another, there hadn't been a war in over a hundred years where men had been conscripted into the Army. He'd been seduced by happiness into thinking this saber rattling in Europe was no different from any other Balkan conflict. What if it were?

"Yes, well, we're speaking of Europe. They'll find a way to drag us in, mark my words. Remember Napoleon? Not that any of the present-day rulers are his match. Far from it. But before he was finished, all of Europe was ablaze."

"You're pessimistic," Rutledge said. "We weren't drawn into the Franco-Prussian War."

"Not so much pessimistic as concerned. France and Prussia had at it in 1870. And France didn't much care for the outcome. She'll not walk away from a chance to get her own back. If Germany comes in on the side of Austria, mark my words, she'll leap at the chance to take on the Kaiser."

If so, a little Balkan war wouldn't stay little or confined to Serbia and the Balkans. "The Kaiser is a cousin of the King. He's not a Chancellor Bismarck. And he's no Frederick the Great."

But even as he said the words, Rutledge remembered glimpsing the German Kaiser on his last visit to England. A pompous man with a withered arm . . .

"That may well be what the French are counting on."

"You can't be serious about the possibility that this man—what's his name?—could be a spy?"

Farraday rubbed his face with both hands, his voice sounding hollow as he answered. "God knows. But we've not much else to choose from." He dropped his hands. "Name's Hartle. Edward Hartle. See if you don't see something about him that raises the hackles."

"Where can I find him?"

"At the ruins, I expect. You needn't go around by land, there are stairs on the cliff that will take you up. I'll show you."

He led Rutledge out into the street, and shading his eyes, he pointed. "That row of houses. Halfway along you'll find the stairs. Can't miss them."

Rutledge thanked him and set out for the ruins. It was warm in the sun, and by the time he was halfway up the steps—nearly two hundred of them—he'd taken off his coat and his tie. Higher up, he began to catch the breeze from the sea, and by the time he'd reached the flat top of the headland, he could feel it ruffle his hair even as the sun baked his face.

The ruins were majestic. There was no other word for them, at a distance or close to. He'd been to Fountains Abbey and a few of the other well-known abbey ruins, but not all of them had such a spectacular setting, here on the headland, the sky above and the sea beyond. He turned for a moment to look back down at the little harbor, the houses straggling below him. He could just make out the bunch of black crepe on the door of the furniture maker's shop. A mother and daughter were stepping out of the tea shop, Mrs. Calder seeing them off and closing the door behind them. Several other women were standing in front of the milliner's shop, admiring the latest display. As he scanned the town center, two men came out of the tobacconist's, conversing earnestly, their heads together.

As a place from which to watch the town, this was an excellent vantage point. Rutledge followed the street patterns toward the Clayton bungalow. Moving slightly to his left, he found he could even pick out the walk leading up to the door.

Had someone stood here and waited for Annie Clayton to leave for her brother's flat above the shop? The days were long, it might well be light enough by ten to see her step out the door and to make certain she entered the shop. Signaling that Clayton was alone . . .

Who had had a reason to kill Clayton? An ordinary man, a furniture maker, a family man, and a widower? Soon to be a grandfather for the first time?

Was it someone in Moresby? Not a stranger, as Farraday seemed to hope, someone Clayton might not recognize at two in the morning, but a friend who had harbored a hatred that finally spilled over into bloodshed?

He turned and walked on toward the ruins, to find this man Hartle.

The tracery of empty windows was sharp against the sky and quite lovely. The remaining walls gave him some sense of what the abbey must once have looked like. Certainly if its builders had feared Viking invaders from the sea, this was the spot to choose for the abbey. The monks could see for miles around, could have been prepared for any attack, and yet the original abbey had been plundered and destroyed by Northmen. This ruin was, like so many others in England, Norman. And they had built for beauty as well as endurance.

The pond just beyond the abbey's west front rippled as the breeze touched it, and the abbey's reflection shivered across the surface.

There was someone in the nave. Rutledge had seen the flash of a white shirt before the man moved out of sight behind a portion of the wall that had once been part of the north transept.

Better, Rutledge thought, to approach in a roundabout fashion, and so, picking up his pace, he crossed the headland in the direction of the pond and the west front of the ruins, walking through the high grass at an unhurried pace, so as not to alarm his quarry. He looked up at the massive and beautiful facade as he made his way through the summer wildflowers toward it. Stepping into the shadows of the nave, he paused for a moment to get his bearings, and then he walked on toward the towering transept wall. There was no sun beating down on his shoulders here, and he felt a distinct chill as the perspiration on his body began to cool.

He cornered his quarry on the far side of the transept, and he said, raising his voice to carry above the whisper of the wind, "Hallo."

The man turned, his face anxious, but he relaxed when he saw Rutledge.

Who was he expecting to come up here to meet him? Farraday? Or someone else?

Rutledge put his age at perhaps thirty, his build slender, his hair sun-streaked fair, although his eyes were brown.

"Beautiful to walk here," Rutledge said casually. "Is it usually so quiet?"

"Yes. Well, sometimes there are visitors." He paused. "What brings you here?"

"I had time on my hands. And I'd never climbed up before. I thought it might be worthwhile. You?"

"I— Working on an essay about Moresby. Its history and construction. I hope to see it published."

"Interesting. A don, are you?" But he was already fairly certain the man wasn't an academic. His voice had given him away, and his clothing.

"No, no. More like an amateur historian, I expect." He stared up at the walls, then turned the subject. "They built well, didn't they, those monks."

"Very well. A pity the years have taken their toll," Rutledge answered, gesturing to where a part of the wall had fallen in, stones scattered in the high grass. "What made you choose Moresby for your work?"

"Its isolation."

Rutledge indicated the man's worn and earth-caked boots. It was evident he'd done quite a bit of walking lately, and in all weathers. "Scrambling about looking for dinosaur bones and pockets of jet, as well?"

There were areas of the headlands here where both had been found. But the other man appeared to be perplexed, as if uncertain whether Rutledge was jesting or serious.

He shrugged, then added. "There hasn't been time so far."

"Where do you live, below? Can you see the ruins from your windows? It must be quite amazing to look up here during a full moon."

It was clear the other man hadn't thought about a full moon. He stared for a moment, then said quickly, "Yes, rising from the sea. Of course."

Rutledge's voice changed as he said, "What really brings you here, Mr. Hartle?"

"Oh dear God. You aren't another policeman, are you?"

"Scotland Yard," he replied tersely.

Hartle sat down quickly on the nearest stone, as if his legs couldn't support him any longer. "I thought I could get away with it. At least for a while." He gestured with one hand, as if giving up. "I just hadn't bargained for the police to take such an interest. At least not quite so soon."

Rutledge reached up to deal with his tie, and then pulled on his coat. "I think you'd better come down to the police station with me and explain yourself."

"For God's sake, no."

"I don't think you have much choice," Rutledge said. "A man has been murdered here in Moresby. We're interviewing local people and strangers like you."

"But I'm not a stranger!" Hartle said quickly. "Look, let me explain. Will you just listen to me for a moment? I didn't want to say anything to Farraday. He might have remembered. You're from London, you'll not be prejudiced by the past."

"Go on." Rutledge found another place to sit, and waited.

"My father is dying," Hartle began. "He has a farm not far from here. We had a falling-out eleven years ago. I was no more than a boy, but he struck me out of his will, and I don't mind that. I can fend for myself. Still, I was hoping he'd ask for me, you see. And I wanted to be nearby, in the event he does. But of course I can't stay at the farm. And so I spend my days sitting up here, wondering what else I can do. One of my cousins has promised to come for me if Papa changes his mind about seeing me. I stay in my cousin's house at night, but his wife doesn't much care for me and has made it clear she doesn't want me hanging about." He made a deprecating gesture. "I was what you might call wild in my youth. I can't blame her for feeling the way she does. But I've settled down. Changed. In more ways than one. Farraday didn't even recognize me as the skinny lad with the spotty face and a sullen attitude. I long ago forgave Papa, but I want his forgiveness as well. Does that make any sense?"

"Why didn't you tell Inspector Farraday that?"

"I told you. I'm here on sufferance as it is. Even my cousin has limits to his forbearance. If the police come around asking questions, trying to find out *why* I'm here, it will be taken in the worst possible way. Don't you see? They'll think I've never changed at all. But I *have*. I've found work, I'm seeing a very nice young woman, and the past ten years I've tried to make up for what I've done."

"What did you do?"

Hartle's face flushed. "I was more or less a ruffian, in with the wrong people. I stole from Papa. Before I ran away, and again the night I left. I've tried to pay it back, every farthing of it, but he refuses to take my money. It's dirty, he says, ill-gotten. But it isn't. I've worked for every bit of it. Honest work."

"What sort of work?"

"I now have a position in a haberdashery in Scarborough. I was never cut out to be a farmer. Mr. Hartle is very kind. He gave me a little time off when I learned that Papa was ill. And come to that, it wouldn't do for *him* to learn about my past. I've lived it down."

"Hartle. Another cousin?"

"No, that's it, you see. I didn't want to hang about and give people time to think back. My name is Mark Kingston. I borrowed Mr. Hartle's name. I doubt he'd approve, but I have not sullied it in any way," he ended defensively.

"A very plausible story. But it will have to be verified."

"But why? I've held nothing back." Kingston's tired face was suddenly haggard. "It will be even worse, with Scotland Yard walking up to the door and asking about me. I don't know who was murdered. I don't really care. But I swear I had nothing to do with it."

"Didn't the Inspector tell you? It was Ben Clayton, the furniture maker on Abbey Street."

"I don't remember the man. For God's sake, it was eleven years ago. And I wasn't interested in furniture then, was I?"

"What about his sons, Peter and Michael Clayton. His daughter, Annie? You must have been in school with some of them?"

Kingston shook his head. "I wasn't much for school. If they were good at their lessons, I scorned them and had nothing to do with them. My loss. Although somehow I took in enough reading and arithmetic to satisfy Mr. Hartle, when it came to hiring me."

Easy to say, hard to prove. Rutledge took another tack.

"Inspector Farraday wonders if you might be a German spy."

Kingston was aghast. "In God's name—" He got himself under control. "I've never been out of England. Never out of Yorkshire, come to that. Why would I spy for anyone, much less a country I don't even know? Besides, why would a spy kill a furniture maker?"

"Money?" Rutledge suggested, although he tended to disagree with Farraday on the subject.

Kingston buried his face in his hands. "It's a nightmare, I tell you. I just wanted my father's blessing, I just wanted to know he's forgiven me. And for him to see what I've done with my life these ten past years."

"Then we'll verify what you've said." He stood, stretching shoulders. "I'm going with you to your cousin's house."

"And tell them what? That I've lied to Inspector Farraday, and I'm suspected of killing a man I wouldn't have recognized if he passed me on the street?" He got to his own feet. "No thank you, I'd rather throw myself off that cliff and be done with it."

"Don't be so ridiculously melodramatic," Rutledge said shortly. "We've a long walk ahead of us, and I'm not in the mood."

Kingston stared at him, then fell in step. "I'm sorry. It's been a difficult time." He was silent until they'd reached the path that led down into the town. Then halfway down he commented, "I like the cut of your suit of clothes. London?"

"Yes."

"Do you have your own tailor? I'm sorry, but I've learned a good deal about men's fashions since I went to work for Mr. Hartle. I've considered learning how cloth is measured and cut. When I left the farm, I'd never seen a bespoke suit. We had the proper clothes to wear to church of a Sunday and the like, but the rest of the time it was corduroy and flannel and heavy cotton cloth seven days a week. Serviceable."

Rutledge let him rattle on. It was partly anxiety and partly curiosity, he knew, and by the time they'd reached the bottom of that long flight of steps, Kingston had fallen silent again.

They walked through the town without speaking, Kingston peering over his shoulder, as if expecting Inspector Farraday to leap out of the shadows at any moment. On the outskirts, he pointed to a muddy lane that wandered off to their left. Behind a stone wall in the distance, sheep grazed quietly, ignoring the pair of black horses higher up on the rising land.

At Kingston's direction, Rutledge turned into the lane and took the second right he came to, trying to avoid the ruts and puddles left over from the last rain. They had covered some distance before he saw the farmhouse in a fold of the land. They were well beyond Moresby now, and the abbey ruins had disappeared from view.

Kingston was even more apprehensive now, his hands clenching and unclenching at his sides.

"What are you going to tell them? Must you say you're from the Yard?"

In a space between the kitchen garden of the farmhouse and one of the smaller outbuildings, a line had been strung. A woman was taking in the washing, mostly bedclothes she must have hung out that morning. She paused in her work, a clothespin between her lips, and stared at the two men approaching her. It was not a friendly stare.

"I told you she doesn't like me," Kingston said beneath his breath. "She has only taken me in because my cousin insisted. But where else was I to sleep? I can't afford to put up at an inn or the hotel."

They were within hearing distance now. The woman called, "I don't recollect Tad sending for you. And who is this with you? Another penniless relative come to take advantage of a dying old man?"

5

There was such venom in her voice that Rutledge could almost feel her anger and contempt like a physical wall, and on the instant he changed his mind about the course this interview would take.

"I'm sorry, Hilda. This is Mr. Rutledge. He—" Kingston turned to Rutledge, his face pale and flustered.

"Mrs. Kingston?" Rutledge said pleasantly. "I apologize for intruding like this. But I knew your cousin, here, and I asked if I could come up to pay my own respects to his father."

"You're not sneaking him into that house, whatever you say about respects. He's not wanted there, Kingston isn't, and if he had any sense at all, he'd accept the fact that his father doesn't want any part of him, death bed or not. Now or ever."

Rutledge didn't stop. He was within thirty feet of her before he paused. "You speak very harshly of your husband's cousin. What has he ever done to you?"

"His reputation is enough. He's a thief. And don't speak to me about the prodigal son, in Scripture. There's no fatted calf or anything else for him here. He's wasting his time and my husband's goodwill, hanging about as he is."

Rutledge rather thought it was possibly sharing the inheritance that angered her, not Kingston's past.

"What is the elder Mr. Kingston dying of?" Rutledge asked.

"His kidneys are failing." She gestured to the line of bedclothes. "I can hardly keep up with the laundry. I don't need this extra work, I've my own to do."

"Where is the elder Mr. Kingston?"

His companion began to speak, but Rutledge held up a hand to silence him.

The woman glanced from Rutledge to Kingston and back again. Narrowing her eyes, she said, "You're not a solicitor, are you? Here to try and break the will?"

"I'm from London, Mrs. Kingston. Where is your husband's uncle?"

She gestured down the road, and Rutledge could see that the lane continued past this smaller holding and snaked across the land for another hundred yards before disappearing.

"The main farm is over there, beyond that rise. But if you're smart, you'll turn about now. Nobody wants either of you here."

A voice came from behind them. Rutledge turned to see a farmer bearing down on them. He was clearly angry, and he must have been close enough to hear some of the conversation with his wife. Rutledge tensed, uncertain what to expect.

But the man's wrath, if that's what it was, was directed to his wife. "I've told you. Mark's my cousin, and you'll treat him as such. His father gave me this land and a start, and I owe him something for that." Still angry, he turned on Rutledge. "And who might you be?"

"My name is Rutledge. I came here with Mr. Kingston. He seems to feel he's not wanted. I wondered why."

"Small wonder, if he's treated this way when my back is turned."

Kingston couldn't help himself. "How is my father today? Is he any better? Has he asked for me?"

"Haven't I just told you he's dying of his kidneys?" the cousin's wife snapped.

But the cousin said in a kinder tone, "The doctor thinks he may not last the night. I've spoken to him. I promised you I would. But I don't think he's in his right mind. I don't think he hears me. Or understands half of what I'm saying."

"Would it upset him if I went in to speak to him? Tad, it's important. I wouldn't ask, except this might be my last chance."

"I'm not feeding both of them their dinner," the woman warned.

Her husband ignored her. "All right. I'll take you to the house. Mary is there, she won't be happy to see you, but I'll try. And you never know."

Kingston turned to Rutledge. "I must go. Please, understand."

"Who is Mary?" Rutledge asked.

"My father's housekeeper." There was more constraint than affection in Kingston's voice. "She never liked me, she swore I led her son into mischief. In truth it was the other way around. He was older and more proficient at not getting caught."

"I've work to do in Moresby," Rutledge said. "I'll leave you to speak to your father alone."

The man's face reflected his gratitude. "Thank you," he said, and reached out for Rutledge's hand. Then he thought better of the gesture and let his drop.

Rutledge stayed where he was, watching Kingston and his cousin until they had disappeared over the hill. The woman had gone on collecting the bedding, not looking at him, as if ignoring him might make him disappear in a puff of welcome smoke.

When he was sure that Kingston was indeed being led to the main farmhouse, he turned on his heel and left.

But the woman couldn't let it go. "There's nothing for him. Or for you," she called. "So don't be getting any ideas about what the will says."

Rutledge turned. "I shan't worry about it. I'll leave it to the police, if anything happens to that man while he's staying with you."

She opened her mouth, then snapped it shut smartly. Reaching for the basket at her feet, already half full, she hefted it to her hip and marched back into the farmhouse, slamming the door behind her.

Back in Moresby, for a time Rutledge sat on a weathered bench near the harbor, his mind busy with the problem of Clayton's murder while idly watching clouds building up over the Yorkshire moors. Finally, satisfied that he must be right, he walked on to the police station and Inspector Farraday's office.

The local man listened to what he had to say about Kingston, then nodded. "So that's who he is. I knew my mind wasn't playing tricks on me. I knew he was up to something. What you don't know," he went on, a glint in his eye, "is that Kingston was a troublemaker of the first water, when he was younger. I can't tell you how many fights he must have started, and he was a thief to boot. Drove his poor father mad, because there was no dealing with him. I was just a constable then, I did what I could, but most people disliked bringing charges, for his father's sake. It was a good week when he vanished in the night."

"He's not the same man now," Rutledge said, frowning. "You can't jail him for what he did before he was twenty. Unless there is an open warrant for it."

"People like Kingston don't change. Oh, yes, in appearance, I grant you. That explains why I didn't recognize him straightaway. And consider this: if he's been given leave to come here in the hope of seeing his father, how is he managing to live?"

"I've told you. He's staying with Tad Kingston and his wife."

"Cold comfort there. What if he'd been standing up there on the headland, wishing he had the price of a meal, and he saw Miss Clayton leave for the evening? He might have thought the house was empty, and if Clayton was there, quietly reading or dozing in his chair, he might not have heard Kingston breaking in."

"I'd agree with you but for two things. No one broke in to that house. And nothing is missing."

"All right, the door wasn't locked. But Kingston had no right to be in that house, did he? He's not likely to steal the candlesticks, he'd have no use for them. But he might've helped himself to a few pounds from Clayton's purse. We can't be sure the daughter knew how much money he carried with him that Tuesday. She hadn't counted it."

"I can't see Kingston hanging his victim. Bashing him over the head with the fire tongs, yes, perhaps. Hanging is another matter."

"It served its purpose, didn't it? Threw us well off the track."

"Where did he learn to tie a hangman's knot?"

"He's been gone nearly eleven years. Closer to twelve, come to that. He could have learned a good many unsavory things in that time."

Rutledge shook his head. "I don't see Kingston in the picture."

"Then who else, pray, fits it?"

"I'd like to look into Clayton's past. His background in Somerset or wherever it was. That shouldn't be too difficult to trace." What's more Sergeant Gibson, at the Yard, was a master at digging out information, no matter how obscure the lead. But he didn't need to tell Farraday how he intended to go about it.

"Wild goose chase. No, of all the people we've questioned, I'd put my money on Kingston. Besides." He studied Rutledge for a moment. "Nearly three pounds were stolen from a house near the harbor just the week before. The day after Kingston arrived in Moresby."

Surprised, Rutledge said, "You never said anything about it before now."

"We thought it was one of the local lads. In fact we've been keeping an eye on him to see if we're right."

"Then it's possible *he* killed Clayton in a botched attempt to rob him."

"He's fourteen and scrawny. How did he heave Clayton up the stairs, much less convince the man to let him in?"

"I'd keep an eye on that boy, all the same. If he's brought in for that theft, then Kingston is in the clear for it." Rutledge took a deep breath. "I'm going to need to consult with the Yard. Before we take this inquiry any further."

"And if his father dies, meanwhile? And Kingston discovers there's nothing in the farm for him, what do we do?"

"He works for a man called Hartle in Scarborough. It should be simple enough to find him there. As you say, he will need to keep that position if his father leaves him nothing."

"If he's killed once, he might take it into his head to murder his own cousin."

If murder lurked in Kingston's heart, Rutledge thought to himself, it would be Tad's wife that he would be tempted to kill.

"He could hardly take over the farm, if he were hanged."

"Still," Farraday said. "Kingston lied to the police, didn't he? What else is he concealing? I ask you."

Farraday had made up his mind. But Rutledge remained unconvinced. He asked, "Is there a telephone nearby? It will be the quickest way to resolve this."

Farraday shook his head. "Not in Moresby."

That settled it.

"Then I'll have to take the first train to London, find out where Clayton's roots are, look to see if there is anything in his background we ought to know about, and return as quickly as I can. Meanwhile, keep an eye on Michael Clayton. He's feeling left out of the family circle just now. Keep another watch on Kingston. If his father has changed the will, I'm more worried about Tad's wife deciding that Mark Kingston should simply disappear. There's a good deal of water out here. What better place to toss a body?"

"My money is on Kingston," Farraday said firmly.

Rutledge started to say that the inquiry was his, not Farraday's, then thought better of it. There was no need to antagonize the man. Nodding, he said, "I'll be back as quickly as I can. Allow Kingston to see his father. If he's not our man, then we'll have done him a grave disservice if we interfere with that."

He went back to his lodgings, quickly packed his belongings, and carried on to the railway station. As he'd expected, the next train to London pulled in twenty minutes later, and he was on his way south. With his last look at Moresby Abbey, he had a feeling that Farraday would act on his own once the Yard was out of sight. It would be necessary to speak to Bowles, and through him to the Yorkshire Chief Constable. A word in his ear would keep Farraday in line.

It was only after they'd reached York that Rutledge realized he'd be in London in time for the Gordons' party. He'd tried to put it out of his mind and concentrate on the inquiry. Now he could allow himself to think about Friday with a clear conscience. He felt a rising excitement at the prospect of seeing Jean so soon.

A man entered the compartment, a newspaper tucked under his arm. He took the seat across from Rutledge and opened it. From where he was sitting, Rutledge could read the headlines on the page facing him.

He didn't like the look of them. It appeared now that the assassination of the Archduke had involved more than a handful of fanatical nationalists, bent on making trouble. There were indications of a Serbian government role. It was no longer a question of hanging a few anarchists. Austria would be well within her rights to march. Meanwhile, Russia's threats to step in and protect a fellow Slavic nation would take on new and ominous overtones. No longer saber rattling but a very real danger of war. The question was, would Germany, Austria's traditional ally, feel compelled to act on *her* behalf? The Kaiser was making it clear that any involvement on Russia's part would be viewed as a serious matter.

And yet—and yet. In the end, wiser heads might prevail, and it would all blow over. Tsar Nicholas would listen to his advisors and recognize that protecting Serbia would cost more than he could possibly gain. The Kaiser could consider he'd done his duty by Vienna by stepping up. And Serbia might take fright and deliver up to Austria all those who had had a hand in the death of the Archduke, allowing them to stand trial.

All the same, Rutledge rather thought that Farraday was right, this business could well engulf most of Europe. In Victoria's day—even in that of the late King Edward—the English royal family's blood ties with the rest of Europe, including Russia and Germany, would have counted for something. The question was, would King George have the same influence?

Time would tell.

He put it out of his mind and watched the passing scene until it was too dark to pick out landmarks. As soon as he reached London, he and Sergeant Gibson would track down where Ben Clayton had come from and find out whether he'd had a past there. Then he'd be free to attend his own engagement party, setting out at midnight if he had to, in order to be at his destination by Saturday morning. There was a pressing need to return to Yorkshire as soon as he possibly could.

Best of both worlds . . . Rutledge smiled to himself. As a married man he would have to learn to juggle both of them.

Dressed and shaved, Rutledge made one stop on the way to the Yard, arriving there late on Friday morning. He ran down Sergeant Gibson and conferred with him for half an hour.

Gibson was a veteran at the Yard, and he had amassed contacts across half of England, or so it sometimes seemed. An irascible man, he had no favorites, and was Rutledge's ally only as far as it concerned Chief Superintendent Bowles. But he was the best at what he did, which was finding out information that eluded everyone else.

No one knew quite why Sergeant Gibson disliked Bowles. He concealed his feelings very well, but there was something possibly left over from a distant past that might also have explained why Gibson had never risen beyond the rank of sergeant.

There was no doubt that Bowles was a difficult man for anyone to deal with, although his superiors looked at his record and either turned a blind eye, or agreed that they were unwilling to promote him further, even to be rid of him.

Rutledge thought the problem with Bowles was simple. He'd begun his career in the ranks, a man of limited education and lower-middle-class roots. He'd taught himself to speak well, had polished his image by choosing a better tailor when he reached the rank of Inspector, but he had never changed his mind-set. Suspicious, jealous, seeking to appear the initiator of any successfully concluded case, he had acquired a reputation for never applauding any effort by someone who might in time challenge his position as Chief Superintendent.

Chief Inspector Cummins had felt his wrath, and so had Rutledge, among others, ostensibly for not following orders, but it was generally felt that the new breed of better educated men from a better social class had drawn his ire simply because they were able to deal comfortably with a wider range of witnesses and suspects. Addressing a duchess or an archbishop came as easily to them as interviewing a guttersnipe or a fishwife.

Listening to Rutledge's request, Gibson said, "It's a wild goose chase."

"Possibly. But according to the records in Somerset House, where I went this morning, our man can be traced to Somerset, to a village just outside Bristol. Netherby is the name of it. What the official records *can't* tell me is why he chose to leave there and never come back. What did he do—or fail to do—that might have led to his death once it was discovered that he was living in Moresby."

"There was no one in Moresby with a better motive? Sir?"

"The interviews in Moresby were well done, and I followed them up for myself. There's nothing in Clayton's present life to explain such a vicious killing. And he seldom referred to his past. In fact, even his children weren't certain just where he'd lived before coming to Yorkshire."

"Then you're as likely to find you have the wrong Clayton. Did you consider the possibility that he'd changed his name with his county?"

"If that's the case, we'll never know what he did. It would also mean that his wife and possibly her family agreed to go along with the change in name. She knew him when he lived in the West Country. And while she might have agreed—it was a love match—her father was a canny man and is said to have looked into Clayton's past for himself."

"I'll do what I can," Gibson told him gloomily. "Sir."

"Will you send a message to the house, if you find anything?"

"Sir."

Rutledge nodded and left him to it. He reported to Bowles, who seemed to have other matters on his mind and brushed aside Rutledge's uncertainty about Moresby. "When a man says nothing about his roots, he's either ashamed of them or wants to forget them. Worth looking into."

With that blessing, feeble as it was, Rutledge cleared his desk and then went home to prepare for the evening.

The affair was to be held at the Gordon house, and he'd had strict instructions to arrive early. Ross Trevor had sent him a message that he'd bring Frances, and she seemed to be relieved to be escorted by him rather than her brother, pleading the need for more time to dress.

Rutledge walked in the open door to find the rooms filled with flowers, their scent heavy in the warm air. He was told that Jean was still putting the finishing touches to her toilette. Her father, on the other hand, was in the study and expecting him.

Gordon was in excellent spirits.

"Hallo, Ian. Glad you returned in time. Jean was fearful you might not be here. Worried all week about that. Even so, the ladies have been busy seeing to all the arrangements. I've left them to it."

"The house is transformed."

"Here, have a bit of courage before the evening's fanfare." He went to the silver tray of drinks and reached for the whisky. Pouring a glass for himself and another for Rutledge, he added, "I've had to retire to my club the last three nights. You'll be complimentary, of course."

"Yes, of course." Rutledge smiled. It was the sort of party his own parents would have given for Frances, if they'd lived. He made a note to speak to Melinda Crawford about standing in for them when the time came.

"What do you think about events in Europe?" Gordon asked.

"I'm hoping it's merely posturing and comes to nothing."

"This is for your ears, only, but I've already been warned that if matters proceed, I'm to be prepared to be called back to duty."

This was surprising news. Rutledge was about to ask if he'd been given a reason when the butler, a slender man in his fifties, came to announce that the ladies were on their way down.

"Thank you, Simpson. All right, Ian, drink up, and we'll face the worst together." He smiled and, as Rutledge set his empty glass on the tray, took his future son-in-law's arm and led him back to the foyer. Mrs. Gordon was just descending the staircase, wearing a dark blue gown with silver trim, and there were feathers of the same color in a silver pin set in her graying hair. She was still quite an attractive woman, and there was no doubt that Jean's beauty had come from her mother.

Mrs. Gordon smiled at her husband and gave her hand to Rutledge. "How handsome you are tonight," she said.

He took her hand in his. "And how beautifully you've arranged everything. I must say, it's like walking into a summer garden."

She thanked him, looking quite pleased. Then, glancing around at the floral displays, she added anxiously, "I hope the heat won't wilt them before midnight. Do you think, my dear, that it will storm tonight?"

"I don't expect rain," her husband answered. "We'll leave the garden doors open. That should help."

He stopped and turned back toward the stairs.

Jean was just coming down. Rutledge's heart stirred. She was quite radiant in a rose gown that set off her coloring. He smiled up at her.

"My dear, I've never seen you so lovely," her father announced and took her hand as she reached the last step. "I'm already regretting losing you."

She laughed then, a little nervously, and said to Ian, "I was so worried."

"I told you I'd be here," he answered, leaning forward to kiss her on the cheek.

The first guests began to arrive just then, and Rutledge stood with the Gordons in the receiving line for over an hour, a whirlwind of names and faces, congratulations and best wishes. And then they were free to enjoy the half hour before dinner.

Jean, cheeks flushed with happiness, took his arm and said, "I would die for something to drink."

He found a lemonade for her and she drank thirstily. "Lovely," she said, handing the empty cup to a passing footman.

"I've never seen the house so beautiful," she went on, looking around at the displays of flowers and laden tables. The summer evening light created a golden haze that made candles unnecessary just yet, but candelabras stood ready to be lit.

"You and your mother are to be congratulated," he said, and meant it. "It's quite marvelous."

"Do you truly think so?" she asked, looking up at him. "It isn't Papa who put you up to saying something?"

He held her hands in his and smiled. "He's as proud of you both as I am. And tonight will be the talk of London."

Laughing, she gestured to the crowded room. "We're expected to mingle. I'll go this way, you go in that direction, and we'll meet on the far side."

Seeing Ross Trevor standing by the whisky decanters, Rutledge walked over. "I'm so glad you could make it," he said. "I'm sorry David couldn't."

"Not half as sorry as he is. He wanted to be here. By the bye, Morag sends her best." Morag was the Trevor family's housekeeper. She'd run the house since the death of Ross's mother and had always treated Rutledge like another child. "She told me you should be marrying a Scottish lass."

"Give her my love. Tell her if she'd been twenty years younger, I might have proposed to her."

Ross nodded. "That will please her. I'm to bring her a detailed account of the evening, and what Jean is wearing, and what we have for dinner." He paused for a moment, then said quietly, "You're a lucky man, Ian. I wish you both well." He lifted the glass he was holding in a salute. "I thought as much when I met Jean at Melinda's."

"Which reminds me, I must go and find Melinda. I wasn't sure she'd come."

"Wild horses couldn't have kept her away." He hesitated. "Frances is taking it hard." He gestured to the room at large. "I expect she thinks you'll be swallowed up in happiness and neglect her. But after the first excitement is over, she'll be glad to have a sister. The Yard keeps you on the go."

"That's why I've had only one drink this evening. I shall have to leave at first light, if not sooner."

"Yes, I noticed you didn't have a glass. Try the punch over there. It's quite good and won't see you into the bushes at the first curve."

"I will. Thanks." Rutledge clapped Ross on the shoulder and moved on, speaking to others as he passed.

Jean's cousin Kate was just finishing a conversation with friends and turned his way as Rutledge was passing. They collided, and he held her shoulders to steady her.

"Hallo again," she said, looking up at him. "Are you enjoying the evening?"

"Immensely." She was a very attractive young woman, with light brown hair and dark brown eyes, and he'd always enjoyed her company.

He was about to say something more about the evening, when she took his arm and whispered, "Here comes Teddy Browning again. Please, Ian, don't abandon me."

She was right. He saw Teddy, tall, slim, and fair, handsome in his dress uniform, bearing down on them. Rutledge smiled at him. "Someone was looking for you just now," he said, pretending to scan the room. "Over by the punch bowl, I think."

Kate's father was standing there, talking to friends. Teddy's face lit up, and he excused himself, weaving his way through the crowded room toward the older man.

Kate said, "My father will never forgive you. I don't think he likes Teddy any more than I do."

"He seems to like you well enough," Rutledge replied in a teasing voice.

She sighed. "He thinks he's in love with me. But he's not. Last month he thought he was in love with Marilyn Whiting. And in May it was Sarah Bellefont."

"And who are you in love with?" he asked.

She said tartly, "I'm going to be a spinster."

He laughed. Kate was charming, intelligent, and well connected. He didn't think there was much chance of that.

She laughed with him, and then in a more serious vein, she said, "I hope you and Jean will be happy."

"Do you doubt it?" He meant it lightly, taking her words at face value.

Kate looked straight at him. "Truthfully? I don't know. Jean has Enthusiasms. She always has. Her friends are out and getting themselves engaged, and she's happy to be joining them in their talk about wedding parties and gowns and how to manage the servants."

"I wasn't her only suitor."

"That's true. Of course. And I truly believe she cares for you, Ian. It's not that. What I see is how much you care for her, and I think it is by far more love than she can give anyone."

"Why are you telling me this? Here? Now?" But Kate had always been honest. About herself, most of all, and always without malice. He'd admired that about her.

"Because I like you, Ian, and I want you both to be happy. If you are content being happy loving *her* and making *her* happy, it should be enough."

He didn't quite know what to say in reply.

Kate smiled, and lightly touched his arm. "Forgive me. I didn't intend to air my own thoughts. Not tonight of all nights. I expect I'm a little jealous. We've been so close, she and I. I miss that. Perhaps I shall have to accept Teddy, and then Jean and I can share everything again the way we used to."

Rutledge laughed, as she'd meant him to. "I shouldn't go that far," he said. "Not Teddy."

But he thought she had been quite serious. He hoped he was wrong.

One of their mutual friends joined them just then, where they stood by one of the open windows, commenting, "Ah, there's a nice breeze here. Kate, would you care for a turn in the garden before it's too dark? It should be cooler."

And with a quick glance at Rutledge's face, she went off with Harry.

Rutledge did his duty once more, circling the room, stopping to chat again and again, then pausing to speak to Mrs. Gordon, who said, her face bright with the success of the evening, "I don't believe I've ever seen Jean as happy as she is tonight. All her friends are telling her what a remarkably handsome couple you are, and I think even dearest Kate must agree. Which reminds me, Jean is looking for you."

"I'll find her," he promised, but before he could make his way to where Jean was surrounded by other young women, her expression animated as she talked, he spotted Melinda with a court of older men around her, most of them high-ranking members of the government or the military. Leaving Jean to her friends for the moment, he crossed to where Melinda was sitting and waited for her to notice him. She held out a hand, and he took it, coming to sit beside her.

She sent her admirers away and turned to him. "I'm glad to see you so happy."

"Are you?" he asked, searching her face. "I thought you had reservations."

"I did, I admit it. She's young, Ian, and I don't mean only in years. You'll need to remember that and help her find her way in a policeman's world. It won't be easy."

"I've thought about that. Especially tonight. She's accustomed to a very different place in Society, isn't she? Which isn't to say she can't keep that place. But she knows how much Scotland Yard means to me."

"Does she? I wonder if her parents do. They like you, Ian. But they might well like you even better, if you were in another line of work. The Army, her father's world, is a very close family. And you're outside it."

He remembered his conversation with the Major. But he said, "She loves me. And she knows what I do. She's accepted that."

Melinda Crawford smiled but didn't answer him. At that moment, dinner was announced, and he rose, ruefully.

"I must take Jean in. Do you mind?"

"My dear, I shall manage quite well. I was Army too, and I must still know half the General Staff. In fact, there's a retired Brigadier bearing down on us now, with a look on his face that tells me he's my dinner partner." She touched his arm. "But thank you for caring."

He moved across the room to where Jean was waiting with her parents, and the procession moved toward the dining room doors. Jean held his arm tightly. "I haven't had five minutes with you," she whispered. "Will you come by tomorrow? We'll have a picnic somewhere in the country. Just the two of us."

"I'd like that," he said, and didn't have the heart to tell her then that he'd be halfway to Somerset before she was out of bed.

6

He left shortly after two in the morning, having stopped by the house to change out of his evening clothes and take up the valise he'd already packed. Gibson had left a message for him: *Start in Bristol.*

This time he drove his own motorcar. It had been an extravagance, but he enjoyed it and had found it surprisingly useful. He'd spoken to Frances before she left the party on Ross's arm. She had been unexpectedly cheerful, and he realized with sheer relief that she'd enjoyed her evening. His sister was tall and very attractive, and there was an abundance of young Army officers who were happy to dance with her. He'd taken his own turn, and she had seemed almost preoccupied before asking him about his friend Richard, with whom she'd danced the last waltz.

"He's engaged, I think," he said lightly. "Don't set your cap for him."

"I shan't have to," she said enigmatically, and then smiled. "Ian, I take back every reservation I've had about Jean. I think you've made a good choice. Truly I do. And I like her parents as well. This is the first time I've really spoken to them. More than the usual polite exchanges at parties or the theater."

He brought her hand up to his lips and kissed her fingers. "It means more than you know," he said, "to hear you say that."

"You've always been my brother, always there when I needed you. I think I was just being selfish. Wanting to keep you to myself a little longer."

What lay unspoken between them was the fact of their parents' deaths. She had had no one else to turn to. And together they had managed to live through the nightmare and all the changes it had brought in its wake.

"I think Jean understands that as well. She's another part of our family, that's all. Not a wedge. Never a wedge."

The dance came to an end. Another officer was there to take his place, and he relinquished his sister with a smile. He went to find his next partner, one of Jean's closest friends, then found a moment to speak to Jean herself before taking another turn.

On the whole, he thought, the evening had gone very well indeed, and after the last guest had left, the Major had taken him into his study and said, "Well, that's past us now." Grinning, he loosened his tie and reached for the brandy decanter. "I swear, I've not danced this much for ten years. I was the wallflower patrol. And I saw you doing your own duty there. Good man." He offered his future son-in-law a drink, but Rutledge shook his head.

"Speaking of duty, I shall have to go to Somerset this weekend."

"Oh, too bad. We were thinking of going up to Henley to have lunch with friends. Jean and her mother are looking forward to it."

So much for the picnic. He was glad he wouldn't have to disappoint Jean.

But he had a feeling he'd disappointed the Major.

Toward three in the morning, he felt fatigue pulling at him, and he found a farm lane where he could sleep for a few hours, half hidden by tall hedgerows. An equally sleepy horse came to lean over the fence and inspect him, then it moved away again.

Stiff and in need of a shave, he drove into Bristol later in the morning than he'd expected, and found a hotel on the hill near the university where there was a little breeze in the rising morning heat. After shaving, changing, and sitting down for a quick breakfast, he made his way to the police station.

There he discovered that Sergeant Gibson had already been in touch with a Sergeant Miller.

The desk sergeant sent him down a passage to a cramped room where Miller had a table desk.

A tall, thin man with prematurely gray hair, Miller was deep in a collection of files. He looked up as Rutledge came into the room, a frown on his face. It cleared when he realized the interloper was a stranger.

"You wouldn't be Inspector Rutledge, by any chance?" he asked, rising. "I didn't expect you this soon."

"This is a rather pressing matter. An inquiry in Yorkshire hinges on what I learn here. You've spoken to Sergeant Gibson?"

"I have, and I've been looking through some of these files. Nothing criminal on a man named Benjamin Clayton. Although I did find he sold the shop inherited from his father." Miller thumbed through the papers before him, and gave the date.

"Did he indeed?" Rutledge asked, interested. The time was close enough to fit Clayton's arrival in Moresby to marry a young would-be schoolmistress. "Tell me more about this shop."

"There are a number of families on the rolls with the surname of Clayton. The great-grandfather of your lot, a man with the Christian name of Harold, was apprenticed to a furniture maker, his son Alfred after him. Then the next in line, also an Alfred, opened his own shop. It sold household goods, mostly from Birmingham, as well as a few handmade pieces of furniture, and it flourished. My next question was, where did this Alfred find the money for such a shop? I looked into *that*. It seems the father of your Clayton married well, and used his wife's dowry."

The names matched what he'd learned at Somerset House in London. Still, he wanted to be absolutely certain. "And we're quite sure that this is the family of the man who went to live in Yorkshire."

He could see Sergeant Miller bristle. "You must look for answers to that in Yorkshire. Benjamin sold up and left. That's as far as our information goes."

"I understand. What I'm searching for is a past that might have followed him there. Does this shop still exist?"

Miller gave him directions, and Rutledge set out to find Netherby. It lay east of Bristol, and Rutledge discovered he'd actually driven through it on his way into Bristol although he hadn't seen a sign giving its name. In the shadow of the larger town, it had never attained more than village status. Still, Netherby had a small church with a tall, elegant tower, and a number of pretty houses on the High Street. He had no trouble finding the building he sought—but it had been converted into a barber's shop many years before. He spoke to the barber, who was busy stropping his razors, and learned that the furniture shop had only survived Ben Clayton's decision to sell up for some ten years.

"The new man didn't have the knack," the barber told Rutledge. "Everyone needs a haircut, man and boy. But it's quite another matter convincing a housewife she needs a new carpet this year, or a more comfortable chair or a sturdier washtub. Mr. Stedman hung on as long as he could, but it was never the prosperous business it was under Alfred Clayton or his son Ben."

To Rutledge's surprise, the barber, a stooped, graying man of perhaps sixty, actually remembered Ben Clayton.

"And for the price of a haircut," he added, folding his razors and setting them away, "I'll remember more than the name."

As the shop was empty, it was a fair trade, and Rutledge laughed as he sat down in the worn chair. "The sign says LOLLY'S. Is that you?"

"Was when I was a lad. I took the name for the shop because Edgar didn't sound quite right, to my ears."

The barber whisked a sheet across Rutledge's chest, and set to work. Rutledge reminded him of their bargain.

"I remember the father best. As a lad I'd do errands for him, and earn a few pence. But I knew Benjamin also. Nice lad, he was. Alfred, now—the father—knew his worth, and he gave good value for the money in everything he sold. Wife died young of her appendix, and so there was only the one child. Clever with his hands, Alfred was, and the boy took after him. Ben was always trying something new. Most of it didn't suit at first, then people began to ask for his chairs. After that they wanted tables to match, and my wife bought one of his tea tables—the top tilted, you could push it against the wall, if you liked, out of the way. But he was quiet, you see, not one to stand about and chat, like his father."

"Was he ever in any trouble?"

"Benjamin? No, not the sort, in my book. Went to church of a Sunday, fell in love with a nice girl from the teacher training school, and married her. But that was after his father had passed on. He was taking a cart to the school outside Wells, chairs I expect it was, and she was in the parlor when he came to the door."

Once more the information fit. "Married her and left Somerset?"

"That's how it was. I can't bring to mind just where it was he went. He did say he had no ties here, not with his father gone, and I was looking for a place of my own to set up shop. But he sold to Stedman and shook hands on it." He turned and pointed to a rosewood chair in one corner. "He did that one for me. My wife's having the cover redone, something a bit more cheerful."

The elegant ladies' chair, with the knot of carved cabbage roses at the peak of the back, was beautifully made, the finish still rich with beeswax and polish, although with time the seat had grown dark with wear, the original pattern of the fabric all but obscured.

"Of an evening she always sits in that chair."

"Did Clayton have any friends to speak of? Anyone he owed money to, anyone he might have had difficulties with? Someone who might have known where he'd gone to live?"

"Benjamin? Not what you'd call close friends, no. Although he was on friendly terms with everyone in the village. He was a hard worker, with very little time to spare for an evening in the pub. Still, people respected him. He was meticulous about money, and everyone knew he was as honest as the day's long. If he gave you a price, he held to it. I never heard any word said against him."

Lolly whipped off the covering and stood back. "Now, then, there you are."

Rutledge looked in the mirror and was satisfied. He'd had his hair cut before the party, but Lolly had trimmed it nicely. He said as much and paid what was asked.

As Rutledge rose from the barber's chair, Lolly said, his head to one side, "You haven't said why you're interested in Benjamin Clayton. I've told you what you wanted to know. It's only fair you should tell me why you come around asking about a man gone these thirty years."

"I never knew much about his past. He never spoke of Netherby to his family. I wondered why. I was in Bristol this morning. It wasn't far to come to Netherby."

Lolly nodded. "I expect Netherby held only sad memories for him. Losing his ma so young, and then his pa before his time too. Horse stepped on his foot, gangrene set in, and the doctors couldn't stop it. Not an easy death. You tell Ben Clayton that old Lolly remembers him right enough, and the chair's still just fine."

Rutledge added something to what he'd paid, and thanked the barber.

But as he went down the street, in the direction of the church, he thought that Benjamin Clayton must have indeed been the good man his children had claimed he was. Then who had killed him?

He stopped by the church, looking for the vicar, and found him changing the numbers on the hymn rack.

He turned, nodded to Rutledge, and clambered down the ladder to come and greet him.

"Good morning! Visitor, are you?"

"I'm doing a little research into family history. I wonder if you remember a Benjamin Clayton, late of this village and now a resident in Yorkshire. He tells me we shared a great-aunt, who lived here."

The vicar smiled. "I've only been here these ten years. I'm afraid I don't know a Benjamin Clayton. But there are Claytons in the churchyard here. One of them might well be your shared great-aunt."

Rutledge was looking around him. "This is a little gem of a church," he said, amazed to find such beauty in a village this size. The wood paneling, the ends of the benches, and the choir were old and exquisitely worked.

"Yes, it was built in the years when wool was king. No expense spared by the Benton family. Benton's wife was from this village, and he rebuilt the church for her. There's gold leaf in the chancel, and the altar was carved by a German woodworker. And the misericords in the choir were done locally, with such vigor. The glass is quite good, and you can see the pulpit for yourself. A marble work of art. So is the baptismal font."

It was clear he took great pride in his church, and for the next fifteen minutes he took Rutledge on a tour. And then, suddenly remembering that his companion was interested in the dead, he said, "But I'm forgetting my manners. I'll show you where to find the Claytons."

They walked outside into the sunny churchyard. Flowers were rampant in front of some of the grave stones, adding bursts of color to the green of the grass. Trees shaded a good part of it, and sun picked out the stones on the east side and lit the details of the tower. Rutledge had been looking at that when the vicar said, "Here are the Claytons. You should be able to read most of the inscriptions."

They'd been buried along the south side of the church, and Rutledge knelt on one knee to look at them. He counted seventeen family members, going back five generations. The stones weren't ornate, but they had all been well carved, and verses from the New Testament had been engraved on most of them. Ben Clayton's mother and father were there, lying side by side.

"You'll find an Agnes Clayton just there," the vicar was saying, pointing out a stone at the edge of the grouping. "Married a cousin, I believe. She may be the ancestress you're seeking."

"She must be indeed." He noted her dates, and then thanked the vicar for taking the time to show him the church and the graves. They made their way around the apse toward the far side, the vicar pointing out various features remaining from an earlier church on the site, and that was when Rutledge saw the stones.

Blackened, smeared, and ugly. An attempt had been made to clean them, but to no avail. Whatever the mixture was—lampblack and paint?—he couldn't read a single name carved into them. It was as if they had been deliberately obliterated.

"What happened here?" Rutledge asked, and almost at once answered his own question. "They've been vandalized by the look of them." Davies's unsolved case? Cummins hadn't told him the village name, but he'd said the churchyard was in Somerset.

The vicar said tightly, "We've never found the guilty party. Or known why those graves were damaged while so many others have not been touched. It's a desecration. I've prayed that the police will find out who has done this, if only to know why he's so disturbed."

Rutledge surveyed the damage. Surely here indeed was Inspector Davies's unsolved case. He remembered how lightly he and Cummins had discussed the inquiry. Looking down at the evidence before him, it no longer seemed humorous. There was a violence and hatred here that was shocking, the black substance layered on with savage intensity, as if the person doing this wished he could tar the body buried here as well. But he said nothing to the vicar of Inspector Davies.

"It's a tragedy," he said, and meant it. "And you know of no connection among these people?"

"They died on different dates of different causes as far as I can ascertain. A farm accident for that one, typhoid fever took another one, cancer two more, and a brain hemorrhage for the most recent. I've made it my business to find out. I even wondered if someone hated doctors. There's a doctor among them." He sighed. "Desecration, that's what it is. Family members have been very upset, as you can imagine." They walked on. "My training says that all men have good in them. And I strive to find it. But this is depravity. The dead can't fight back."

Rutledge thanked him again as they reached the churchyard gate and took his leave.

As he walked back to where he'd left his motorcar, he thought that he must tell Cummins what he'd seen here. And that the vicar had been right to fear for his church. But that was all that he'd accomplished here in Somerset.

Unless there was a connection in Netherby with Clayton's death that he hadn't found.

Yet.

He was no longer so convinced that there might be.

Clayton's break with the village had been amicable and permanent. Hardly the stuff of murder thirty years later.

Now he must return to Moresby and look into the possibility that the killer had mistaken his target. There had been the older man living next door to the Clayton house. Talmadge, his name was. His past would bear looking into next.

Which was certain not to please Inspector Farraday.

As he turned toward London, Rutledge wondered if Jean was enjoying Henley with her parents. For all the good he'd done by rushing to Bristol, he could have stayed in London and spent the day with the Gordons.

When Rutledge reached London, he looked at his watch and saw that there was still time to call in at the Yard before going home.

Bowles was not in, but Rutledge stopped to thank Sergeant Gibson for directing him to Sergeant Miller.

"Little good it did you," Gibson said. "Or you'd be more pleased than you are. Sir."

"True, but there's another possibility I'd like to look into when I get back to Yorkshire. A man by the name of Talmadge."

"There's no need. A suspect's already in custody."

Surprised, Rutledge said, "Inspector Farraday's found Clayton's killer? Who is it?"

"You'll have to ask Himself on Monday. He sent for you and wasn't best pleased you were haring about in Somerset when the murder was in Moresby."

Rutledge swallowed the retort he'd been about to make. Bowles had agreed to his going on to Somerset. It wasn't Sergeant Gibson's fault, but it would delay his return to Yorkshire if he must wait to speak to the Chief Superintendent.

He went to his office to see if Bowles had left anything on his desk. But there was nothing.

The rank and file referred to Bowles as Old Bowels, and with good reason—his ill temper was legendary. When Rutledge walked into his office on Monday morning, Bowles glared at him and snapped, "There's an inquiry come in that needs your attention.

You had no business taking yourself off to Somerset without my authority."

"I went because I haven't closed the inquiry in Yorkshire," Rutledge said as pleasantly as he could manage. "It was my belief that you concurred in that decision."

"It's been closed. Yorkshire. And without your help, I might add. The local man informed me that you didn't wish to act, and he was forced to do it for you. And I'm told you hurried back to London for a party on the Friday night."

"There was a dinner honoring my engagement to Miss Gordon," he said. "Yes. But you knew about that. And I took my time in Moresby."

"I won't stand for insubordination, Rutledge. Do I make myself clear?"

"*Who* was taken into custody?" he pressed.

"Man by the name of Kingston."

Rutledge felt anger sweeping through him in a red tide. He tried to count to ten before answering but didn't quite make it past six. "I told Inspector Farraday that the case he presented against Kingston wouldn't stand up in court. That's why I went to Somerset, to look into the victim's background—"

Bowles didn't wait for him to finish, abruptly interrupting. "And did you find anything?"

"My opinion is—"

"Did you find anything." It was no longer a question.

"No—"

"Then Inspector Farraday's decision stands. The matter is closed."

"I'd wager my life that Kingston is innocent."

"We'll see how you feel about that when he's tried and found guilty." Bowles took up a file lying on his desk and gave every appearance of being absorbed by it. But Rutledge saw his eyebrows twitch in annoyance.

He left the office, feeling the roil of an anger so fierce he kept going, out of the building and down the street, unaware of where he was until he heard Big Ben strike the half hour and realized that he was just by Westminster Bridge.

He wasn't sure whether Bowles had been in the police force so long that he had lost any driving need to see justice done. If Inspector Farraday was satisfied that the inquiry was closed, then closed it must surely be.

Or was it the fact that Bowles had no imagination? He'd long suspected that. No ability to look beyond the obvious and see where supposition and possibility might lead.

Swearing, Rutledge turned back toward the Yard.

And then there was Farraday's decision.

Was *he*—Rutledge—wrong about Kingston? Or for that matter, Michael Clayton, the dead man's son? Had he looked into every corner of the inquiry before—as Bowles had put it—haring off to Somerset?

In his considered opinion, he had. And yet Farraday had won the day, Kingston was in gaol, and it would now be up to a jury, not an Inspector of police, to decide if the charges stood on their own merits or not.

Yet it *felt* wrong. He'd dealt with murderers before this, he'd had to sift through evidence and interviews, he'd had to come to a conclusion based on facts he could prove. Kingston had neither the courage nor the weakness necessary to kill.

He had reached the door to the Yard, but his anger was still molten, and he stood there for a full minute, debating what to do.

Just then Inspector Cummins came out of the building and nodded to him.

"You could give thunderclaps a bad name," he said. "Run-in with Bowles, was it?"

"Yes. He's cut short the inquiry in Yorkshire."

Cummins put a hand on his elbow. "Let's walk, shall we?" He

headed in the direction of Trafalgar Square and carried Rutledge along with him. "More of those blackened graves have come to light. This time in the village of Beecham. South of Bristol, a few miles from the first village. Davies was sent to have a look, and it appears to have been the same vandal, because whatever was poured on the first graves appears to be the same substance used here. Or else news of what happened earlier has sparked someone else to copy what was done."

"Davies must be beside himself." He turned toward Cummins. "While I was in Somerset, I happened on the first of the damaged graves. In Netherby." He went on to describe what he'd seen. "It was rather macabre, the way the names had been eradicated as the black substance, whatever it was, spread into every crevice. As if the dead were sinners, not fit to lie in a proper churchyard. The vicar hasn't found an answer, although apparently he's still looking." For a moment Rutledge watched the traffic moving around the square. "I did wonder if they might have some connection with Clayton. Now it seems unlikely."

"I'm sorry there isn't. Davies has two vicars and a local squire pressing him for answers. The latest theory is that someone is targeting churches. My feeling is that it's more personal than that."

"Male, again? The grave stones."

"Yes. One of them the squire's late nephew who owns a cottage not far from the church. Owned, I should say. Although his widow lives there still. She's as perplexed as everyone else is."

"The count is seven, now?" Rutledge asked, wrenching his mind away from his own thoughts. "Five in Netherby, two in Beecham?"

"I believe it is. Davies has looked at everything from wills to disputes over an inheritance. And he's no closer to the truth."

"What about a jury? Could these men have served on one?"

"That's quite clever, Ian." Cummins considered the suggestion, then shook his head. "Still, I don't see how that fits. At some point in time, all these men would have had to live close enough to have been called upon to serve together. According to the information Davies has, three of the five in the first churchyard hadn't died in the village but had been brought back there for burial in the family plot. And one of the two in Beecham had been brought back as well. Quite a scattered population, in fact."

"Another possibility is that they shared a secret of some sort. Or someone believes that they did."

"That has possibilities. I'll pass the suggestion along to Davies. He'll be grateful."

"At least he's not faced with an innocent man sitting in prison, awaiting trial."

"Yes, well, if you feel that strongly, then the jury might also. What's the proof against this man?"

"Circumstantial, all of it. And the local man's memory of a troublesome lad who left town under a cloud. Farraday was a constable then, and he seems to think Kingston escaped his just deserts."

"That shouldn't affect his judgment now."

"I believe it has."

They had reached the small restaurant where Cummins usually bought his lunch, and Rutledge followed him inside. He wasn't hungry, but he ordered a cup of tea to be polite, and then changed his mind and asked for a sandwich as well.

He liked Cummins, he always had, a fair-minded man who took care with his cases and supported those under him. But he didn't think there was much Cummins could do about Yorkshire. And Kingston would have already lost his position in Scarborough, and perhaps the girl he wished to marry as well.

As if he'd heard the thought, Cummins said, "Have you decided where to live after your marriage?"

"For the time being, I expect I'll stay where I am. There's my sister to think of, you see."

"Well, take my advice. Two women in the same house, vying for the attention of one man and eager to make him happy, can be difficult."

He was considering the ramifications of that—after all, it was Frances's house—when he realized all at once that Cummins had changed the subject and was waiting for an answer or at least a comment about what he'd just said.

Rutledge lifted a hand in apology. "Sorry. I seem to have lost my train of thought."

"Engagements do tend to destroy a man's concentration," Cummins said with a laugh. "I was asking if you'd had a chance to look over the new file on your desk."

"The new file? No. Truth to tell, I haven't seen it."

"Odd case. I think Bowles gave it to you as punishment. He was not happy that the local man in Yorkshire gave him the news before you did."

Rutledge stirred his tea and said, "I doubt he's ever happy. Yes, all right, I'll go back and have a look."

"Good man."

For the rest of their meal, the two men discussed other Yard business, and then Cummins summoned the waiter and paid the bill, insisting that he settle up for Rutledge as well.

Rutledge wondered if the Chief Inspector had happened to see his abrupt departure from the Yard and come looking for him with an eye to smoothing over whatever it was that had disturbed him. As a rule Rutledge kept his temper well in hand, but Farraday's betrayal and Bowles's complacency had struck him as callous and deliberate.

He said wryly as they rose to go back to the Yard, "I know better than to lose my temper. But injustice rankles more than I care to say."

"You're young," Cummins replied, an echo of bitterness in his voice. "The time will come when you tell yourself you've done your best, and that it must be enough."

I hope I never reach that stage, Rutledge answered, but not aloud, for he saw that Cummins himself had already come close to that point.

The odd case, as Cummins had called it, took him just west of Wells, to Stoke Yarlington. It was a village of pretty thatched cottages, a venerable square-towered church, and a small manor house set behind tall gates at the far end of the High Street.

Rutledge drove again, as he had done to Bristol, and when he arrived it was rather late. He'd snatched a brief moment with Jean before leaving London. He looked for a place to spend the rest of the night, and found it not far from the narrow green in the heart of the village. The building appeared to have been a coaching inn at one point in its history, but now it housed the only pub to one side and a tearoom on the other. Above there were six bedchambers, if they could be called that, and tall as he was, his head brushed the rafters in the largest one available. He'd asked for it after seeing the others. At least the bed in the one he'd chosen appeared to be long enough for him. The woman from the pub left him with an oil lamp, and the admonition that if he wished his breakfast, he must ask in the tearoom.

"My sister runs it," Mrs. Reid said, preparing to shut the door. "Just tell her you've taken a room."

"Where is the police station?"

She regarded him suspiciously. "It's the front room in the constable's cottage. Look here, is it the murder brought you from London? If so, this room's taken. We don't cater to the newspapers or the people they send down."

"I'm from Scotland Yard, Mrs. Reid. I was asked by the Chief Constable to look into the murder. I'm afraid you must take your objections to him." It was late and he was tired. His voice brooked no discussion of the matter.

She nodded after a moment, her face uncertain, but she shut the door smartly. He rather thought the news of his arrival would have reached every ear in the village by first light, but there was nothing he could do about that.

After an early breakfast, he went to find the constable. The police station, if it could be called that, was indeed the front room of the cottage, but another room had been added to the rear to compensate for the lost space.

Constable Hurley was in his undershirt, his suspenders hanging down at his sides, when Rutledge knocked at the door, then walked in. Middle-aged, running to weight now, and balding early, he gave the impression at first glance of being incompetent.

Hurley said, "You're the man London sent down? Sir?"

"I am. Tell me about what happened to Joel Tattersall."

"Surely you've seen the report, sir?"

"I have. But you saw the body, according to what I've read. I'd like to know what else you saw and what you felt when you arrived at the scene."

"His sister found him. Miss Tattersall. A spinster. She was quite frantic, and I heard her crying for the doctor to come quickly. Dr. Graham is past seventy and slow. I went ahead to see what I could do, and there he was, Mr. Tattersall, lying there on his side just back of the door. She'd seen him as she came down the stairs, thought his heart had given out, and rushed for help, as there was no one else to send. The daily, Mrs. Betterton, hadn't arrived, for it had just gone seven."

"What did Dr. Graham have to say?"

"He thought it was Mr. Tattersall's heart as well. But he sent for his son, who lives in the next village, and the younger Dr. Graham took Mr. Hurley away to his surgery and told us later that afternoon that he hadn't died of his heart at all."

"He had died of an overdose of laudanum, according to the report I saw. Why was he taking it?"

"But that's just it, neither Miss Tattersall nor her brother had been prescribed it by Dr. Graham. Mrs. Betterton, who does for them, takes it sometimes to help her sleep because she has a neuralgia in her back. But she never carries it with her to the house."

"Is Dr. Graham certain of that?"

"He is, indeed, still having all his faculties, in spite of being slow afoot. Laudanum is a freakish thing, Mr. Rutledge, as you well know, sir. It gives the body rest, and frees it of pain, but too much and a person dies. Or can't stop craving it."

"Who was in the house at the time?"

"Only Miss Tattersall, and she swears the door was on the latch when she opened it to run for Dr. Graham."

"And what does gossip have to say about Mr. Tattersall's death?"

"He had a falling-out with his solicitor some weeks ago. Sorry to say, no one likes the man. He has chambers in Wells, but his firm has handled the affairs of the Tattersall family for generations. The trouble is, Mr. Simmons has developed an unfortunate taste for gambling. Mr. Tattersall accused him of embezzling certain funds. Mr. Simmons replied that Mr. Tattersall's refusal to listen to reason resulted in poor investment choices."

"And has anyone spoken to Mr. Simmons since Mr. Tattersall died?"

"He was drunk as a lord when Inspector Holliston went to call on him. Asking about the will, you see. There was no making any sense of what he said."

"Inspector Holliston is the man in Wells?"

"Yes, sir. It was he who asked that we summon the Yard. I'd not have done it on my own account."

"Why?"

"We like to do things in our own good time, you see. No offense intended."

"None taken. What in your opinion happened to Mr. Tattersall?"

"It's possible he took the laudanum of his own accord. He was something of a hypochondriac." He stumbled slightly, as if the word were unfamiliar to him. "I know it's what Dr. Graham had to say about him, always coming to the surgery with this or that ailment, most of them in his head."

"But he wasn't prescribed it."

"And then there's the man who does the outside work of the house. Bob. He and Mr. Tattersall were always at odds over the pruning. Bob having an aggressive hand with the shears."

"Hardly a reason to murder a man."

"You don't know how those two fought over the years," Constable Hurley answered darkly.

Rutledge had seen it before. Men who deliberately tried to aggravate each other, to the point of madness. Something in their personalities, something in their mind-sets that led to bickering and sometimes beyond. Yet the loss of one often led sooner rather than later to the death of the other. But not always.

Rutledge read the statements that had been collected and then nodded. "We'll begin with Miss Tattersall, I think. And then Dr. Graham."

Miss Tattersall's red eyes spoke of sleepless nights. But she was of a class where duty was paramount, even overruling grief. Tall, slim, with an intelligent face and no pretense at beauty, she was wearing a plain black dress with jet beads at the throat.

Leading them back to a small sitting room overlooking a bed of roses, she offered them tea, but Rutledge politely declined, instead offering his sympathy on the loss of her brother.

Following up on that, he asked gently, "Can you tell me just what happened when you discovered your brother's body? I've read the interview, but it will help me to see that morning more clearly."

She moistened dry lips with the tip of her tongue, and then said quietly, "I came down as usual to put the kettle on. I like the early morning, and I enjoy the quiet before Mrs. Betterton arrives to bustle about. You passed the stairs as you came in. I'd just started down them when I saw my brother lying there at the foot. My first thought was his heart, because he was lying so still. I called to him as I hurried down to him and put out a hand to touch his cheek. It was already cool. Unnaturally so. I realized then that he was still dressed, that he hadn't gone up to bed. That he must have been lying there for quite some time, while I was sleeping. There was no one else to summon Dr. Graham, although I opened the door to see if there was anyone on the street. I was wearing slippers, although I was dressed, of course. I looked at them for a moment and decided they didn't matter at a time like this. And so I walked quickly down to Dr. Graham's house. He was already awake. I'd been afraid I might have to pound on the door. I told him I feared something had happened to my brother. He could see that I was in my slippers and distressed. He came at once, just stopping long enough to fetch his bag."

She looked away then, staring out the window where a climbing rose the shade of blood framed the glass, one or two blossoms still visible despite the July heat. Her fingers smoothed the dark blue chintz arm of her chair. Rutledge waited.

After a moment, she picked up the thread of her story. "He asked me—Dr. Graham—if I'd tried to resuscitate Joel. I said no, explaining that his skin was already cool to the touch. But perhaps that was from the night air, and I thought then that I ought to have *tried*."

Rutledge stopped her. "Had your brother had trouble with his heart before this?"

"No. Not at all. But our mother had, you see. We came to the house, and he asked me to allow him to go in first. I hadn't told him that Joel wasn't in his bed. He was quite surprised to find him lying there by the door. But, of course, there was nothing to be done. Dr. Graham insisted that I go into the kitchen and make both of us a cup of tea. I really didn't want it, but he's an old man, and I thought it might be best to make it for his sake. I even asked if he'd like a little something in it. Joel often took a drop or two of whisky in his tea. But he said no. And so we sat there, with my brother still lying at the foot of the steps, and waited for the kettle to boil. I asked Dr. Graham then if it was his heart. He said he feared it must be. By that time Mrs. Betterton had arrived, and we had to give her a cup of tea as well. While I was occupied with her, Dr. Graham saw to it that Joel was removed to his son's surgery and he also had the floor cleaned where—where my brother had died."

"And at that time you still felt it was a natural death?"

"Oh yes, anything else never crossed my mind. It wasn't until the constable, here, told me about the laudanum that I knew it was something vastly different. Joel never used laudanum. I don't think he approved of it. But what I don't understand is how it came to be in his stomach. I didn't find a glass by his chair or in the kitchen. Where I'd expect to see one if he'd had something to drink before retiring. I also looked in his room. A little later, however, I found a broken glass in the dustbin."

"Where is it now?"

"I expect it went to the tip."

"Was your brother in any pain? Did he have any problems that would make him look for relief, and then swallow the wrong dose?"

"If you're asking if he were anxious, the answer is no. And he never complained of pain. But then he wouldn't. We'd been brought up not to complain, you see."

And yet the constable had told him that Tattersall was something of a hypochondriac. Was he careful not to worry his sister with imaginary ailments? Or afraid she would make light of them in her blunt, practical way?

"When the possibility of murder was raised, what did you think?"

"I didn't know what to think. I had been asleep just up those stairs. If someone had come into this house, they must have known that."

"And nothing was taken?"

"Nothing. Inspector Holliston asked me to look, and I did. Not so much as a matchstick was missing."

He was reminded of the inquiry in Moresby, where nothing had been taken except for a man's life. But Tattersall hadn't been hanged.

"Is there anyone you can think of who might have wished to see your brother dead?"

She shook her head. "No. I'd have said he wasn't the sort of man who would ever be murdered. It's odd—and it's troubling. I find myself looking at people in the village and wondering. But of course that's ridiculous. I don't know of anyone who would do such a thing to him."

"Which suggests that someone could have entered this house without breaking in. He could have come through the door and found your brother still downstairs?"

"Yes, sadly, that's true. We thought we had nothing to fear. How foolish we were. But I expect if someone had wanted to come in badly enough, he'd have found a way. We leave the kitchen door off the latch as well, so that Mrs. Betterton can come and go without disturbing us."

"Why do you think your brother was lying there by the stairs, so close to the door. Was he looking to find you—or to follow someone out? You told the doctor that the door was on the latch."

"If someone had come in and wanted to harm him, he would try to stop this person. I don't think he would have considered coming up the stairs until he knew I would be safe. Possibly he intended to lock the door after whoever it was left."

There was a stoicism in her voice that had the ring of truth in it. Setting aside her pain and her grief, she was looking at her brother's last moments as objectively as she could. She was of an age and a class that demanded it of her, and she would not fail in her duty. Mourning would have to wait.

Rutledge thought it very likely that she was right. The dying man's effort to lock the door behind whoever it was who had killed him was a natural instinct to protect his sister. But he'd never reached the door. Then why had she thought it was locked?

Unless the killer had locked it when he came in, and then let himself out the back way, so as not to be seen.

Rutledge asked to see the kitchen door. The back garden, protected by a high wall and shaded by tall trees, ran down to a small shed at the bottom. He went to have a look at it, then tested the wall's height himself.

It was just possible for him to pull himself to the top of the shed and then swing himself over the high wall. It was a long drop on the far side, but into heavy grass. Beyond lay a plowed field and beyond that a thin copse of trees.

If the killer had left by this route, he must have been tall enough to do what Rutledge had done.

But by the side of the house, there was a narrow passage with a small gate into the garden and flagstones leading across to the kitchen door. The way that the housekeeper arrived and left each day. If the killer had watched the house, he would have seen her regular movements, and perhaps late at night even tested the gate and the back door himself.

Not a random killing, then. A premeditated murder?

7

Dr. Graham was in his surgery. Rutledge and Constable Hurley waited for some ten minutes before he was free to speak to them.

The man's hair was white, as was the mustache that bristled above his upper lip. His hands were blue-veined and thin, but there was no quiver of age in them as he gestured to two chairs in front of the table he used as a desk. And his gray eyes were sharp, steady. His nurse, who looked to be thirty, had also been steady and unflappable in the face of a visit by Scotland Yard.

Dr. Graham said, before Rutledge could ask his first question, "I never said anything to Miss Tattersall about suicide. But I must tell you that under the circumstances, I've considered the possibility. The problem is, I know of no reason for it. Tattersall was in reasonably good health for his age, and he had no financial worries. Rumors about that sort of thing usually get out sooner or later, and I'd heard none. Nor was there any note. I looked upstairs in his bedroom while Miss Tattersall was putting the kettle on. And yet murder seems to me to be equally far-fetched."

"Why?"

"I can't think of any reason for it any more than I can for self-destruction."

"He came often to your surgery, I'm told, with imaginary ailments."

"Well, yes, that's true, but I think he was mostly lonely. A good many of his friends had passed on or moved away to live with a son or daughter. We'd discuss whatever problem he claimed to have had, I'd prescribe exercise or avoiding a last cup of tea at bedtime, or simply tell him he was mistaken, that he was not ill. He'd thank me, settle my bill with the nurse, and be on his way. He was never insistent or rude."

"I've been told he had had a long-standing feud with the man who kept the grounds at the house."

Dr. Graham chuckled. "So he did. If it led to murder, I'll be hard-pressed to believe it. I have never seen two more stubborn men. But the odd thing is, they were never that way in any other situation. There was something about the pruning that began the feud. Have you see the back garden? Yes? To tell you the truth, I think they rather enjoyed their verbal battles."

"And his quarrel with the solicitor? A matter of possible misappropriation of funds?"

"There may be some truth to that. The man was no fool when it came to money. Simmons must have been desperate indeed if he tried to embezzle from the accounts of Joel Tattersall. But Simmons might well be guilty of raiding the funds of other clients, if his gambling got out of hand. I've heard that he frequented several clubs in London."

"And Tattersall might have threatened to tell those other clients, or at least make his suspicions public."

"That's very possible. And he would have opened the door to

Simmons, if he'd come to eat humble pie. Or pretended to have done. Something to consider."

"It appears that you and the constable here knew of the problems with Simmons. If others knew, what would be the point of killing Tattersall?"

"We learned of it after the murder. There was the draft of a letter in Tattersall's desk. Holliston read it and told us that it indicated the dead man's suspicions and his intention to call for an audit of the books. Tattersall and his sister enjoyed a considerable trust fund, jointly held. Simmons and his father before him had the administering of it."

But Rutledge hadn't been told about this letter.

He said as much. Constable Hurley cleared his throat. "The doctor and I felt it best to mention nothing about it until there was time to judge whether it was true or just Mr. Tattersall's suspicions."

Interesting information. It might even prove motive.

"Could you tell whether or not the house had been searched, as in Simmons trying to find this letter?"

"Miss Tattersall assured us nothing had been disturbed."

"Why did Tattersall use a solicitor in Wells, rather than one closer to home?"

"It was his father who selected the firm of Simmons and Simmons. Or so I was led to believe by Miss Tattersall."

"Would she have killed her brother in order to inherit his share of the fund?"

"I can't imagine why. My understanding is that the fund is more than sufficient for their needs now and well into the future."

"Anything else you've chosen not to share?"

Color rose in the constable's face. "No, sir."

Dr. Graham added with almost Victorian righteousness, "I didn't wish to ruin a man's reputation without good cause."

"But you told the sister about the possible embezzlement?"

"Not at this stage. It was unlikely that whoever killed her brother would return to kill her."

But nothing was unlikely yet.

Rutledge rose. "It might have set her mind at ease. She fears that whoever killed her brother knows she was in the house at the time. And whoever it is might decide at some stage that she can identify him."

"Still."

He realized that a man of the doctor's age would have been accustomed to sparing women ugly or sordid details. In matters of illness, he would have told their fathers or brothers how their female relatives should be treated, naturally assuming that the male members of the family would see that instructions were understood and properly carried out. An old-fashioned and outdated point of view. He wondered briefly what the very capable Miss Tattersall would have made of it.

"I'll like to speak to Inspector Holliston and possibly to Simmons. Thank you for your time, Doctor. Constable."

He turned and left both men in the office, staring after him.

It was not a long drive to Wells, and he found the town bustling in the summer morning sun. Inspector Holliston was easily found in the main police station.

A man of medium height with the springy step of an athlete, Holliston ran his fingers through his fair hair and said, "Sorry to put this matter off on the Yard, but we've had a rash of trouble. The heat, I expect. No relief from it. And so you got Mr. Tattersall."

"What sort of trouble?" Rutledge asked, curious.

Holliston sighed. "A hanging. We haven't decided if it's suicide or murder. A man killed in his farmyard, but we aren't certain whether it's murder or an accident. Fell out of the loft window onto his own pitchfork. A drowning that could be suspicious. There were enough people eager to kill the bastard. I wouldn't be surprised if one of them did it. And now Tattersall's death."

"Which you treated as murder from the start."

"For one thing, he's a prominent man. For another, where did the laudanum come from? Finally, a man doesn't kill himself without good reason. No health issues, no money worries, no enemies. A quiet man living a quiet life. A sister to look after, for that matter. Not a likely suicide. And yet it appears he drank that laudanum himself. No bruising of the lip or tongue. No sign of a struggle. One wonders why."

On the table behind where Holliston was sitting were three rowing trophies. Rutledge wondered where he rowed, and if they were past or present achievements. The way the sun shone in the window above them, he couldn't read the dates. Or the inscriptions, for that matter.

"Why, indeed. The only change in his life appears to be the problem with the solicitor. The possibility of embezzlement."

"That's the odd thing," Holliston said, moving the papers in front of him so that they marched with the border of his blotter. "It appears that there was a break-in at Simmons's chambers not long ago. Nothing taken, but some of his files had been rifled. We've not found out any more about that. But it's worth noting."

"Constable Hurley said nothing about a break-in."

"I doubt he knows. It was our patch, not his."

Rutledge said, "It might have some importance in both inquiries."

Holliston shrugged. "I don't see how. Besides, Tattersall hadn't written his letter to Simmons when that happened."

"Then how did he learn of the embezzlement?"

"I expect he was careful of his business matters. In his desk were a number of small ledgers listing various transactions about his and his sister's trusts."

"Do you think Miss Tattersall was worried about that trust—and poisoned her brother with laudanum?"

"She seems an unlikely candidate for murderer. What's more, given the sums in question, it would have been sheer greed, not necessity. The ledgers indicated that she had more than the usual freedom of access to her monies and spent them as she saw fit. My conclusion was that the trust was unlikely to have become an issue between brother and sister."

Unlikely . . .

That policeman's caveat again. And yet Rutledge had to agree. His conversation with Miss Tattersall had given him no reason to doubt her testimony. She was straightforward, almost blunt at times, and gave no impression of hiding anything.

"It's certain nothing was taken during the break-in at the solicitor's chambers?"

"According to Simmons and his clerk."

"If it was incriminating material, perhaps they preferred not to admit that to the police."

Holliston frowned. "If it were only Simmons, I might agree with you. That's to say, if the man *is* stealing from his clients. But William Barry, his head clerk, is a different matter. I can't quite see him lying to us. He worked for the elder Simmons, and he has a reputation for integrity and honesty."

"How can he not know? It's possible he's aware of embezzlement and is afraid of losing his position once he confirms your suspicions."

"I stand by my belief that he's what he appears to be."

"Then either Simmons is brilliant in hiding his affairs from his clerk, or it's been a fairly recent problem. And there's his gambling."

"All right, I'll give you that."

"I'm told that he was drunk when you called on him to take a look at Tattersall's will. Is this a frequent occurrence? Does Simmons often drink more than he can hold?"

"I've never known him to do that. I was as surprised to find him in that condition as my constable was. And at that hour."

"Perhaps his conscience was troubling him."

Holliston raised fair eyebrows. "You're suggesting that he killed Tattersall, and then was overcome by remorse?"

"It's happened before. I think it's time to have a word with Simmons."

Holliston gave him directions to the solicitor's chambers, and then said, "He's a likeable man. Simmons. I'm not sure where the gambling came from, or why. Unless he fell in with a bad crowd at that club in London."

"It's always possible," Rutledge agreed, and took his leave.

He found the tall, handsome house with the brass plate by the door that read SIMMONS AND SIMMONS, and lifted the matching brass door knocker.

The clerk who answered his summons was a plump man with white hair and steady brown eyes.

He invited Rutledge inside and led him to the reception room. "I'm sorry if I kept you waiting, sir," he said. "Mr. Simmons has gone to see a client, and I was in the back. Can I help you?"

"I've come to speak to Mr. Simmons in regard to the Tattersall trust fund. I understand he administers it for the late Joel Tattersall and his sister."

"May I ask why you are inquiring?" the clerk replied, giving nothing away as he faced Rutledge.

He gave his name, and after a moment, he added, "I'm from London. Scotland Yard."

"Ah. I was uncertain whether Mr. Tattersall's death had been determined to be murder or perhaps suicide."

"Why should he have killed himself?"

"I have no idea. But I have held this position for many years, and if I have learned anything at all, it's that people often do things that one never expects them to do."

"For instance, your employer's enthusiasm for gambling? I was given to understand that this was a recent—er—pastime."

The clerk considered Rutledge. "Mr. Simmons is a good man. And a fair man. But he doesn't have the same dedication to the law that his father had. If anything, I would say he took up gambling out of boredom."

"This is his livelihood."

"I daresay it is. But there is no law that prevents a solicitor from enjoying himself."

"None at all, unless his habit of gambling has led him into deep waters, and he finds himself in need of more funds than he's able to raise. Unless he turns to the trust funds that are in his keeping and helps himself to them."

The clerk never blinked an eye. "To my knowledge, Mr. Simmons has never broken the promise he made to his father, to conduct his business honorably."

"Then you're saying—"

The outer door opened and a man with dark red hair and sharp blue eyes walked in, interrupting them.

"I say, Barry, can you lay your hands on that inquiry about the—"

It was his turn to break off as he saw Rutledge sitting in the antechamber speaking to his clerk.

"Sorry," he said, nodding to Rutledge. "I'll be with you shortly."

But some sort of signal must have passed between Barry and his employer, because Simmons frowned, then said, "If you'll forgive me," and walked on to the inner door, passing through it without looking back.

Barry excused himself and followed Simmons.

From where he was sitting Rutledge could hear their voices but not what they were saying.

After several minutes, Simmons returned and said to Rutledge, "I can see you now, but I must tell you I have an urgent meeting in ten minutes."

He showed Rutledge into a large inner room with a desk and several chairs. It was clearly where he met with clients, for the carpet and the window hangings and the dark wood of the furnishings spoke of longevity and trust. Even the paintings, dark and Elizabethan, save for the white ruffs of the sitters, added to the feeling of timelessness and respectability. The only thing out of place in this setting was the bright green blotter on the massive desk.

Sitting down, and gesturing to Rutledge to follow suit, he said,

"I've been told you're from Scotland Yard and that you wish to see me about the Tattersall trust. Is that correct?"

"More precisely," Rutledge said pleasantly, "I wished to discuss a report from Inspector Holliston that you were drunk the morning he came to report Mr. Tattersall's death to you. And later you couldn't account for your whereabouts when asked where you were on the night your client died."

"I couldn't because I couldn't remember." Simmons ran his fingers through his hair. "Look. I'd just proposed to the young woman I thought I wanted to spend the rest of my life with, and she turned me down. Not even a 'Do let me think about it, Thomas,' or an 'I'm not ready to consider marriage just now, Thomas.' A resounding *no*. I wasn't expecting it. And I wasn't about to relate that story to Holliston because he's acquainted with the young woman and could, for all I know, be my rival. I went home and got drunk. The first time I've done that since I was at university, and rather stupid, yes, but at the time I couldn't think of anything better to do."

Remembering the rowing trophies behind Holliston's desk, Rutledge smiled. Holliston might well turn a young woman's head. "And your gambling habit?"

"That's a rumor that got started after I'd been up to London. I put some money on a horse race, just for a lark, and by God I won. Quite a large sum, in fact. I shouldn't have told anyone, but I was elated. After that I was occasionally invited by people I knew to sit in for a hand or two of cards. Friendly games, hardly wallowing in dens of iniquity, and I won as often as I lost. That experience changed my mind, gave me the courage to try my luck. I determined to speak to Rach—to Miss Barclay. Apparently my luck was short-lived."

"Do you play cards often?"

"Two or three times a year? Whenever I'm in London. Never locally. And certainly never more than I can afford to lose. But I'd give much to know who started the rumors that I was in over my head," Simmons ended grimly.

"Then how do you account for the fact that Mr. Tattersall had come to question your stewardship of his and his sister's trust?"

"I can't. Unless those rumors reached his ears. Holliston also asked me about Tattersall's concerns. I will say this. Sometimes Tattersall would decide that this or that would be a sound investment, and he would ask me to look into shares. If I couldn't dissuade him, and the London banks warned me off from that particular investment possibility, I'd drag my feet rather than argue with him. It was simpler. South American gold mines, Trans-Africa railways, coffee plantations in Kenya—they all appear quite tantalizing when you read the brochures. As do the unbelievably good rates of returns guaranteed. The fact is, most of them never pay back a farthing, and as often as not the principal is lost as well. If you want to talk about gambling, there's the real danger."

He was right. Financial bubbles usually burst.

"Why did Tattersall take a fatal dose of laudanum?"

The question took Simmons off guard. "God. I don't have a clue. I'd have said he was the last man I would think of as a murder victim. Tattersall and his sister lived a settled life. He walked every morning, whatever the weather. He read every afternoon. In the evening they occasionally entertained but most often played a two-hand game of whist. Hardly the sort of people you expect to arouse strong passions in anyone."

"What becomes of the Tattersall trusts?"

"Nothing. Miss Tattersall inherits her brother's share, and that's that. There's no charitable distribution or the like. It isn't like a will. The funds simply go to his sister."

"Would she have killed him for it?"

"Miss Tattersall?" he asked, eyebrows climbing up his forehead. "I can't imagine that, either. As it is, she has enough money to see her through this lifetime and several more. I quite like her, as a matter of fact. Very different from her brother. He enjoyed the solitary life. I expect she would have traveled more, if the decision had rested with her. But they were devoted to each other."

"What happens to the trust when she dies?"

"As I remember it goes to Eton. Hardly the sort of people who might try to collect early on their money."

To Eton. Where Tattersall and most likely his father had gone to school. Her share of the trust was not in Miss Tattersall's gift.

Rutledge left with a handful of names and began the tedious process of interviewing their owners. Holliston had most likely covered the same ground earlier, but given Simmons's suspicions about the man, he thought it might be best to work independently.

He began with Rachel Barclay and found her at home in a fashionable part of Wells where old money still lived. The house was handsome, and the maid who answered the door wore a uniform so well starched that it gave the impression she was imprisoned in it.

He told her his name but not his connection with the Yard, and a few minutes later, when he was shown into the sitting room where Rachel Barclay had been writing letters, she frowned on seeing him.

"I fear you have the advantage of me. Are you a friend of my father's? I don't believe we've met," she said quite coolly, rising.

"I doubt that we have," he answered equitably. "I'm from Scotland Yard, Miss Barclay. I'm looking into a murder that occurred recently, not far from Wells."

"I don't see why this requires you to call on me."

"Because it appears that you can provide proof that Mr. Simmons was with you on the evening in question," Rutledge said, meeting bluntness with bluntness. And he gave her the date of Tattersall's death.

He'd expected her to be surprised.

Instead she stared at him with distaste and said, "If you are asking me if he got himself drunk later that night, after I had turned down his proposal, the answer is, yes, he was here."

"You were a witness to his drinking?"

For the first time she appeared to be taken aback. "Most certainly not."

"Then a member of your family witnessed this fall from grace? Your father? Perhaps a brother or a cousin?" he inquired, his voice polite, his face giving away nothing. But he thought he already knew the answer to his question.

"Of course not," she snapped.

"You are, perhaps, clairvoyant?"

At that she flushed and walked across the room to the bell pull. "I will ask you to leave now."

"I'm afraid I can't. Not until you've answered my question. This is a murder inquiry, Miss Barclay, not a temperance meeting. However disgusting it may appear to you that a man who has just asked for your hand in marriage should go out and drink himself into oblivion, you must tell me how you came to know he'd done such a thing."

Flushed and angry, clearly not accustomed to being told what to do, she said, "I shall tell my father how you have behaved, Mr. Rutledge. But to answer your question, I was informed by a friend, who felt I should be aware of the true character of the man who had so recently asked me to be his wife."

Rutledge smiled. "Ah, yes, the man who found him in that condition. Inspector Holliston. Thank you, Miss Barclay. I can find my own way out."

He turned on his heel, leaving the room and nearly colliding with the maid who was hurrying to answer her mistress's summons. She begged his pardon and rushed on in the direction of the sitting room.

Inspector Holliston had overstepped his authority by using information he'd collected in the course of his duties to further his own interests. Rutledge found himself wondering if Holliston had also broken into the solicitor's chambers in search of any damaging information he might find there.

His next stop was the bank on the High Street, where he learned from the assistant manager that Mr. Simmons's accounts were in good order and had not been overdrawn at any time.

"I was told that he had a problem with gambling. Perhaps the horses?"

The assistant manager, a short heavyset man called Jenner, laughed. "I daresay any number of our clients may make small wagers from time to time, but these don't show up in their accounts. It's usually in notes and on the spur of the moment. I can tell you as well, since it's on this list you've given me, that the accounts of Mr. and Miss Tattersall are also in good order. While their trust is administered by London through Simmons and Simmons, the income is paid into an account in our bank, enabling them to withdraw such monies as they may need for their personal use." He peered again at the list that Rutledge had. "Mr. William Barry, clerk at Simmons and Simmons, has been saving toward his retirement, and everything is in order there. He lives frugally—a widower with grown children—and takes one holiday a year, traveling to Lyme Regis where he has a cousin."

"He doesn't visit his children?"

"They come to Wells, it seems. He was saying not long ago that they appear to like coming home, that they enjoy the quiet here. His daughter lives in London and his son in Manchester. Metropolises compared to Wells."

"And Mr. Holliston?" Rutledge gently pressed.

"He has his income as a policeman of course, but also a small legacy from his mother. He tries to live within his means."

Hardly the suitor that Miss Barclay might prefer. But Holliston had successfully blackened Simmons's character in her eyes.

Thanking Mr. Jenner for his time, Rutledge found a small pub where he ordered his lunch at the bar. Moving on to a table, he began to organize what he'd just learned.

Holliston had not directly accused Simmons of being involved in the death of Mr. Tattersall, but he had most certainly suggested it was possible. But how had the story that Simmons was an embezzler reached Tattersall's ears?

Or perhaps it was the other way around. Inspector Holliston had seen the letter that Tattersall had written, asking Simmons for an accounting of his stewardship. A letter never sent. And Holliston had seized the opportunity to interpret Tattersall's request as suspicion.

On the other hand, Tattersall's might well have been the largest account that Simmons administered. He couldn't afford to lose it, either financially or from the standpoint of his reputation. Which made Simmons suspect if Tattersall was murdered before the man could make accusations public or move his business elsewhere.

But Rutledge favored the view that if the trust was withdrawn from Simmons and Simmons, it might make the solicitor a far less eligible suitor for Miss Barclay's hand. It might even level the playing field in the rivalry. And once started, whispers spread. Of Simmons's gambling, of his possible misappropriation of funds to pay for it, even of his drunkenness. Whether they'd reached Tattersall's ears, or his letter had offered Holliston the chance he needed to ruin his rival, there was no way of knowing.

He finished his meal with a plate of cheeses, and then walked back to the police station.

Holliston was in a meeting, Rutledge was told, and would be available shortly.

In another five minutes a tall, well-dressed man strode purposefully out of Holliston's office and passed Rutledge without a glance.

Holliston had followed him to the door, and his face changed as he saw Rutledge waiting.

"I didn't know you were here. Otherwise I'd have let you speak to Mr. Barclay and explain yourself. You've been harassing his daughter."

"Nothing of the sort," Rutledge said breezily. "I've been asking her to help the police with their inquiries."

"I don't see how interviewing Miss Barclay could possibly help with your inquiries," the Inspector retorted, an edge to his voice. Clearly, whatever Barclay had said to him had stung. "Tattersall wasn't killed until very late. Simmons left the Barclay house shortly after nine-thirty."

"I'd like to read for myself the letter that Tattersall wrote to Simmons but never posted."

Holliston frowned. "It's in the file. Constable Hurley must have told you the contents."

"The letter, if you please."

Holliston turned and went back to his desk, glancing through the files in his current box, and finding the one he wanted. He opened it, thumbed through the contents, and pulled out the letter.

Rutledge read it through quickly, then a second time.

The pertinent passage was very different from what he'd expected.

I shall ask you for an immediate accounting of my affairs. I feel that you are not properly administering them as I would like, and I shall make my suspicions known to London. I have requested on at least two occasions, in writing, that you consider purchasing shares in the Republic of Colombia mines owned by Gower and Healy for our portfolios, but my understanding is that you have failed to do so. This is contrary to our agreements, and I will have an explanation for this dereliction of duty on your part.

Hardly an accusation of embezzlement, but an angry request to explain the solicitor's actions.

Rutledge had seen the advertisements for Gower and Healy in the financial pages of the *Times,* although he hadn't read them. They appeared to claim that a new vein had been discovered in the Minero River region and was calculated to produce the finest stones of the last two centuries. Shares were being offered to finance the costs involved in mining them.

He knew very little about mining emeralds and even less about the Republic of Colombia, but as a policeman Rutledge was well versed in schemes that promised vast fortunes for the gullible investor. Whether the emerald mine was one of those he couldn't say, but Simmons was well advised not to allow his client to act rashly.

He handed the letter back to Holliston, who stood there behind his desk, his expression wooden. Looking at his face, Rutledge realized that the Inspector had found Tattersall's letter and read only the pertinent parts to Constable Hurley and Dr. Graham, leaving them with the impression that the solicitor was guilty of mismanaging funds.

"You've been running a quiet campaign with an eye to discrediting Simmons," Rutledge told him then. "Your personal affairs are none of my business, but ruining the man's chances with Miss Barclay is abuse of your authority." Rutledge was curt. "In my view, you and Miss Barclay deserve each other, but what you've also done is muddy the evidence regarding Tattersall's death. I'm going back there now, to do what I can to sort out truth from fallacy. Any further use of your position for personal gain and you'll find yourself reduced to rank of constable, if not dismissed from the police altogether."

He turned on his heel, leaving Holliston standing there. It wasn't until he reached the outer door that he heard the man call his name, but he didn't turn. And Holliston didn't follow him.

R eturning to Stoke Yarlington, Rutledge sought out Constable Hurley and asked if there had been any strangers in the village in the past weeks.

Hurley was just finishing his tea, and he wiped his hands as he considered the question.

"I don't think there's been anyone of late. Not since early June, and that was an itinerant peddler selling ribbons and lace and the like. He didn't find the ladies here very eager to buy, and he moved on. Short man, graying hair, missing a tooth in front. I don't know that he had anything to do with the Tattersalls. He wasn't likely to call at their house. His custom came mainly from young girls and a few of the younger maids he encountered on the street."

"No one else. Not someone passing through who attracted little attention to himself?"

"If there was, I never saw him, nor did anyone mention him to me."

So much for that line of questioning. He went back to Tattersall's sister.

Rutledge asked her much the same questions that he'd put to Hurley, but she was unaware of anyone who might have shown an interest in the house.

But when asked, Mrs. Betterton said, "I was leaving one night about a week before Mr. Tattersall's death, and there was a man some twenty yards from the gate, repairing his bicycle tire. He didn't look up as I came round the house and walked down the path. It was getting on toward dusk, but I'd stayed late to hang the new curtains, helping Miss Tattersall get them to fall just right. I haven't thought twice about the man since then. He seemed to be just an ordinary sort."

"What did he look like?"

"He was wearing coveralls and a blue shirt. Middling tallish, as far as I could tell, and slim. He didn't strike me as the usual run of beggars, and so I didn't give him a second's thought. I did notice the bicycle appeared to be new, and thought what a pity it was he'd already had a flat."

"Did you see his face?"

"He was wearing a cap, and bending over the tire, putting on a patch. I walked on into the village, and he didn't pass me. I expect he'd been heading the other way."

He turned to Miss Tattersall. "Did you or your brother see this man?"

"No, Inspector, I expect we were having our dinner. It was rather late that night because of the curtains, and my brother was anxious to dine."

"Did you make the curtains yourself?"

She gave him a withering look that said he knew little about such matters. "No, certainly not. I ordered them from London, and when they came, I thought it was not impossible to hang them myself, rather than have someone in to do it. My brother never cared for people traipsing, as he put it, through the house."

Which brought Rutledge back to Bob, the handyman.

It was Mrs. Betterton who told him where to find Bob.

He lived in a small stone cottage down a narrow lane that crossed a little stream. There was a wood just beyond the cottage, and the ground rose on the far side of the stream.

Bob was in the kitchen of the cottage, apparently staring at the walls when Rutledge was ushered in by the woman who had called herself "Bob's wife." She was a few years younger than her husband, a pretty woman who had retained her looks into middle age.

Bob by contrast had the broad shoulders of someone who had been a laborer all his life, and strong, square hands.

He looked up as Rutledge came into the room, saying, "Who may you be?" in an irascible voice with a heavy Somerset accent.

"Dear, he's a policeman, come to speak to you about Mr. Tattersall, I should think."

"I've already spoken to two policemen, Hurley and that fool from Wells. What does this one want?" He addressed his question to his wife, all the while watching Rutledge.

"I'm from London, Mr. Bryant. Scotland Yard to be precise. I've taken over the inquiry into the death of Mr. Tattersall. I was wondering what you could tell me about that day and whether or not you have any suggestions about who might have wanted to see your employer dead."

"I didn't live in his pocket," Bob retorted. "I cut his lawns and took care of his flower beds and pruned the bloody shrubs and trees."

"You had worked for him how many years? In all that time, you never formed an opinion about Mr. Tattersall, or speculated on his activities?"

"Twenty-some years, I expect. More like twenty-five. And it wasn't my place to form opinions or speculate. I was there to see to the grounds and argue with him when we disagreed on the most sensible way of doing that."

"Did you argue over anything else?"

"No. Nothing else was my responsibility."

"Will you continue to keep the grounds, now that he's dead?"

"I don't see any reason not to." He looked at his hands, at the earth caked under the nails and the calluses on his palms. "Miss Tattersall has said nothing to the contrary."

"And I don't expect she will. Who did you see loitering around the grounds one day?"

Bob frowned. "I never saw anyone hanging about. Who says there was?"

"Mrs. Betterton saw someone repairing his bicycle tire, just outside the gate to the path. Did you see him?"

"Here, I never did. If she says I did, she's lying."

"I'm asking if you saw him," Rutledge replied patiently.

"No. I start work at seven, leave just at four twice a week. Those were the terms that old fool and I agreed to, and then he set about trying to change them every chance he got."

"That's not fair, Bobby, dear," his wife put in. "He was very good to you, and he even paid the doctor's bills, when you hurt your foot."

"Was the injury severe? Did it require stitches, laudanum for the pain?" Rutledge asked Mrs. Bryant.

"My heavens, no," she answered, smiling. "Dr. Graham put a plaster on it and that was that. But Mr. Tattersall insisted he go back to be sure it'ud healed properly."

"He disliked me and I him," Bob said stubbornly.

"Then why did you work for the man?" Rutledge asked, letting his impatience with Bob show.

"I needed the position. Besides, I thought, given his age, he'd leave me to it. Old fool that he was." But there was something in his voice that belied his words, a lack of force, as if he'd said such things for so many years he couldn't retreat from his position. As if, underneath the gruffness, there was a feeling of loss he didn't know how to deal with.

Rutledge glanced at Mrs. Bryant. She was watching her husband with fondness in her gaze and some sadness as well. As if she too knew how much he was hurting.

"And you know of no enemies or anyone who might wish this man dead?"

"I've told you. He was a difficult man to deal with. His enemies might be legion—but I know nothing about them."

Mrs. Bryant said, sadly, "He never bothered anyone. Why should he have enemies? Why should anyone want to kill the poor soul?"

Which was the question he carried with him as he left.

If Bob had wanted Tattersall dead, he could have taken the pruning shears to him, or a hammer, any time in the five-and-twenty years of employment. An overdose of laudanum was not the sort of weapon he'd have used. Indeed, how would he know how much was an overdose? It was Mrs. Bryant who would see to such things. But he called in at Dr. Graham's surgery to be sure.

Rutledge spent the next several hours interviewing Tattersall's neighbors, seeking out the vicar of the little church, and speaking to the postmaster in the tiny booth set up in the greengrocer's shop.

The vicar put it best. "There has to be a reason for killing, isn't that true? I don't think Mr. Tattersall ever raised his voice to anyone, with the exception of Bob Bryant. And then it was more a game than anything else. He was never unkind, and if there were parishioners in need, I'd find extra money in the poor box that week, left there anonymously, but of course I could guess where it came from. He worried about his trust, for fear he'd outlive it, and so he watched it carefully."

"That may be the man you know now. But what about ten years ago? Twenty? Thirty?"

"A wild youth? Mr. Tattersall? I think not. He did his duty, he voted in every election, and he paid whatever he owed. You've met his sister. They were very much alike."

"And no problems between them? They've lived in the same house for how many years?"

"Wild horses couldn't have forced her to do anything against her conscience."

Rutledge was to remember those words in the weeks ahead.

8

H e spent two more days in the village, taking his inquiry farther afield, even interviewing farmers' wives who came in to market. But neither the shopkeepers nor the farmers had taken on anyone new in the past year, and no one had inquired about possible work. Stoke Yarlington was far enough off the main road to Wells that it saw very little traffic from the outside world.

And he was no closer to the truth than he'd been when he drove down the High and looked for the police station that first morning.

Constable Hurley was unconvinced that Simmons was clear of any suspicion. He held on to the whispers of gambling and the accusation of embezzlement in Tattersall's unfinished letter. The doctor was of the same opinion. His son, who lived in Wells, had passed the story of drunkenness on to his father, and Dr. Graham believed him.

Irritated with their intransigence, Rutledge suggested they read the entire letter for themselves.

He went back to Wells to speak to Simmons, found him out of the office for the next hour, and walked on to the cathedral. With its exaggerated west front and wishbone pillars holding up the roof, it was a beautiful building, and the swans on the moat by the bishop's palace moved majestically in the shadows cast by the trees overhanging it.

He was reminded of Jean's wish for a lake and for swans. He wondered what she was doing on such a lovely day, and missed her more than he'd thought possible.

On his way back to Simmons's chambers he decided to make a detour to find a telephone, and when he had, in the largest hotel in town, he called the Yard. It took several minutes before Sergeant Gibson came to the telephone, his voice rumbling down the wire with its usual brusqueness.

Rutledge identified himself and asked Gibson to speak to the headmaster at Eton, where Tattersall had gone to school. "Any trouble there? Any problems that might spring up years later?" When the conversation ended, he went to find Simmons.

The man looked tired. "Trying to scotch rumors is the devil of a task," he said with a heavy sigh. "I'm a drunkard who has squandered his clients' money on horse racing and cards. Holliston has tried to make things right, but it will take years to undo the harm done. And Miss Barclay is not speaking to either of us." He shrugged ruefully. "Well, at least Holliston's chances are as dead as mine now."

"Serves him right, don't you think?" Rutledge asked.

"I feel no sympathy for him, if that's what you mean. Any closer to solving Tattersall's murder?"

"The inquest brought in the verdict of person or persons unknown. I've found no reason to dispute that."

"It would help me if you found Tattersall's killer."

"I'm sure it would." Rutledge shifted in his chair. "There's something we're missing. There must be. But I've found nothing. I shall have to tell the Yard as much, and ask if they wish to send someone else in my place to close the inquiry."

"I don't relish digging all this up again."

"I wish I could have avoided it."

"Well, we have larger worries, it seems. The news from Europe isn't improving."

Rutledge recalled what Major Gordon had said, that the Army was keeping a close eye on events. "It's the middle of July," he agreed. "Russia will have to choose—if she backs down, lets Austria punish Serbia as she sees fit, there won't be any war."

"Friends in London are saying that if the Germans cross the Rhine into France, the Government will consider it a purely European war and try to act as a broker of peace instead. You're from London. Any truth in that?"

"God knows. I can't afford to await events. I have a murderer to find." Rutledge rose. "I'm running up to London. There are several matters I need to look into. You're still on the suspect list, in the eyes of Constable Hurley in Stoke Yarlington. Both Dr. Graham and his son feel the same. I'd watch my step, if I were you."

"Thanks for the warning. I've volunteered to help out in the church fete. God forgive me, it was the only way I could think of to mend fences. At least for a few of my clients, this will appear to have the Church's blessing." He grimaced. "And to be honest, I'll be very glad to see the end of you. Every time you walk through my door, there are those waiting to see you drag me out in chains."

"Then they'll be surprised to see me drive away without you."

With a nod to Mr. Barry in the clerk's room, Rutledge left.

He stopped in Eton, found a telephone, and put in a call to the Yard. Gibson had elicited the information he needed, and he walked into the headmaster's rooms in Eton, to ask if anyone recalled a student by the name of Tattersall.

Apparently the man had not left a strong personal impression, but his marks were high and he appeared to have been liked by his fellow students. His sport was cricket, and he had been a good batsman.

The playing fields . . .

They had made men who helped rule the Empire. But Tattersall had been content to return to the village where he'd been born and to live out his life there. He'd surrounded himself with books rather than people, and yet he had done his duty when called upon to do so.

There was nothing in his record here to account for his murder some forty years on. Or his suicide.

Rutledge drove on into London, intending to confer with Chief Superintendent Bowles. But he had gone to a conference in Oxford and wasn't expected back until the next morning.

Rutledge went home, spent an hour with his sister, and then drove to Jean's house.

He rang the bell, only to be told by the butler that Miss Gordon and her parents had gone to Warwick to visit a cousin. They weren't expected back in London until the weekend.

More disappointed than he cared to say, Rutledge thanked Simpson and turned to go.

Just then Kate came down the stairs and called to him. He waited for her, and she smiled at the butler. "Thank you, Simpson. I'll see to him."

And to Rutledge she said, "I'd just stopped by to borrow Jean's lavender gloves." She held them up like a trophy. "If you like, you can drop me in town."

"I'll take you to lunch. And you can tell me why you require lavender gloves."

"Lovely." She closed the door behind her and followed him down the short flight of steps to his motorcar. "I thought you were in the hinterland chasing murderers."

"I was. But the Chief Superintendent is away today, and so I must wait for him."

"Ah. Well, Jean's misfortune at missing you is my good fortune at finding you. Dear Ian, would you mind terribly taking me to the theater tonight? We've got up a party, and we're well chaperoned by the Merrimans. But I lack an escort, and I shall have to beg off."

"What happened to your escort?"

"Timothy's grandmother is quite ill, and he's accompanied his parents to Canterbury to look in on her."

"Yes, of course. Is this why you needed the gloves?"

"It is, and I was desperate enough to consider asking Teddy to take me, when you appeared like a gift from heaven. Besides, you know everyone who is invited."

He laughed. "A gift from the Yard."

"We won't quibble. Now. Where is the most interesting place to have our lunch?"

"We'll go to the Monarch Hotel. The dining room there is perfectly proper."

And so he took Kate to lunch, and later called for her to escort her to the play. He could tell she enjoyed it immensely, although it was a Shaw revival. She looked quite beautiful in a white gown with the lavender gloves and shoes with a sprig of silk lilac flowers in her hair. The play lived up to its reviews, and Rutledge found he was enjoying himself.

They went as a party to have a light supper afterward, and then Rutledge squired Kate to her door. Her family lived two squares over from the Gordons, and her maid was waiting up for her.

She thanked Rutledge for saving her evening, stood on tiptoe to kiss his cheek, and then went inside, shutting her door.

He drove back to the house. Frances had also been out most of the evening, and over a pot of tea that she made, they exchanged accounts.

"I do like Kate. I hadn't met her before the party. She's great fun," Frances said. "My evening was lovely as well." She hesitated. "Richard was there. He asked me to say hello."

"He's to be married soon," Rutledge reminded her. He recalled that this was the second time.

"Yes, of course he is. He's still allowed to speak to other women."

He went up to bed soon thereafter. It worried him that Frances had neither parent nor aunt to chaperone her here in this house. But there was no one to call on but Melinda Crawford. And he wasn't sure whether she'd leave her beloved Kent for London even for Frances. Still, he'd write to her in the morning for advice.

When he arrived at the Yard shortly after eight, he found Chief Superintendent Bowles already there. He was surprised to see Rutledge.

"I thought you were in Somerset. Or was it Devon?"

"Somerset, sir."

"Indeed. Have you made any progress there?"

"Not as much as I'd have liked. The case is proving to be difficult."

Bowles considered him, his eyes narrowing. "You got nowhere in Moresby. Are you telling me that you haven't made an arrest in this inquiry?"

"I've been as thorough as possible. But the victim, Tattersall, appears to have lived an exemplary life. I'd appreciate any views on the matter." He recounted what he'd learned thus far, but Bowles shook his head.

"What's wrong with you, man?" Bowles snapped. "You're sent out to do your duty, and instead, you rush back to London on the smallest excuse, pleading confusion. But my wife saw you at the theater last night, roistering with that party in the boxes. You've let your personal life overtake your good sense, and I'll have no more of it."

"Hardly *roistering,* sir. But yes, I was waiting to speak to you this morning, and in the interval, I went out with friends," Rutledge snapped. He had done nothing to deserve a dressing-down.

"Everyone speaks of your brilliant rise at the Yard, how you never fail to find the evidence and bring in your man," Bowles went on ruthlessly, ignoring the interruption. "'Brilliant,'" he repeated, as if the word had caught in his throat. "And now you're engaged, and you can't find your hand in front of your face. No, don't tell me that has nothing to do with it. I have the proof before my eyes. Well, you'll have to make a choice, Inspector. The Yard or this social fling you've been putting before everything else." He didn't wait for Rutledge to reply. Instead he went on with rising anger, "Now get yourself back to Stok Yarlington or Wells or wherever it is you ought to be instead of dling in my office, and bring me back a killer."

With that he picked up a file, opened it, and began to study it as-
siduously, leaving Rutledge with no alternative than to leave.

He had come to Bowles to talk over the facts in the inquiry and
look for new insights he might have missed. And he had learned a hard
lesson. In the future, he would find his own way. Bowles be damned.

He got out of the Yard without encountering anyone or having to
control what was left of his temper.

Stopping at the house for fresh clothing, he left a note for Frances,
and then set out for Somerset once more.

It took a good two hours for him to calm down. He wasn't sure
whether Bowles's antipathy was personal or professional—or both.
He'd had glimmers of it before, but never such a bald display of what
Bowles was feeling. *Was* it his engagement? Or was the engagement a
convenient weapon to use against him? He resolved to keep his life as
private as he could from now on. There were one or two men he could
trust—Chief Inspector Cummins, for one. And that was the end of it.

He'd had no idea that Bowles's wife had gone to the theater last
night. As luck would have it, she had spotted him, but Rutledge hadn't
noticed her.

Because he'd been relaxed, enjoying himself, off duty as it were?
There had been no reason to scan the sea of faces in search of friends
or suspects.

What's more, he'd had nothing to hide. He'd enjoyed the evening
with Kate. He had no regrets.

Rutledge saw the headlines of a newspaper when he had stopped
briefly for petrol. Affairs in Europe were looking increasingly
ominous.

He'd begun to think that Paris was not the best choice just now
for a wedding journey. There was no certainty that these rumblings

of war would end anytime soon. It might be a wise idea to ask Major Gordon what he'd recommend. His father-in-law appeared to know more about the situation abroad than the newspapers.

Back in the motorcar, his Thermos filled with fresh tea, he concentrated on the case in hand.

He'd made very little headway by the time he reached Stoke Yarlington.

Beginning with Miss Tattersall, he said, "I want to go over your brother's life day by day, if need be. We're missing something."

"But I've told you everything," she replied, "I've hardly had time to mourn, thinking about his death. I'm tired, I can't give you what I don't have, myself."

Rutledge smiled encouragingly. "Let's begin with Eton. Did he enjoy his years there? I understand he was quite good at cricket."

Astonished, she said almost accusingly, "You've been digging." As if it were ill-mannered.

"I have indeed, Miss Tattersall. But you're the only person left who shared your brother's life. And so I must see the bare facts through your eyes."

"All right, yes. He enjoyed Eton. His interest in so many things stemmed from those years. History, mathematics, art, music. Our father was a plain man with plain tastes. I've always thought he'd have made a fine monk. His life given over to contemplation and prayer, only in his case, it was his interest in his books. It was fortunate that he didn't have to earn his daily bread. He wouldn't have been good at it. My mother ran the household and my father. Without any fuss or dramatics. She just got on with it."

"And when your brother came down from Eton, what then?"

"He wanted to go on to university, but my father viewed that as a waste of time. My brother then suggested that he read law, and he went up to London for six months or so, until he realized that the law was not his forte. He came home again and cast about for something else to do. My mother was ill just then, and so for her sake he stayed close.

He was twenty-seven when she died of a lingering illness. I think her death affected him terribly. He told me he couldn't bear to stay here, it brought back too many memories for him. Our maternal grandfather had left him a house in Bristol, and Joel opened it and lived there for a while. He took it into his head that he might stand for office. But he didn't have that way with people that makes one a successful candidate for public office. Eventually he sold the house in Bristol and came home. After that, he seemed content to remain here."

What she had failed to say—but Rutledge could read quite clearly between the lines—was that she herself had never been offered her brother's opportunities. She had probably been educated at home and trained to run a household. If she didn't marry, she would be expected to take her mother's place in due course, keeping her father and brother comfortable. The trust fund should have afforded her financial freedom. Freedom to live on her own in London, if she chose, to travel, to make new friends. What use was it to her, here in Stoke Yarlington?

"Were you jealous?" He asked it outright.

Miss Tattersall smiled whimsically. "There were times when I thought I was. But I had more of my father in me than I knew. I was comfortable here. Safe. And so I stayed."

"Will you lead a different life, now that you can choose your own future?"

Taking a deep breath, she said, "I'm afraid it's too late for that. No."

"Let's return to Bristol. Tell me about the house there."

"It was simply a town house my mother's father used when he did business in the city. He had large estates, and he spent time in each of his holdings. He had a very fine manager, but he loved the land and took great joy in keeping it healthy and productive. His son, alas, wasn't as good a steward. I'm happy to say *his* son, our cousin, took after his grandfather."

"Your brother never married?"

"I expect he might have, if he'd found the right girl. Someone like Mama, who would take him in charge and leave him to his own pursuits. For all I know, he found her but she failed to see him as her life's work. He never spoke of it."

"Could he have made enemies in Bristol?"

"I seriously doubt it. He took a course or two at the university. But he found history more satisfying than science. I think he enjoyed his brief independence. And when it palled, he came home."

He asked her for the dates of Joel Tattersall's time in Bristol, and it overlapped the time of Benjamin Clayton's life in the village of Netherby by no more than a few months. Rutledge could see no real link there. Tattersall came from old money while Clayton had earned his by working with his hands.

Miss Tattersall put her hand on his arm. "You're trying very hard to find my brother's murderer. But what happens if you don't?"

Rutledge had no answer for her. But he said, "The inquiry won't be closed. It will stay open as long as it takes." He paused for a moment. "I must remind you that you had the best opportunity to bring your brother a glass of milk with a little more medicine in it than usual. And when it was too late, when he realized that something was wrong, he tried to go for help. But you had quietly locked the door, then waited until morning, when you were certain he was dead, before going for the doctor and raising the alarm."

For a moment she regarded him with those clear, intelligent eyes, then she shook her head firmly. "Of course it's entirely possible, isn't it? You must consider the likelihood that I did just that. But tell me what I had to gain by it? I had no reason to kill my brother. I didn't need the money. I'm too old to start a gay and lavish life in London or Paris. He wasn't the perfect companion, and nor was I. Still, we managed to rub along together. You do, after so many years. Now I shall be alone for the rest of my life, rattling about in this great house, achieving nothing but filling my days as best I can with reading and good works. If Joel had wanted to punish me, he would have killed himself and left me behind."

"Are you certain he didn't do just that?"

She said practically, "We never got to the point where we hated each other. I don't know if we ever would have done. But Joel was quite content, I think, to have me look after him as Mama had done. And content people seldom look at suicide."

Rutledge said, "Did he fear his mind was going? I'm told he kept an almost obsessive eye on your trust funds. Was he really afraid that Simmons had played fast and loose with them? Or was he unable to be sure what he remembered, and therefore he suspected they were being manipulated by someone else?"

Her open friendly manner stiffened. "I can't think what you're getting at, Inspector. My brother had all his faculties. To the very end. You can ask Dr. Graham if you don't believe me."

It wasn't the question he'd asked. But he had no choice but to be satisfied with her answer.

In the end he went back to Wells and told Inspector Holliston what he had found out—that there were no realistic suspects in the death of Joel Tattersall.

Holliston smiled. "My money is on Simmons. No matter what you say to the contrary."

"Who drank himself blind out of sheer guilt? Or a lost love? There's no evidence that would survive the skills of a reasonably competent lawyer. The banks show no loss of funds, no replacement sums he's hastily shifting from one account to the other. There has to be a trail to follow, in embezzlement."

Inspector Holliston grimaced. "I'll keep looking."

Rutledge said, "Not too hard, if you're wise. Neither of you will gain from it." He rose and walked to the door. "What I suspect—and can't prove any more than you can your own theory—is that Tattersall might have taken his own life, and at the last, when he changed his mind, left it too late."

Holliston stared at him. "How do you reckon that?"

"The broken glass in the dustbin. Why would the killer tidy up after himself, if the postmortem is going to show an overdose anyway?"

"Miss Tattersall was adamant that it couldn't have been suicide."

"And so she would be, if she wanted to bury her brother in the family plot."

That gave Holliston something to think about. Rutledge on the other hand was not completely convinced. Likely? Yes, if Joel Tattersall's memory was slipping. But he had run out of questions. There had been the man with the bicycle. But if no one had been seen entering or leaving the house, then the killer must have been inside. And he couldn't believe that Miss Tattersall had murdered her brother.

He left soon afterward and set out for London.

He toyed with the thought that this case and the one in Moresby had certain factors in common. Somerset, for one, but people moved about now more than they had done in the past. That someone who'd once lived in Somerset had ended his life in Yorkshire was not astonishing. Laudanum for another. But it had probably been used to kill more people than had ever been discovered by the police. Finally because there was no clear-cut solution to the crime. No single piece of evidence that led to an arrest.

But no one had tried to hang Tattersall. The style of the stairs in the Tattersall house hardly lent itself to that, but there had been a number of trees in the garden that might have served, if the killer had been determined to try.

Rutledge smiled to himself. He would have been happy enough to name Holliston as the killer. Simply because he'd disliked the man.

He settled himself for the long drive ahead. By the end of it, he realized that while he hadn't found any sound reason for suicide, it was quite possibly the answer. Without a note, there was no way to look into Tattersall's mind and explain such a decision. Still, that meant only that Joel Tattersall, always a private man, had carried his reason with him to the grave rather than giving others the satisfaction of gawking at his torment, whatever it had been.

He wouldn't have been the first to keep his own counsel. Nor the last.

9

Jean had returned from Warwick, pouting prettily as she accused Rutledge of neglecting her for someone in Somerset.

While laughing with her, he found himself remembering Miss Tattersall with her red-rimmed eyes, calmly accepting it as her duty to answer his questions to the best of her ability. He assured Jean that on the contrary, it have been a dull inquiry that had dragged on too long.

He'd learned early on that it was best not to share his work. Not with his sister, not with Jean or any of his other acquaintances. Murder was something few people ever encountered in their lifetimes, and yet he dealt with it every day. An unpleasant business at best, but someone had to speak up for the victim, or the killer went free.

She was soon telling him about all the decisions she and her mother had been making, from caterer to florists to the right organist for the church, quickly losing him in the details of hats and dresses and matching shoes for her trousseau. And then something she was saying abruptly brought him back to the conversation.

"Oh, Ian, it's so wonderfully exciting. We've found just the right dressmaker, and I'm to go in a fortnight to choose my gown. And you must give Mama a list of the guests you wish to be invited. Jenny will stand up with me. She's asked me to be in *her* wedding next April. And there's Patricia of course. And Margaret. I mustn't forget Georgina, I've known her since we were in leading strings. But I can't decide between Maud and Elizabeth. What do you think?"

"I'd like Frances to be in the wedding party."

Her face fell. "Mama says five bridesmaids. More would be pretentious."

"Still." To soften the request, he asked, "And what about your own cousin, Kate? I'm sure she would like to be asked as well."

"I'll speak to Mama. Kate will understand if she's not included, I'm sure she will. Besides, I'm not speaking to her," she added, glancing up at him teasingly. "You took her to the theater."

"She was coming down the stairs at your house, just as I called to see if you were there. She asked to borrow me."

"As long as it doesn't happen too often," she said archly. "I won't share you. And speaking of sharing, I have a box of chocolates that my godmother sent to us."

She crossed the room for a box wrapped in silver paper, bringing it to him to open. He did, and offered her first choice. The chocolates were Belgian, and delicious. Jean went on, chatting about all the arrangements, whether to be married in the smaller family church or to choose a larger one. Her face was alight, and he'd never seen her so beautiful.

Christmas seemed a long way off.

When he reported to the Yard the next morning, he made a point of knocking on Bowles's door first thing.

The Chief Superintendent appeared to be in better spirits, looking up to greet Rutledge and asking him what the conclusion of the inquiry in Stoke Yarlington had been.

"I'm not completely satisfied that it's suicide, but there are more facts pointing in that direction than to murder."

He gave the Chief Superintendent his reasons, and after several pointed questions, Bowles nodded.

"Sad case, then. Very well. There's another file on your desk. This one in Kent. If you have any questions, speak up."

"Any news, sir, from Moresby?"

"The reconvened inquest agreed with Inspector Farraday. Kingston will be tried for murder."

Rutledge wondered if he'd been sent to Stoke Yarlington in order to distract him from Moresby and the verdict of the inquest. It was the kind of thing Bowles would think of. He himself hadn't been asked to give evidence . . .

"I still disagree with Inspector Farraday," he said briefly. "I could find no connection between Kingston and the dead man, Benjamin Clayton."

"Kingston was looking for what he could steal. He got caught, and tried to make Clayton's death appear to be suicide. And you won't be meddling in that decision."

It was a warning.

Rutledge ignored it. "With respect, sir, I suggest you ask Inspector Farraday where Kingston found the rope he used to hang Clayton."

Bowles stared at him, tight-lipped. Then he said with barely concealed contempt, "It's a harbor town. A port. There must be ropes to be had anywhere along the water."

"I agree, sir. But if Kingston only intended to rob Clayton, and then found himself forced to stage a suicide, where did he find the rope? Did he go rummaging in a shed behind the house, risking awakening the neighbors? It's worth pursuing."

"It's no longer your inquiry."

Rutledge left, walking back to his own office and standing for a time, looking out the window. He could feel the summer heat through the glass, and set his hand on it for a moment.

He would be called on to testify in Moresby, when the trial began. That was a certainty. And he would do what he could then to present his case to the jury. Until that time, he would have to put it out of his mind.

But he would ask Gibson to keep him informed. In the event Farraday persuaded the court that Rutledge's evidence wasn't needed.

He turned and sat down, trying to concentrate on the murder in Kent.

The Chief Constable had sent copies of interviews taken down immediately after the body was discovered.

They were vivid, the shock still echoing through every word, especially in the statement by the housekeeper.

He could almost imagine what had happened.

One Jerome Hadley walked out to his hop gardens after his dinner on Tuesday evening, to inspect the crop. Hops were a vine, a preservative for beer, and at an early stage, as they emerged from winter dormancy, they were trained to run up strings attached to tall frames, fields of them in spite of the fact that in Kent, they were called "gardens." In the spring poorer families came down from places like London to put up the frames and help string the vines. The trellis frames came from coppices of young sweet chestnuts that grew straight and tall and weathered well. Even the children did their bit, and the fresh air and good food were a welcome change for them. Many of them returned in the autumn to harvest the crop and remove the frames. In winter, the "gardens" were flat and nondescript, but in summer they could look like living sails that had lost their way inland. Rutledge had seen them often on his visits to Melinda Crawford.

There was a glorious sunset that evening (according to Tom, the footman, who had stood in the stable yard for a quarter of an hour watching it. It was thought that Hadley had also stayed out by the fields as the sky faded to apricot and rose, before turning to gold and lavender. For it was late when Hadley had finally walked home by way of the oast houses where eventually the hops would be dried. One of the tenant farmers had seen him there, or so he believed.

The staff had either gone to bed or returned to their homes in the village of Aylesbridge, and so Hadley must have let himself quietly into the house without disturbing them. According to the housekeeper, his wife was in Canterbury, visiting friends, but she was expected to return the next evening. Inspector Watson had verified this information.

The next morning, Hadley was found in the room he called his library, lying by the long windows, which stood open, and he was already beginning to stiffen with rigor.

The maid—Peggy Goode—who had come in to open the curtains and look for empty glasses on the drinks tray, raised the house with her screams.

That brought the cook and the housekeeper and the one footman, Tom, running from the kitchen where breakfast was under way.

The footman took one of the horses and set out for Aylesbridge for Dr. Wylie.

By the time they returned, the maid had been settled in the kitchen with a cup of tea laced with a little whisky, the library door had been shut, and the kettle was still on the hob, ready for the doctor if he cared for a cup.

Mrs. Tolliver, the housekeeper, had been particularly upset, and according to her statement, she had said to the staff, "I can't think what I'm to tell Mrs. Hadley. If she'd been here, she might have noticed the spell he took and sent for the doctor sooner. She won't forgive herself."

"But how could she have even known—sudden as it was?" Mrs. Bowers, the cook, had asked just as the doorbell rang. The housekeeper went herself to answer it, admitting the doctor and sending the footman round to the stable yard with the horses.

Coming in briskly, the doctor had said, "Good morning, Mrs. Tolliver. Where is he?"

"He's still in the library, sir. There was no use to move him—we *knew*, you see." She'd led the way down the passage and unlocked the door.

Wylie had taken up the story at this point. "Wait here, please." He'd walked carefully into the room and went to stand beside the body before dropping to his haunches and reaching out to feel for a pulse. But Mrs. Tolliver was right—Hadley had been dead for some hours.

"When did you last see him yesterday? Do you remember?" he asked from where he was squatting. "He hasn't changed for bed."

"He went out to the hop gardens after dinner. I left a little lemonade for him, in case he was warm after his walk, but he never touched it."

Wylie stood. "He drank something." He pointed to the glass on the desk. It was empty, but there was a rind of milk around the top.

"He must have gone down to the kitchen for it himself," she said, frowning, trying hard not to look directly at her employer's body. "The only thing is, he never cared for milk. I don't remember ever seeing him drink a glass."

"Well, he managed to down one last evening." He lifted the glass and smelled it, then with a finger, wiped up some of the residue in the glass. "It's already turned in this heat," he said with a grimace. "But I'd swear there was laudanum in it as well." He lifted the glass and looked at it. "It's of a size, depending on how much laudanum was in the milk, that it could have killed him. But I've never prescribed that for either of the Hadleys. Where did it come from?"

The question wasn't meant for Mrs. Tolliver, but she answered it anyway. "One of the maids had a little, when she broke her leg. Peggy."

"The one who found him. Yes, yes, but that was in the spring, and it was just enough to take the worst of the pain away at the start. I can't

imagine there would be any left, certainly not enough to kill anyone."
He put the glass down, precisely where he'd seen it sitting on the desk.
"I'll stay here with the body. Send that footman back into Aylesbury
for Constable Roderick. And give me the key, while you're about it, so
that I can lock the door. Were the long windows open when you first
came in this morning?"

"They were. All I could think was, it got stuffy in here with the
heat, and he opened them for a little air. He did sometimes. Mr.
Hadley was never one to be shut up into a room." She was taking the
key out of her pocket as she spoke, but before she could cross the room
to pass it to the doctor, he hurried to meet her at the door.

And then her statement followed the main thread of the story, and
she wrote that as she'd stepped into the passage, she realized that she
had pictured poor Mr. Hadley dying alone, unable to make anyone
hear his cries for help. But the doctor had given her the impression
that this was not the tragic death of a healthy man in his prime, falling ill while he was alone, and it had come as a terrible shock to her. A
police matter. In this house? She had refused even to think the words
to herself and instead had dispatched Tom posthaste for Constable
Roderick. She had told the rest of the staff that he'd been called because someone had to reach Mrs. Hadley in Canterbury.

It was more than half an hour before Constable Roderick arrived,
and Tom hurried down to the kitchen, demanding to know what had
been happening.

He admitted he'd fired question after question at the village policeman, only to meet with a solid wall of silence from the older man.

But Mrs.Tolliver had shaken her head and refused to say any more.

There was the statement from Peggy, who had found the body, but
she had been so shocked at seeing her employer lying there, his eyes
staring blankly at her, that she'd noticed nothing else. She added that
he was never down at that hour of the morning, and she hadn't even
bothered to knock at the door before entering.

Inspector Watson, from the town of Maidstone, had decided to ask for help directly, and in his message, attached to the interviews, he commented that so many of the hop pickers who came with any regularity lived in London, and if the inquiry was expanded to include any of them, it would be a mare's nest for Kent to try to track them all down.

He'd added, to be fair, *Neither Constable Roderick nor I is aware of any problems existing between the hop pickers and Mr. Hadley, nor have I uncovered any after speaking to the three tenant farmers. Good people, one had called them, no trouble at all. One or two of the men had gotten themselves drunk of a Saturday night, but had caused no trouble to anyone but themselves the next morning.*

As he finished the file, Rutledge realized that he had calmed down a little, but the determination to give evidence in Moresby when the time came remained just as strong.

He took out his watch and looked at it. If he hurried, he could reach Kent by nightfall with an early start the next morning in Aylesbridge. And because he would be away from the Yard for the next few days, he stopped by Gibson's office and left the names of Constable Roderick and Inspector Watson with the sergeant, in the event he needed to be reached in a hurry. Bowles might not tell him when Kingston's trial began, but he rather thought Gibson would, if only to spite Bowles.

As he picked up a newspaper from the boy who seemed to haunt the Yard, hawking the papers in a voice that sometimes cracked, dropping precipitously from soprano to baritone, the heavy black headlines from Europe leaped out at him.

Whitehall was expressing growing concerns that Germany might use the tiny kingdom of the Belgians as a route into northern France as opposed to the heavily contested eastern border where the two countries were separated by the Rhine. The fear was, Belgium and the broad flat fields of Flanders offered a back door into Paris, as well as control of the Channel Coast.

Once more he left notes for Jean and for Frances, then he drove to the house where Melinda Crawford lived. It was no more than forty minutes' distance from Aylesbridge, but late as it was, Rutledge had his doubts about finding a place in the village that could accommodate him for the night. And he had no desire to be left alone with his own thoughts about Bowles and Moresby.

Melinda fussed over him, seeing that he was well fed even though he hadn't arrived in time to share her dinner—and what's more, had arrived without any warning.

"Never mind the whys," she said, cutting his apology short. "I've been trying to think how I was to amuse myself this evening, and here you are, breaking the monotony very nicely. Now tell me the news of Frances, and how Miss Gordon's wedding preparations are going." She sat beside him at the long table, their voices echoing in the large rectangular dining room, with two ornate—and working—fireplaces opposite long windows leading out to a wide terrace beyond.

Rutledge told her about Frances—"I've seen very little of her of late, and I was meaning to speak to you about that. She needs a chaperone, someone who can be certain she's all right when I'm not there. At least until Christmas, when I bring Jean home."

"You may not realize it, but Frances can look after herself. Still, I'll find a suitable woman to come and stay, for appearance's sake. Will that do?"

"It will, yes. And perhaps you can convince my sister to accept her."

"Oh, that won't be a problem," Melinda replied, and smiled.

He told her about the wedding plans, and that he'd asked Jean to invite Frances to be one of the wedding party.

"And so she should. I wouldn't worry about it if I were you. Leave it to Mrs. Gordon. She'll be sure that everything is done properly. What does Miss Gordon's father have to say about this business in Europe?"

"Very little. But I think he's more worried than he wants anyone to know."

"Colonel Crawford tells me not to worry, but I think he wishes to spare me. He's officially retired, but he knows everyone in the War Office." Richard Crawford, Melinda's cousin, had retired from his regiment—the same one Melinda's late husband had served with—but still had many contacts where it mattered. He was young enough to be called up again if there was war.

The Major had also retired from active duty, but Rutledge said nothing about that.

It was early the next morning when he drove into Aylesbridge and found Constable Roderick already in the police station.

The door was standing wide to let in as much of the morning's cool air as possible, and as Rutledge pulled up in front, Roderick stepped out to run an admiring eye over the motorcar. He whistled under his breath.

"She's a beauty all right," he said. "What I wouldn't give to have one like her."

Rutledge got down and introduced himself.

He greeted Rutledge man to man, without deference to his position at the Yard, one professional to another. Rutledge was reminded of Sergeant Gibson.

Nearing forty years old, Roderick sounded much like his own statement, solid, not easily misled, and a good judge of character.

"It was a tragedy, that death. Made no sense. A thoroughly nice gentleman who kept the hop farm prosperous after his father-in-law died. Even though they seldom saw eye to eye, the land mattered, and I think Mr. Graves knew that at bottom."

"The farm came to Hadley through his wife?"

"Yes, I've known her girl and woman, and there's no one kinder. She keeps an eye on the families who come for the hop picking and takes care that the children are fed and healthy. She's summoned the doctor for more than one, and paid his bill too. Even if one of them took against her husband, the rest would see to it that he kept it to himself. I don't see them hurting her."

There were women in every village who knew how to look after those in need, to volunteer for handing out school prizes or Garden Day awards, and who did it with a graciousness that set everyone, even the losers, at their ease.

"And she was in Canterbury, visiting friends?"

"She was. Dr. Wylie went there to give her the news himself, since there was no way to reach her. He said he was glad she was with friends. It was the friends who brought her back here."

"Surely someone has a suspicion about who did this? In as small a village as Aylesbridge? People gossip."

"There's none that I've heard. Mostly shock and disbelief. Mr. Hadley was no easy mark, mind you, he knew his business and he ran it with an eye to profit. But he wasn't one to take advantage of people just because it lined his pocket."

A man with no enemies . . .

He'd heard that often enough—indeed, as recently as Stoke Yarlington and Moresby. Sometimes it was true, and sometimes it was not.

It was easy to sift through a list of ill-wishers and find a killer. It was the victims who seemed to have lived an exemplary life who were hard to fathom. Sometimes there were secrets, hidden depths that no one saw behind the surface kindness and generosity. But it could be there, nevertheless, and the police had to dig for it, often hurting the innocent along the way. Even the truly good man could rouse jealousy, fear, and intense hatred.

And even a good man might kill himself and leave no note behind to satisfy his sister's questions. Or be sitting in his own chair, half asleep, when an intruder came to his door.

"This time of year, the hop pickers have gone back to London? Yes? And so there is only the regular farm staff on the property. Have any of them seen anything out of the ordinary? Someone hanging about in the vicinity of the Hadley farm or asking unusual questions about the owner or his family? Even directions to the house."

"We spoke to everyone. Surely you've read the interviews? I saw to it that the Inspector had extra copies."

A lot of work to have them copied either by hand or by typewriter. Most small police stations didn't run to a typist. But it was clear Constable Roderick took his work seriously.

Roderick quickly added, "My wife has a fine hand, sir, and I often ask her to do the copying for me. She's discreet as well."

As the wives of vicars and policemen often had to be, living in two worlds at the same time. His own mother, Rutledge remembered, had talked over cases with his father, because she could often bring an objective eye to the subject. And yet she lightly professed to have no knowledge of her husband's clients, adding that she had no head for law. As she was a pianist of some note, she was believed.

"Yes, I've read them. Thank you. It was good work."

They discussed the murder for several minutes more, and then Rutledge rose. "I think I'd like to speak to Mrs. Tolliver first. The housekeeper. She appears to have her wits about her."

Roderick said, "I'll be happy to take you up to the house, sir. But you might consider talking to her on your own. She might say more to someone from London. It's worth a try."

"Thank you, Constable. I'll take your advice."

And so he left the police station, directions in hand, and found his way to the Hadley farm. Driving to the house, he could see the lines of greenery, like lacey curtains blowing in the light wind, and he was reminded of the frame his grandmother insisted on using for her lace curtains after they'd been washed, to keep their shape.

He'd been intrigued to learn that it was the female blossoms of the hop plants that were harvested and then dried in the oast houses, which in his opinion looked rather like truncated brick windmills. One could see them across the Kentish landscape, with their small white turrets that moved to keep the drying process going. The number of oast houses usually indicated the size of the hop gardens any given farm owned.

The Hadley farm boasted three. He could see tenant cottages beyond them, like a miniature hamlet, and then the drive split, the left turning leading up to the house.

It was a lovely old farmhouse that could even be called a small manor, brick with stone facings and newer wings to either side of the center block. They matched very well, but he could see slight variations in the brick that indicated they'd been added at different times.

He left the motorcar by the door, where the drive swept in a wide circle that in its day would have accommodated carriages and coaches. Walking up the shallow steps, he lifted the knocker.

A maid came to the door and asked his business. He didn't want the staff gossiping until he was ready. And so he gave his name but not his rank and asked to speak to Mrs. Tolliver.

He was invited to step in and shown to the stairs that led down to the nether regions of the house. As there wasn't a large family in residence, the kitchens weren't bustling, but he saw several faces peering out at him as he followed the maid to the small sitting room that served the housekeeper.

Mrs. Tolliver was sitting at an old-fashioned upright desk, working on accounts. A slim woman with graying hair and a kind face, she looked up, frowned, and turned her attention to the maid.

"Mr. Rutledge, Mrs. Tolliver, to speak to you."

She rose, frowning, and said, "Thank you, Peggy. That will be all." When the door had closed behind the girl, she offered Rutledge a chair and said quietly, "Constable Roderick mentioned that someone might be coming down from London. Scotland Yard?"

"Yes." As he took the chair she offered him, he asked, "Is that the young woman who found the body?"

"It would be a kindness if you don't have to speak to her. I doubt she could tell you very much, even if you did. I don't think I've ever seen anyone more frightened. I don't believe she sleeps well, even now."

"She had entered the room going about her usual morning duties?"

"Yes, that's right. This time of year, we needn't lay the fires for use, but we open the curtains, fluff cushions, set a room to rights before the downstairs maid begins to dust it. If the weather is fair, we might open the windows to catch what breeze there is. It's been quite hot for the most part, and airing a room as early as we can is important."

"And what did you see when you walked in?"

"I saw Peggy first, of course, and went directly to her to ask what was wrong. It was then I saw Mr. Hadley, and the long windows standing wide, as if he'd just come in from the terrace."

"And you hadn't seen him since early evening of the day before."

"That's true. As he was finishing his dinner, he said that as it was such a fine evening, he thought he might take a turn down to the hop gardens. As a rule he took the dog with him, but she died of old age at the end of May and he hadn't got around to replacing her. He was quite fond of her, and he said not just any dog would do." She paused, and looked across the room, where a small framed tintype of the house with only one wing added on held pride of place. "I did wonder, if he'd had a dog, if that wouldn't have made a difference somehow."

"Did you touch him?"

"No, there was no need. I've seen the dead before this." It was said with a sadness that told him that she spoke from a sense of great loss still.

"Tell me about the glass."

"It was odd, I never noticed it. Not even while I was waiting for Dr. Wylie. I was trying not to think, to tell the truth. And yet my mind was running on—that he hadn't gone to bed, that the windows were standing wide, that Mrs. Hadley hadn't been here to help him or comfort him—what I was to do about Peggy. I'd left her in the hands of Mrs. Bowers, the cook, and I could hear her still having the hysterics. For that matter we were all in a terrible state, I can tell you."

He could hear the words of her statement in her voice as she spoke.

"Dr. Wylie saw the glass?"

"He said the milk had turned. But I've never known Mr. Hadley to drink milk. He must have walked down to the kitchen rather than wake one of us—he was thoughtful in that way. Perhaps he didn't find anything else to his liking, or perhaps he thought it might settle his stomach, although I don't recall his dinner being troublesome in that way. No spring onions, or the like. I wish now he had asked me to bring it—I'd have *known,* you see, if something was wrong. Dr. Wylie says it wasn't his heart, but I still wonder. They do say that a sense of being gassy can be the first signs of a heart attack. Pressure in the chest."

"But Dr. Wylie thought there was laudanum in the glass?"

"Yes, he tasted it. That's when he told me the milk had turned. Well, it was that hot in the night, it very likely had."

"Did Mr. Hadley's body give you any reason to believe that he'd struggled with anyone, or that he'd been forced to drink the milk?"

She stared at Rutledge. "By whom?"

"That's just it, I don't know."

"Nothing was amiss in the library. Even the glass was set tidily on the blotter, the sort of thing he'd be likely to do. But Dr. Wylie couldn't explain where the laudanum came from in such a quantity to kill Mr. Hadley."

No enemies. No signs of breaking in, no struggle. And that glass of milk laced with laudanum. These appeared to link three deaths. But why? How could they have been tied to a murder in Moresby, in Stoke Yarlington, and now here in Aylesbridge?

The connection had been slowly dawning on him, but the hanging in Moresby had confused the issue. Was that what it had been intended to do? Or had a killer been afraid that the laudanum hadn't done its work?

Rutledge felt a surge of excitement and a fervent wish for access to a telephone. He needed to put in a call to Sergeant Gibson to find out if there were any other cases similar to this, cases handled by other

Inspectors at the Yard, cases he hadn't heard about. Something that might just indicate a pattern . . .

But it would have to wait. He must finish this interview and keep his mind on what he had come to do.

He said, "Do you think Mrs. Hadley is up to seeing me? I should like to ask her a few questions."

"She wasn't here—" Mrs. Tolliver began, then went on, "Of course, you'd want to know if anyone had a reason to kill him. For my own part, I'd have said no, that he was the last person to be murdered. I can name a name or two in the village, people who are always causing others hurt or bullying them, who might be more likely. But everyone seemed to like Mr. Hadley. He was that sort of man."

Like Tattersall. Like Clayton.

She rose, leading him up the steps he'd just come down and putting him in a small drawing room, rarely used except for guests.

Unable to sit still, he paced the floor, oblivious to the pale cream walls and the heavy Turkish carpet under his feet.

If Tattersall *hadn't* killed himself. If Clayton *hadn't* been hanged. Take out the distractions, and look only at the similarities.

And these three cases fit together. Three men killed not at random but as part of a whole.

But what whole?

He didn't have all the pieces. Not yet.

By the time Mrs. Hadley came into the room, nearly a quarter of an hour later, it was all Rutledge could do to conceal his excitement.

He began by offering her his sympathy. Her eyes were swollen from crying, and she looked as if she might have been resting. He felt a sudden distaste for having to disturb her.

A pretty woman with red-gold hair and blue eyes, of medium height and build, she had walked across the room with steady determination, as if to make certain she didn't show any sign of weakness. And yet it was there, the shock of a loss so great that she hadn't managed to absorb it yet.

"I must apologize for asking to speak to you today, but for the fact that the sooner we begin our inquiries, the better chance we have to find the person behind your husband's death."

She said with a steeliness that surprised him, "It's the one thing in this world I want just now. Other than to bring my husband back to me."

"You weren't here, of course. But you knew your husband better perhaps than anyone else. I'd like to know if there was anything on his mind. Anything in the present that worried him, or in his past that might have come back to find him."

"No. He was such a good man. Yes, I know, every new widow says that, and means it at the time. But even saints are human. Jerry looked for the best in everyone, and expected to find it. And so sometimes he did, even when everyone else thought he must be mad even to try." She caught her lower lip in her teeth as if to stave off tears that were far too close to the surface. After a moment she added, "I don't see what anyone had to gain from his death. And sometimes that's the only reason for murder, isn't it?"

"I'm afraid so."

"I'm his only heir. And as this farm was my father's, that's how it should be. We don't owe large sums of money. We haven't ill-treated our people here, either the household staff or the temporary workers from London. In fact Jerry is rather generous in paying them, with the forward-looking idea that happy people seem to work all the harder. I'm told by Mrs. Tolliver that nothing appears to be broken or stolen. My husband had small treasures in this room and his study, but nothing of such great value that he might have become a target for thieves. We entertain friends from time to time, we've had a few small house parties, but they were always great fun, without any incident to mar them. No one has stormed out in anger."

It was unexpectedly comprehensive. He thought she'd already gone over and over these possibilities, trying to make sense of the senseless. But he had to ask another question that would surely hurt her.

"Was there anyone else in his life? A woman . . ."

She smiled sadly. "If there were, I'd die of the shock. Ours was a love match. I'd have given my life for Jerry. And he for me."

"I'm told you didn't live here in this house, just after your marriage."

"My father wouldn't have been satisfied with the Prince of Wales, much less Jerry. And as a consequence we visited infrequently. And yet Papa left him this estate, when he might have tied it up for me alone. I've always believed it was because he'd come to know that Jerry would be a good husband in every sense. To me, to the land, to the people we employ."

"Where did you live before coming here?"

"Bristol of all places." She smiled again at his look of surprise. "Jerry was the heir of his Uncle Thaddeus, and so we lived in a town house there. Quite a lovely old one. We'd met in London when I came out, and I knew straightaway that it was Jerry I wanted to spend my life with. When my father died, we turned the Bristol house over to my husband's cousin and his family. They were looking for a larger home, and so it was suitable for them."

Bristol. Even in Moresby, even here in Kent, the road led back to Bristol. Why Bristol?

He asked if she or her husband had by any chance known the Clayton family, or the Tattersall brother and sister. But she shook her head. "Should we have known them? Were they connections of my husband's? If so I don't believe he ever spoke of them or introduced me to them."

And he believed her.

She considered his question from another perspective. "Are you saying that someone among these families, the Claytons or the Tattersalls, wanted to harm my husband—that this might be why he was so willing to move to Kent, when I asked him to take over the farm?"

"I don't have any reason to think so, no," he replied. "They were involved in other cases concerning Bristol. It's a matter of thorough-ness, that's all." He kept his voice level, his expression neutral, but it took all his willpower to conceal what was going through his mind.

Bowles would call it another of his leaps of the imagination, not founded on fact or backed up with evidence. But here were three cases revolving around this singular business of Bristol and a glass of milk. Surely there had to be something connecting them? A killer. Why had he singled out three such different men?

Annie Clayton had left her father in the house. But only for a night. Miss Tattersall had been asleep upstairs, as the staff had been here. How had a killer found his victims so alone?

He tried to concentrate, to finish his interview, but his mind was jumping from one possibility to another.

If these murders *were* connected, Kingston, sitting in a jail in Moresby, couldn't have committed the last two. But did that clear him in the first death? Was one man at the bottom of this, or was it a con-spiracy?

He said, "I've kept you longer than I should. Perhaps we could finish talking tomorrow?"

Gratitude flooded her eyes. "Yes, if you wouldn't mind. Unless, of course, what I could remember would speed your investigation?"

"I think we have enough to be going on with."

"Then would you mind ringing the bell, there by the hearth? Mrs. Tolliver can show you out, and afterward, help me back up the stairs."

She was pale, and Rutledge wondered if she had eaten or slept since she had been given the news.

He did as she had asked, waiting for Mrs. Tolliver to appear. When she stepped into the room, Rutledge said quietly, "I can find my own way out. I think your mistress needs you."

He turned to go, but Mrs. Hadley said in a stronger voice, "If you find out who did this to my husband, or why, will you come at once and tell me? I need to *know*."

Rutledge promised, nodded to her and to Mrs. Tolliver, and left.

Through the still open door he heard Mrs. Tolliver say, "I was afraid it was too much for you. Let me help you back up the stairs."

And Mrs. Hadley answered, "Too much for me? When Jerry is lying God knows where, dead? I would do anything to find his killer."

He found himself wondering if she had meant him to hear.

R utledge finally ran Dr. Wylie to earth.

He was not in his surgery, but his nurse explained that there had been an accident out at one of the farms. Following her directions, Rutledge reached Sunrise Farm, only to learn that the doctor had dealt with the mangled foot and was now on his way to look in on a newborn at Foxhole Farm.

Rutledge had just turned into the muddy farm lane when he saw the doctor's carriage with its smartly stepping black mare in the harness, coming toward him.

Waiting for him, Rutledge looked out across more hop fields, and beyond them to orchards already heavy with late summer fruit.

Wylie was younger than he'd expected, perhaps thirty-five, tall and slender with a shock of unruly black hair and intelligent blue eyes.

"Am I needed?" he called when he was close enough to be heard.

Rutledge introduced himself and said, "I wanted to ask you a few questions about Jerome Hadley's death."

"It's better for you to join me here than for me to get down. Nellie is not accustomed to motorcars."

And so Rutledge climbed up beside him in the small carriage.

"What made you suspect it was murder even before you'd done a cursory examination of Hadley's body?"

"I knew he had a sound heart, and although that's never a guarantee of a long life, I couldn't believe it was that. When I saw the glass of milk on the blotter, Mrs. Tolliver told me that he never drank milk.

Some people can't, you know. It upsets their digestive system. And then I smelled the milk—a doctor uses his nose as often as he uses his eyes—and despite the sourness, I thought there was something else in the glass. I tasted it. And I realized at once that it must be laudanum. Where had it come from, and why was Hadley taking it? This was altogether too suspicious for me to say nothing. I told the constable what I suspected. He was worried about contacting Mrs. Hadley in Canterbury, but I must admit I was curious enough that I volunteered to go there myself."

"Did you suspect her?"

"Not really. No. But I was concerned about the laudanum, and I wanted to ask her if she used it. I'd never prescribed it for her—there was no need, she's a healthy young woman—but women sometimes use it in small amounts to help them sleep, and she might have got it in Canterbury. Women used to take arsenic, you know, to give them that ethereally pale complexion so desirable at one time. In such small amounts, it's not deadly, but there could be an accumulative effect if users aren't careful. As a matter of fact, I *had* prescribed laudanum for the maid Peggy. But it was a dilute solution and a small vial because she was so young. In the night, she might not count her drops properly. Or follow my instructions to call the housekeeper to help her. That's trouble waiting to happen. Or perhaps she decides to rid herself of another maid who has made her life wretched? Young, impetuous, thoughtless."

"You have an extraordinary interest in murder, for a healer."

"Not murder. I've been a doctor long enough that nothing surprises me. Human nature being what it is. Medical training shows you the best and the worst of life. You don't deal with only the nice people. There are drug addicts and botched backstreet abortions and abuses that turn your stomach. And attempted murder that winds up on a table in front of us and we have a matter of minutes to determine what we can do to save the poor victim. I've run across more than my share of laudanum cases. Best way to rid yourself of that elderly aunt sitting on all that money, or a clinging wife who has long since become a burden. Even an unwanted child. The list goes on."

"How could someone kill a man with laudanum, without leaving any other trace of his presence in a house? As in Hadley's case? If it wasn't someone who lived there?"

"I've pondered that myself. No robbery, no rummaging through the house looking for private papers, no attempt to torture Hadley into giving him whatever it was he wanted. And yet someone went down to the kitchen for that glass of milk. And someone had the laudanum to put into it. I did the post, you know. That's what killed him."

"Yes, I thought as much. Although it was essential to have that confirmed. Any possibility of an affair? Either partner might have reached a point where he or she wished to be free without the scandal of divorce."

Wylie shook his head. "They were close, the Hadleys. And very happy."

"No children?"

"Sadly, no. My wife tells me that's why Mrs. Hadley does so much for the hop pickers and their families."

"Any idea how the will stands?"

"I was one of the witnesses. There's a Hadley cousin in Bristol, I think, but the property was Mrs. Hadley's to begin with, and Jerome didn't wish to leave it elsewhere. The cousin would have been an absentee landlord, and besides, apparently he's doing too well in the shipping business to think of taking on a farm of this size."

"Are you sure of that?"

"Jerome spoke to him before drawing up the will. He wholeheartedly agreed."

"Then what happens to the farm?"

"It goes to Mrs. Hadley, of course. And if she dies, it will be sold and the proceeds donated to various charities."

"So the property isn't at issue. Anything else that might be?"

"I was talking to my wife about that last night. Mrs. Hadley had inherited some rather nice pieces of jewelry, and her husband had given her other bits and bobs. But they were all there. She looked when she got home. That rules out theft. Unless of course the intruder, whoever he was, had no idea they existed. Apparently he never even looked. The bedroom hadn't been touched, any more than the library had. Not so much as a drawer opened."

"Interesting," Rutledge said. "I've had two other cases closely resembling this one, each of them separated from the other by quite some distance. Wells in Somerset and Moresby in Yorkshire. And yet threads of both of them led back to Bristol. A shopkeeper, a man with a trust that enabled him to live a life of leisure. And now a farmer."

"Were they the same age? Had they been to the same school?"

"The man with the trust was the eldest, the shopkeeper was some twenty years younger, and Hadley must have been ten to fifteen years younger still."

"And they're not related? Distant cousins, or even through marriage?"

"No relationship at all. Not that we've turned up."

Wylie shook his head. "I can't think what it might be that they shared. Hadley was to all intents and purposes a gentleman farmer, but he worked as hard as any man I know."

"Anything else that you think might be useful? What about all those workers out from London?"

"If this had happened when they were here working, I'd say you must interview the lot. But they weren't. Still, it's possible that one of them held a grudge, it simmered, and we've seen the aftermath of it."

"But that wouldn't explain the shopkeeper and the man of leisure."

"No. I doubt a farm laborer down from London would have any knowledge of the other two." Wylie shrugged. "I know this village. There's not a soul in it who would harm one of the Hadleys. And I can't picture Jerome taking advantage of his wife's absence in Canterbury to kill himself. I'd seen him just this past week, and he was cheerful, looking forward to her return, and even thinking about driving down to spend a day or two in Canterbury, then bring her home. Hardly the attitude of a man depressed enough to kill himself."

"Unless he'd had bad news about the farm and felt he'd failed as its steward."

"Not Hadley. He'd have faced it squarely and dealt with it."

Rutledge thanked the doctor, got down, and drove back to the Hadley farm. He asked permission to look through Hadley's desk in the small room where he kept the farm accounts. The local police had been there before him, but he spent three hours searching for anything that might explain Hadley's death.

The accounts were in order, the farm was prospering, and the death duties for Mrs. Hadley's father had been paid off long ago. Nothing to indicate that a man had felt it better to take his own life than to have to face his wife with dire news.

He thanked Mrs. Tolliver, left the farm, and instead of going to Maidstone to speak to Inspector Watson, he drove instead back to Melinda Crawford's house.

She had paid to have a telephone installed as soon as it was possible to do so, and from there, he could call London.

10

Rutledge had tea on the terrace with his hostess, and then asked for the use of her telephone.

She grinned at him. "Is that why you came back? Why didn't you say so straightaway instead of fidgeting for half an hour."

"I didn't fidget," he answered her.

"Not literally, perhaps, but figuratively, definitely. Go on. Call Jean if you like."

"Not Jean. The Yard. There's something I need to know before I can go any further with this present inquiry."

"By all means. And then come back and satisfy an old woman's curiosity."

He kissed her on the forehead as he passed her chair on the way to the telephone closet just off the main hall.

He was in luck. Sergeant Gibson was still at the Yard.

"Having any success there in Kent, sir?" the sergeant inquired when he was summoned to the telephone.

"I need information, Sergeant. And it's rather urgent."

He went on to explain what it was he was after. Had any of the other Inspectors on duty at the Yard recently handled a case where the outcome was uncertain, but the weapon of choice was laudanum in glasses of milk that the victim drank without a struggle.

"As to that, sir, I don't know."

"Look into it for me, will you? It's important enough that I'll wait by the telephone to hear from you." He passed on Melinda's number, thanked Gibson, and hung up.

As he walked back out onto the terrace, Melinda turned to study his face. "Your telephone call. It had a satisfactory conclusion? It must have done, for here you are, back again this quickly."

She alone of all his family and friends had that uncanny way of seeing through him. Not that he had much to hide from her. But she seemed to read his moods and his distractions with ease, and sometimes it was trying to be so transparent.

He said, "I was looking into this case in Aylesbridge." He proceeded to tell her about Hadley's death. She was surprised.

"But I know him, Ian. Not well of course, but he and his lovely wife were often at county functions I bothered to attend."

Melinda had created quite a stir when she had bought this house and staffed it with Indian servants she'd brought back from Delhi with her. Her Sikh chauffeur drove with skill and speed, frightening horses and small children. Her personal maid, a Hindu with what appeared to be an endless assortment of saris, had a reputation for being a shrewd businesswoman, making certain her mistress was never cheated by purveyors of goods to the household. Shanta also treated Rutledge as a favored member of the family, indulging him when his parents weren't looking. He knew Melinda turned a blind eye, and so he'd enjoyed his popularity in the kitchen as well as the stables.

Melinda Crawford was nothing if not clever. She listened to his account of the inquiry in Moresby and again in Stoke Yarlington, then nodded as he finished and sat back.

She rang for more tea, then said, "This killer has a scheme, I should think. He's not acting randomly. He's selected his victims with care, always coming upon them when they're alone. He's studied them and knows when it's safe to approach them. The question remains, what is that scheme?"

"I don't know yet." Rutledge got up to pace. "So far these have all been men."

"Yes, that's true. Which points to business affairs, I should think, rather than personal matters. Only they've never shared a business relationship that you know of. The only link I can find, then, aside from the laudanum, is Bristol and its environs."

"They were all reasonably successful men. Even Clayton had sold his shop for a goodly sum. It's possible each of them refused to help someone desperately in need of money. And he's taking his revenge. But why wait so long? Was this man in prison? Out of the country? Ill? Shut up in an institution?"

"A good question. The Army perhaps? Posted in the Empire somewhere and unable to return to England?" Melinda shrugged elegantly. "My dear boy, it could be any of these things. A veritable needle in a haystack. How do you propose to find that needle?"

"I don't know yet. Much will depend on what Sergeant Gibson has to tell me. Surely if this killer has had other victims, he must have made a mistake, left a clue, or in some way tipped his hand."

"We can only hope he has."

But it was late when Sergeant Gibson returned Rutledge's call. Well after ten.

They had just finished their Madeira and set their empty glasses on the drinks tray. Melinda was on the point of going up to bed when they heard the trill of the telephone from the hall.

"Ah," she said. "That must be for you. Answer it, Ian."

And so he had, not waiting for one of the staff to summon him.

It was Gibson, as he'd hoped.

"There's been another such case, sir. Inspector Penvellyn in Northumberland."

Rutledge remembered discussing that inquiry with Inspector Cummins, considering the possibility that the Cornish Inspector hadn't dealt well with the people in the far north of the country.

"What about his successor? Martin, I think it was."

"No luck there, either, although Inspector Martin was convinced the wife had killed her husband. She had had laudanum after her surgery to remove her gall bladder, and had even begged more from the local doctor. The problem was, there was no way to prove his suspicions."

A frustration Rutledge recognized.

"Will you have a copy of that file on my desk? I'll be back in London tomorrow morning to have a look at it."

"I don't see how it's pertinent to Kent, sir. With all respect."

"Nor do I. But I'm hoping I'll find what I'm looking for once I've read it. And, Sergeant? Not a word of this to either Inspector Martin or Penvellyn. And most particularly not Chief Superintendent Bowles."

"Mum's the word, sir," Gibson said, doubt still large in his voice.

When Rutledge returned to the sitting room, Melinda took one look at his face.

"You're leaving tomorrow for London." It was a statement, not a question.

"Yes, there's a file I must read for myself."

"Will you be returning to the inquiry here in Kent?"

"I don't know. I expect I shall have to."

"Well. I have enjoyed your company, my dear. And Ian. You know my door is always open."

With a smile, she said good night and left him there.

Rutledge watched her go, affection in his gaze. She was a remarkable woman, and he was very fond of her.

Without waiting for breakfast the next morning, Rutledge was on the road a little before six, making his way toward London. Traffic was fairly light at first, and then it picked up as he neared the city.

Sunlight filled the air, but there had been a red dawn when he set out, brilliant and blazing. If the old saw about red skies was true, then there would be storms before the day was out. It had been a remarkably fine summer, with very few breaks in the weather.

He reached the Yard before Bowles had appeared, and walked quietly through the passages to his office. There he'd had to search for the file that Sergeant Gibson had promised him, finally discovering it in a stack of innocuous documents that Rutledge had been meaning to return to the files. He wondered briefly if this had been a hint from Sergeant Gibson, or if the man had tried to conceal the file from casual searches for one of Rutledge's court documents.

He'd shut the door behind him, and now he sat down in his chair, his back to the room, and opened the file.

First he scanned Inspector Penvellyn's reports. The Cornish Inspector had got nowhere. Part of the problem was his lack of experience in dealing with Northumberland. But the local man had not been thorough in his interviews before Penvellyn arrived.

A Northumberland schoolmaster, living just outside Alnwick, had been found dead in his sitting room by his wife, who had come downstairs after waking shortly before four in the morning to find her husband hadn't come up to bed.

In the beginning, there had been no mention of a glass of milk. Inspector Martin had discovered there had been one during a third interview with the victim's wife after the postmortem had revealed the death was caused by an overdose of laudanum. The local man had failed to note it.

The initial view was suicide. Mrs. Stoddard had sworn to the police that her husband had had nothing on his mind, but it was soon discovered that he had been very worried about the future of the small boarding school. The history master and the French master had tried to cover up the school's problems, until Penvellyn had had a discussion with Stoddard's bank manager. There he'd learned that Stoddard had been using his own money in a desperate attempt to shore up the school for another term.

Nothing had been stolen from the house nor had it been searched, reinforcing the belief that Percy had killed himself while despondent over the future.

At that stage the doctor had suggested that Stoddard had surprised a housebreaker, and then in order to sleep, had taken some of his wife's laudanum without properly measuring the dose. It was even suggested that Stoddard had come downstairs in the first place because he was having trouble sleeping, and walked straight into the housebreaker, who had fled empty-handed.

Inspector Martin, arriving to replace Penvellyn, soon realized that the doctor had tried to protect Mrs. Stoddard from the stigma of suicide by describing the death as accidental.

Martin was a straightforward man who brooked no interference with the facts. He ascertained that the laudanum had indeed been prescribed for her after surgery and that she had kept the bottle upstairs in the drawer of the table by her bed.

The glass was finally discovered when Martin took over the inquiry. It had been set in one of the drawers of the desk, and he began to suspect the dead man's wife.

A neighbor had heard arguments about the money from his personal funds that Stoddard was using to prop up the school, and Martin surmised that Mrs. Stoddard had killed her husband to stop him from bankrupting them.

The servants had indicated that the Stoddards were not the most devoted of couples, and it was Martin's opinion that household often knew more about what was going on in a marriage than either the husband or wife realized.

Try as he would, Inspector Martin couldn't shake Mrs. Stoddard's testimony that she had not killed her husband and had in fact supported his use of personal funds to help the school. And there was no record that Mrs. Stoddard had purchased more laudanum than her physician had prescribed. Nor could he prove that she had been hoarding her supply in order to kill her husband.

He did suspect from a comment that the doctor's nurse had made, that Mrs. Stoddard used any excuse she could think of to visit the doctor's surgery, and he wondered if there was any relationship between them. But it appeared that he was not her lover but rather the source of the laudanum that she needed.

Martin spent nearly a week in Alnwick, tracing every possible thread.

All he could elicit was the fact that Mr. Stoddard had been born in Bristol, owned property there, and had moved to Alnwick when he had been appointed headmaster of Riverton School.

Laudanum and Bristol. A glass of milk.

There it was again. And in a case not his own.

What the hell was in Bristol? Rutledge asked himself.

It was not the size of London. And yet four dead men had lived or worked in the town or its environs. They had moved in different social circles, and had left there at different times in their lives. Furniture maker, man of independent means, gentleman farmer, and now a schoolmaster.

No, they hadn't simply lived there. They had owned property there. And they were all male.

Wary of jumping to conclusions, he went down a mental list of possibilities. And as he did, he realized that there was only one place where men of such varied backgrounds might have touched each other's lives.

So ordinary as to be overlooked: serving on a jury.

He remembered that he'd even suggested as much to Cummins in the case of the blackened grave stones. And Cummins had shaken his head, considering it more far-fetched than the idea of a shared secret.

And it went beyond a simple matter of jury duty. These men hadn't been brought together to decide a petty theft or an assault. Very likely not fraud or embezzlement. Not housebreaking or horse stealing. A capital case. Murder.

His office felt suffocating, too small, too hot on this warm day, too confining when he needed to think. Rutledge rose, putting the file back where he found it, and left, turning toward Parliament, as he so often seemed to do, his feet taking him in that direction out of habit. And as he walked, his mind was engaged in sifting all the facts at his command. He couldn't go to Bowles with this until he was absolutely certain that he was right. And he wouldn't put Chief Inspector Cummins in the middle by talking to him. Not yet.

Bowles was satisfied that they had Clayton's killer in custody. He'd agreed that very likely Tattersall had killed himself for reasons he'd kept to himself. And Martin was certain Mrs. Stoddard had murdered her husband. It would take more than theory to overcome the Yard's certainty.

This was a battle he would very likely lose, Rutledge was all too aware of that. He had a fine career ahead of him, and he was engaged to the woman he wanted to spend the rest of his life with. It would be wiser not to engage in such a battle in the first place.

But there was Mark Kingston. Rutledge could tell himself that the jury that tried the man would realize that Kingston couldn't have murdered Benjamin Clayton and refuse to find him guilty.

What if they did?

He looked up at the tall spire of Big Ben, shading his eyes from the hazy sunlight. He could feel a storm in the air, but he catalogued that in the recesses of his brain, just as he noted the traffic over Westminster Bridge or the sounds of ships coming up from the river, without any of it entering his conscious thinking.

How in God's name could he find out if these four dead men had served on the same jury? Much less those whose grave stones had been blackened. But the seven who lay beneath blackened grave stones could wait.

Rutledge had a good memory for names and faces. He went through the long list of barristers his father had worked with, many of them later becoming QCs and then KCs. One of them might know where he should begin.

Who was still alive, who could he turn to, to ask for information?

And then he came up with the answer.

Fillmore Montagu Gilbert. Famous in his day for his successes, but even more famous for the dramatic way he conducted his crosses, sometimes shaking the prisoner in the dock to his very boots. Gilbert knew people, and he had had an uncanny feeling for guilt, even when the evidence seemed to point in the other direction. And he could ferret out details that led the prisoner to contradict himself or stumble over a fact that was pertinent to the case.

What's more, Gilbert was still alive. In his eighties if Rutledge's math was correct.

Where was he now?

Rutledge turned back to the Yard, thought better of asking Gibson, and instead went to his motorcar and drove to the house he shared with his sister.

She was there, arranging flowers for the main rooms, a skill she'd inherited from their mother.

Surprised to see him, she said, "If you're here to beg lunch, you'll have to take me out to dine. Mrs. Holly has found ants in the pantry, and she says it's a certain sign of heavy rain. Ants *know,* she says. And the kitchen is being given a scrubbing it probably hasn't experienced in twenty years."

He laughed. "God forbid that we should find an ant swimming for its life in the consommé. All right, if you can help me find what I need, I'll take you anywhere you'd like to go."

"Promise? You won't go haring off to the Yard instead?"

"Promise. Besides, it's a personal matter, not Yard business."

But when he told her what he needed, she looked stricken.

"Ian. Everything was boxed up after the funerals. All the cards and letters and the names on the floral arrangements—everything. I can't—I can't do it."

With a surge of guilt, he realized how thoughtless he'd been in his hurry to find what he needed. Taking her hand, he said, "Of course I can't ask you to relive it. All I need is to know where to look."

"Melinda had it all taken up to the attic. I didn't ask—I didn't want to know."

"Then I'll start there."

"And still take me to lunch?"

"Yes, I've given you my word."

But the grief he'd awakened hadn't gone away.

He took the stairs two at a time, walked on to the attic door on the second floor, and went up the next flight of steps just as quickly, although they were narrower and shorter.

The attics of this house held memories for him as well. His rocking horse, the cradle where Frances had slept for the first few weeks of her life, the collection of walking sticks that had belonged to father and grandfathers, a chest full of his mother's favorite hats, chairs and bedsteads and armoires and tables that had long since been replaced in fits of modernization, including the heavy Victorian table under which he'd played with his vast army of lead soldiers on rainy days. Its multiple branching legs had provided battlefield and barracks, parade grounds and cemeteries for fallen warriors.

He tried to shut out the past, searching for the boxed history of his parents' untimely deaths. He found what he was looking for under the eaves, in a corner where the boxes were safe but not intrusive. And he recognized them because they were labeled in Melinda Crawford's copperplate script.

Rutledge began with the labels, squatting there as he scanned them. He had told himself he could do this, but it was no less painful for him than it was for his sister.

Memories came flooding back.

Standing in the passage at the Yard as Cummins was walking toward him, a telegram in his hand, his face drained of all color. The feel of the telegram in his own hands as Cummins wordlessly passed it to him. The blurring of the type as he tried to read the message, and the wave of sheer disbelief that swept him, followed by shattering anger. Then the terrible realization that he would have to break the news to his sister.

Nearly two years had passed since the accident on the Isle of Skye that had killed his mother and father. They had been returning to the Kyle of Lochalsh on the small ferry that carried visitors, residents, goods, mail, and even the occasional Highland cow or sheep back and forth between the island and the mainland. It had been dusk, and there were no witnesses. It wasn't until the ferry was overdue that those waiting at the Kyle realized that something was wrong.

When the bodies were recovered, Rutledge and his wife were clinging together, almost impossible for anyone to separate.

After, everyone had said that it was good that they had gone together. That they would have wanted it that way. But Rutledge had refused to believe there was any goodness at all in what had happened, what had been so suddenly taken from them.

Shaking his head to clear it of the past, he concentrated on the task at hand.

It was then he located the box marked *CONDOLENCES* and against his will remembered sitting at the desk in his father's study, responding to each and every one of the many messages of sympathy that had poured in. How do you find the words to say at a time like that? And yet many people had found them. And he had had to thank them with a rote statement he'd written out to copy because it caused less pain than answering each message with an individual response.

Thank you for your kind words at this time in our lives. My sister and I are more grateful than I can express for your sympathy and your thoughtfulness in writing.

Brief, to the point, his duty to his parents handled to the best of his ability. But Melinda, a hand on his shoulder, had approved.

"No one expects an outpouring of your feelings, Ian. Only an acknowledgment of their offer of comfort."

Shoving that memory aside as well, he sat down on the dusty attic floor and opened the box. With resolute fingers he began to lift out the stacks of cards, a few at a time, and then a handful. He told himself he needn't open them or the emotions they evoked. He need only to look at the sender's name.

Forty-five minutes later, he had what he wanted: the letter of condolences that Fillmore Gilbert had sent. He remembered the contents all too well, the references to his father's infinite wisdom and experience in the law, and his mother's grace in every circumstance. *A rare woman,* Gilbert had called her, *and well suited to be the wife of such an extraordinary man.*

He noted the address under Gilbert's name, and then he carefully repacked the box, closing it up again with a sense of finality.

Brushing off his trousers, he followed his own footsteps back to the stairs and went down them.

Frances was waiting for him in the sitting room.

Looking up as he came through the door, she said, without really wanting to know, "Did you find what you were seeking?"

He took out his notebook to show her that he hadn't removed anything from the boxes. "An address I couldn't find anywhere else. I need information, and this was the best person I could think of to help me."

"Yes, they knew so many people, didn't they? It was a great comfort at the—the time."

"Are you still hungry, or have you found something in the ant-ridden kitchen?"

She grimaced. "Mrs. Holly won't let me through the door. I asked if she'd found mouse droppings too, but she exclaimed 'Weovils' as if they were the devil himself."

"Not surprising this summer."

He took her to the Monarch Hotel with its famous restaurant, and enjoyed watching her greet friends and examine the menu. They talked of this and that, and finally Jean's name came up.

"Her mother has written. Asking me to be one of the bridesmaids. I was so pleased. You didn't put her up to it, did you, Ian?"

"I've never spoken to Mrs. Gordon about the bridesmaids." It was the truth, and he was glad he could tell it with conviction. "I stay as far away from discussions about veils and slippers and church decorations as possible. It's a foreign language no man can comprehend."

Laughing at him, she said, "We're to go to see the gowns they've picked out. I'm rather looking forward to it. It isn't often your favorite brother is married."

He smiled in return. "Melinda sends her love. I was in Kent on Yard business and stopped to see her. She's worried about you."

"I can't imagine why. Because I haven't decided to marry? I never lack invitations or dance partners. Early days, my dear Ian. I'm enjoying myself too much." Then she was suddenly serious. "You'll be the first to know when the right person comes along. And I dare you to tell me he's not the right one for me."

Yet she had done just that when he'd told her he'd proposed to Jean. A stir of worry suddenly wormed its way into his heart.

That was when he broached the subject of a companion for her.

There was fierce resistance. And that worried him more. Frances was one of the most sensible women he knew. But she was only twenty, not a great age for wisdom where the heart was concerned. He found himself wondering if she would have married before this, had it not been for the long period of mourning for their parents. Mandated by grief, not etiquette, it had taken some time for both of them to come to terms with that loss.

"Think about it," he said. "And speak to Melinda. Between the two of you, you can surely find someone who would suit."

"I thought you were giving me a sister, so that I wouldn't be lonely anymore," she reminded him.

"And so I am. But Christmas is five months away. And I've been out of London this summer more often than I like. You wouldn't want to find yourself the subject of gossip. No matter how unfair or untrue it was."

"I will never find myself the subject of gossip," she retorted, lifting her chin. "Mama taught me well."

Rutledge took a deep breath. "Speak to Melinda. I'll agree to whatever you decide."

But the mood of their luncheon had been spoiled now, and he regretted it.

Soon after, he took her home, changed the clothing in his valise, and set out again. He left without telling the Yard what he was about or why. As far as they knew, he was still in Kent.

It would be viewed as insubordination. But the fact was, Bowles would never agree to what Rutledge was doing, and permission would be refused out of hand.

A risk, but if he was right, then whatever had happened while these four men were living within shouting distance of each other in Bristol had come back to haunt them.

He drove to Kent, but not to Aylesbridge. Instead he headed for Swan Walk, no more than thirty miles southeast of London, where Gilbert lived presently, having given up his house in town some years ago. Swan Walk was not far from Penshurst Place, the great ancestral home of the Sidney family. Gilbert's was a placid estate set on high ground that gently sloped down to a narrow winding stream. Sheep grazed in meadows or rested in the shade of walls and copses as he made his way down the winding road leading into the tiny village of Swan Walk.

Less than half a mile on, he turned in through the gates and took the long drive through an avenue of trees that led up to the house. It was cool there, branches arching high over his head like the ribs of vaulting. Rutledge savored it. And then he came out into the last of the long twilight. The view spread before him was of more fields and meadows, distant church towers and green countryside. But in the west, far to his right, there was heat lightning, constant flickers in a bank of dark clouds. He pulled up by the main door and got out, stretching his legs for a moment before mounting the steps and lifting the brass knocker.

A middle-aged maid in crisp uniform opened the door to him, peering out into the dusk at the tall stranger on the doorstep.

He gave his name, asking if he might speak to Mr. Gilbert, and was told to wait while she inquired if he were receiving visitors at this late hour.

Apparently Mr. Gilbert was in a mood to receive this visitor, and Rutledge was shown to a room overlooking the gardens. Through the long windows—the curtains hadn't been pulled—he could see his reflection and just beyond it, those flickers of light across the dark sky.

The room smelled faintly of cigar.

As he turned to greet his host, Rutledge was shocked by the changes in Gilbert. He was shrunken, a thin man where there had been a robust one, a paisley India shawl draped over his shoulders, in spite of the heat.

But his gray eyes were as alert as ever.

"Ian! Forgive me for not rising—I have a confoundedly painful big toe at the moment. Gout, they tell me, but I refuse to believe a word of it. Good God, man, you're as tall as your father! Come in and sit down. What can I offer you? I have an excellent Madeira, a French brandy, and a single malt whisky, none of which I am allowed to taste unless I have a visitor."

"The brandy, sir," he replied, well aware that it was Gilbert's favorite tipple.

"There are glasses on the tray. If you bring me one, I can tell the confounded doctor I was coerced."

Smiling, Rutledge poured two small glasses and took one of them to Gilbert before joining him by the windows.

"What news of Claudia?" Rutledge asked. She was Gilbert's daughter.

"She and Sidney and the boys are still living just outside Portsmouth. They come when they can, but of course his practice is growing by the day. He should be in Harley Street, but they much prefer the countryside."

The town of Portsmouth was hardly countryside, the docks and shipping lanes dominating it, but with three young sons, it offered all the amenities that Sidney had known at their ages. They rambled, they fished, they went to the seaside, hunted birds' nests and held mock sea battles with a fleet of small wooden ships on the stream at the bottom of their garden. And then Rutledge realized that the boys were most certainly at school now, for the youngest must be all of nine.

He looked at the old man sitting hunched in his chair, alone and lonely.

As if aware of his visitor's scrutiny, Gilbert changed the subject, saying pensively, "Always liked the night. I can't say why, but even as a boy, the dark intrigued me. What brings you to Swan Walk? I'll wager it's not for news of Claudia nor my scintillating conversation. Tell me it's something interesting, before I die of ennui. I should never have retired from the law. Biggest error of my life."

"The story I've come to tell could be interesting. I can't say. I'm still trying to decide that for myself."

"Are you indeed?" He sipped his brandy and sighed softly with sheer pleasure. "All right, begin."

"I'm looking to find a trial that might have been held in the Crown Court in Bristol. I can't begin to guess just when this was. But I have four dead men whose only connection appears to be that they owned property in Bristol at some point in their lives. The only way that these men could have met is when they served on a jury. And now I believe someone has tracked them down and is killing them."

"Then it couldn't have been a capital charge. If the man had been sent to the gallows, there's no possibility of revenge."

"All right then, his wife," Rutledge answered. "Or perhaps a child? Who had reason to think the verdict was wrong. That would explain the delay between the trial and seeking revenge."

"Or he has been brought up on the theory that it was wrong."

"Yes, there's a difference, isn't there?"

"When a man serves on a jury, he's enjoined to silence on the deliberations and the verdict. Your four victims wouldn't have talked about this trial."

"Which of course will make my task all the harder," Rutledge agreed. "Even so, a man's family might recall that he'd served on a jury at such and such a time, and perhaps even the charges, if not the name of the accused. With luck, someone might even have followed accounts of the trial in the newspapers."

"For that matter, the family of the accused is free to think or say whatever it wishes," Gilbert pointed out.

"Sadly I don't know who they are. Not yet."

"Yes. Which brings us to another question. If no one remembers—or never knew about it—how are you going to find when this trial was held? You don't know the crime, the defendant's name, or the judge's."

"That's why I'm here. My father always said you were a walking compendium of information on the English judicial system."

A shadow passed across his face, and was gone as quickly. "A jury's task is the finding of fact on the question. Yes. Did you know that trial by ordeal was halted when the Catholic Church refused to support it any longer? And so a jury was the solution, much wiser than hoping the better man with a sword was also the innocent man. Or trusting that torture could reveal the truth. Still, a jury is not always right either."

The gray eyes were distant now, as if Gilbert had slipped into the past. Rutledge sat there for a moment, and then was rewarded by a sharpening of the man's gaze again.

"You say there are four men dead. A jury is twelve."

"In a month's time, he's managed to find and kill four. If I'm to find the others, I'll have to get ahead of him." He said nothing about the blackened headstones.

"When did these four men live in Bristol?"

"I'm not in possession of the exact dates, although at a guess between twenty-five and thirty years ago."

"Great God, even my memory isn't that good."

Rutledge smiled. "I daresay it isn't. But you may be able to point me in a direction that will help."

"How do you know he's killed only these four?"

"I don't. They're the only recent deaths I can find where laudanum was added to a glass of milk that the victim apparently drank of his own free will."

Gilbert shivered. "No one does that. Not without good reason."

"Once I have the information I need, the reason may make itself apparent."

"Twenty-five to thirty years ago? Some of your precious twelve may already have met their Maker. Have you thought of that?"

"I have. Which will mean that I don't know whether he's finished his goal and has disappeared into whatever normal life he stepped away from. Or if he has his eye on other unsuspecting targets. There's no mark of Cain to ease a policeman's lot."

"Nor a barrister's. Tell me more about the four."

Rutledge gave him an overview of the three inquiries he'd conducted, ending with what had happened in Alnwick. Gilbert listened intently, posing a question now and again.

"Your Inspector Farraday is a piece of work," he commented at one point. And when Rutledge had finished, Gilbert added, "That still doesn't answer my question. What about the dead, Ian? He won't forgive them any faster than he's forgiven the living. He'll turn to them next."

Rutledge said slowly, "He may have already seen to them." And he related the troubles Inspector Davies had encountered trying to solve the puzzle of who had tried to permanently stain the grave stones. "I've seen several of them myself. I'd even spoken to Chief Inspector Cummins about the possibility that Davies's inquiries have to do with a jury. Now—now I am in the process of rethinking all I know."

"Good luck convincing the Chief Superintendent," Gilbert said, giving Rutledge a look that spoke volumes. "I remember him, you know. Giving evidence in the courtroom. Pedantic and unimaginative. He'll see this as a confession of incompetence on your part. Reaching for a solution to cover the fact that you've failed to find your man."

It was too close for comfort.

Rutledge said, "Still, if I could find the trial, could confirm that each of these men had served on the jury in question, it would go a very long way toward convincing Bowles."

Gilbert was tiring. Rutledge could see the strain in his face, the slurring of his voice as he tried to concentrate.

Rutledge rose. "I've overstayed my welcome," he said, finishing the last of his brandy and taking the empty glass from Gilbert's hand.

"I don't sleep very much, Ian. As often as not, I sit here in my chair and watch dawn coming in the windows. Hadn't you realized that no one had interrupted us, telling you it was past my bedtime?"

Rutledge gestured toward the night, where the lightning was more serious now, sheets of it on the horizon. He listened but failed to hear the thunder. "You'll not be sleeping here tonight, sir. Or if you do, you'll be wet to the skin. There's a storm coming, and with it cooler air, I hope."

"Damnation. Very well, then, ring for someone. And ask them to make up a room for you while they're about it. I won't see you driving off into this, if you're right."

Rutledge tried to decline the invitation to stay the night. But Gilbert wouldn't hear of it, and in the end, he was shown to a room on the western side of the house, not far from his host's own bedroom. There were large windows here, and as he prepared to undress and get into bed, he opened the curtains to the slight breeze that had come up. He lay there, listening to the thunder as it grew closer, watching the night turn nearly to day in the ever brighter flashes of lightning.

And he had a sudden sense of foreboding, as if the breaking storm was a sign of what was to come. He got up and closed his windows.

Morag, his Scottish godfather's housekeeper, who claimed to have The Sight, would have crossed herself and told him to beware.

He closed his eyes against the approaching storm and tried to convince himself it was a sign of fatigue compounded by a glass of brandy and the excitement of the evening. Nothing more.

II

Rutledge breakfasted alone. Gilbert, he was told, seldom appeared downstairs before ten, if he'd gone up to his room the night before.

He walked out to the terrace with his teacup, sniffing the rain-washed summer morning, and watched bees hunting nectar in the hollyhocks in the gardens on either side of the terrace, although many of them, like the delphiniums, were beaten down by the storm.

As he finished his tea, his thoughts turned to Jean, and he wondered what she was doing today—shopping with her mother or her bevy of bridesmaids, or sleeping in after coming home late from a party. He wanted her to enjoy herself, to do the things she had always loved doing. But he would have liked to be there at her side, watching her face light up with happiness. Once this inquiry was closed, he would ask for a week of leave to make up for so much time away from London.

That brought him to consider his work, the Yard, the long hours in London and the frequent days away from the city. For the first time he doubted that it was suitable employment for Jean's husband. Perhaps Major Gordon had been right after all. And there would be children, he'd be away from them as often as he'd be away from their mother. Was it really for the best that he'd stubbornly resisted any suggestion of a change? That he clung to what had seemed to him the work he wanted to do, without weighing the cost?

For that matter, he'd left Frances to her own devices more often than he should. More often than was wise.

Was a man's desire to do what he felt he'd been born to do merely a selfishness that he was blind to? Was it the excitement of the chase, of outsmarting the murderer, rather than his concern for the victim, who no longer had a voice? Was that victim merely an excuse to clothe his own shortcomings?

He'd never looked at the Yard from that angle before, and it was unsettling.

Turning, he walked back across the terrace and stepped in through the sitting room windows. Half blinded by the sunlight, he blinked.

Gilbert was sitting there in his chair, the shawl around his shoulders, looking up at Rutledge as if he'd never moved last night.

Startled, he said, "Good morning! I was told you never showed yourself until ten at the earliest."

Gilbert chuckled. "I told you I seldom slept. I've written out a list of QCs who may've tried cases in Bristol. It's not complete, but it's the best I could do. A few names had to be struck from the list when I remembered that the poor devil was already dead. But there it is."

He took a folded sheet of paper from his pocket and passed it to Rutledge. "You were right about the storm, of course. Best display of pyrotechnics I've seen in quite a while. But we have long views here, we can watch storms roll in. At least I enjoy that. I daresay the women on the servants' floor pull their coverlets over their heads and wish it was over as quickly as possible." He watched as Rutledge scanned the names on the sheet of paper. "It will take you some time to run down all of them. And still you might not have the answers you seek. What about newspaper files?"

"It may come to that, of course. And that will take time as well. In fact, I might have to hire someone to research it for me. London will start asking questions about my absences if I'm not careful."

"I can recommend someone to do the research, if you need it. Let me know."

"I shall. Thank you, sir. I don't know how I'd have managed without your help."

"You'd have managed very well. You're an intelligent young man, Rutledge. God help us if you ever take to crime."

Rutledge laughed and reached down to take the thin, veined hand offered him. "And thank you for refuge from the storm."

Gilbert seemed reluctant to let go Rutledge's hand. "You've inquired about Claudia, while I've been remiss in not asking about Frances. How is that lovely sister of yours? She's so much like your mother at that age. Breaks my heart to see her. Is she happy?"

"I think she is. I hope she is. I'm to be married in December. Major Gordon's daughter, Jean."

Gilbert relinquished his hand. "Don't meddle with the Army, my boy. Stay with your own kind. The law. You'll be happier."

Rutledge smiled. "Too late. And Major Gordon has been very kind."

"Army men see things differently, that's all. You're a thinker, Ian, you work things out in your head, and know where you're going. Military minds rush into action. It's what's leading Europe into war right now. Clearer heads didn't prevail, and now everyone wants to teach the other fellow a damned good lesson. No one has considered the thousands if not millions who are going to die, the miles of good land laid waste, the starvation and disease and cruelty that marches in an Army's wake. For God's sake, the Austrian Emperor didn't even *like* his heir. Now he's willing to slaughter the Russians to punish the Serbs. God help us."

"Your name isn't on this list," Rutledge said, to shift the subject.

"I can't remember that far into the past. The law, now, I haven't lost that, I can give you chapter and verse on any matter. It's burned into my memory. But the individual cases—they're blurring. Bristol has always been a commercial center, and as it happened, I knew more than most about Admiralty Law. Commerce, salvage, navigation. That sort of thing."

Rutledge nodded. His father had sometimes conferred with Gilbert on such matters.

"You can't go wrong with Edgerton, though. There at the top. His favorite sister lives in Gloucester, and he was always looking to try a case in Bristol."

Rutledge took his leave soon after, and once on the high road, he pulled to the verge and gave his next move some thought. He was eager to speak to Miss Tattersall in Stoke Yarlington and that was possible. Moresby and Alnwick were beyond his reach at the moment. And there was the barber in Netherby.

Stoke Yarlington, then.

He looked at the map he carried in his head, chose his way, and set out in the direction of Wells.

Miss Tattersall had just come in from attending a small afternoon gathering of women who were planning the Harvest Festival in the autumn.

Taking off her hat, she greeted him as the housekeeper moved aside to allow him to step through the door.

"Inspector?" she said in some surprise. "Have you news for me?"

Rutledge glanced at Mrs. Betterton, all ears, and said, "Could we speak somewhere a little more private, please?"

She stared at him, then dismissed the housekeeper and said,

"Come this way." She led him to the room where he'd interviewed her before. The windows were open to the fresh breath of air that had followed in the wake of the storm, and he could smell the scent of flowers carried on the breeze.

Offering him a chair, she considered standing, then sat herself, as if she might need to face whatever news he brought with him.

Rutledge said at once, "I have no new information for you. I'm truly sorry. Still, there is information you might have that would be useful to me." He tried to word his request as if there was no urgency about it, just another lead he was following.

There was disappointment in her face. "I daresay I've answered every question you could think of. How can there be more?"

"We are trying to locate several people who might have known your brother during his time in Bristol. Does the name Jerome Hadley mean anything to you? Or Benjamin Clayton, for instance? Or a schoolmaster by the name of Stoddard."

She shook her head. "If I met anyone by those names, I've long since forgotten them. I would say therefore that they were passing acquaintances of my brother's, if that. Hardly friends."

"Did your brother ever serve in a trial as a juror?"

"No, I'm sure he didn't—" She stopped in midsentence. "But yes," she went on more slowly. "I vaguely remember something about that." Frowning, she tried to bring the memory to the fore. "And then only because I was quite curious about how such things were done. Women aren't called upon, of course, but everyone says that serving as a juror is what makes English law superior to what is found in most of the world. He was living in Bristol at the time, and I must have bombarded him with questions. But he told me he was sworn to secrecy—not just at the time of the trial, but ever after. So there was an end to it."

"Surely you followed the trial in the local newspapers?" he asked, striving to keep hope out of his voice.

"My dear Inspector, you didn't know my brother. He felt that the lurid information contained in newspaper accounts wasn't fit for a woman's more delicate sensibilities." There was irony in the words. "He subscribed to the *Times* of course, but had no patience with the local newspapers. They weren't allowed in the house. And of course this important case that required his presence every day for nearly a week was not important enough to warrant so much as a paragraph in the *Times*. My father was much the same sort of man. Women were not to be troubled with something like murder."

"You're saying it was a capital case?"

"Not at all. I have no idea. I was just thinking that while I was never *troubled* by murder while my parents and my brother were alive, now I've been pitched right into this horror, and I don't have the faintest useful knowledge about what to expect or how to cope."

He felt the sadness behind that remark. She was an intelligent, able woman, and in London might once have marched with Mrs. Pankhurst and the suffragettes. Instead she'd been relegated to a life of Good Works.

"Do you by any chance remember the year that your brother served on this jury?"

"It was during the time Joel was living in Bristol, but I can't tell you just when. That was nearly thirty years ago."

They talked for several minutes more, but there was nothing else she could tell him.

All the same, it was a first step. Tattersall *had* served on a Bristol jury.

For the sake of thoroughness he would have liked to drive on toward Bristol, to the village of Netherby, and ask Lolly the barber if Benjamin Clayton had ever served on a jury. But he needed to reach Kent as soon as possible.

Rutledge drove through the night, taking the most direct way he could think of across Wiltshire and Surrey to Kent. His sense of direction, sharp as he left Wells, dulled as he tired. He concentrated on the powerful beams of the motorcar's headlamps. The roads seemed to be swarming with wildlife and not a few domestic animals. Badgers and hedgehogs, foxes and prowling cats, a grazing horse, and once a rooster that for some reason stood in his way and challenged him. He had to step out onto the road and coax it to the verge, before it finally dashed through a break in the hedgerow and vanished. It occurred to him to be grateful that last night's rainstorm had not chosen tonight instead and drenched him and the arrogant rooster as well.

Finally, for fear of falling asleep and running into a ditch, he pulled over somewhere in western Surrey to rest.

He reached Melinda's house at seven in the morning, bathed and changed before breakfast. Despite her attempts to persuade him to rest a little longer, he set out for Aylesbridge and the Hadley farmhouse.

Mrs. Hadley had not come down by the time he arrived. He was taken to the sitting room, where he paced impatiently.

When she finally appeared, she looked tired in the morning light, as if she were still having trouble sleeping. He felt a surge of sympathy for her as she asked politely if there was anything he needed from her, and he responded with the question that had been burning in his mind on the long journey east across half of southern England.

"Jury duty? I'm sure he never served. I'd have remembered."

"Perhaps before you met? Before your marriage?" He didn't want to put words in her mouth, false memories in her head, but his need was desperate.

"Now that was possible. Before we were married. Let me think. I went to spend three weeks with an aunt who was quite ill. Jerry wrote to me, of course, but they were the letters a man writes." She smiled with sadness, remembering. "Things like 'The dog flushed two rabbits this afternoon during our walk.' Or 'I had dinner with Freddy'—a friend—'and we talked about this new corn seed that is supposed to be resistant to many of the ills we see in damp weather.' I was grateful, mind you, but there could have been earthquakes and floods, and the Fifth Ice Age, and he'd never had thought to mention it."

"When was your aunt taken ill?"

She frowned. "Oh, dear. How precise do you need me to be?"

"As close as you can recall. It's rather important."

"Let me think. It was late May, early June. I remember that the lilacs came out while I was there, and I could smell them below my window when the wind caught them. So yes, that's about right. The year? 1887, I should think. No, that's not right. 1888."

Not as far back as Rutledge had thought. But then Hadley had been the youngest of the three victims.

"And you're quite sure?"

"Oh, yes, Aunt Lydia died late the next year. She never fully recovered her strength, and we had to postpone the wedding twice for her sake. Not that I minded, she was a lovely old girl, the sort of favorite aunt everyone should have."

"It would have been in Bristol, this trial?" he repeated, to be absolutely certain.

"It must have been. Jerry was living there before we married."

And then with her hand to her mouth, she said, "How stupid of me. Come with me!" She was walking briskly to the door, and he followed her down the passage to a room at the back that someone— perhaps Hadley himself—had turned into an estate office. Shelves ran around the small room, and a desk with two chairs in front of it stood between the outside windows.

Ledgers filled many of the shelves, going back a hundred years or more, Rutledge thought, glancing at their dates. Farm records? And then more rows of what appeared to be tenant accounts. But Mrs. Hadley ignored them, going instead to a cabinet next to the hearth. Opening it, she scanned the leather-bound personal diaries that marched across the shelves.

"Jerry was urged to keep diaries when he was a boy and he never fell out of the habit. His grandfather gave him a new one every Boxing Day, and later he bought his own. They're not terribly personal— mostly jotting down what he'd done in a given day and what the weather was." She looked up at Rutledge with tears in her eyes. "On our wedding day, he simply wrote, 'I have married Helen. Now our happiness together begins.'"

Without waiting for him to respond, she reached for a volume on the top row and opened it. Thumbing through it she found the place she wanted. "Here it is, 1888. Look at May. Or early June."

She handed him the diary.

He found the end of April and scanned the pages forward. And there it was. Monday, May 14—and the entry: *Reported to the Crown Court this morning to serve as a juror.*

Rutledge turned to the following pages, but the notations were cryptic.

Trial continues for successive days, and then on Friday, *Delivered our verdict.*

He felt a surge of frustration. If only Hadley hadn't taken his oath quite so seriously and had put something in his diary that was germane. The charges, the name of the accused, the name of the judge.

Mrs. Hadley was studying his face. "Will this help you find my husband's murderer?"

"I don't quite know," he told her honestly. "Not yet. What it will do is tie together an unsettling series of events that could finally point the Yard in the right direction."

Taking the book from him and restoring it to its place in the row, she smiled, wry humor mixed with heartbreaking sadness. "That's not terribly reassuring, Inspector."

He felt he owed her something more, regardless of the Yard's policy not to divulge information to potential witnesses.

"There have been other murders, very similar in fact to the way your husband died. The question was, how could these be related?"

"I remember now. You asked me about several other men. I couldn't think why they mattered."

"They might have been known to your husband. Somewhere in their pasts, these three men, possibly a fourth one, crossed paths. Joel Tattersall served on a jury in Bristol, and so did your husband. If it was the *same* jury, perhaps that's where this inquiry actually began. If such a connection can be shown for the other two, we can narrow our search for answers."

"How awful," she said with a frown. "I don't think I'm quite comfortable with such a thought. *Four* men?"

"Still, if this terse entry in your husband's diary can be tracked down, it's possible that he's given us the information we need to stop a killer."

"Too late for him," she said regretfully. She led the way back down the passage after closing the estate room door behind them. "I don't want to learn any more. Not until you make an arrest and I can see this man's face for myself." And then, her control breaking, she said angrily, "Why should something Jerry did as a very young man make my husband a victim now?"

"Because some people," he told her, "have very long memories."

"How very frightening." She glanced anxiously through the open door of the sitting room, as if wondering if the windows there were locked.

"I don't have any reason to believe that the suspect we're after will return to disturb you."

"No. He's already taken what I held most dear. There is nothing left to steal."

Rutledge went to look for Constable Roderick, but he had gone to one of the outlying farms to talk to a father about his rowdy sons. Or so Rutledge was told by his wife, who came to answer his knock.

"Tell Constable Roderick I'll be back as soon as possible. I have work to do in London first."

"I'll do that, sir. Thankee."

But as a matter of fact, he went back to Melinda's and slept for five hours straight before turning toward London. If he intended to beard Chief Superintendent Bowles in his den, then he needed to have his wits about him.

There was a message from Jean waiting for him at home, asking if he could join the Gordons for dinner that evening. Rutledge wondered what frame of mind he would be in by seven in the evening.

However, Chief Superintendent Bowles was not in his office at the Yard, forcing Rutledge to postpone their meeting. It was useless to leave a message. What he had to say was best related face-to-face.

And so at the hour given in Jean's note, he presented himself at the Gordon house and was welcomed warmly.

He hadn't had a chance to look at any of the newspapers, which surprised the Gordons and their guests, all of whom were following events anxiously.

"France has indicated that if Russia is attacked by either Austria or Germany, she will go to war on Russia's behalf, against both countries," Gordon said over cigars and port. "This will not end well. The Foreign Office has already acted, informing Germany that as guarantors of Belgium's safety—have been since the country was set up in 1830—we'll brook no interference there."

"I can't see Germany taking on France, Russia, and Britain simultaneously. It would be madness," an older officer by the name of Strickland said.

"There are those who say the Kaiser is just mad enough to try." Gordon shook his head. "The General Staff will have contingency plans. If the worst happens, an Expeditionary Force will be sent as a stop-gap measure while we fully mobilize. My view is that the French Army can't hold back the German tide on two fronts."

"We'll see some fierce fighting at the start," a young Captain said. Rutledge had met Harvey before and liked him. "But I daresay it won't last long, this war. There's no reason for it to. By Christmas everyone will have come to their senses and the talking will start."

"From your lips to God's ear," Strickland said under his breath, just loud enough that Rutledge heard him.

"None of this before the ladies, gentlemen," Gordon said as he rose to leave the dining room. "No need to worry them before we know where we stand."

Rutledge managed a few minutes alone with Jean. She was in a restless mood and finally said, "Papa won't tell me what's going on. There's talk of war. But everyone stops the minute I enter the room."

"Let's hope it comes to nothing," he said cheerfully. He knew what she was afraid of, that her father would be called back to active duty. Privately, he thought there was a very good chance of it, although not necessarily to serve in the fighting.

"*And* you've been neglecting me terribly, Ian. I've had to attend three parties this past week with my parents. Everyone asks where you are."

"I'm sorry, my love. Blame it on the hot summer, if you like. The Yard has been very busy."

"Yes, but will we blame it on the rainy autumn next time, or the frigid winter? We're engaged, it's supposed to be the happiest of times. I sometimes feel that people are talking about me behind their hands. *There she is, alone again. I thought she was engaged. Oh, but she is. Her fiancé is always somewhere else.*"

"You know I'd be here if I could," he said gently. Some of the older guests were already calling for their carriages or motorcars. "Shouldn't you join your parents in saying good night?"

"Don't change the subject, Ian. I really wonder if you love me as much as I love you. If you did, you wouldn't find it so easy to stay away."

"It's never easy. It's just that I have responsibilities. As your father did when he was a serving officer."

"He wants to serve again," she said, her voice anxious. "He misses the Army. Will you enlist if we go to war with Germany?"

He was taken aback. "I haven't thought about it."

"Oh, Ian, we could be married in September, you in uniform, the two of us running down the church steps under an arch of swords. I've been to military weddings—they are exciting, romantic."

"And what happened to your dream of being married at Christmas, like your parents?" It was said half teasingly.

"But Ian—"

"And if there *is* a war, I'll be marching off with my brothers-in-arms, rather than leaving with you on a wedding trip."

That stopped her short.

"I'll make certain you're given leave for the wedding journey," she said after a moment. But he thought even she knew it wouldn't happen quite that way.

And then Kate walked up. Jean frowned at her. "We're trying to have a little time together, Kate."

She looked from one to the other. "So it appears," she said dryly. "Anything I can do?"

"Just go away," Jean told her sharply.

"I can't. Marianne Hayes and I are faced with a small problem. I was hoping that Ian could drive the two of us home."

"I thought you came with Teddy Browning."

"So we did. But he's just got a message from his commanding officer. All leaves canceled. And so he's going straight back to barracks. That leaves us without an escort."

Jean said, "Oh, very well, take him then." Turning on her heel, she marched away without saying good night.

Kate watched her go. "You've been neglecting her," she said to Rutledge.

"So I've just been told," he replied ruefully.

"Yes, well, I'd pay attention if I were you. Where *have* you been, come to that?"

"On business for the Yard."

"I don't think Jean bargained for murder topping romance. There's Marianne. Do you need five minutes to make your peace with Jean? She must be on the terrace. We can wait."

He took a deep breath. "I think it's all this talk of war that's upsetting her."

"It's upset all of us. I've three friends in the Army. All they can think about is showing the Kaiser a thing or two. Ridiculous men! But as Teddy said, they've trained for years to fight for King and Country, and all they've done is travel from one outpost of Empire to another. They're spoiling to get into this war in Europe."

"They may well have their chance." He touched her arm. "Hold the fort for me, will you? Let me see if I can find her."

But he didn't find her. If Jean had gone out to the terrace, she'd come in another door and slipped upstairs without his seeing her.

When he got back to Kate, the evening was nearly over, and Marianne was looking distinctly anxious. Kate took his arm and walked with him to the door. "Send her flowers tomorrow. With a kind note. That will help," she said softly, and then louder, "Here is our dashing chauffeur, Marianne. He went to say good night to Jean." She smiled, and Marianne answered it, looking archly at Rutledge, as if she understood completely.

He appreciated Kate's attempt to lighten the moment, but he said to her after seeing Marianne to her door and inside to where her maid was waiting for her, "What am I to do, Kate? We're busy at the Yard at the moment. I'll probably be away again tomorrow."

"It's called pen and paper, Ian. Write to her every day you're away.

Not just a short note saying you're off to Manchester or St. Albans. Take the time to say the things she wants to hear, that you miss her, that you're thinking about her, that you are looking forward to getting back to London. It will make a huge difference."

He was suddenly reminded of Mrs. Hadley's comments on her husband's diaries.

He walked Kate to her door and bent to kiss her lightly on the cheek. "You're very wise," he said with more cheerfulness than he felt.

"Not wise, Ian. I'm a woman too." And with that she went inside without looking back over her shoulder, as Marianne had done.

T he next morning, Rutledge made it a point to be at the Yard early. In his office he listened for sounds of the Chief Superintendent's arrival and hoped for some barometer of his mood.

It didn't appear to be very encouraging. Rutledge could hear him shouting at Chief Inspector Cummins, then marching into his office and slamming the door.

He winced. Changing tactics, he went to find Cummins, and said quietly, "Can you spare a few minutes?"

"I can," he said. "It would seem that I'll have quite a few minutes in which to contemplate my sins." With a wry smile, he opened the door to his own office and ushered Rutledge inside.

"You look like a man with something on his mind."

Rutledge grinned. "Is it so obvious? But yes, something has come up, and I was intending to broach the subject to the Chief Superintendent before I heard his door slam."

"Give him an hour. Meanwhile, what's afoot?"

Rutledge had already mapped out what he intended to say to Bowles, and so it was a simple matter to explain the question of a jury to Cummins.

The Chief Inspector listened intently, then blew out a breath in a soft whistle.

"Ye gods, that's convoluted thinking. Didn't you mention that to me before? Yes, about the blackened grave stones. Not about the murders. But I'm damned if I don't believe you may have something here. It would solve the problem that Davies faced, it could clear up four cases that haven't been closed to everyone's liking, and it could find us a killer. Who do you think he is?"

"Assuming it was a capital case, the accused is probably dead. Convicted and hanged. But there may be a son who is probably a man now, and for some reason launched on this vendetta."

"It's certainly no way to clear his father's name," Cummins said dryly.

"I don't think he has any intention of doing that. He may simply wish to punish the people he blames for taking his father from him. Children don't always see things clearly. Guilt or innocence doesn't really matter, does it? But loss does. And for some reason he hasn't outgrown that loss, and he's still angry enough to kill."

"But why laudanum?"

Rutledge shrugged. "Perhaps he had access to it. And it's quiet."

"There's the man Clayton he strung up in Moresby."

"The house was empty. He wasn't so lucky in other cases. Nor was there a suitable place. Or perhaps he didn't care for what he'd done. It may have smacked of his father's death, and turned him away from hanging the others."

"Makes sense, in a macabre sort of way. But how does he persuade them to drink the milk laced with the drug?"

"Perhaps they don't know. I've not thought it through that far," Rutledge said. "We've a long way to go before we know if I'm right. I've got to show that these victims did serve together. And then there's the question of how he manages to find his quarry."

"The same as we do? Somerset House with its lists of births, deaths, and marriages. He could possibly work it out from there. That's assuming he knew the names of the jurors."

"Yes, he would have to know that, wouldn't he? Someone would have told him. His mother. Grandfather. Someone."

"And he remembered the names. Or they were written down in some way. A newspaper cutting?"

"I've confirmed the names of two of the dead men. Tattersall and Hadley. But only two. That could be viewed as coincidence. Especially since I have no proof they were on the same jury. I've been warned off Moresby, worst luck, and I can't think of a reason to go to Northumberland."

"And it would take a dozen men weeks of work to run down the names of men under those ruined tombstones and ask their families. No, I can see you need to start with the facts, not chase them."

"That's to say, if Bowles will countenance such a search."

"What about this man Edgerton. The KC? Where does he live?"

"In Surrey, I think."

"That's not unreachable. Thirty miles? Before you see Bowles, speak to Edgerton. He might well know something that will take you to the next level. He may even have personal notes of the trial, if indeed he was the QC you're after."

Cummins got up and silently opened his door. "The coast is clear. On your way. And stop in when you get back. I want to hear what you've discovered."

Rutledge nodded, slipped out the door, and walked quietly down the passage to the stairs. He made it out of the building without raising any eyebrows, and was on his way to Surrey five minutes later.

Edgerton lived near Guildford in a Georgian house on the outskirts of town.

Flower beds bordered the drive, full of summer bloom. Rutledge went up the slight incline and pulled up at the door.

He had no official appointment, he told the footman who answered his knock, but there was a matter of law that had come up at the Yard, and he needed to speak to Mr. Edgerton, if at all possible.

He was available, Rutledge was told, but busy writing his memoirs.

Memoirs meant information to hand. If writing them wasn't an excuse to retire to the country, as it had been in Gilbert's case. Rutledge smiled and said, "Mr. Gilbert suggested that Mr. Edgerton was the man we should be seeking. Ask him, please, if he could spare half an hour?"

Ten minutes later, Rutledge was in Edgerton's study. He was a tall, cadaverous man with graying hair and green eyes. He looked Rutledge up and down, saying, "If I don't care for your questions, you're out on your ear. Understood? I have better things to do with my time than research legal niceties for Scotland Yard."

"It's a question of a case, a capital case, that was tried in Bristol in May of 1888. As far as we can determine, the outcome was likely to be a guilty verdict, and the accused was condemned."

"Good God, man, you must be mad to think I can remember every detail of every case I ever tried."

"I'm told you're writing your memoirs. That suggests to me that you have kept notes on the cases you did try. And if you have, I'm sure they're catalogued in some fashion."

"You are impertinent, sir."

"I'm sorry. There have been at least four murders that could well be connected to this trial. And there could be other victims unwittingly being stalked."

"A fresh murder, not an ancient one."

"Precisely."

"Tell me what you have, and then go away. If I can find anything, I'll contact you."

Rutledge hadn't anticipated finding answers that morning. But this sounded to him like a rebuff: *Go away and if I feel like it I might look at my notes. If I don't, I won't.*

He said, standing his ground, "I can't tell you how urgent this need for information is."

"I am no longer an officer of the court, young man. I can do as I please."

Rutledge hesitated, then said, "Mr. Gilbert was kind enough to give us your name. I see no reason for you to be less generous with your time."

"Gilbert is an old man looking God in the eye. I have memoirs to finish. There's a difference in emphasis here."

"Which tells me that you don't after all have notes you kept from your various trials. You're making up the memoirs as you go along."

For a moment Rutledge thought he'd gone too far. Edgerton's face turned as dark as a thundercloud. And then unexpectedly he laughed.

"All right, you proper nuisance. Let's see what we can find."

Edgerton took him upstairs to a bedroom where bookshelves had replaced most of the usual furnishings. And on the bookshelves were lined up row upon row of small black leather binders, each one with a month and a year stamped on the spine in gold.

Reminded of Jerome Hadley, Rutledge was impressed and said as much.

Edgerton answered dryly, "I found it cleared my mind to write down exactly what I knew about a case and then what I thought about it, initially and without preconceptions. Then I kept a log of what I did from my first interview with the accused, straight through the trial, to what the verdict was. Whether there was an appeal and what the outcome was. A tedious pastime. But I sometimes went back and read a similar case, to see what I'd made of that one. Law, my young friend, is not what you think it is. It's a compendium of human experience in learning to judge men fairly."

And so they settled down to search.

Almost three hours later, they had to agree that the Crown prosecutor in the murder trial Rutledge wanted to find was not Edgerton.

He had been in Derby on the week in question. Not in Bristol.

Edgerton invited Rutledge to stay for lunch. "It's the least you can do, since you've spoiled my morning. I want to hear more about these abominable murders."

But at the end of Rutledge's recital of the evidence, Edgerton shook his head. "Mind you, I think you may be on to something. But the fact is, I don't think you're likely to find it. Much less be able to prove it in a courtroom."

"There must be court records. Something—"

"Oh, of course there are. Moldy boxes of them in the attics of chambers or the cellars of courthouses. If they were pertinent to new law or the interpretation of an old one, raised questions of jurisdiction or details of successful appeals, and the like, you'll find them in books on jurisprudence. Or in a judge's memoirs, if you're very lucky. If we had the name of the accused, it would make a huge difference. That's your task now. Find out who he was."

But the men who could have told him that were dead, Rutledge thought, and even before that they'd been enjoined to secrecy about the trial and its outcome.

But there was still the barber . . .

The question was, should he return to London or go directly to Netherby? If he spoke to the Chief Superintendent, and he was warned off this particular line of inquiry, there would be an end to it.

If he didn't go back, if he went on to Netherby, Bowles would demand to know why he wasn't clearing up the inquiry in Aylesbridge.

He found himself ruefully thinking that if all else failed, he might be joining David Trevor's firm of architects sooner rather than later.

Still, if Lolly was able by some miracle to confirm that Benjamin Clayton had served on a jury, in fact, the same jury as Hadley and Tattersall, that would make three. And three was less of a coincidence than two.

If Netherby led nowhere, then he'd wasted his time, and what's more had nothing to offer the man defending Mark Kingston in Moresby.

To Bristol, then, and Netherby. Calculated risk though it might be.

Rutledge turned the bonnet toward the West Country and settled himself for the long drive.

Before he reached Netherby, however, he changed his mind and swung south of Bristol. Finding the road that led off to the village of Beecham, he followed it. It was in Beecham that the smaller number of churchyard stones had been damaged, and he realized that he'd never been there.

Rutledge ran the local vicar to earth in his back garden, where he was on his knees weeding the vegetables. As his housekeeper opened the kitchen door, he looked up.

"Someone to see you, sir," she called, and he nodded. As Rutledge stepped out into the path, the vicar rocked back on his heels and frowned.

"I'm sorry, if you need me in my professional capacity, I'll be with you in a few minutes." He dropped his handful of weeds into the basket by his elbow.

Rutledge gave his name and rank. "I've come for information. I was hoping you could help me."

The vicar slowly got to his feet, dusting off the knees of his trousers. "Has Inspector Davies sent you? Is it about that trouble in the churchyard? Come along. There are benches over there, by the gooseberries."

"I'm afraid not. Not directly."

Rutledge followed him, and they sat down across from each other. The vicar said, taking out a handkerchief to wipe his hands, "God made everything, including the weeds. I accept that. I just wish he'd been a little less generous with the weeds."

Smiling, Rutledge said, "You won't have been the first gardener to think so."

"No, I expect that's true. How can I serve you?"

"I need to find someone who has lived in this village for a very long time—twenty years or more. I'd like to know more about the men whose graves were painted black. At the moment this is in regard to another inquiry."

"I can tell you, there's really no connection among them. Inspector Davies and I made a thorough search of the church records."

"Setting those aside for the moment, I need to know whether they were men of property or not."

"Property? Let me see. Thompson was the squire's nephew, but he owned the cottage where he lived. Died out in Kenya, his body brought home. As for Mr. Mayfield, he and his brother owned the general store. Quite prosperous, it was. Still is, for that matter."

"Mayfield lived here all his life?"

"Yes, that's true."

"I'd like to find out if they had served on the same jury in 1888."

"Mayfield's widow is dead as well. I expect you could speak to Thompson's widow," the vicar went on doubtfully, "but they weren't wed until 1890. Of course, there's Lucy Muir. She's not old enough to remember such things, but she's set herself the task of compiling a history of the village. It's to be printed and sold in the church."

"I don't think," Rutledge answered carefully, "that what I'm after would be of any interest to church visitors."

"I'm sure that could be true. But in gathering information that might be of interest, Lucy has surely come across a good bit that isn't. I'd start with her." The vicar looked down at his hands, at the earth that was caked under his fingernails. "Give me a few minutes to change, and I'll take you to call on her. My housekeeper makes a fine lemonade, if you'd like a cooling drink while you wait."

And so Rutledge was settled in the parlor with a tall glass of lemonade while the vicar took the stairs two at a time, disappearing above to change.

The vicarage parlor was bright, the windows standing wide and white lace curtains lifting in the gentle breeze. There was a glass case on beautifully carved feet that held an assortment of treasures, from enameled snuffboxes to thimbles. He was standing there admiring them when the vicar returned.

"My mother's collection," he said. "She loved pretty things and my father found ways of indulging her. How was the lemonade?"

"As good as you promised. Thank you."

They walked out to the motorcar, and the vicar said with a sigh, "My weakness. Mechanical things. It's new this year, is it not? Yes, I've seen some of the quite enticing advertisements Rolls has put out. You do realize that I insinuated myself into this visit with Lucy just to be driven there in this marvelous machine?" He walked around it, admiring it.

"My pleasure."

They drove along the High Street to a lane that ran down to a fast-moving little stream crossed by an old stone bridge. Beyond that, a drive led from the lane up a slight rise to a cottage with a thatched roof and one of the prettiest gardens Rutledge had ever seen.

"Quite beautiful, isn't it?" the vicar agreed. "She advises me on the vicarage gardens from time to time. But I fear she wastes her knowledge." He got down as the motorcar came to a stop, and said, "Don't be misled by what you see. She's really marvelous."

The young woman who came to the door to greet them wore a simple white dress with a gold locket at her throat. She was no older than Rutledge, and her hair was the color of honey, her eyes hazel. Quite taken aback, for he'd pictured a middle-aged spinster, he smiled as the vicar presented him, and tried to think what to say.

Her eyes twinkled. "Yes, I know. The aged white witch in her cottage, musty herbs hanging from the rafters, and a black cat on the hearth," she said. "Well, I don't have any herbs, I'm afraid, but I do possess a black cat. Come inside and meet Abigail."

The vicar led the way, saying, "Mr. Rutledge has come down from London to look into the past of our village. I thought of you at once and promised that you could help him. Don't let me down, I beg of you."

She grinned as he kissed her cheek. "I shall try my best. But you shouldn't make such promises."

The front room of the cottage was tastefully decorated, a smaller version of a Welsh dresser against one wall showing off a fine display of china figurines, and the tea table was certainly Queen Anne. But she took them through that room and up the stairs where the smaller of the two bedrooms had been turned into a study of sorts. Windows at both eaves let in the summer air, and he saw that besides a small desk and chair, the room held mostly papers—on shelves, on the floor, on the windowsills, and even under the cat's bed, raised two feet off the floor. A black cat with golden eyes stared at them, then lost interest, going back to sleep.

"We needn't sit up here—well, there's really no place *to* sit, is there?—but if you will tell me what you're looking for, we can take what I need downstairs again." She smiled up at him.

Rutledge found himself wishing he could ask her about anything but a murder trial. It seemed to be far too ghoulish a subject for this pretty cottage on this sunny day. But he said, "There was a trial in Bristol, I think. Some twenty-five years ago. In 1888? I don't know who the accused was. But I believe I know the names of several of the jurors. Or at least I hope I do. I desperately need to know the name of the man who was tried for murder, if I'm to find a record of his trial. And I must find that record in order to prove a case. It sounds like a hopeless task. I hope it isn't, because this is an urgent matter."

Lucy frowned. "Murder cases. Yes, they would be over here." She walked to a low stool set where the cottage roof sloped almost to the floor and retrieved a sheaf of papers.

With them in hand, she nodded to the door. "Let's go back downstairs."

They followed her and sat in the front room. She glanced at the papers, refreshing her memory.

"Beecham hasn't had many murders. In 1792, 1848, 1860, 1867, 1870, and 1888, 1897, and 1901. Most of these, interestingly enough, were committed by the same family. The first five, at least. They were highway robbers, and sometimes killed their victims. The highwayman was not as romantic as he's been painted. People were terrified of them, and nobody talked. That allowed them to continue their way of life until the Lord Lieutenant in 1867 took it upon himself to rid the neighborhood of them. And he quite ruthlessly did. That leaves us with only local murderers."

She looked up at her two guests. "Shall we try 1888, then?"

Rutledge said, "Yes. Please."

She shuffled through the pages to find what she was looking for.

"Here it is. One Evan Martin Dobson. I've grown accustomed to my own scrawl, so I'll read it to you. Mr. Dobson, who was a leatherworker by trade, had a falling-out with the son of the greengrocer in early April of that year. No one is quite certain what the falling-out was about. There was some feeling that it was wages owed for a new bridle with silver buckles that Mr. Dobson had made for the greengrocer's son. The greengrocer's son—here's his name—Thomas Atkins—saw himself as something of a dandy, but of course his father wasn't the squire and couldn't afford his son's extravagances. Atkins and Dobson had a falling-out over the harness, and in the end, Mr. Dobson applied to the father for payment."

She turned the page she'd been referring to. "The father refused, saying that it was his son's purchase and his son would have to settle the account. Two nights later, the greengrocer was set upon on his way home from church. He died of his injuries without ever regaining consciousness. The maker of that bridle was taken up for questioning, and he swore he had nothing to do with the beating. There was some evidence to the contrary, the print of a boot in the muddy lane where the assault happened, and a copy of Dobson's account lying under the body. The inquest found Mr. Dobson as the murderer, and he was bound over for trial."

She looked up at Rutledge. "Does this sound in any way familiar?"

"I never knew the details. But it's possible that Dobson is our man."

The vicar said, "He's interesting, is Dobson. The son, Henry, that is. His mother was buried in our churchyard at the end of June. Dobson left the village as soon as she was buried. He was a quiet sort, rather dogged. But devoted to his mother."

"Tell me about her."

"She struggled to put food on the table. The previous vicar felt no compassion for her or her child. He held rather Victorian views about sin. In her last illness, I contrived to have her medicines put on my account, but it was to no avail. She was simply worn out from overwork and unhappiness."

"And the son?"

"Henry? He was rather stiff-necked about charity. When I was still new here, I once offered him work in my garden, to help him make a little money, but he felt it was pity and not his skills that moved me. Sometimes helping the least of His children is not as easy as it ought to be."

"How did he earn his keep?"

"His mother took in washing and ironing. For a time he ran errands for the greengrocer—the new man—and picked up whatever other work he could find. He helped in the lumberyard when he was older, and tried to take up his father's trade, but there were too many who remembered the bridle, and what it had led to."

"His mother is buried in the churchyard?" Rutledge repeated the vicar's words, considering the possibility that that was why the other graves were defaced—because those lying beneath them weren't fit to lie in hallowed ground with Dobson's mother. A first step in a murderous journey.

"Yes, as I said. Henry told me there and then that he would be sending me the money for a proper stone. He wanted something with a sunrise in the upper part, and her name and dates. The next morning, when I went to the cottage to look in on him, he was gone. He'd taken everything that mattered to him, I expect, and just abandoned the rest. No one seemed to take notice of his departure. I doubt most people even knew he'd left, except when he failed to show up for work. Sadly, there was no one at the burial but Henry and myself." The vicar sighed. "I count him as one of my failures, but truly his path began long before I was ever here."

Lucy Muir had been listening intently. "I didn't know. I'd gathered this material about this man's father, and I had no idea—it's more personal somehow that I could have passed him on the street how many times?—and yet never connected him with the man who went to the gallows for murder."

"He probably preferred it that way," the vicar said.

"Why did he stay, if life was so unbearable?" Rutledge asked.

"Money. His mother. Where were they to go?" the vicar answered.

"Do you know if she took her husband's death hard? If she, for instance, told her son that he was innocent?"

The vicar shook his head. "I don't think she considered guilt or innocence. He had done the work on the bridle, he hadn't been paid because he was caught up in the argument between the greengrocer and his son. And he needed the money. The boy must have been very young at the time. The silver buckles alone would have cost Dobson dearly. I'm not excusing what happened, but from his wife's point of view, the greengrocer and his son destroyed her family."

"Then why didn't Dobson think in terms of righting that wrong?"

"Atkins was dead. His son sold up a year or so later and left the village. What wrong could he right?"

"Is the Dobson cottage occupied at this time? I'd like to see it."

"No one has shown any interest in it. It's probably just as Dobson left it. I'll take you there."

Rutledge turned to Lucy Muir. "What is your interest in the history of the village?"

"I needed something to do when my grandmother was ill. And I came to like living here. When the visitors' brochure is finished, I'll stay on."

"How did you find so much material?"

"My grandmother. Her friends, who must have been at least her age if not older. Gossip at the Women's Institute or at teas and flower committee meetings. The church records—some of the early vicars were quite chatty. And I've used my father's name to gain access to newspaper files in Bristol." She shrugged ruefully. "They refused unequivocally to allow a woman to search those files. It's amazing what they thought important to publish at the time. There were stories of runaway bulls, of gypsies suspected of stealing a little boy who later turned up safe and sound, of the miller being accused of mixing chalk into his flour, and someone who went around stealing pansies from graves and gardens. That thief was never found, nor were the pansies. My view is that they were sold to unsuspecting gardeners in another village."

"Do you think you could find out more about the trial of Evan Dobson in the newspaper files?"

"I could try."

"I'll pay your expenses. Gladly."

"Done. I shall treat myself to a short stay in my favorite hotel. Where shall I send whatever I find?"

He gave her his home address, not that of the Yard. "I'm not always in London," he said in explanation. "I don't want it going astray because I wasn't there to receive it."

She rose, indicating that the interview was over. "Then I must be getting back to my work. Shall I send you one of our little visitor books when it's completed?"

Surprised, he said, "Yes, I'd like that very much." And he found he meant it.

"That will be six pence in advance." She held out her hand, and laughing, he gave her sixpence.

"If I don't receive my copy, I'll have the Yard bring you to justice for misleading a policeman and swindling him into the bargain."

Her head to one side, she considered him. "You wouldn't be willing to tell me why you're so interested in the Dobsons? It might lend a little excitement to the story I'll write."

Rutledge shook his head. "It won't be a good story for another fifty years," he said.

She saw them to the door and told the vicar she would speak to him later about going into Bristol.

"Thank you, Lucy," he said as he waved good-bye. In the motorcar, driving back toward the village, he added, "She's a remarkable young woman. Her grandmother thought her brilliant. I don't believe Lucy knows it yet, but Beecham will soon be too small and provincial for her. She'll find another place to live and new work to do. And I shall miss her cheerfulness and her brightness."

Rutledge turned to look at him. "You're fond of her."

"I am. But I'm no fool, Rutledge. She treats me like a favored uncle, and I'm happy with that." And then on a lighter note to show that his heart wasn't breaking, the vicar added, "One can't keep a butterfly in a glass jar. However lovely it might be to dream about it. Besides, think what she'd be like as the vicar's wife. Half the women in the village would turn on her, and the other half would feel sorry for her. No, I need a plain and kind woman who will support the church—and me— and raise no hackles amongst the ladies of the parish."

There was nothing Rutledge could say. They drove in silence to a farm track on the far side of Beecham, and at the end of it was a small cottage that had seen better days twenty years before. It needed paint and new thatching and better glazing in the windows. The door was closed, and although the vicar offered to take him inside, Rutledge contented himself with looking through the windows.

The furnishings were much like the exterior. Plain, hard used, worn. A poor man's dwelling, and probably filled with bitterness as well as hopelessness.

"Can you describe Dobson for me?"

"He's rather ordinary. Light brown hair, blue eyes, a little above medium height—good shoulders—and while he knew to keep his place, he was a stiff-necked man."

Rutledge changed his mind then and asked the vicar to open the door. Walking from room to room, looking at the dust, the large wooden washtub in the little addition on the back, the lumpy mattresses and hand-me-down curtains, he felt a surge of sadness. Dobson and his mother had been made to pay every day of their lives for what the father had done. Guilt by association, wearing away at them like drops of water on stone until it must have scoured the soul. Until they couldn't forget the past, even if they had wanted to.

But it was in the little shed that he stopped and knelt.

On the floor was a smudge of something black. Hardly more than a speck, but his sharp gaze had found it. He scraped at the spot with his fingernail, then gave up.

He said nothing to the vicar, but to himself it was a different matter.

Rutledge would have been willing to wager his life that whatever had stood here only a few months ago must have been a pail or even a pair of them, filled with a thick black, tarry paint, rancid fat, and chimney soot.

12

The vicar offered Rutledge lunch, and he accepted the invitation. They ate their meal in the sitting room where a small table had been drawn up to the window.

"I often dine here," the vicar said. "The dining room is by far too large for one poor clergyman." He waited, making general conversation, until his housekeeper had served them and gone back to the kitchen to enjoy her own meal.

And then he said, "You haven't told me much about the business that brought you here. Was it the blackened grave stones? Yet you seem to feel that Dobson is a killer. Like his father before him. I could judge that by your questions."

"I'm afraid that may be the case."

"I find it hard to believe. Or rather, I find it painful to believe. Perhaps because I feel young Dobson never had a fair chance at a decent life."

"I'm sure he didn't. Still, who knows what drives people to choose to do murder? He could have started a new life in Cornwall or Herefordshire where no one knew of his past. I daresay many of the villagers living in Beecham today don't remember the whole story—only that Dobson was a murderer's son. Not why."

"That's probably true." The vicar shook his head. "Villagers have long memories."

"How ill was his mother? Do you know?"

"She was in some discomfort at the end. Her heart simply stopped. But according to the doctor, she had a tumor in her breast that spread. It was too late to try to do anything about it. She refused even to consider a doctor's care for months. I think she worried about the cost, but she very likely didn't wish to hear the truth."

"Was she given something for the pain?"

"Yes, the doctor was quite liberal there. Laudanum." He was helping himself to the pudding and didn't see Rutledge's sharp reaction. "And she took a long time to die, poor woman. Her spirit simply wouldn't admit defeat. As if she hadn't finished with life. I sat with her sometimes, but I don't think she believed in God any longer. My presence made it possible for her son to leave for work. That was what mattered to her."

Had she too thirsted for revenge? Or feared that her son did? Rutledge started to ask the vicar what he believed, and then thought better of it.

As he was leaving, the vicar said again, "You won't forget to keep me informed?"

"I will do my best."

He nodded, and turned to go back inside, his shoulders slumped, as if under a burden too heavy to bear.

Rutledge drove on to Netherby, stopped at the barbershop, and had to wait ten minutes while twin boys were given matching haircuts.

He sat in the chair without being asked this time, and let Lolly trim his dark hair again. And as the barber worked, he asked his question.

"We spoke before. When I was here about Benjamin Clayton. Do you recall?"

"I do."

"While he lived here in Netherby, was he ever summoned to Bristol to serve on a jury?"

The scissors stopped while Lolly stared at Rutledge. "Now how did you come to know that?"

Rutledge swallowed a surge of excitement. "I didn't. But I've encountered two other men who had once lived in or near Bristol in the same period that Clayton was still here in Netherby. They served on a jury, and it was possible that Clayton had as well, since he had very likely met these men at some stage in his life."

"You're the clever one then." Lolly was still staring at him.

"Not clever, Lolly. Used to finding connections between people and events."

"Yes, well, it was true. He was summoned, but he was reluctant to go. He never spoke about it again—at least not to me—except to say that it was an experience that troubled him, and he wished he'd never been a party to it. I'll say this for him. He wasn't a man to judge others, Benjamin Clayton wasn't. Always trying to see both sides."

"Do you know when this was?"

Lolly laughed. "When he served? Now I must think about that." He frowned, considering. "I'd say it was no more than a matter of months before he sold up and went north to be married. If that."

How old was Benjamin Clayton then? Twenty-seven? A young man, engaged, looking toward the future. A man much like himself . . .

He paid Lolly for the haircut and thanked him for the information.

He spent the night in Bristol, then set out for London. He was, he thought, finally ready to speak to Bowles. He didn't have proof, but he had sufficient evidence now that his thinking was correct, that there was indeed a connection among the victims that pointed to one killer, not four. And certainly not suicide. He should have been able to discuss his conclusions with the Chief Superintendent and receive his blessing to continue searching. But Bowles wasn't given to encouraging his men. Unlike Chief Inspector Cummins, he measured those under him on their results, not their insight.

As it was, Rutledge would have to be very careful not to let Bowles know the support Cummins had provided in this quest. And that meant any consequences would fall on his shoulders alone. He was prepared to accept that.

Passing through villages and towns along the road to London, Rutledge could see apples ripening on laden trees, corn heavy with golden heads in rolling fields, livestock grazing peacefully. A Sunday morning alive with promise and beauty. He tried to enjoy it, but his thoughts kept returning to Dobson and whether or not he was capable of killing. The vicar had pitied the man, but how much had he really known about him, when it was all said and done? That cottage was proof enough of the suffering a child and his mother had endured. And suffering could turn a mind toward vengeance.

It was late when Rutledge reached the city, but he stopped by the Yard anyway.

The passages were quiet, doors closed, the only sound of voices coming from the night staff. Neither Chief Inspector Cummins nor Chief Superintendent Bowles was there. Even Sergeant Gibson had gone home, although there were those who swore he had no home to go to.

In the morning, then. He was almost glad of it.

Frances was already in bed, the rooms downstairs dark and stuffy, although the lamp burning in the hall welcomed him.

He walked into his father's study and poured himself a small whisky. Draining it in two swallows, he went upstairs to his own bed.

There was no chance in the next morning to confer with Chief

Inspector Cummins, but when Rutledge asked for a meeting with Bowles, he requested that Cummins sit in on the conference.

It was taking a risk, and he knew it. Without a prior meeting, Cummins wouldn't be able to back his position. On the other hand, Cummins's presence could mean that Bowles would at least listen.

As they walked into the Chief Superintendent's office, Bowles said irritably, "I hope this meeting is to tell me you'd made an arrest in Kent."

"I think it's very likely that we can, and soon," Rutledge began confidently. It was the best way to handle the Chief Superintendent. He had a knack for scenting weakness as soon as it stepped through the door. "Meanwhile, I've discovered a strong connection between the Tattersall murder and the Hadley inquiry."

"I thought we'd discussed the likelihood that Tattersall was a suicide. With the Yard's blessing, the reconvened inquest agreed."

"So we believed at the time. It wasn't until I was in Kent that I learned that Hadley and Tattersall had once served together on a Bristol jury. A capital case that ended in conviction. What's more, it appears that Benjamin Clayton, who later went to live in Moresby, was also a member of that same jury." He was choosing his words carefully. And he'd already decided not to include the schoolmaster Stoddard. Not until he was more certain of his ground. "Here are three men who lived ordinary, blameless lives, respected and respectable, who share only two things: their connection with Bristol and having been summoned to serve on a jury there. And yet they were murdered in similar circumstances within a matter of weeks of each other. The surprising thing is, those men whose grave stones were recently desecrated, the case that Inspector Davies was called to investigate, could very well be connected to this inquiry. I'm waiting for information that will confirm the names of all twelve jurors."

Bowles was glaring at him impatiently, purposely being obtuse. "You're reaching for straws, in the hope of making bricks. If it was a capital case, either the accused was found not guilty—in which case he would have no quarrel with the men who set him free—or he was convicted and hanged, and not likely to be your murderer so many years later."

"Evan Dobson was hanged in Bristol in 1888. I'm looking for his son, Henry. Mrs. Dobson died at the end of June this year, in poverty and despair. Henry left the family home as soon as she was interred. And very shortly thereafter, the killing began. What's more there is evidence that Henry Dobson had access to laudanum prescribed for her."

"All very well and good. Now explain to me how this man Henry, poor and no doubt with only a village school education if that, managed to trace his victims? With luck he might have found Tattersall in Stoke Yarlington, but you claim he reached Aylesbridge and Moresby as well."

"He worked at various times in a greengrocer's shop and a lumberyard. He knew people of his own kind, poor and making their own way as best they could," Rutledge responded. "Such a man could cadge lifts to any part of England. It's not how he got there that troubles me. It's the question of how many names are left on his list—if those damaged stones aren't connected to Dobson, then it's a long one."

Cummins cleared his throat, speaking for the first time. "In late June, early July, there was a rash of breaking and entering at greengrocers along the southern coast. Three pounds taken here, five there—someone was even lucky enough to find ten on one occasion. The seaside has been quite popular this summer, and crime has taken a holiday there as well. A London pickpocket was just apprehended in Brighton, and two well known housebreakers were taken into custody in Lyme Regis and Plymouth respectively only last week. I daresay there are other instances of petty theft elsewhere. Sufficient for a determined man to put food in his stomach, find a bed for the night, and even pay his way if necessary."

That was news to Rutledge, but Bowles ignored his Chief Inspector.

"Then tell me how this killer of yours managed to find men he'd never seen, or seen only as a small child—several of whom had long since moved some distance away? It's far-fetched, Rutledge, even you must see that."

"I haven't explored that yet," Rutledge answered frankly. "The first step was to ascertain whether I was right about the jury. It's not impossible to find someone if the pursuer is determined enough."

"For us at the Yard, perhaps. But an untutored man? It's a good theory, Rutledge, I grant you that. But there are too many holes in it. The tarred grave stones? I wouldn't doubt you could be right there. It's something a man like this Henry Dobson might do out of spite. Inspector Davies will be happy to hear of it if that's true. And that confounded vicar as well, who made such a fuss about what was done. Besides, we've got our man in Moresby. The trial is coming up in late September."

Rutledge opened his mouth to say something but caught Cummins's eye and shut it.

Bowles went on without interruption. "And as for the inquiry in Kent, there's the maid who found Hadley's body. Statement says she had access to laudanum. You need to sort that out."

"Dr. Wylie has confirmed that it was not full strength and certainly not a lethal amount."

"Yes, well, it might have given her the idea. Search out the chemist's shop that sold it to her. Hadley wouldn't have been the first man to try to take advantage of a pretty young housemaid while his wife was away. If he pressed her too far, she could well have considered getting rid of him before Mrs. Hadley came back and gave her the sack. It's even possible she only intended to put him to sleep, so that he'd leave her alone, but got the amount wrong."

"You haven't spoken to Mrs. Hadley—" Rutledge began.

"The wife is often the last to know in these matters. But the housekeeper might have an inkling. Speak to her. Make certain before you pursue this Henry Dobson that you aren't blind to what's right there under your nose."

It was final. And arguing with the Chief Superintendent was the surest way of making him dig in his heels.

Bowles reached for a sheet of paper on his desk. "While you've been running about chasing hares, that Inspector in charge of the Kent murder is wondering where you've been. You haven't kept him informed. See that you do. The sooner the better." And then he turned to Cummins. "I've had two men in here this morning, threatening to enlist if we go to war. Cates and Johnstone. They've run mad. Have a word with them, if you please, before this gets out of hand."

Reports indicated that the Kaiser's forces had entered tiny Luxembourg, no match for the invaders, and were now poised on the Belgian Frontier. Whitehall had sent a stern warning to Berlin. Germany could field whole armies, while Belgium had hardly more than a hundred thousand men under arms to defend her. However gallant a fight she waged, it would be impossible for her to hold out.

There had been prayers in churches across Britain on Sunday, solemn pleas to the Almighty to make the combatants see reason and asking that the King and the Government be given strength and wisdom during this ordeal. These had been comforting to many people.

Rutledge and Cummins were dismissed. They walked out together, not speaking as they moved down the passage.

They reached Cummins's office, and he beckoned the younger man inside. When the door had closed behind them, he walked to his window and stood looking out, hands clasped behind his back.

"Interesting possibility," he said after a moment. "But perhaps a little premature in expounding it."

"Yes," Rutledge admitted. "Still. What happens if someone else is killed while I'm going through the motions in Kent, to satisfy Bowles? Besides, I've met Peggy Goode, the housemaid in question. If Hadley had made advances, she would have run screaming through the house instead of calmly plotting to be rid of him. And how did she convince him to stop and drink a glass of milk, if he was intent on raping her?"

Cummins turned. "I must ask. Are you sure it wasn't what you viewed as the wrongful arrest of that young man in Moresby that sent you down this road?"

A hot retort formed on Rutledge's lips, only to be replaced almost at once by a wry shrug. "It's a fair question. The answer is, yes, that's still troubling me. But the possibility grew out of the same exercise you and I tried when we were talking about the Davies inquiry. The first and second deaths were slightly different. By the third, I could see a pattern. I looked into the Stoddard case, which Martin had investigated, and that made four. The next question was what had these victims shared? They hadn't been to the same schools, they hadn't served in the military, they weren't related, they didn't have the same solicitor or doctor or tutor. But there was Bristol. We don't usually consider a jury as forming a bond among men. They serve at the pleasure of the court, are dismissed, and are expected never to speak to anyone else of what they did. Not their deliberations, their decisions, their findings. And unless a trial is scandalous in nature or attracts the attention of the gutter press, it's forgotten in six months' time. And yet for those few days, twelve men are extraordinarily important to the prisoner in the dock, whose future rests with them. And just as important to the prisoner's family."

"Dobson would have been old enough to attend the proceedings?"

"I very much doubt it. I find it hard to believe that his mother didn't attend the trial. But the verdict touched both of them deeply. It had to."

"Yes, I see that. But where is Dobson now?"

"God knows."

Cummins sighed. "You've got yourself a very interesting possibility, Ian."

He ticked them off on his fingers. "I have someone searching for information on the jurors. The next step is to discover a means by which Dobson found his quarry. And I must find a sighting that proves Dobson was in the vicinity of each murder. Even though I myself don't know what the man looks like, I've got only a general description to be going on with. But I think it can be done, with time and perseverance."

"Good. Meanwhile, get yourself back to Kent and speak to the local man. I'll keep an ear to the ground here."

Rutledge rose. "Thank you, sir."

"If war comes, will Major Gordon be returning to active service?"

"There have been whispers that he will."

"Then spend some time with your Jean today before you leave for Kent. She'll be worried. God knows we all are." He picked up a pen, looked at it as if he'd never seen it before, and then said, half to himself, half to Rutledge, "What am I to tell these hotheads eager to go out and get themselves killed?"

"To wait and see. Germany might well pull back. If they don't, then give the Army a chance to do what they've been trained to do. If Germany comes through Belgium, it will be facing the French as well as the British. And the French have fought them before."

"Our regiments are scattered throughout the Empire. If the French can't hold Germany long enough to get them here, then we'll need every man we've got."

"Germany has to contend with three armies. The Russians, the French, the British."

"With respect to the Tsar, I don't know that the Kaiser is particularly worried about his eastern flank. I *am* rather surprised that he's baiting the British by massing an Army on the Belgian Frontier. Or perhaps it's a feint, and he's trying to keep France guessing. I can't see why he would wish to bring us into the war if he could avoid it."

"His sights are set on Paris, not London. And he might not believe that we'd go as far as war on Belgium's behalf." Rutledge put his hand on the door. "The problem is, if he tests us too far, there will be no turning back."

He took Cummins's advice and went to call on Jean. It was just as well not to be under the Chief Superintendent's feet at the moment, he thought wryly as he lifted the knocker at the Gordon house.

Jean, he was told, was upstairs lying down with a headache. But as soon as she was informed that he'd called, she asked him to wait and hastily dressed.

"Ian, what a wonderful surprise," she said, lifting her cheek for his kiss. "Let's walk in the garden, where it's cooler."

She was wearing a white dress inset with lace panels in the bodice and around the line of the hem, and there was a blue sash at her waist and a blue enameled locket at her throat. He had never seen her look lovelier and told her so.

She smiled. "I was going out walking this afternoon, but it's far too warm. This is much more comfortable. You look tired. Is it the war news? Young officers have been running in and out of the house all morning, until Mama banned them from coming more than once. I found it quite thrilling and dashing, but I daresay she's worried about Papa. Everyone is dancing on the Kaiser's convenience, which is silly, if you ask me. Lieutenant Rodgers calls him Mad Willy. I don't see why we shouldn't simply send our Army to France and block his way. He'll retreat quickly enough then."

It wasn't as simple as that. But he let her chatter on, happy to walk arm in arm with her and listen to her.

"And the Humphreys have canceled their ball tonight. I was glad, since you weren't going to be here to accompany me. But now you are, and I'm of a mind to tell Sarah Humphrey that she's ruined my evening."

"It would have been a crush," he said lightly. "You know you wouldn't have enjoyed that."

"No, that's true. Oh, Ian, I've found the loveliest design for my wedding gown. I do wish I could show it to you. Or even describe it to you. But that would invite all manner of bad luck, so I must simply wait, until you can see it for yourself."

"It will be the finest gown in England," he said, smiling down at her. "You'll be wearing it, and that's all that matters to me."

She squeezed his arm. "Will you enlist, if war comes? Our footman is already excited about going. And the Nevilles' chauffeur, and even the Haldanes' son-in-law is considering doing the same."

"I've far too much work to do at the Yard," he told her. "I'm a policeman, not a soldier."

"But you'd fight for King and Country, wouldn't you? If it comes to that?"

"Are you saying the Army is in such dire straits that it needs me? I doubt it."

"I just don't want to be the last person who is sending someone to France," she said, and he saw she meant it. "Yesterday, after the church service, it was all everyone was talking about."

"Jean. I'm not going to make a fool of myself, rushing out to enlist. By the time half these men have been trained sufficiently that they can sail for France, the war will be over." But even as he spoke the words, he wondered. Europe had gone up in flames so quickly—barely five weeks had seen the worst happen. Before that there had been peace for such a long time. And now everyone was mad for war. As if the excitement was all they saw.

"If you feel that way," she said angrily, "then I'm going inside."

"Jean," he said again, but in a different voice. "I won't quarrel with you over this. You've no idea what war can be like. Neither do I for that matter. Your father can tell you, he was in the Boer War. People die. People are maimed. It's not all parades and bands and uniforms, it's cruelty and misery and destruction. When the lists of the dead come in, will you be quite so happy to find your friends' names there? Or the footman, or the neighbor's chauffeur? The men you've danced with and played tennis with won't all come back, you know."

She turned away. "You make it all sound so dreadful."

"It is dreadful. I'm sorry, but there it is."

She turned back to face him. "Please don't tell anyone what you've just said to me. Particularly not Papa or my friends. Pretend, a little, that you're eager to fight. I don't want everyone thinking you're a coward."

13

Jean's words stayed with him all the way to Kent.

Rutledge told himself it was her upbringing, her father's career, but he was reminded of something that Gilbert had said, that the Army had its own circle of obligation. It was truer than he'd been prepared to believe at the time.

The young officers who were Jean's friends would see the darkening clouds in Europe as a chance to cover themselves in glory. Promotion was notoriously slow in peacetime. Even Major Gordon had seemed very pleased to hear he'd be expected to serve again. He himself was happy to leave them to it. Not out of fear for himself, but from the knowledge that war was what they were trained for, just as he was trained for police work, and just now, with Dobson on the loose and four dead men to account for, adventuring in France as a lark to prove his mettle was not something he dreamed of.

Still, the words had stung. Would she realize that and take them back? He thought it was very likely she would. And he held on to that thought.

When Rutledge was shown into Inspector Watson's narrow office, the man on the far side of the desk considered him, then said, "You've taken your time coming to see me." He was older, experienced, and competent, with steady gray eyes and a strong square chin.

"You laid the groundwork for this inquiry with thoroughness. I didn't need to speak to you until now."

"Still. It would have been a courtesy."

"It would have been," Rutledge agreed, "but we have reason to believe this isn't the first time our man has killed, and it's likely he's going to kill again. I've been trying to stay ahead of him."

"And have you done that?"

"So far I haven't located him. The question we're wrestling with now is how he found his victims. That might help us narrow down the search."

"You're telling me they were chosen, not picked at random?"

"I believe so. In all fairness, there are those at the Yard who don't."

"Who are the other victims?"

Rutledge took a deep breath and launched into an account of what he'd uncovered so far. "Meanwhile, someone in Bristol is searching for a list of those involved in that particular case. If there are more victims, we can warn them in time."

"All well and good. But you haven't explained why Hadley drank that glass of milk. I knew the man. It's not like him to sit there meekly and let himself be killed. And even if he was told that he'd helped convict an innocent man, why should he believe a word of it? He was practical, clearheaded. He wouldn't beat his chest and fall on his sword."

"I don't have an answer there. Yet."

"Your notion is interesting, but it doesn't stand up to scrutiny."

"Then tell me why *you* believe Hadley drank that milk?"

Watson frowned. "I don't know. Unless he was offered a choice? Laudanum or a far more painful death. It might even go deeper than that. If you are right about this man, he could well know more about his victims than we do. Blackmail that allowed the killer to arrange a quiet little murder, with a long night ahead in which to escape."

Rutledge rose from his chair and went to lean against the office wall. "Do you know something about Hadley's past that the killer could have used?"

"Not here in Kent. But he lived in Bristol before coming here. It would have to be something that happened in Bristol. Besides, there hasn't been any gossip about him here. If there was, I'd have heard it by now." Watson cleared his throat. "I'd give much to know why his wife went to Canterbury alone. Visiting friends, she said, but why didn't he go with her? There was no pressing reason for him to stay at the farm. Were there strains in that marriage that we haven't heard about?"

Rutledge remembered the Chief Superintendent's suggestion that Hadley had tried to force one of the housemaids. Was this the source of his suspicions?

"In my conversations with her and with the servants, there was no hint of trouble. According to Dr. Wylie, she was devastated when he gave her the news."

"That could be true enough. Well, time will tell."

T he interview with Inspector Watson had not been very satisfactory, but Rutledge himself took most of the blame for that.

Once more he chose to spend the night at Melinda Crawford's house.

And after dinner, he asked her, "How would you go about finding an old friend from India, if you didn't know where she was living now?"

"I'd ask a mutual friend for her direction," she answered promptly.

"Let's say she's remarried and your mutual friend has also lost touch with her."

Melinda, her head to one side, examined him. "Are you purposely making this difficult?"

"I am."

"Then I expect you won't like my next answer. I'd call Richard Crawford and ask him if the regiment knew where my friend was."

"But her husband wasn't an Army man. He was a solicitor."

"If I mailed a letter to her at her last known address, I'd hope that the present residents would forward it to her."

"But then you'd be waiting for her to decide to contact you. If she didn't wish to for some reason, you'd have no way of knowing that your letter ever reached her."

"I'd leave it to the telegraph office to find her."

"Possible, but again, if she doesn't respond, you'd have no way of knowing if she received your telegram."

She gave the matter some thought. "There must be a way. I can't seem to find what it might be." Her face brightened. "I'd ask the vicar in the last place she lived."

"Ah, but he's a new man and never knew your friend."

Melinda frowned. "Has this person you wish to find lived in the same place for very long time?"

"As it happens, he has."

"Is he on the telephone?"

"I shouldn't think he is."

"Ian!"

"Try again."

She stared at him, her mind busy. "Is my interest in finding my friend, malicious or friendly?"

"Possibly malicious."

"Then I'd have kept up with her somehow."

Rutledge said, smiling, "You have hidden depths, Melinda. You should have been a policeman. How would you go about keeping up with her?"

"If I were really intent on knowing her business, every year I'd send a Christmas note. Everyone has friends or relatives they hear from quite regularly but don't know from Adam. I'd scribble a name to the card, and if someone received it and opened it, it would tell them nothing. But I'd have a *poste restante,* where the letter could be returned to sender if they'd moved away. It would cost me a few pennies, but it would be worth it. And then if I decided to speak to this person, I'd send someone to their door with a box of chocolates or a bouquet of flowers, and if my gifts were accepted, I'd know I was safe to do more."

Had Mrs. Dobson kept up with twelve jurors over the years? But how?

"Someone would remember the arrival of flowers or chocolates, surely?"

"Ian, I could stand on the doorstep with anything in my hand, and make up a name. If you know what you're doing, you can persuade the person at the door to divulge any amount of information." She went on, changing her voice, "'Is this where Mrs. Cranford lives? I have a delivery for her.' And the reply would be, 'I'm afraid you have the wrong house. This is the Crawford residence.' Or if he were uncertain of the address, he might stop at a neighboring house, in which case the maid would answer, 'I'm sorry, Mrs. Crawford lives in the next street, at number two.'"

Rutledge was intrigued. In each house, the victim had been the only male resident of the right age. Michael Clayton had left Moresby for York, but even if he hadn't, he wouldn't have been mistaken for his father. Nor Hadley for the footman, Tom.

He rose, kissed her on the top of her head, and said, "Don't wait up for me. I'll let myself in when I get back."

"Nonsense. I'll be sitting here waiting for you to return. And then you'll tell me what this is all about."

He drove through the late evening afterglow to the Hadley farm and asked for Mrs. Tolliver.

She was downstairs in her small parlor. "Inspector," she said, rising as he was shown in, "I hope there's nothing wrong." She glanced at the pretty little clock on the chimneypiece. "It's quite late, I'm sure Mrs. Hadley has retired."

"I've a question to ask you. If you can't answer it, I'd like to summon the rest of the staff and ask them."

"The older ones have already gone up. I think the younger ones may be sitting out by the kitchen garden. What is it you need to know so urgently?"

"Did anyone bring a parcel to this house in the week before Mr. Hadley was killed, only to be told he'd come to the wrong address?"

"I don't remember any such caller," she said. "And either the maid or the footman would have informed me of it."

"You're certain of that?"

"Oh, yes. It could have been a parcel for a visitor either Mr. or Mrs. Hadley expected to arrive."

"Will you ask the staff, all the same? I'll call tomorrow to find out what you've learned."

"I will do that, Mr. Rutledge. But don't pin your hopes on it. I can't think when we last had someone at the door."

He thanked her and prepared to leave. She accompanied him up the stairs and to the main door to see him out. She was about to shut it after him but stopped and said into the night, "What was in the parcel? It might help if I knew?"

"Very likely nothing. It would have been an attempt on someone's part to elicit information. The contents of the parcel aren't important."

"Indeed, sir?"

He had been about to turn the crank on the motorcar. Straightening, he said, "It needn't have been a parcel. Flowers, perhaps. A query about a lost dog."

"I see. Well, I will ask. Good evening, sir."

"Good evening." He had cranked the motorcar and taken his seat behind the wheel when the door opened again, letting a shaft of light fall across his face. Mrs. Tolliver stepped across the threshold and said, "Inspector?"

"Yes?" Her face was in shadow, but something in her posture as she leaned toward him made him cut the motor.

"The only stranger I recall coming here shortly before Mr. Hadley was—before it happened—was the poor man looking for work. But he came to the wrong farm. One of the maids gave him a glass of cold water, and told him how to find the other lane."

"Did you see this man?"

"Actually I did, because we thought it was the fishmonger at the kitchen door. He came half an hour later."

"Can you describe the man looking for work?" He realized he was holding his breath, waiting.

"I didn't get a good look at him. The kitchen maid had just finished mopping the flagstones by the door to the kitchen garden when he came up. She said he doffed his hat and asked if this was the farm looking for someone to do the mucking out in the stables. He thought this was Pennythrift Farm. The maid said afterward that he didn't know Kent very well and had likely taken a wrong turning. He'd put his cap back on by the time I reached the door. He was footsore and dusty by the look of him. But tidy enough, good shoulders, polite. Middling tall. He drank the water, thanked the maid, and went on his way. I didn't give him another minute's thought. This time of year there are any number of people looking for seasonal work."

"Is there a Pennythrift Farm?"

"Oh, yes, it's on the far side of the village."

"And you haven't seen this man before or since?"

"No."

All the same, late as it was, he found Pennythrift Farm and asked the middle-aged woman who came to the door if they'd taken on a new stableman in the last few weeks. They had not. Nor had they advertised for one. What's more, the man claiming to be looking for work there had never appeared at Pennythrift.

Feeling much himself again, Rutledge drove back to Melinda's house.

Good to her word, she was waiting in the sitting room where she kept all her treasures from her travels. It had seemed to be Aladdin's cave to an impressionable boy brought to visit by his parents, and was his favorite room in the house.

She looked up as he came through the door. "There you are. I was about to give you up. Shanta is bringing us tea. Sit down and tell me if you've found someone delivering parcels?"

"No," he said slowly. "But I did find an itinerant laborer looking for work."

By the time they had finished their tea and were ready to go up to bed, he'd told her what he'd learned and why he'd been looking for ways to trace an old friend. Or enemy. And Melinda, who had looked death in the face as a child, never flinched as he described what he'd learned about a killer's mind.

"That's very clever of you, Ian," she said as they were mounting the stairs on their way to their beds. "Seeing the link with a jury. But I expect Chief Inspector Cummins is right. You will require hard evidence before you convince the naysayers."

"I'd give much to know where Dobson is now," he said, turning to walk down the passage to his room.

"You must pray that he isn't already stalking his next victim."

The next morning after a brief conversation with Mrs. Hadley, Rutledge left for Stoke Yarlington, outside Wells, driving straight through without stopping in London.

In every village he passed through, there were little clots of people standing in the streets, talking. He'd been in the middle of many inquiries where small groups stood as close as possible to where the police were working, asking in hushed tones for information in the aftermath of a crime. This was different, worried faces turning to stare at him as he drove on, wondering if he'd heard more than they had.

He found Miss Tattersall at home and asked her if she or her brother had over the years received Christmas letters from someone she didn't know.

"Not Christmas messages," she said, smiling at a memory. "But my brother often got birthday messages from someone he'd known at university in Bristol. Or more likely someone who thought they knew *him*. And the date was always wrong, so whoever it was had thoroughly confused him with someone else. Every year, without fail, on the twenty-eighth of June. It quite tried his patience. But of course there was nothing he could do, he didn't know anyone at the return address, and as I pointed out, even if he did, and he wrote to this person to inform him of the mistake, very likely his correspondent would take that as acquaintance and begin writing to my brother in earnest. He was quite put out, but I found it rather sad and even amusing."

"What did the messages say? Do you know?"

"Oh, the sort of thing anyone might write. A few lines on the order of 'Thinking of you on your birthday and hoping it's a happy occasion.' It was signed Fred or Frank, we never could decide, and the hand was copperplate and rather florid."

"Did you save any of these letters? Or do you remember the postmark on them?"

"Good heavens, no. They went directly into the dustbin. As I recall, they were posted in Bristol. But still we couldn't think who it might be."

"Lately has anyone stopped at your door looking for employment?"

"We do our hiring through an agency, like most people. The

agency supplies solid references. But I suggest you speak to Mrs. Betterton. She would know." She rose and went to pull the bell.

When he put the same question to Mrs. Betterton, she shook her head. "No, sir, no one has come by looking for work. He's not likely to find it on this street."

"A parcel then, or an inquiry about a neighbor?"

"Well, there *was* the man with the bundle of clean wash under his arm." She smiled. "His wife was ill, and he'd been asked to bring the sheets back for her. But he got the wrong street, poor man, and tried to insist they were Miss Tattersall's. Mixed up the bundles, he had. He'd already delivered three, and he could only pray they went to the correct houses."

"When was this? Do you remember what he looked like?"

"It was a few days before we lost Mr. Tattersall. He was rather ordinary, sir, as I recall. Not the sort you'd take a second look at. Stooped, his hair in need of the barber. He said he'd been too busy helping his wife to see to himself."

"And you didn't think to report him to your employers?"

"No, I did not," she said stiffly. "Neither Miss Tattersall nor Mr. Tattersall, God rest his soul, would thank me for disturbing them to gossip about another family's sheets."

And yet it seemed that here and in Kent, the stranger had been affable enough to find out what he wanted to know.

Assuming of course that the itinerant worker and the washerwoman's husband with the bundle of clean sheets were one and the same, but Rutledge was ready to wager they were. The descriptions were too close.

He thanked Mrs. Betterton, and Miss Tattersall said as he walked to the door, "Is this important, Inspector?"

"I can't be sure," he replied. "It's early to be drawing conclusions. But I have some hope now."

From there he went to find the village constable. Hurley hadn't seen the man with the bundle under his arm.

"But if it was market day, and if he was minding his own business, I'd have no reason to take particular notice of him."

Rutledge thought to himself that the washerwoman's husband would have taken great care not to encounter Constable Hurley.

He was tired when he reached London and left his motorcar in the mews. The house was dark when he walked around to the door on the square and let himself in.

The warm air was stuffy, the August night slipping toward the morning of the fifth. He tried to move quietly—after all, he knew the placement of every chair and carpet, every door and stair. He could walk—and had—in nearly pitch darkness from the door to his room without waking anyone, coming in from school late and unexpectedly, sent down for incurring his head's wrath.

He smiled at the memory. And froze with the smile pinned to his face as the study door opened, casting a bright shaft of light into the passage, catching him off guard.

Off stride, he heard his sister's voice.

"Ian? Is that you?" She appeared in the opening of the door, a black silhouette, slim and uncertain.

"Or else it's a very clumsy housebreaker."

"Don't make light of anything tonight," she said, moving back into the room.

He was down the passage in a half a dozen swift strides. "What is it? What's wrong?"

She turned to face him, and her eyes were bleak.

"My dear," he began, uncertain what to say.

"Charles just came to the door to tell us," she told him. "The Germans haven't replied to our ultimatum. They've marched into Belgium, and there's heavy fighting."

Charles Talbot was with the Foreign Office, he would know the latest news. It wasn't a false alarm.

"Oh, God." There was the end of hope that cooler heads might prevail.

It seemed they hadn't.

"We're at war. It's real," she whispered, echoing the words she had heard not half an hour earlier.

He stood there, his gaze holding hers for a moment, then he went past her straight to the drinks cabinet to pour a little whisky into a glass. But he didn't drink it, he set it down again and simply stared out the window. It occurred to him—he'd had no idea at the time—that he had asked Jean to marry him on the same fine summer's day that the Archduke and his wife had been murdered.

Somehow it seemed his life and their deaths had become inextricably linked.

Frances said, her voice trembling, "You won't enlist, will you, Ian? I couldn't bear it if you did. I couldn't bear it if something happened to you so soon—well, so soon."

He cleared his throat, turned and held out his hand. "I'm a policeman," he said quietly, remembering that he'd said it before, and only recently. "Not a soldier. I don't kill people. I arrest those who do."

14

Afterward he couldn't have said when they went up to bed. They has sat in the study without talking for a time, then called it a night.

He hadn't expected to sleep. But the driving he'd done in the past few days caught up with him, and the morning was well advanced by the time he opened his eyes.

Frances hadn't come down to breakfast when he left for the Yard.

The streets were quiet, the Yard subdued. He made an effort to find Chief Inspector Cummins and tell him what he'd learned about two of the linked cases.

If he'd expected praise, he would have been disappointed. But it was in the way of a report rather than an announcement, and Cummins took it that way.

"It's amazingly fine work, Ian. But we still need that list of jurors, and we'll have to see if the Clayton family and Stoddard's wife have had similar experiences. Still, we may have a better description now. Even if it isn't earthshaking. You've spoken to Watson, you say?"

"Yes. He's a good man. I need a few hours. I haven't been to see Major Gordon. Or Jean. I must say, he was expecting this."

Cummins squared his blotter with the edge of his desk, then moved the tall jar that held his pencils and fountain pen. "Sergeant Hunt went to enlist this morning. You'd have thought he was prepared to win the war singlehandedly. I expect Inspector Perkins may do the same before this day is out."

"They're both young."

"At a guess, Hunt is a year older than you."

Rutledge shook his head. "It doesn't matter. Before this is finished, old men will be called up for duty."

"They're already saying it will be over before the year ends. That's why so many men are rushing to enlist. They don't want to miss a tidy little war."

"I hope it is finished before Christmas." He made an effort to smile. "After all, if my future father-in-law is in France, the wedding will have to wait for him."

"Good God, I hadn't thought of that. All right, off with you. For once in my life I'm very pleased that I have daughters."

Rutledge found the Gordon house in turmoil. Officers were coming and going, and Private Meecham was waiting in the entry for Major Gordon. He gathered from the chaos that Gordon was leaving for duty.

Just then Jean came to the head of the stairs, her face streaked with tears. She spotted him below and hurried down.

"Ian! I'm so happy to see you. Could you drive us to the railway station? Mama and I can't leave with Papa, but we both want to see him off."

"He's not on his way to France?" he asked, surprised.

"No, he's taking over the training of men from the Midlands. We don't know when he'll have leave. Mama thinks he'll lead his men when they go over."

The Major appeared then, his wife on his arm, and started down the stairs. He was already giving her instructions, but Rutledge thought she was heeding only one word in ten.

"Yes, George, of course I'll see to that. Yes, yes, I'll remember. This isn't the first time I've had to do this, my dear. Jean? Oh, you've found Ian. Thank you for coming, Ian, there's simply been no time to think. Where is your motorcar?"

"In front of the house." He took the hand the Major held out to him. "Good luck, sir." And then they were swept outside, and it was time to leave.

The railway station was in turmoil. Trains were being allocated to the Army's use, and the platform even at this hour of the morning was almost impossibly crowded. Steam from the railway engines wreathed everything, making the heat seem more intense. One young woman had fainted in the crush, and several people were bending over her, ministering to her.

Rutledge left the motorcar where he could and followed the Gordons to the carriage waiting for the Major, again shaking his hand.

"Look after them, Ian," he said briefly, then turned back to his wife and daughter for a final farewell. Carriage doors slammed shut, the signal was given, and the train began to move.

Mother and daughter waved the train out of sight, then took Rutledge's arms, clinging to him as the crowds buffeted them. Another train was pulling into the track, and men were pressing forward to find their carriages. He did his best to protect them, guiding them through the throng of weeping families and grim-faced soldiers. He got them to the barrier and then through it. Mrs. Gordon, who had bravely held herself together seeing her husband off, began to cry into her handkerchief. Jean's grip on his arm was so tight he could feel her nails through the cloth of his coat.

Mrs. Gordon, choking back a sob, said, "It never gets easier. I really don't know why I think it should."

Rutledge had to offer both of them handkerchiefs by the time they had reached his motorcar.

Handing them in before turning to the crank, he said, "Back to the house, Mrs. Gordon?"

"Yes, please, Ian. It will take most of the day to settle everything down again. The Aldriches were to have us to dinner tonight, but I expect that will change. The Captain was on the train. I saw him just as it was pulling out, stepping into George's carriage. Or perhaps Mrs. Aldrich will want us there anyway. Can you be here at seven, Ian?"

He'd intended to leave for Yorkshire by five o'clock. But he smiled and said, "Yes, count on it."

"Thank you, my dear."

Jean went upstairs with her mother, and after a few minutes came down again.

She said, appearing in the doorway to the morning room, "Mama will be in a frenzy for days, trying to see to all Papa's instructions. It's her way of coping. His solicitor was here this morning to make certain that everything was as Papa wanted it."

"And how will you cope?" he asked gently.

"By being Papa's brave girl. As always. We never went with him to his postings, you know. He always said it was a greater hardship for everyone if we were uprooted every few years. So it really won't be much different now, will it? He could be on his way to South Africa or Egypt. Somewhere safe."

"Who will take over the running of the estate?"

"His solicitor has already found an excellent man. Papa met him last evening and he was pleased. Their agreement is only for six months. With clauses for extensions of time as required. But that won't be necessary. Don't let's talk about it any longer," she said, pacing the room. "Tell me where you've been, what you've been doing."

But he was fairly sure she didn't mean that literally. And so he said, "To Somerset and to Kent."

"But you're back in London now? Because with Papa away, Mama and I will be counting on you to stand by us."

"There's a matter I must see to tonight. It won't take too long." He hoped he was telling the truth.

The Aldrich dinner party was canceled, as expected, and so Rutledge dined with Jean and her mother. Leaving there, he stopped at his own house long enough to collect what he needed, and by just after eleven, he was on the road north.

He arrived in Moresby late on the second day, which actually suited his plans better than driving into the village in daylight. Leaving his motorcar on a farm lane, he walked the rest of the way into the town and went first to the Clayton house.

To his surprise, it was Annie Clayton who came to the door, her face tight with uncertainty until she saw who it was.

"Inspector? I thought—are you here for the trial? But you can't be, it's far too early."

"Actually, no, I haven't come for it. When is it?"

"With the war and all, it's been moved again. Two weeks from tomorrow. You can't imagine how I dread it."

"May I come in? There are a few questions I'd like to put to you."

"I—yes. Of course."

He followed her into the front room, surprised to see that the walls had been freshly painted, and the stairs had a new bannister and balustrades.

She noticed his surprise, and said, "Michael and Peter couldn't get along. And so this was the compromise. I agreed to come back to the house if they would change—would improve on the room."

"It's quite well done," he said.

Offering him a chair, she added, "Michael should be home soon. He's working in the harbor with one of the chandlers. It's not work he particularly cares for, but he hopes something better will come along, with so many young men enlisting. But I heard him tell a friend that he was considering the medical corps." She bit her lip. "He hasn't said anything to me yet."

Rutledge said, "I've run into something that intrigued me, Miss Clayton. And I've come to ask you if your father ever received birthday greetings from someone from his past, someone he couldn't remember?"

Her eyebrows went up in amazement. "How did you know? Mama always teased him, saying that it was his lost love. He thought perhaps it was the young man who worked in his father's shop at one time. You could barely read the scrawled name. Papa said he was never good at penmanship, but it was the thought that mattered. Only he got the date wrong. Papa didn't have the heart to tell him. So he just let it pass."

"Did he reply?"

"I don't believe so. The return address was a scrawl as well. But the greetings came faithfully. I always thought it rather sweet. And I did wonder if it really was a girl he'd known before he met Mama."

"Do you have any of those letters by any stroke of luck? We'd like to have a look at one."

"I don't think it ever occurred to us to keep them. And there wasn't one this June. Papa thought Danny might have taken ill or even died. Why are you interested in Danny? Does this have anything to do with what happened to Papa?"

"Just tying up loose ends. There's one more question. In the week before your father's death, had anyone come to your door with a parcel or to ask for work? Possibly even bringing clean sheets to the wrong house?"

"Do you mean to speak to Papa? No. I don't remember anything like that."

"Could your father have seen this person, if you didn't?"

"He was usually in the shop from early morning to later in the evening. There was always something to be done, turning a piece or staining it and waxing it. After Mama's death, he tried to stay as busy as possible."

That was a disappointment. But Rutledge persevered. "Would your father have mentioned such a visit to you?"

"I don't know. I don't see why he should."

So much for that. At least he'd verified the birthday message. And surely all Dobson would have had to do was follow Clayton home from the shop one evening.

Rutledge thanked her and walked back to where he'd left his motorcar.

Some miles back from the headland, he found a room for the night in a small inn along the road.

It wasn't until he was preparing to drive on to Northumberland that he remembered the Clayton neighbor who had been so helpful on his first visit. She hadn't given him her name, but he knew which house was hers.

Taking a chance, he drove back into Moresby and went to her door.

She was as surprised to see him as Miss Clayton had been, saying, "You're that policeman, aren't you?" and she invited him in for a cup of tea.

It was clear she wanted to gossip about the upcoming trial, and it was some minutes before he could bring her around to the question he had come to ask.

"Strange that you should bring that up," she told him. "Such a nice young man. I was walking home from a friend's house, and there he was, looking rather lost. I asked if I could help him, and he told me his brother had done some work at number seventeen, repairing a chair, and he was to meet him there so that they could walk home together. I had to smile, coals to Newcastle, you know, repairing a chair for the Clayton household. I told him that number seventeen belonged to the man who owned the furniture shop in Abbey Street, Mr. Clayton, and he wasn't likely to hire the young man's brother. He looked again at the scrap of paper in his hand, and laughed at himself—he'd got the number right but the street wrong. He thanked me and was off."

"Do you remember him well enough to give me a description?"

"It was nearly dusk, and of course he wore a workman's clothing." She considered Rutledge. "Not as dark as you, nor as tall. Wide shoulders. But rather thin."

"Would you recognize him if you saw him again?"

"Oh, I doubt it. I was in a hurry, my cat was waiting. I wouldn't have remembered just now if you hadn't asked." Her face slowly changed. "Are you saying—does that young man have anything to do with Ben Clayton's death? Is that why you're asking?"

He smiled, unwilling to worry her. "It's important to question everyone who might have been out and about in the week before his death. Who knows what he or she might have seen that could help us?"

"Yes, of course," she replied, reassured. "I quite understand."

Dobson had had long years of practice at hiding his feelings. At knowing how and when to please the people around him, so that he and his mother could eke out an existence in a hostile village. And he had probably learned to lie as well, discovering early on that a glib tongue was a shield against prying questions and callous indifference. He could hate in secret, and survive.

It would stand him in good stead as a murderer too.

Rutledge had reached the corner, on his way to his motorcar, when a constable approached him.

"Inspector Rutledge?"

He was wary, uncertain whether the constable had spotted him or was actually looking for him. The face was familiar, but Rutledge didn't recall his name. He said with a nod, "Yes?"

"Inspector Farraday is looking for you, sir. He's asking if you would step into the station."

"I'll be happy to." But he was on his guard. He and Farraday hadn't parted on the best of terms, and the man had gone against his express orders when he arrested Mark Kingston.

He turned toward the center of the little town, expecting the constable to continue on his rounds. Instead, the man fell in step with him, walking briskly at his side.

"A fine morning," Rutledge said.

"It is that, sir." The sun was warm on their faces, and the sea shimmered.

They went the rest of the way in silence, the constable staying with him until he opened the door to the police station and stepped inside. Was he under escort?

Farraday was at his desk, and it was clear at once that he'd been waiting for Rutledge.

"Nice of you to stop in and let me know you were on my turf. Still smarting over the arrest of Clayton's murderer?"

Without waiting for an invitation, Rutledge pulled out the chair next to the desk and sat down.

"There has been a connection with another inquiry I'm pursuing," he said easily. "I came to Moresby to find out if we might be looking at Kingston for another murder."

Farraday wasn't expecting that. He sat there, rearranging whatever was on his mind, and finally said, "Indeed? And why wasn't I informed?"

"Because at the moment there's more work to be done before we muddy the waters of Kingston's trial." He kept his face and his voice bland.

"Care to tell me what it is you're after?"

"I asked Miss Clayton if there had been an unexpected visitor to the house before her father was killed."

"And?" He was already jumping to the conclusion that this might have been Kingston.

"She said there was not."

"This is what you were doing when Constable Blaine found you?"

"It was."

"Why was it important enough for you to come all the way to Yorkshire to ask a question one of my men could have answered for the Yard?"

"Because I am on my way to Northumberland to ask a similar question."

Farraday considered him for a long moment. "Well." He reached into his desk drawer and brought out a telegram. Rutledge could see that it was already open. Farraday held it for a moment, then tossed it across the desk to him. "This will change your plans."

Rutledge's name was on the envelope. He lifted the flap and drew out the sheet inside.

The telegram was brief.

If this reaches you, return to London at once. Urgent.

And the name at the bottom was unexpected.

It read simply *Cummins*. Without a title.

"Personal or professional?" Farraday was asking, his gaze sharp.

"I expect there has been a development in the inquiry I've been pursuing," Rutledge said, giving the impression he was resigned to his orders. "The Yard has been waiting for other information to come in."

But his mind was racing. What had happened in London that had made Cummins try to find him? The answer was, it could be anything, including Bowles demanding to know where Rutledge was. And it had been a risk on Cummins's part to send a telegram here. Farraday was no friend. Unless Bowles had already guessed where he might be? Rutledge had made it clear enough that Kingston's fate concerned him.

"They'll ask me when I reach London. Has a date been set for Kingston's trial?"

"As a matter of fact it has. The third Monday in September."

"As a matter of interest, did Kingston's father agree to see his son before he died?"

"I don't know," Farraday replied with some relish. "That had nothing to do with the inquiry, did it?"

"It was what had brought Kingston to Moresby."

"So you said. There is a witness who claimed he was intent on setting aside the will by claiming to have reformed. But of course he hadn't reformed, had he?"

"His cousin's wife. Why doesn't that surprise me?" Rutledge rose. "I'll be on my way. Good morning, Inspector."

He was not going to argue Kingston's case here and now. Not until he could be sure he was right about Dobson. To try would do more harm than good. He left the office door open as he walked out, and behind him there was the sound of a fist coming down hard on the solid wood of a desk top.

Rutledge drove farther than he'd intended, reaching Lincoln before stopping for the night. He made an effort to close his eyes and rest, but his mind was busy with speculation. In the small hotel not far from the cathedral where he usually stayed, he'd had difficulty finding a room because so many men had come into the city to enlist. Several of them had come down very early to breakfast, as soon as the dining room had opened at six-thirty, unable to sleep for the excitement of what they were about to do.

He put their ages at nineteen, and from their conversation, he gathered they worked on neighboring farms and appeared to know each other well. They had decided that joining the Army was far more exciting, and they had walked this far only to find the recruiting office closed for the evening.

One of them asked Rutledge where he was from, and when he told them London, they bombarded him with questions he couldn't answer. What was the war news? Were they still in time? Did the fact that the recruiting office was closed indicate that the Army already had as many men as it needed?

He wanted to tell them to go back home and await events. But their excitement was high and reason didn't interest them. They had told everyone they were leaving to fight the Kaiser, and if the Army would have them, it was what they meant to do.

"They'll be sending seasoned troops to France first," he told them as he finished his meal. "Not raw recruits. Even if you manage to take the King's shilling today, you'll need to be trained before you fire a shot, and by that time, the Germans could well have decided to back off."

But they wouldn't hear of it, demanding to know if he intended to enlist as soon as he reached London.

Rutledge ignored the question, asking instead who would work the farms they'd left behind while they were away.

"There are enough men to bring in the harvest," one of them said. "And if we're home by Christmas, there will be plenty of time to think about next spring's planting."

He wished them well and went on his way. But he thought about them as he drove south. Three of how many hotheads on their way to join an Army they wouldn't have considered a month ago? Drawn by visions of glory and the chance to kill Germans. And how many young Germans and Frenchmen and Austrians and even Russians had rushed out to do the same? What had happened to this quiet, peaceful summer? What had brought on such madness? Not just the assassination of an Austrian Archduke. It was as if a plague of blood lust had spread on the wind, infecting everyone it touched.

He was young enough to feel the pull of adventure. To feel the blood run hot with excitement. He wasn't immune to the plague. But he'd seen his share of bodies in the course of his time as a policeman, and there was nothing glorious about death. Parades and bands and banners were all very well, but after these had passed by, the dead didn't rise up and go on with their lives. They were collected and buried, the hero together with the coward. And medals handed out by a grateful country did nothing to comfort the bereaved the dead left behind.

War was best left to the Major Gordons of the world, who were prepared and trained to deal with it.

Trying to shake off his mood, he picked up speed and made an effort to think about London, and why he had been summoned.

T he first person he encountered when he walked into the Yard the morning of the second day was Sergeant Gibson.

"You're back," he said. "Sir. There's a file on your desk. Chief Inspector Cummins asked that you look at it first thing."

"Is the Chief Inspector here?"

"He's at a meeting in Bloomsbury. There's been trouble over German waiters at a restaurant there. Spy fever. He's trying to make people see sense."

"I don't envy him. All right, thank you, Sergeant."

He found the folder placed conspicuously on his desk so that he couldn't miss it.

Setting his hat on the top of the file cabinets, he sat down and stared at the plain cover. Clipped to it was a small square of paper where Cummins had written, *URGENT*.

Rutledge opened it and stared at the name of the victim. It seemed to leap out at him.

F. M. Gilbert.

He must be dead, Rutledge thought, and not of natural causes. Not if his name was in a file at the Yard.

He forced himself to go through the file logically, familiarizing himself with the details.

One Fillmore M. Gilbert of Swan Walk, Kent, had been found in his study by his housekeeper, unresponsive and to her eyes dying, his breathing so shallow she couldn't be sure she could see it.

She had sent for help, and Gilbert's physician had come posthaste. He had done what he could, then sent Gilbert to Tonbridge and hospital.

"The man's got the constitution of an ox," the doctor had said in his preliminary statement. "He should have died."

He had taken an overdose of laudanum. But because Gilbert took small amounts quite regularly, he hadn't died.

Rutledge stopped there, and went to ask one of the sergeants on duty if Cummins had returned. He hadn't.

And there had been nothing in the file to indicate whether Cummins believed this to be Dobson's work or had left the file for him, knowing Gilbert's connection with the Rutledge family. What's more, the local police hadn't requested the Yard's assistance.

But family connections wouldn't account for that urgent telegram. Rutledge went back to stand by his window looking down at the canopy of leaves below.

"Gilbert claimed he hadn't prosecuted that particular case," he said aloud. "He couldn't remember anything about it."

Catching himself, he turned back to the file.

Rutledge came to a decision. Cummins wasn't available. The file was on his desk. He could swear he believed it was a request for assistance, not a routine notification in the event the Yard had an interest in the man or the situation.

He flipped the folder closed and took his hat down from the top of the cabinet, walking out of the office and down the passage. It was no more than thirty miles to Tonbridge. He could be back before the end of the day, if he hurried.

Traffic was heavy as he left London but thinned as he turned south. He passed a carriage of young men, waving their hats and cheering, clearly on their way to enlist, and flushed with a precelebratory drink, no doubt. And on the road were other men walking purposefully toward the nearest town.

What would the Army do with them all?

When he arrived at the hospital, he was told that Gilbert had regained consciousness and insisted he be taken back to Swan Walk. The doctor's carriage had left not half an hour before.

Rutledge stopped for sandwiches and a cup of tea, then drove after the carriage. It had already arrived by the time he reached the house, the horse standing there quietly, swishing his tail at the flies and waiting patiently.

He knocked, was admitted, and told that Mr. Gilbert was not accepting visitors today.

"Please tell Dr. Greening that this isn't a social call. I've come from Scotland Yard."

Dr. Greening himself came down then. He was younger than Gilbert but not by much. "Whatever business you have can wait," he said testily from the stairs. "My patient needs rest."

"I'm afraid my business is official and urgent." He gestured in the direction of the room where he'd talked to Gilbert on the night of the storm. "But I have no objection to beginning with you, sir. Shall we?"

He led the way without waiting to see if the doctor was following. And then he heard the footsteps coming the rest of the way down the steps and after the briefest of hesitations, turning toward the passage.

The maid who had admitted him was still in the hall. He heard her close the outer door and cross the floor in the direction of the servants' stairs. That door opened and shut as he waited for the doctor to catch him up.

"There is no need for this," Dr. Greening said stiffly as he walked into the study and faced Rutledge.

"A file was waiting for me today. I must presume it was placed on my desk because it has been reported that Mr. Gilbert had attempted suicide."

"As a matter of fact, one of the staff had mentioned that you had called on Mr. Gilbert fairly recently. Inspector Williams in Tonbridge felt that Mr. Gilbert's decision to kill himself might have been a result of your visit."

It was not what he expected to hear. After a moment he said, "Sit down, this may take some time."

"My patient—"

"Is he stable?"

"Well, yes, but his age is a matter for some concern."

"Then you can spare me ten minutes. Why should my visit have led Gilbert to a decision to kill himself?"

"His mind is rapidly failing. He skates the issue rather well, but it has been causing increasing distress. That's why as a rule he doesn't go out or receive visitors. Did you press him? Make him feel the loss more particularly?"

"We talked about an old case. He told me he sometimes confused the older trials, but he most certainly still understood the law. That last was clear enough. And he gave me a list of other barristers practicing at the period of time in question. It's possible one of them will remember the information I need. In the scheme of things, the trial I'm after was rather commonplace. Certainly nothing that would disturb Mr. Gilbert or drive him to suicide."

"Yes. Well, he's quite good at concealing his ailment. There are days when his memory functions remarkably well. And others when he is sadly muddled."

"Tell me what happened here, what sent him to hospital."

"He often sits up at night. He doesn't sleep very much, and he finds it easier not to make the effort to go up to his bed. I think he breathes a little better as well. Where was he when you saw him?"

"Where you are sitting now. Only the chair had been turned to face the open window."

"When the housekeeper came in to bring him his morning tea four days ago, he was slumped over, his breathing slow and labored. She couldn't rouse him. She was afraid he'd had a stroke, and she sent for me at once. By the time I arrived, he was unresponsive. I knew it wasn't a stroke, it was more like an overdose. I had him taken straightaway to hospital, where they emptied his stomach and took other measures to bring him back. In the end, he survived, much to our surprise. For one thing, despite his age and his appearance, he's a strong man. For another, he'd been taking laudanum for a painful toe. To help him sleep at night when it throbbed like the very devil. His body was used to a certain level of it, you see. And what might have killed an ordinary man failed to do more than render him deeply unconscious. It's one of the problems with the drug, I'm afraid. The body becomes accustomed to it, and requires more and more to be efficacious. In effect, the same problem found by those who take such drugs to obliterate rational thought. They require larger and larger doses until it kills them."

"In Gilbert's case, how was it administered?"

"In a glass of milk."

"Milk? I think if Gilbert had been given a choice in the matter, he'd have taken it with French brandy."

"And just as well he didn't."

"Then who brought him the milk? And who put the drug into it? Gilbert couldn't make it down to the kitchen on his own. Not the man I saw a few days ago."

"On the contrary, I believe he could, if it was the only way." Dr. Greening pointed to a small box on Gilbert's desk. "As to the drug, he has laudanum available down here as well as in his room. He administers it himself as needed, because he says the staff can't get the hang of the drops. I think he believed he was more in control of his life if he could make his own decisions on how much or little he needed. And I must say, he's never had a problem with an overdose before."

"If his memory is failing, how can he be trusted with drops?"

"There is a sheet of paper in the box, with days of the week and times of day. He simply fills it in and replaces the sheet in the box. The housekeeper looks at it every morning. On the night in question, he failed to fill it out at all. I myself looked at the vial, but the level didn't indicate such excessive use. I came to the conclusion he'd been hoarding it, lying about taking it, in order to build up a sufficient amount. Perhaps for this very purpose."

"Then where is that second container? He couldn't be sure the housekeeper wouldn't grow suspicious when the amount in the vial stayed at the same level day after day."

"The point was to spare the family pain," Dr. Greening said coldly. "If I had come across the container, I should have had to acknowledge the possibility of suicide rather than an accidental overdose while confused by pain. Look, he most likely tossed the container out that window. I didn't go and search."

Rutledge stood and went out through the lace curtains that had been pulled across the open windows to keep out the sun. He spent several minutes carefully examining the terrace and the plantings surrounding it. There was nothing that might have been used to hold the laudanum.

He did however find a boot print in the soft earth of a bed of tall delphiniums near the side balustrade of the terrace. He reached down to touch the edge of the print. There had been no rain to wash it away, but it was fast losing its shape in the dry soil. He stood inches from it and looked up. He could see the doctor sitting there in Gilbert's chair, fingers tapping impatiently on its arm.

Rutledge went back inside. Sitting down again, he said, "There's nothing out there. I should like to suggest something else to you. That someone tried to murder your patient. And failed."

"That's a ridiculous assertion. Fillmore Gilbert? Who would wish to harm him?"

"Someone from his past? One of the reasons I've come to Swan Walk today was to question him. If he's awake and alert, he can give us an answer to that."

"I tell you he's too weak, he will need several days to regain his strength."

"And in several days, this person, whoever he or she may be, will have killed again."

Dr. Greening stared at him. "You know more than you're telling me."

"I think—I believe that I do. There have been other deaths, far too similar for coincidence. Not just in Kent but across the country. And each one seems to point to a trial in the past. In fact, the one I'd come here earlier to ask Gilbert about. He told me he didn't remember it, and he sent me to someone else. Unfortunately that man wasn't able to help me either. Now, given what has happened to Gilbert, I'm beginning to think the killer found him first."

Greening shook his head. "Are you suggesting that someone he sent to prison is now free and bent on revenge?"

"It's possible. But if I'm right, it's the son of a man Gilbert sent to the gallows. His mother died recently, and that, I think, set him free to commit these murders."

"Because his father was not guilty?"

"I don't know what this man Dobson believes."

"All right. I'll give you five minutes with Gilbert. And I'll see that a nurse is brought in to stay with him at all times. Good God, the man who did this could very well try again!"

Greening rose and led the way up the stairs, limping a little as he neared the top of the steps. Down the passage to the right, he opened the door to a handsome room with wall hangings and furnishings that harked back to Tudor times, although there were comfortable chairs set before the hearth.

Gilbert's skin was gray and dry, as if what he'd gone through had cost him dearly. His gaze had lost its sharpness, and he seemed to have shrunken even more, almost lost in the great canopied bed.

Rutledge took his hand and spoke to him, but Gilbert didn't seem to know him.

He tried again, saying, "It's Ian, sir. I've come to see how you are."

Gilbert searched his face. "Where's Claudia?" he asked in a whisper.

"She's at home, sir. The doctor is about to send for her—"

The dry hand on the coverlet curled around Rutledge's with an iron grip. "No. I don't want her here. No, I tell you." He turned to the doctor. "Bring me the milk," he said in a stronger voice. "I didn't finish it. I couldn't have."

And then as if the effort was more than he could handle, his hand fell back to the coverlet and he closed his eyes.

" . . . couldn't have," he said again after a moment. Then clearly, "Dear God, what have you done?"

Rutledge stood by the bed for several minutes more. But Gilbert seemed to have slipped away from him, unable to struggle back to consciousness again.

Greening finally motioned to Rutledge, and they walked as far as the door.

"You see?" Greening said, "he knew what he was about. Your fears about a killer notwithstanding, Fillmore Gilbert tried to end his own life. He did empty that glass of milk, you know. On purpose."

"I spoke to him quite recently. He wasn't suicidal then. It makes no sense that he could change so drastically in such a short space of time. Just now I found a footprint in the flower bed outside the window where he generally sits. Was that made while you were trying to save his life? Or has someone been watching him from the shadows?"

"It makes sense if you consider what he just admitted he wanted to do. As for the footprint, it could have been made by one of the staff, worried about him and not allowed in the room."

"What else has he said about what happened? Has he spoken before?"

Dr. Greening looked away. "As to that, he muttered from time to time, but it's been unintelligible. Not even the ward sisters attending him could judge whether he was lucid or not." He turned again to Rutledge. "Now that he's back in his own bed, his own house, he may be able to push aside the shadows and remember why he felt he needed to take his own life. He's old, Rutledge, in pain, and no longer the brisk, decisive man he once was. Can you blame him for tiring of his present state?" He glanced toward his patient. "Meanwhile I've removed all the laudanum from the house, and I'm putting a watch on him for fear he may intend to try again as soon as he's able. I'm also sending for his daughter."

"He's told us he doesn't want her here."

"Nevertheless, she ought to be at her father's side. I expect he will find it easier to accept living, if she's here to support him. How would you feel if you couldn't remember the last inquiry you handled? If the names of a suspect and the evidence were muddled? He refused to let me tell his daughter anything about his loss of memory. He would put off her visits, to keep her in the dark. Of course he doesn't want her here now to see him as a failed suicide."

But Gilbert had left Rutledge with the impression that she was busy with her children and her husband's career.

"Set your watch. The nurse should wait until he's more stable before sending for Claudia. Look at him. Seeing him in this state will only distress her. Have you considered that in his drugged, confused mind, he thinks she may have tried to kill him?"

"*Claudia?* Good God, man, you can't believe that?"

"I don't know what to believe. I won't, until he's fully awake and coherent."

He left the doctor with his patient and ran lightly down the stairs, walking on to the door that led to the kitchens.

He found the servants standing in their hall, whispering together, as if speaking in a normal tone of voice might reach the man in the bed upstairs. They broke apart as soon as they saw him coming through the doorway.

The housekeeper stepped forward and asked, "Is there any news?"

Her eyes were dark-circled from lack of sleep. "Dr. Greening wouldn't tell us anything except that Mr. Gilbert needed rest."

Rutledge had dealt with Mrs. Thompson when he spent the night in this house. He had found her capable and very concerned about her employer.

He said, "It's true, I just saw him. The quieter he is, the sooner he'll recover. There are to be no visitors. The only people allowed in this house will be Dr. Greening and the nurse he's sending for to attend his patient."

The housekeeper exchanged glances with a heavyset woman wearing an apron. The cook, he thought. Then she turned back to Rutledge. "Are they saying he tried to kill himself? I won't believe it. Not Mr. Gilbert."

"He isn't able to tell us what happened. Which of you brought him a warm glass of milk the night he was taken ill? Do you remember?" His gaze met that of each member of the staff in turn.

There was a general shaking of heads. The housekeeper said, "I can't think that he came down for it himself. But then if it was late and we were asleep, he might have tried. He isn't an invalid, you know. Walking is painful and difficult, with that toe. The night you stayed here at Swan Walk, you saw how he needed help to manage those stairs. Still, if he was determined enough, he might've. If it had been his French brandy now, I'd believe it. I can't think why he should want milk. He generally took his drops in water."

"There's another question I must put to you. Have any of you seen a stranger hanging about? Coming to the door to ask directions or to speak to anyone in this house?"

"There's been no one," the housekeeper told him. "We don't see many people. You yourself were our only guest for months now—since Miss Claudia was last here in the early spring."

"I don't mean a policeman or a guest. I'm talking about a laborer, a peddler, a mender of pots and pans—anyone who isn't a member of the staff or who wasn't sent out by the greengrocer or the miller with your orders—not someone you know well by sight because he comes regularly?"

But they couldn't think of anyone. Scanning their faces, he wondered if they were telling the absolute truth. Or if one of them had seen someone and was afraid to mention it. He waited for several seconds, to give everyone a chance to speak. But no one did.

There was the footprint in the earth by the delphiniums. Perhaps Dobson hadn't come to the door because he'd already spotted his quarry in the sitting room.

Still, how could the killer be sure that this thin, stooped man was once the robust figure of one of the old Queen's finest barristers? The doctor was right, Gilbert had changed.

But if Dobson had never seen him at the height of his career, he would have no means for comparison.

What's more, Swan Walk hadn't changed. It had been in Gilbert's family for centuries. His own home from childhood. Perhaps that was all his killer needed to know.

And yet it was the weak voice of the old man lying in the great bed that haunted Rutledge all the way to his motorcar.

Gilbert was intent on finishing what he'd begun. Driven to finish it.

That sounded more like suicide than murder. And it might well be Rutledge himself who was trying to make this man into another of Dobson's victims.

15

Rutledge drove to the little village of Swan Walk, clustered less than half a mile from the gates to the house. It had a dozen or so shops, a tobacconist, a church that had been built by an ancestor of the Gilbert family, and a post office that served the estate and the surrounding farms and smaller manor houses.

Sandwiched between a shop that sold a variety of goods, from thread and needles to brooms and buckets, and the ironmonger's shop, the post office itself was so narrow that Rutledge felt that if he put out his arms, he could touch both walls at the same time. It was an illusion created by the fact that the space was far deeper than it was wide.

The man behind the brass grille looked up. "May I help you, sir?"

"I'm looking for Swan Walk House," he said. "Mr. Gilbert's residence."

"The gates are on the far side of the village, sir. You haven't gone far enough."

"Thank you." He turned as if to go, and then swung around. "I sent one of my people here last week with a parcel for him. I expect he was lost as well."

"A parcel? I don't remember one, sir. A young man did come in asking directions as you've done. But he said he was to fetch a horse that was sold to a party in Tonbridge."

"Who was he?"

"I didn't ask. The buyer's groom, he said. Mr. Gilbert doesn't drive out any longer, and I expect he sees no need to keep so many horses these days."

"Do you remember what he looked like?"

"A groom," the postmaster said, frowning. "Young, polite, I'd say shorter than you. They can probably give you his name at the house, if it's important."

Rutledge thanked him and left without telling him that the groom had never appeared at Swan Walk, because no one on the staff had seen him.

The pattern held. A simple query that elicited the right information, without drawing attention to the questioner. And a footprint in the earth by the terrace windows, where Gilbert so often sat of an evening. A glass of milk instead of brandy.

Only Gilbert hadn't died, and if he survived, as Dr. Greening believed he would, then he was a witness who could not only identify the killer but also tell the police what had transpired as victim and murderer came face-to-face.

The niggling fear at the back of Rutledge's mind was that his brush with death had hastened Gilbert's decline. Why else would he feel he'd not completed what he'd set out to do? Why would he seem to feel he'd botched his own death?

Had the encounter been wiped from his memory, save for that single moment when he'd drunk the drug-laced milk?

Scotland Yard desperately needed Gilbert's evidence. Not to mention Kingston, awaiting trial in Moresby.

And what would the killer do, when he learned he himself had botched his latest murder?

Rutledge drove directly to the Tonbridge police station, where he asked an Inspector by the name of Williams to send a constable to Swan Walk, to keep an eye on Gilbert.

Williams said, "I heard he tried to top himself."

"I don't buy it. We're working on a similar inquiry where the cause of death was murder. This may well be another such case. If Gilbert is this man's victim, he could well decide to come back to Swan Walk and make certain Gilbert doesn't talk."

"Look, two of my constables are going on about enlisting. I've been told Chatham dockyard was overrun with enlistees. The world's gone mad. I'm not sure I can spare anyone for more than a day or two."

"That's a start. Dr. Greening is bringing in a nurse. But a constable on Gilbert's door throughout the night would be best. I think he's safe enough during the day."

"You're quite serious about this."

"Never more so. If I'm right, Gilbert is the only one of this man's victims to survive. And he's the only one who can identify him. Or testify in court against him."

"What's this man got against Gilbert?" Williams asked, his dark eyes sharp with curiosity and speculation. "And why weren't we informed here in Tonbridge that this killer was hanging about?"

"We didn't expect him to strike in Kent a second time. It appears that a man in Aylesbridge was a victim as well."

"I heard about that inquiry. Good God, you mean whoever killed Hadley is the man who tried to kill Gilbert?"

"I'd bet on it."

"That's a different story," Williams said. "I'll have a constable out there straightaway. He can enlist next week. The war can wait."

Rutledge thanked him and left, returning to Swan Walk to find Dr. Greening pacing anxiously in the passage outside Gilbert's door.

He stopped when he saw Rutledge coming up the stairs and said, "He's half mad, he's shouting at me to let him die. I can't make head nor tails of it."

Rutledge walked into the bedroom.

Gilbert was lying propped up by half a dozen pillows. He looked ghastly.

Dr. Greening, coming in behind Rutledge, said quietly, "He needs a sedative. But I can't give him one this soon. It could stop his heart."

Gilbert, hearing the doctor's voice, jerked his head around so that he could see them. "Damn you," he said, his voice thick with emotion, "I meant to die. And you've prevented me. If I had the strength to get out of my bed, I'd find that shotgun in the estate room. Ian? What are you doing here? Make this fool see some sense."

"A doctor can't be a party to your death, sir. He'd hang for it."

"Then bring me that gun. I can still load it myself."

"I can't. I'd be taken up as an accomplice, and tried. I'm to be married soon. It's not on."

"By God you will find a way to help me! Or I'll know the reason why."

Rutledge moved closer to the bed. Gilbert was not raving. He was racked with fear. There was sweat on his brow and his hands were shaking.

"What are you afraid of?" Rutledge asked softly, for his ears alone.

"I keep telling you—I want to die. My life is over, finished, an empty shell. I'm sick of it. Let me go in peace."

Dr. Greening started to speak, but Rutledge held up his hand to stop him.

"Will it do," he asked the man in bed, choosing his words with care, "if we put black crepe on the door knocker and tell the staff and even the village that the effects of the laudanum are irreversible, and you're dying? That it's only a matter of time?"

Greening stared from Rutledge to his patient and back again. "You're both mad," he said.

"No, not mad at all," Gilbert said at once. "For God's sake, do it. Quickly!"

Rutledge turned and left the room.

He sought out the housekeeper, asked her to find black crepe for the door knocker, and inform the staff that Mr. Gilbert had taken a turn for the worse. "There will be a nurse in his room at all times, to care for him until the end. The staff will not dust or mop the passage outside his door until further notice. Will you see to it?"

Her eyes filled with tears. "The poor man. But shouldn't we wait until the end? Crepe is for the dead. And there's his family to think of."

"That's been taken care of. I'll contact his solicitor when I'm back in London to see about a notice in the *Times*. And the nurse will take her meals in that room. I'm putting a constable on the door to see that Mr. Gilbert is not disturbed."

"A constable? I don't understand."

"A precaution. Mr. Gilbert might become violent before it's over. Please see to the crepe at once."

"Yes, of course," she agreed, although Rutledge could tell she was mystified. Before Mrs. Thompson could ask more questions, he left her there in her sitting room.

His next stop was the village. He told the postmaster and the vicar that Mr. Gilbert was dying, having failed to regain his senses. "He's physically strong," he said, using the doctor's words. "It could be today or next week. But the accidental overdose of his nightly drops has undermined his health to such a degree that it's only a matter of time."

The postmaster sympathized and promised to pass the word that Gilbert's death was imminent.

The vicar wanted to call.

Rutledge told him that Mr. Gilbert was no longer able to respond. The vicar took some convincing. But in the end, he understood that the dying man had seen a priest at the hospital and his soul had already passed into God's hands.

By the time he got back to Swan Walk, there were already two or three small bunches of flowers left by the gate. Rutledge glanced at them grimly, and made certain he closed the gates behind him, then sat there in the motorcar.

How long could they keep up this charade?

With any luck, until he himself got to the bottom of whatever was happening.

Making himself useful—and keeping the curious away from Gilbert's room—Rutledge went up to the maids' section of the servants' floor to help bring down a cot for the nurse. She was expected momentarily, for Dr. Greening had gone to fetch her himself.

The cot's mattress hadn't been used in some years and was deemed unsuitable. While the housekeeper and one of the maids went in search of another one, Rutledge stood at the window in the room where he'd slept during the night of the storm and looked out over the sunny countryside.

He could just see the church tower from here, fields of sheep, and to his surprise, from this angle, the gates to the drive were just visible. He was idly staring down at them, his mind on London and the Gordon household. He'd promised to be there to help Mrs. Gordon and her daughter. Instead, there was no way he could get a message to Jean, explaining the delay.

His attention sharpened as a man pedaled into view from the direction of the village. He slowed, then stopped, looking at the gates.

The door to the house, hidden behind the rows of trees, wasn't visible from where the man stood. But he studied the little bundles of flowers wilting in the sun.

From the other direction another man on a bicycle pedaled up the slight rise, and Rutledge saw him first. He caught the glint of the sun on the badge on the rider's helmet, and realized it was the constable from Tonbridge.

Rutledge's hand clenched on the window ledge. The two men were going to meet.

The first cyclist, dressed as a groom, mounted and prepared to move on as he heard someone coming toward him, then paused when he saw who it was.

Rutledge watched the constable nod to the cyclist, then open the gates and push his bicycle through before closing them again. He then headed up the drive, vanishing from Rutledge's line of sight among the trees.

The other man stared after him, then moved on, heading in the direction of Tonbridge.

Rutledge was already out the door of the bedroom and racing toward the stairs, shouting for Mrs. Thompson.

She came out of another room, alarm in her face. "Mr. Rutledge—what is it?"

"Leave the cot for now. Take more of that black crepe down to the gates. Straightaway."

"But it's too soon. I can't feel that it's right."

"Just do as I say. *Now*. I'll explain later."

He took the stairs at speed, sprinted for the door, and reached it just as the constable rang the bell.

Rutledge flung open the door, ushered him in and to the stairs. Speaking rapidly, he said, "I'm from Scotland Yard. I want you to stand guard on Mr. Gilbert's door and let no one—no one—in or out except for Dr. Greening and the nurse he's bringing. Do you know Dr. Greening?"

"Yes, sir, I do."

"Then follow me. Quickly. I have to leave."

He took the constable as far as Gilbert's room. "They'll be bringing down a cot for the nurse. Leave it in the hall until I get back. And ask Mrs. Thompson to find a chair for you."

"Yes, sir, thank you, sir."

But Rutledge was already on his way back down the stairs. He cranked the motorcar, blessed it again for being there when it was needed, and set out for the gates. It took a moment to open and close them, and then he was off, speeding after the man on the bicycle. He'd had a head start, but the motorcar was faster.

Rutledge had no reason to think that the man was Dobson. But something in the way he'd stopped by the gates and stared at the flowers had indicated more than mere curiosity. He'd been weighing what they meant. Deciding what to do.

As he drove, he tried to tell himself that the man might have worked for Gilbert on the estate, or remembered him from some chance encounter, but his intuition was shouting at him that Dobson had discovered that Gilbert was still alive. And so he'd broken his rule of vanishing into thin air once he was certain his victim was dead.

But this time he couldn't have been certain, could he? Gilbert had taken a long time to die, and dawn came early in the summertime. Dobson dared not linger.

"Damn it," Rutledge said aloud as the realization struck him, "no one had sent for the undertaker. Instead, it was an ambulance."

He sped down a long hill to a sharp left-hand bend in the road, leading to the gates of Penshurst Place before it turned sharply right again, to continue straight on to Tonbridge.

He'd overtaken no one on the road, and there had been no turning that the cyclist could have taken. But here in tiny Leicester Square just outside the gates to the great house, part of the village of Penshurst, there were dozens of places where a man could disappear. Even into the churchyard of St. John the Baptist, enclosed by the cottages and tall houses of the Square.

He reached for the brake, pulling hard and coming to a slamming halt in a bow wave of dust and loose chippings. Looking over his shoulder to make certain the way behind him was clear, Rutledge reversed until he could pull off the road next to the tall wooden gates let into the high walls of the estate.

A bicycle was propped just inside the archway leading into the churchyard, barely visible from the road. He couldn't have seen it if he'd rounded the bend and gone straight on to Tonbridge. But where he was sitting now, he could just glimpse the handlebars.

Was it the same bicycle? He couldn't be sure. But looking the other way, he could see that the long straight road to Tonbridge was empty. Leaving the motorcar where it was, he walked over toward the church. It was handsome, set as it was in the churchyard shaded by great old trees, surrounded by equally handsome old dwellings, some of them black and white Tudor houses. He went up the steps, through the archway, and stopped.

He still couldn't be sure it was the right bicycle. He went across to it and felt the front tire. It was warm, even here where the sun hadn't reached it.

Cautious now, he walked on. Grave stones spilled out of the high summer grass, and there was a large stone table near the porch doors. No one else was in sight. For all he knew, he was the only person in the Square. He made himself slow his pace to stroll leisurely through the empty churchyard.

If he couldn't recognize Dobson, then it was very likely Dobson wouldn't recognize him. Then why had he come in here? Had he caught sight of the motorcar thundering down on him, and already wary from his encounter with the constable, decided to take no chances?

Rutledge paused occasionally, pretending to study the inscription on a stone here and there, glancing toward the faded one under a tree where legend said a murdered man had been interred in the last century. The slightest movement caught his attention, from the pigeon scratching in the grass near the church porch to the sparrows squabbling by the west front.

The Square was cool, serene. The houses were silent, their doors closed.

Had he been wrong about the bicycle? It could well belong to someone else, from the rector to one of the residents of the houses facing into the square.

If he was wrong, then he'd lost his chance to catch Dobson up.

A crow suddenly took wing, cawing raucously, startling Rutledge. He saw it then, rising from the far side of the church, climbing high above the roof and turning sharply in the direction of the grounds of the great house.

What had startled it? Someone on the far side of the churchyard?

Rutledge stopped, gazing up at the oddly set pinnacles on the tower. Every sense was alert now. Still appearing to stare upward, he walked on to where he could see down the north side of the church.

No one was there. He moved swiftly now, toward the apse, hoping to catch Dobson playing tag with him around the Square, but when he reached the south porch once more, and was still empty-handed, he turned and in three strides, went through the heavy wooden doors into the nave.

It was bright, airy inside, with heavy well-spaced pillars and a delicate wooden chancel screen.

His senses were at fever pitch now. If his quarry had come in here, where was he? Under the tower? In the south chapel hidden by one of the monuments to dead Sidneys?

He stayed where he was for a moment longer, putting himself into his quarry's shoes, then he began to walk down the aisle.

And stopped, suddenly realizing that he was cold, well off the scent.

He'd been tricked. The church was empty.

Turning, he dashed for the porch doors and shoved his way through them, his gaze at once going to the arch that led out to the sunlit road beyond.

Where the hell had Dobson gone?

He'd hardly framed the thought when he saw someone running out from the shadow of the tower across the grave-strewn ground, headed for the arch. The man looked up as he heard the porch doors scrape loudly, spotted Rutledge, and in the same instant, caught his foot on a stone half hidden in a thick patch of grass.

Rutledge was certain Dobson was going down. He saw the grimace of pain twist Dobson's face, followed by desperate determination. His arms windmilling frantically, he kept his balance somehow, kept running, despite the cost, and reached the arch before Rutledge could catch him up.

He already had his handlebars in his grip, was swinging his leg over the saddle even as he was rolling through the arch and bumping down onto the road, quickly disappearing out of Rutledge's line of sight.

As Rutledge reached the arch, he could see the tall wooden gates of the estate closing behind a cart piled high with straw. And just behind the cart, where he was invisible to the man holding the reins, was Dobson, astride the bicycle and out of reach.

Fast as he was, by the time Rutledge had reached the gates, there was no room even to squeeze himself through, and as he watched, the gates closed with a snap of the latch on the far side.

He pounded on them with his fist, realized it was useless, and swearing, ran on to his motorcar.

As he turned the crank, a woman came out of one of Leicester Square's handsome houses, staring around to see what the noise was. Climbing into his seat, he called to her, "Is there a back way into the stable yard?"

The woman looked him up and down. "And who is asking?" she demanded.

Rutledge yelled, "It's urgent, a man has been hurt."

"Why didn't you say so?" She told him how to find the lane that ran in beside the garden walls, and he thanked her.

Rutledge drove directly there, bounced down the wide, rutted lane and spent half an hour searching for his quarry.

There were fields of sheep to his right and ahead of him as he kept the wall to his left. It turned, then ran along the bottom of the gardens. Here the vast eastern front of Penshurst came into view, rising high above the wall. It might well have been mistaken for a royal palace, he thought, with its great battlemented wings and towers. He finally discovered a back way into the gardens, but by that time Dobson could have gone in any direction, even back toward Swan Walk.

Still he searched, as determined in his own way to find Dobson as Dobson had been to escape. And when someone from the estate came to ask his business, he questioned them about a man on a bicycle. No one, apparently, had noticed him. Rutledge thanked the gardener and drove back to the main road.

It was a near run thing.

But he had seen Dobson's face.

He was trained to remember faces, and he would know this one again when he saw it. No distinguishing features. Long, thin, brown from the summer sun, and ordinary. Intelligent. High cheekbones. Straight nose. Light eyes, most likely blue, straight medium brown hair. Useless in finding him, of course, because the description would fit hundreds of men. But for Rutledge it was enough.

There was the other side of that coin, as well.

Dobson had seen his face, just as clearly.

As he drove empty-handed back to the Gilbert house, Rutledge tried to put himself into Dobson's shoes.

How would I manage it? Getting about England without leaving tracks?

The answer lay in his very ordinariness. Dobson belonged to the class of people he moved among. He'd grown up in a village, shunned and looked down on. He'd learned to make himself inconspicuous. In spite of the native wariness of strangers, there was also an empathy for their own kind in most villages. A man passing through, with a simple story to tell to explain away his Somerset accent, neither tinker nor Traveller, having an honest face and nothing to sell, a workman's hands . . .

Perhaps. It would depend on the village and it would depend on the local constable. But it could be done.

Still, he'd already established himself in Swan Walk, the young groom waiting to take a horse to its new owner. It was certain he wasn't staying there, easily trapped.

Rutledge went to the village and asked people on the street and in the shops, and was rewarded by shakes of the head. The groom hadn't been seen lately, although one man thought he might have seen him pedaling through not more than an hour past.

By the time Rutledge reached the house, Dr. Greening had returned, and the burly constable had helped manhandle a bed and a mattress from the old Nursery into the sick room.

They were just finishing as Rutledge came up the stairs. Mrs. Thompson, disappointed that she wasn't even allowed to snatch a glimpse of her employer, left the nurse to make up the bed and was in the hall, listening to the doctor give instructions about meals.

"A tray each for the nurse and the constable," Dr. Greening was saying, "and one for your master."

"He can eat, then? Mr. Gilbert?" she asked, her face lighting up.

"I don't count on it," Dr. Greening said, glancing at Rutledge. "But we must try, of course. A soft diet, if you please."

When they had all gone away, Rutledge went in the room to see Gilbert for himself. The nurse, a matronly woman in her late thirties, said out of her patient's hearing, "He won't speak or open his eyes. If I've ever seen a man willing himself to die, it's that poor soul."

"The point is to keep him alive," Rutledge said grimly. "At any cost. Let no one in, give no bulletins as to his condition. And no gossiping with the constable or the staff."

Affronted, she said, "In my profession we do not gossip."

He was firm. "I'm sure you don't. But this man's life could depend upon it."

He went to stand by the bed, then bent over it to whisper, "There's crepe on the door and on the gates. The village believes you're dying, that it's only a matter of time now. But you must live, because you are the only witness I've got. And I'm damned if I'm going to face this bastard in trial by combat. He's going to stand before a judge."

For an instant he thought he saw a flicker of response on Gilbert's wan face. Rutledge touched his shoulder lightly, and then, nodding to the nurse, left Swan Walk for London.

16

Chief Superintendent Bowles was livid.

"You've been dashing about the countryside like a cavalry horse. I've warned you that motorcar was going to be the end of you. One way or another."

The dressing-down had gone on for ten minutes, and Rutledge had had to stand there and listen.

As Bowles ran out of words, all but reaching the point of spluttering in helpless fury, Rutledge said quietly, "I've told you. I believed I knew who murdered those four men. Clayton, Tattersall, Hadley—possibly even Stoddard in Alnwick. Now Fillmore Gilbert has nearly died at his hand. Once he recovers, Gilbert will give us a statement. What's more I've seen Dobson for myself—he's no longer a faceless killer."

Bowles came up out of his chair. "You're like an old dog with a bone, you won't leave Clayton alone. I've told you, that inquiry had been *closed*."

"Very well. Set him aside. Someone has attempted to kill Gilbert, one of the foremost barristers of his day. Is the Yard going to investigate that attempt? Or leave it in the hands of Tonbridge? If you won't assign me to that inquiry, then assign someone else."

But Bowles wouldn't listen. "I warned Cummins. I *told* him not to give you that file. But he insisted, because your father knew the man. And precious little good has that done Gilbert or you. Kent hasn't asked for assistance—they list Gilbert as a near suicide. Now get back to Aylesbridge and bring me the person who killed Jerome Hadley."

Rutledge had no choice but to leave. He finished paperwork at his desk for the next twenty minutes, then went home.

He walked in the door to see the housekeeper roll her eyes at him, and then he heard Frances calling from the sitting room.

"Ian, is that you? Do come in—we've been waiting for you."

The stiff, artificial tone of his sister's voice warned him that something was wrong. Summoning up a smile he hoped appeared genuine, he handed his hat and his valise to the housekeeper and strode down the passage.

And stopped short in the doorway.

Amid the remains of afternoon tea, sat four women. His sister Frances, his fiancée Jean, Jean's cousin Kate, and the woman he'd met in Beecham who was writing the little guide book to the village and its church. Lucy Muir.

She had been dressed in simple country clothes when he'd met her at her cottage. Today she was wearing a very stylish London walking dress of periwinkle blue with white lace at the throat. The effect, he thought, would have left the vicar in Beecham stunned. As it was, her companions in the room were regarding her with a very brittle politeness.

Jean rose, moving gracefully to his side and holding up her face for a light kiss, establishing her position as his fiancée. Frances gave him a smile that he correctly interpreted to mean that he would have to earn her forgiveness for the awkwardness she'd endured for his sake. Kate's eyes twinkled, as if she had found the long afternoon amusing. Behind the twinkle was curiosity.

Miss Muir's gaze held an apology. As he came into the room and greeted her, she said, "I had to travel up to London on a family matter. And so I brought what you were looking for, rather than trust it to the post."

He said quickly, "You found it? Bless you! It's even more urgent now than it was before."

She reached into the elegant traveling bag beside her chair and drew out an envelope. "I do hope you can read my writing. I had to copy everything, and there sometimes wasn't enough time to do it as carefully as I'd have liked. There was quite a bit that I thought might be of interest. No one realized what I was trying to find, by the way. They thought it was just more of what I'm generally looking for. You seemed to want to keep it quiet."

"Yes, that's right. For the present." Above anything else, he wanted to rip open the envelope, pull out the contents, and read them now. If this was what he hoped it was, it could well silence Bowles, if not bring him around to Rutledge's way of thinking. But good manners required joining the ladies at the table while Frances asked for a fresh pot of tea. Thanking Lucy, he set the envelope to one side, and did his duty as host with every appearance of pleasure.

Jean often claimed his attention, full of news about friends who had been called up or enlisted, and Frances, much less enthusiastic, named a good number of their own friends who were either enlisting or seriously considering it.

Changing the subject, Kate asked him where he'd been, and Rutledge replied that he'd come from the Yard. But Jean pressed him, as if to prove that his every move as a policeman was fascinating to her. "I was briefly in Kent, Tonbridge, in fact," he added lightly. "Conferring with a colleague."

He turned to Lucy, attempting to draw her into general conversation. But a few minutes later she set down her cup and said, "You'll be looking forward to your dinner and a quiet evening." Rising, she took her leave of the others, and he accompanied her to the door, asking if he could find a cab for her.

"As it happens, I'm just in the next street. Staying with friends. It was good to see you again, Ian. If this isn't what you need, you have only to send word to the cottage."

"I must tell you this information comes at a good time." He lowered his voice so that it didn't carry beyond the two of them. "You've read it. Do you see a connection with the vandalized grave stones?"

"I didn't tell the vicar. I didn't think you wished it to become general knowledge until you'd seen what I'd discovered. However, I did walk in the churchyard. I couldn't read the names on the damaged stones, of course, but I could piece together who these men were by looking at the graves next to them in the family plots. And there they were, in one of the reports about the trial. It seems to validate what you suspected."

He smiled. "You would make a great detective."

"But I am," she replied, returning the smile. "It's what I do, hunting for clues to the past."

"I've paid my sixpence," he reminded her. "I expect a copy of the visitors' guide."

"You'll have to wait a bit longer then. I hope you'll allow me to use what you've discovered. When—if—it can be made public."

He made no promises, reminding her instead, "You'll have fresher village information very shortly, if this war lasts any time. There will be heroes the villagers will want to remember."

She looked away. "The war has claimed its first victim in Beecham. Four friends went to enlist. One was turned down, something to do with his eyes. He went home and hanged himself."

"Good God." It was all he could think to say.

Lucy took a deep breath. "Good luck finding your man. Anyone could have bought a newspaper during that trial and learned the same information I've copied for you. It was public knowledge then."

He thanked her, and watched her as far as the corner before shutting the door and returning to the sitting room.

Jean said, "What were you two whispering about?"

"A tragedy. You don't want to know. It would distress you."

"I didn't realize you knew Lucy Muir," she added archly.

"I met her in the course of an inquiry. She was able to provide information that was critical."

Kate said, rising, "I'm awash in tea, Jean. And I have an engagement for dinner. Are you leaving?"

Jean smiled up at Rutledge. "Unless you can be persuaded to take us to dinner?"

"My dear, I have to finish a report for the Yard," he told her. It was his first intentional lie to her, but his mind was on the contents of the envelope lying beside the teapot. They were urgent—and difficult to explain without going into details that would trouble Jean, her cousin, and Frances.

Kate touched Jean's arm. "Your mother will be wondering where you are."

Frances, ringing the bell for the housekeeper, didn't press them to stay.

Rutledge asked, "Shall I drive you home?" It was the least he could do.

"Would you, Ian?" Jean asked.

It was well over an hour later when Rutledge came back to the sitting room. "They're safely home. And the motorcar put away."

"She wouldn't leave, Ian. Not after Miss Muir arrived. Kate did her best."

"Are you all right?" he asked, looking more closely at her.

"It's just this war. Everyone seems to be so thrilled. So in a hurry to fight. I've had what felt like an endless stream of visitors, calling to say good-bye. It's terribly depressing."

He said, "Men at the Yard have been resigning, intending to enlist. I expect it's just the beginning."

She roused herself. "You've been away a great deal of late. Jean has been complaining. I think Lucy was the last straw. Was it just to Tonbridge?"

"Today, yes. Although I think I've driven over half of England in the past month."

He didn't tell her that it was Fillmore Gilbert who had almost died. He knew it would distress her, as would his encounter with Dobson. He said, "Would you care to dine out? I owe you an evening pleasanter than your afternoon." He tried not to look in the direction of the envelope.

Shaking her head, she said, "Thank you, but no. We'll only be told about a dozen more friends who've gone mad with war fever. There's a roast from last night, I think. We will dine well enough here." And then what was troubling her came out in a rush. "Jean says you're trying to wind up all your cases so that you'll be free to fight. Like all the rest. That that's why you've been away so much of late. Is that why Miss Muir brought you that envelope? To hasten the conclusion to whatever it is you're working on at the moment?"

He laughed, though he didn't feel like it. "It wouldn't do for Jean's fiancé to appear to be less patriotic than her father." After a moment, he added more seriously, "I've found satisfaction in what I do as a policeman. The British Army is made up of men who feel the same way about protecting their country and its interests. Thank God for it. They have their duty as I have mine. I don't need to prove my courage, Frances. I've seen people die, and it's not pleasant."

It was the first time he'd let her hear the darker side of his work. She looked away.

And then she went on, as if goaded by her worry. "But what if it's a longer war than we think it will be. Or we start to lose, Ian? Like Belgium. *They* can't possibly stand up to the German Army. What if *we* can't? If France can't?"

"Then I shall have to reconsider. I shouldn't worry, if I were you. It's not likely to happen."

He realized suddenly that her concern might not be only for him. He said in a different voice, "Frances. Is there someone you care for?"

She turned back to face him, saying brightly, "No. No, of course not."

Just then the housekeeper came to ask when they wished to have their dinner, and he wasn't able to judge whether his sister was lying or not.

I t wasn't until much later that he was free to go up to his room and look at the contents of the envelope that Lucy Muir had left for him.

He whistled under his breath as he realized just how much work she must have done on his behalf. Unable to obtain copies of the newspaper columns, just as she'd said, she had written it all out in longhand. There was a word here or there that he'd had trouble making out. But the substance of all the pages spread out on his desk was clear. Evan Dobson had been desperate to recoup his losses on the bridle. It was a substantial sum for a poor man, and realizing that he would be out of pocket for the lot, even though he'd delivered the bridle as promised, he'd turned to the father when the son proved to be a scoundrel.

Whether Dobson had killed the greengrocer or simply taken his fists to him in frustrated anger, leaving the son to finish what he'd begun, was hard to say. But the son had sworn that he hadn't touched his father, and he was believed. Patricide was an unthinkable crime. The jury had heard the evidence and found Dobson guilty. And Atkins's son had walked away without paying for the bridle, inheriting his father's property as well.

What had become of the younger Atkins?

He turned to Lucy Muir's list, but there was no mention of his name there, after the trial.

The names of the jury seemed to leap off the closely written sheets of paper.

Hadley, Stoddard, Clayton, Tattersall. All of whom must have put the trial behind them and moved on. But not so the Dobsons. They'd never really recovered.

And Fillmore Gilbert, who no longer remembered it, who thought someone else must have been given that brief, had acted for the Crown.

Rutledge looked for the name of the judge—and found it. A man named Vernon Abner, who, given his age at the time, must have died long since.

Somehow Lucy Muir had even discovered that bit of information in the obituaries. He silently blessed her again.

Abner had died at age sixty-eight of a digestive disorder. His wife and only son had predeceased him, and he'd been buried beside them in one of the fashionable London cemeteries.

Lucy had ticked off the names of the jurors whose graves had been vandalized, with a footnote to that effect.

Eleven men accounted for. That left one man still in danger. Someone by the name of Chasten. Tomorrow, he'd ask Sergeant Gibson to find him, so that he could be warned.

No, there was one more. The policeman who had come to the Dobson house and taken away Henry Dobson's father. Taylor. Sergeant Ralph Taylor.

Rutledge sat back. It was all there. Everything he needed to prove his case. One man had done it all. The vandalizing. The murders. The attempted murder of Gilbert.

That was one short week among so many as the years had passed, but it had cast its shadow over the lives of more than a dozen people.

But what was it Dobson had held over the heads of the four men who had willingly drunk their milk, knowing it would kill them?

What had his mother told him that he'd remembered and used as an excuse to kill?

Even Lucy Muir hadn't been able to find an answer to that.

The graves had come first. And then the murders. Appetite whetted? Or had it just taken a little longer to find his victims?

Rutledge was up early the next morning, driving out to the London cemetery where, according to his obituary, Judge Abner had been interred. It wasn't a necessary visit, but he was curious to see if the black substance had been poured out there as well.

There was a morning fog, lying heavily over the Thames Valley, giving the landscape a featureless sameness that twice nearly made him miss his turn. But he found the cemetery, opened the unlocked gates, and let himself through.

He found himself thinking that it was a good thing he didn't believe in ghosts. The funeral monuments here were far more ornate that those found in most village churchyards. Tall plinths bearing urns draped in marble shrouds loomed over his head, angels with outspread wings seemed in the murky light about to take flight, and grieving figures reaching toward tombs had about them a Gothic air. Mausoleums designed like miniature houses or Greek temples seemed to shut him into the narrow avenues that led between plots of graves. He made a mental note at each intersection which direction he'd come from, uncertain if he could find his way out again. And the mist was getting heavier.

He had no idea where he might find Abner's grave, and at this early hour, there was no one else about. The man had died some fifteen years ago, and so Rutledge searched for an older section.

A pair of doves, asleep in the lea of a stone bench, flew up almost at his feet, and he started before he could stop himself, then smiled. What had he thought they were? The spirits of the dead?

Two more turnings, and then at the corner of the next intersection, he saw it.

The monument to the man who had sent Evan Dobson to the gallows.

At first it appeared to be part of the design of the monument. A rough-hewn marble obelisk broken off at a little less than midshaft, as in a life cut off before its time. But as he drew nearer, he could see that it hadn't been rough-hewn at all. Someone had taken a heavy hammer to it in a frenzy, smartly bringing down what must originally have been quite a tall shaft, then striking it again and again until the splintered shards lay like pebbles at its base.

Abner's name was still visible, as if that was intended. All around it was desolation. The smaller stones for his wife and son, his father and his mother, hadn't been spared. It appeared that the frenzy hadn't stopped until the marble had been utterly destroyed.

Whoever had done this wished he could reach into the grave itself and grind the very bones to powder.

17

Rutledge made his way out of the mist-shrouded cemetery, still feeling the shock of what he'd seen.

It was obscene in its way, a glimpse into a fury so violent that who-ever had done this must have been spent when he had finished.

The destruction had never been reported to the Yard. Rutledge was fairly certain of that. The groundskeepers must have notified the cemetery authorities, who could well have contacted the family or heirs of the dead man. But nothing had come of it yet. He didn't even know when this had been done. After the other graves had been van-dalized, but before Benjamin Clayton had been killed?

Or was this destruction what had sent Dobson to Moresby, to begin killing anyone from that fateful trial who was still alive?

Rutledge found a caretaker just arriving for his day's work. Dressed in coveralls and pushing a barrow, he was whistling to himself as he approached the tall cemetery gates. He started when he saw a figure looming out of the gray wall of mist that nearly obscured them.

Setting down the barrow, he waited until Rutledge came closer, a man and not a spirit, then said, "You could age a man fast, coming at him like that out of thin air. Looking for a family grave, are you?"

"There's a damaged stone in the eastern part of the cemetery. Someone by the name of Abner. How long has it been that way?"

The workman tilted his cap forward and scratched his balding head. "That obelisk pounded into rubble? Seems it was about the first week of July. One of the lads found it. We searched the cemetery, but there wasn't no other trouble. Whoever he was, he'd gone. One of the sheds was broken into, but nothing was taken."

"Was there a heavy hammer in the shed?"

"Aye, the big one we use to drive in stakes. But he never took it."

But he'd used it. Dobson couldn't have carried a tool like that with him. Not all the way from Somerset.

Rutledge thanked him and went on to where he'd left the motorcar.

He wished he could bring the Chief Superintendent here, to show him what they were dealing with. Not a twisted mind, but a passionate one that could take at least four murders in stride as deaths owed to him.

For a moment he wondered if the polite young man witnesses had described was one and the same as this angry slayer.

There would be no way to answer that until Henry Dobson was brought in for questioning

He drove on into the city and to the Yard.

Chief Superintendent Bowles, he was told by the first person he encountered, was attending a function with the Lord Mayor. The averted eyes of the constable he'd stopped left Rutledge with the feeling that the raised voices from Bowles's office the day before had raised more than a few eyebrows among those within hearing.

Cummins, however, was in, and Rutledge asked him for a few minutes.

As the Chief Inspector shut the door he grinned. "I gather you have survived the dressing-down, although a little singed around the edges."

"Unfortunately it was a day premature," Rutledge answered ruefully. "Last evening I was given more pieces of our puzzle. Today there was another."

He told Cummins first about what he'd learned about the killer's way of discovering the information he needed about each victim. "I suspect his mother had intended at some stage to take matters into her own hands, but she'd never been free to carry out whatever she'd had in mind. Or perhaps she expected her son to act for her one day. It's the only explanation for keeping in touch with the jurors and Gilbert over the years. I have even wondered if perhaps she'd hastened any of the dead to their graves. But we'll never know the answer to that."

"Go on."

Moving on to Fillmore Gilbert and spotting the man on the bicycle from the upstairs window of Swan Walk, Rutledge said, "I wanted to ask the Chief Superintendent to send a description to every police station in Kent to be on the lookout for this man. But he wouldn't even consider the possibility, much less act on it." He took a deep breath. "Then last night, I was given this. It's a handwritten copy of Bristol newspaper accounts of the Dobson case and trial."

"Very thorough work," Cummins commented as he read it through.

"All the names are there. Including Gilbert's. And the judge's name as well."

He glanced out the window. The mist was lifting, and in an hour or so, it would be replaced by bright sunlight. "I went to the cemetery this morning to look for him."

Cummins listened, appalled, as Rutledge described the grave site.

"Gentle God," he said softly. "I expect we can ask the cemetery authorities for a statement on when the destruction was done and what they think they know about it. I'll send Gibson or someone out there this afternoon."

"Not Gibson. I need him. There are two names left on the list of victims. A man named Chasten. And a policeman—most likely retired—by the name of Ralph Taylor. The arresting officer. We must find both of them as soon as possible. Still, it's just as well to document what happened in the cemetery. I can tell you, in the mist it seemed to take on a horror that it might not have had on a sunny morning."

"No doubt." Cummins studied the man across his desk. "This is a damning piece of evidence, Ian. The newspaper cutting. It all hangs together, just as you predicted. The question is, how are we going to find this man and take him into custody? Will he come peacefully, do you think, or will he make us pay dearly for it?"

"I can't answer that. I can only say, if we don't find him quickly, we might never put our hands on him. If I were in his shoes, as soon as I'd finished the last name on my list, I'd enlist. Under my own name or another, it wouldn't matter. I'd be out of reach."

"I have a feeling you may be right. If so, he's the only man in England that this war is bringing any good to. We've had more resignations tendered. For the duration. Most of them tell me they'll be back before the year is out. I pray to God they're right."

"I must return to Kent as soon as may be. I was ordered to see that inquiry through, and I can interpret that to mean I now have freedom to hunt for Dobson. And I've got to make Gilbert talk to me. I know everything now except why these men willingly died."

"Who defended Evan Dobson?"

"Now that's one of the interesting discoveries. It appears to be the father of the man who handled Joel Tattersall's trust. Simmons, the solicitor. Someone broke into his chambers in Wells fairly recently, but nothing was taken. I expect Dobson might have been looking for the file on his own father."

"How did Mrs. Dobson afford a barrister from Wells?" Cummins asked.

"I don't know. It will be worth looking into."

"Leave Taylor and Chasten to me. I'll see they're located straightaway and send word to you as soon as I have the information. Your task until then is to locate Dobson. Do you think he's still hanging about Swan Walk?"

"I doubt it. I'm sure I put the wind up him when I followed him into Leicester Square, there by Penshurst Place. He must know who I am by this time. The village of Swan Walk does. But then I know who he is."

"Be careful, Ian."

"What about the Chief Superintendent?"

"He ordered you to Kent. I'd go if I were you."

Rutledge grinned. "Yes, sir."

He packed a valise, sent messages to Jean, and left another for Frances, who was attending one of her meetings with volunteers.

Dr. Greening had just left when Rutledge arrived at Gilbert's house later in the afternoon. The nurse shook her head when he asked if there had been any change.

"I'm afraid not. I think he's asleep just now." She hesitated. "It might be time to summon his family."

"A day or two more won't matter."

He asked Mrs. Thompson if she could prepare a room for him.

"It will be ready when you are, sir. Is there any change in Mr. Gilbert?"

"I'm afraid not," he said, unconsciously quoting the nurse. "Is there a firearm in the house? A revolver?"

"There is, in the estate office. I haven't seen it, but I'm told it's locked in one of the desk drawers."

"Then if you will, leave the key in my room."

Soon after that he went back to Penshurst Place. But there was no bicycle propped against the arch. And of course no one in the church. He hadn't expected there to be.

When he came back to Swan Walk, he drove his motorcar around to the rear of the house and found a space large enough for it in one of the barns, to the dismay of the horses. Coming back around, he collected the constable's bicycle, still leaning against the house wall by the door, and stowed that in the barn as well.

He took his dinner in his room and waited there until the house was quiet. It was close on ten when he walked down the passage and spoke to the constable on duty. The man yawned. "They've made up a bed for me as well," he said. "I sleep during the day, when the servants are up and moving about, and return to my post in the evening. If that's all right."

"Yes. Good man. It's the night I'm worried about."

"In what way, sir?"

"It wasn't suicide. Whoever tried to kill Mr. Gilbert came into this house late at night and found him still awake. I don't think he'll risk coming when the staff is going about their duties. But the servants' rooms are well away from the rest of the house."

"Understood, sir." He lifted the heavy truncheon beside his chair. "I'll be ready."

Rutledge walked through the rooms of the ground floor, checking to see that the windows and outer doors were well and truly locked. Satisfied, he went back to the study where he'd met Gilbert on his first visit. Without turning on the lamp, he set about his preparations.

He took a cigar from the humidor, but before sitting down in the chair that faced the long windows, he unlocked and opened them wide. As he stood there a moment, he could hear a frog calling from a pond. He poured himself a small glass of Gilbert's favorite brandy and put it on the table by the arm of the chair.

In a dressing gown that was too big for him, wrapped in shawls, and slumped in the chair, he tried to shrink into himself enough that he might pass as Gilbert sitting there. The masquerade wouldn't have passed muster with the lamp on, but in the dark he hoped that it would appear to be natural enough.

It was a risk, waiting here when the danger could very well be upstairs, but he thought, on the whole, with the constable and a nurse guarding him, Gilbert was safe enough. And he had Gilbert's revolver now.

He cut and lit the cigar, drawing on it until he could see the glowing tip. He held it between two fingers, keeping an eye on it.

An hour must have passed, and then two. The house was quiet, settling around him with the sounds of the day's heat cooling off a little. A fox barked somewhere in the dark, and he refreshed the tip of the cigar for the tenth time. Rutledge had never been a smoker, but Gilbert was, and very likely he did most of it when there was no one about to tell him he couldn't.

It must have been easy for Dobson, here and at Hadley's farm, Rutledge thought, with windows open to catch the coolness of the night after a long hot day. He could have watched his victim for some time before stepping in and confronting him. It had been easy as well at the Tattersall house, using the unlocked kitchen door for access.

Just as another half an hour had ticked by, there was a sound. Barely on the threshold of Rutledge's hearing, keen as it was, and he tensed. The revolver was by his right hand, under the blanket, and he closed his fingers around the grip.

Footsteps on the grassy lawn—or in the drying beds of delphiniums by the terrace?

Or had he imagined it, because he'd been listening so long for it?

He could feel the hair on his arms stir as he waited. Something was out there. Or someone.

Lifting the cigar to his lips again, he made the tip flare out. It cut into his night vision, but he could still judge that the terrace was empty.

He stared out into the night. And someone stared back at him.

Minutes passed.

And then as surely as the presence had come, it began to fade away. Going the opposite way around the house? Looking for the motorcar out of sight in the barn?

Flinging off the scarves and shawls, dropping the cigar into the ashtray, Rutledge was through the windows and after him.

But Dobson moved in the night with the swiftness and certainty of someone who knew the terrain, and Rutledge was hard-pressed to keep him in sight as he used every bit of shadow he could find.

Along the west side of the house, Rutledge began to gain ground. He saw his quarry turn the corner closest to the drive.

There was a soft clink. And Rutledge heard the pedals of a bicycle begin to turn. He ran flat out, narrowed the gap, snatched at the handlebars, almost had his man, and then felt rather than saw the foot lash out at him. It caught him on the flat of his knee, and he was forced to let go as pain shot through his leg.

Dobson had reached the harder earth of the drive now, beginning to make better time. Through the shadows of the trees, Rutledge could see that the gates stood open. A matter of seconds, and the man would be out of range. It would be too late. Rutledge still held the revolver. He swung it up, took careful aim, and fired.

The bicycle jiggled wildly, then steadied.

Rutledge whirled and raced toward the barn and his motorcar.

But he never found the cyclist again.

As soon as it was light enough to see, Rutledge went inch by inch down the drive to the spot where he'd seen the bicycle wobble, and searched for blood.

He found it, large drops that led almost to the gates of Swan Walk; and there they stopped.

He'd hit his mark in the night as the bicycle moved toward the uncertain patchy shadows beneath the trees that lined the drive. But just how badly was the man hurt?

It was impossible to tell whether the wound had simply clotted or Dobson had managed to wrap something around it before he betrayed which way he'd turned.

Rutledge searched the dusty road for fifty yards in either direction, without any luck.

Lights had gone on in the servants' bedrooms at the sound of the shot, and the constable had come running, flinging open the house door, his truncheon at the ready. Rutledge had waved him back into the house as the motorcar sped down the drive. The study doors still stood wide, and Gilbert was still in danger.

But there had been no further excitement.

Over breakfast the constable had asked question after question, preparing his report, but Rutledge had had to shake his head in answer to most of them.

"No, I didn't expect him to come. I did hope that he would. No, I never saw his face. I fired in the hope of stopping him. No, it's not my revolver, it belongs to Mr. Gilbert. I tried to follow him, but it was useless. No, I don't know how badly he might be wounded. Yes, I believe I can put a name to him. Henry Dobson. No, I can't prove it. But who else would have come here, prowling about the house at that late hour? We'll have to wait until Fillmore Gilbert is well enough to tell us what happened to him. That should help us explain the events of last night."

"Will he come back, do you think? If he's been here twice now, will he try a third time?"

"I don't—" Rutledge broke off. "My good God," he said, and pushing back from the breakfast table, he ran for the stairs.

Sending the protesting nurse out of the room, he shoved a chair closer to the bed and said, "Gilbert. You've got to talk to me. What does Claudia have to do with this? Does she know something about this trial? Are you afraid the man who did this to you discovered she does, and will go after her next because of it? Is she holding something for you that he wants?"

But Gilbert ignored him, turning his head away. His breakfast tray sat untouched on the table by the bed, as if the man had already left life behind but hadn't yet found death.

"I know who we are dealing with. I know he's Evan Dobson's son.

We're going to find him, now that we have a name. But until we do, is Claudia *safe*? Should I warn her? Bring her here? Gilbert, for God's sake, you have to tell me what it is you're afraid of. He was back here again last night. Dobson. And he failed a second time to kill you. Damn it, man, *speak to me*."

The man in the bed moved until he could look Rutledge in the eyes. His own were blazing, the only part of the shrunken figure that was alive.

"Damn you. Leave it alone." His voice was rasping, as if his throat was parched. Rutledge reached for the glass of water, offering it to him, but Gilbert shoved it away with surprising strength.

"I can't leave it alone," Rutledge said. "You aren't Henry Dobson's only victim. There are at least two more out there who are in danger. And there's Claudia, unaware of the danger she may be in. I've got to find him. And I can't do it all on my own. What does Claudia know? What if he harms her sons?"

He waited, but Gilbert had nothing more to say.

After a moment Rutledge turned and walked out of the room, gesturing to the impatient nurse that she could return to her duty.

Why was Gilbert refusing to help?

Rutledge could think of several reasons. That what had happened to him was a shock. He'd been a barrister all his life, and a Crown prosecutor. He'd sent men to jail and to the gallows, and no one had ever touched him. The man he had been would have put up a stiff fight against Dobson, and possibly even won. This shrunken shell had been helpless, vulnerable. Already losing his grip on the mind that had made him famous, he was now beset with physical infirmities as well. Death had nearly snatched him away, and at the last moment, he'd been brought back to a world he didn't want to face.

Was that it?

Or did Gilbert even know why he had nearly been murdered? Had Evan Dobson receded so far into the shadows of his memory that the appearance of the dead man's son was confusing, inexplicable? Was he hiding from himself there in the darkness of his mind, because he had been helpless to understand, helpless to save himself by comprehending what Dobson wanted?

It was a shocking possibility.

Rutledge thought about his own father, who had still been vigorous and strong when he died. Cut off too soon, everyone had said. But perhaps the other way to see it was that he'd never had to grow old, ill, forgetful, and dependent.

He went down the stairs and out to the motorcar.

If Gilbert refused to tell him what he needed to know, perhaps Claudia could.

He stopped in Tonbridge long enough to speak to Inspector Williams, giving him the little information he had about Dobson.

"Wounded, you say? By whom?"

"I used the revolver belonging to the victim. I was interviewed by your man at the house, it's all there in my statement. Dobson has killed several times over. We're not convinced he won't kill again. And so I fired."

"Pity you didn't bring him down," Williams said harshly. "And saved the rest of us a good deal of trouble. All right, I'll send out a request to report anyone coming in to hospital or a doctor's surgery with anything that could be seen as a gunshot wound. Give me a description."

Rutledge told him. "Others who have seen him," he added, "have said that he was not the sort of young man anyone would expect to be violent."

"If he's what you claim he is, a man of little education, how has he been able to elude the police so long?"

"Because we didn't know where to look. It's as simple as that. No one connected the deaths, no one looked beyond them. It took time. Sadly, more time than we had. I don't want to hear that someone else has died."

"I'm glad my own patch is relatively quiet," Williams said, shaking his head. "We haven't had to deal with anything like this. But then ever since the Ripper case, we've known such a thing could happen. I'll stay with simple lust, jealousy, and greed, thank you very much." As Rutledge rose to leave, Williams added, "What's the news in London? Any hope that the Belgians will hold?"

"They're fighting hard, but they can't possibly go on much longer. Outnumbered, and without the weaponry to match what's being thrown against them? Still, long enough to get our men over there to back them up. I think that's what Belgium is hoping for. I've heard that the French are ready. But once Belgium is finished, it will be Paris the Germans want."

"For my part, they're welcome to it. Never cared for the French. A stiff-necked people."

Rutledge smiled. "You shouldn't speak ill of our Allies. We may soon be standing shoulder to shoulder with them along the Marne."

"I'll leave the fighting to the young." Williams pointed to his graying temples. "We'll need someone left in England to keep the criminal class from taking over."

From there Rutledge drove to Portsmouth.

Claudia Upchurch's husband had a surgery in the town, but he'd chosen to live just outside, in a village where the house had a distant view down to the sea.

Rutledge found Claudia at home. He'd met her a number of times over the years, but she had been older and so he hadn't known her well. She had always struck him as sensible and clearheaded, very like her father in his prime.

All the way to Portsmouth, he hoped he was right in his judgment of her. The last thing he needed was panic.

She walked into the room where he was waiting, and she looked harried. His first thought was that she must have heard the news about her father from someone else. Dr. Greening?

But her welcome was cheerful and warm, not fearful. "Ian? My goodness, it's been a while. How are you?"

Claudia had inherited her mother's auburn hair and her father's features cast into a more feminine mold. Rather than pretty, she was striking, and she had the taste in clothing that emphasized this. Today she was wearing a soft sea green summer dress with white lace trim, and it gave the appearance of cool elegance.

"I'm well, Claudia. And Sidney, the boys?"

"The boys have been taken to the seashore today. It's Sidney's birthday, and I've arranged a small surprise party for a number of his friends. Trying to keep a secret from three active youngsters has been a nightmare. And I had to lie to Sidney these past several days because we've been cleaning and polishing everything in sight. Of course he *would* notice, just when one doesn't want him to. You will stay, of course, and wish him many happy returns of the day?"

"As much as I'd enjoy staying, I'm afraid I can't. Can you spare a few minutes? I need to talk to you."

"It sounds serious," she said, gesturing to a chair.

"Your father's memory isn't what it once was. I'm sure you're aware of that. I'm curious about a trial in Bristol some years ago. You were a child, but I wonder if he ever spoke of it to you. One Evan Dobson was charged with the murder of a greengrocer by the name of Atkins."

Frowning, she considered the question. "The name doesn't mean anything to me, Ian. He talked to Mama about his briefs sometimes, but seldom to me. Did you know he started to write his memoirs? But I don't think he actually got very far. I've wondered if that was an excuse to withdraw from London and his friends there, to hide the fact that his memory had started to fail." She shook her head sadly. "That's been a burden to him. The worst possible thing for a man who remembered everything."

"Was there any trial that particularly worried him—that he seemed to wish had turned out differently?" Rutledge pursued.

She stared at him. "Are you asking me if he ever felt an innocent man was convicted?"

"I don't think it's that sort of thing." He gestured ruefully. "I really don't know what I'm looking for. Did he ever confide in you? Give you something to keep? Something he might have felt was safer in your care? Perhaps something in his files that he discovered or heard or learned too late to save a convicted man?"

Something in short that Dobson might think would exonerate his father?

"That doesn't sound like Papa. He was a good judge of character, he said, and he was thorough. I know, because I asked him that very question once when I was sixteen and thought I knew everything." She glanced toward the sitting room door. He could hear one of the maids calling to another. "I must be sure they have what they need. Is that all, Ian?"

"Not quite. Someone has attacked your father. No," he added quickly as she turned to him in alarm, "he doesn't want you to rush to Swan Walk and make a fuss. But we haven't caught the man yet. And I'm concerned that he might be mad enough to come here, looking for you."

"For me?" she said blankly.

"It has to do with the case I just asked you about. I may be wrong, but it's foolish to take chances. Lock your windows and doors tonight. Don't let anyone in after dark. I'll ask for a constable to come and keep watch."

Her eyes strayed to the sounds in the passage. "But the party—what am I to do about that? And the boys? What shall I tell them?"

"You know the people who have been invited. You'll be safe enough. But let the constable walk with you through the house afterward, to make certain all is well. This is no idle threat, the man is dangerous. I'm sorry to worry you, Claudia, but I wouldn't have come if I hadn't believed it was important."

"But you'll stay, won't you? And explain all this to Sidney?"

"I can't. There are others at risk, I must go. But don't trust *anyone* you haven't known for quite some time. This man has tricked his way into a number of homes, because he doesn't look threatening. Remember that." He carefully described Dobson. "He could even claim he has a message from your father, or that your father is dying and you're to leave at once for Swan Walk. He might tell you someone has been badly hurt and Sidney is urgently needed, in order to get him out of the house. Don't believe him." He rose. "You're needed elsewhere. Just promise me you won't take this lightly. Even if Sidney thinks it's a foolish precaution."

"I promise," she said uneasily, standing up and following him to the door. "I must say, you've frightened me more than a little."

"I'm sorry." He took her hand. "Keep your wits about you."

She went with him to the door and stood outside in the warm sunlight, but she had wrapped her arms around her, as if she were cold. "You're telling me the truth, Ian? That my father is all right?"

Not wanting to lie to her, he said, "He's a stubborn old fool, and Dr. Greening is despairing of him."

Claudia managed a smile. "Yes, that's just like him. When you see him, give him my love."

He bent to turn the crank. Claudia hurried back inside and closed the door firmly.

Rutledge took a deep breath.

Now to find the nearest police station.

It was in the village, and Rutledge had to use his authority as an Inspector at Scotland Yard to convince the constable on duty that the threat to the Upchurch family was real and immediate. To be on the safe side, he drove the man back to the house, to be sure he got there sooner rather than later.

Claudia's relief at seeing him went a long way toward convincing the man that Rutledge had been right to take precautions.

I n for a penny, in for a pound. He filled the motorcar with petrol, and turned toward Wells.

The solicitor, Simmons, was in, he was told.

The man looked up as Rutledge stepped into his office and said, "Oh God, what is it now?"

"A different matter from the Tattersall inquiry. At least I hope it is. Your father was a barrister, wasn't he? It says 'Simmons and Simmons' on the door."

"My father and I were solicitors. The barrister was his elder brother. My uncle. He had chambers in Bristol. When he died, most of his files came to us. Why?"

"Can you tell me if he defended one Evan Dobson against a charge of murder?"

He gave Simmons the date and the details.

Simmons shrugged. "God knows. We've got his files somewhere. Barry—my clerk —could probably put his hands on them."

"Would you ask him to have a look? It's rather important."

"I can't see how that will help you. It's ancient history."

"I'm sure it is. But there may be something in the file that will help me understand the dead man's son." And perhaps explain, he added silently, why Gilbert's daughter was at risk.

Simmons rose and came around his desk. "Very well. Let's get on with it."

Simmons had been right about his clerk. The man led Rutledge into a back room where the firm's history was shelved by name and date.

In twenty minutes' time he'd pulled down the box that held what Rutledge wanted.

He was given the clerk's desk to use as he sorted through the file. The papers from the Bristol chambers were yellowed, the ink fading in places, but he could read the lot.

The elder Simmons had had no illusions about his client's guilt or innocence. But he did what he could to convince the jury that there *was* doubt. Enough that a clear conviction would be impossible.

And here, amongst these papers, was something that Lucy Muir hadn't discovered, or hadn't realized was important.

Atkins, the greengrocer's son, had been represented by the elder Simmons in another case five years after the Dobson trial, for his role in a drunken brawl. The note pointed the reader to that file, describing Atkins as "now a resident of Wells."

Five years after Evan Dobson was hanged, young Atkins had already sold the greengrocer's shop and moved away from the village of Beecham to the town of Wells.

Rutledge finished the file a few minutes before the clerk came in to ask if he wished to keep the box out for a second day. It was a polite way of telling him that Barry was ready to go home, and Rutledge was keeping him from his dinner. He passed the box to the clerk, saying, "I believe I'm finished. Can you tell me if anyone else has looked at this material recently?"

"I don't believe anyone had looked at it since the elder Mr. Simmons—the present Mr. Simmons's uncle—died in 1903."

"Not even when someone broke into this office?"

"Nothing was taken. Nothing seemed to be disturbed."

But Tattersall's box was here, and Evan Dobson's as well. And Dobson's son had known where to find them.

Rutledge said as he watched Barry restore the box to its rightful place, "Why would a man of Simmons's standing in the legal community agree to take on an indigent leatherworker as a client? I'm certain the Dobson family had very little money at the time Evan Dobson was tried."

The clerk led the way out of the storeroom and locked it behind them. "Mr. Simmons felt it to be his Christian duty to represent the poor. He often took on at least one such case a year."

"Do you know anything about a Thomas Atkins? He moved from Beecham to Wells in the 1890s," Rutledge asked as they walked to the door. "He was something of a troublemaker. The elder Mr. Simmons represented him at least once."

The clerk's eyebrows rose. He repeated the name. "Odd that you should ask, sir. Thomas Atkins fell out of the loft of his barn and impaled himself on his own pitchfork only last month. A nasty business that. And not too many days before Mr. Tattersall was found dead." Barry was careful not to use the word suicide.

Rutledge remembered Inspector Holliston's words when first he'd called on him about the inquiry into Tattersall's death. He'd been listing the reasons why he'd sent for the Yard in the Tattersall case. He'd already had his hands full.

A hanging. We haven't decided if it's suicide or murder. A man killed in his farmyard, but we aren't certain whether it's murder or an accident. Fell out of the loft window onto his own pitchfork. A drowning that could be suspicious. There were enough people eager to kill the bastard. I wouldn't be surprised if one of them did it. And now Tattersall's death.

Rutledge had had reason to believe that Holliston had wanted to stay clear of anything to do with the solicitor Simmons. There had seemed to be no reason for the Yard to inquire into the other cases.

A departure from Dobson's usual method of dispatching his victims? He had chosen a brutal way to see to Atkins. What's more, it hadn't drawn the Yard's attention. The connection with Tattersall and Henry Dobson hadn't been discovered, to cast a new light on Atkins's death.

Rutledge thanked Barry, said good night, and walked on to the police station.

He found Holliston just leaving his own office, on his way home to dinner.

"Rutledge," he said, grimacing. "I thought we'd seen the last of you. I'd heard Joel Tattersall's death had been put down to suicide, but out of courtesy to the man's sister, that hadn't been listed as the final verdict."

"It's still open to question," Rutledge replied. "Meanwhile, there's another matter of interest to the Yard. Thomas Atkins's death."

"How the hell did you hear about that?" Holliston stared at him.

"You told me yourself. While giving me the reasons you had handed the Tattersall case to the Yard. You never mentioned a name— even if you had, it wouldn't have mattered. I didn't know Atkins existed at that stage. He was involved in a murder in Beecham some years ago. I don't think the fall from the barn loft was an accident. Someone had found him and killed him. Very likely around the time of the break-in at the solicitor's chambers."

"I don't know anything about that," Holliston said. "Come inside, this is no place to discuss Atkins."

They went into Holliston's office, and he paused to light the lamp. "The days are drawing in," he said as he sat down at his desk. "About Atkins. His death was determined to be an accident. He was alone at the time, and he often worked in the barn. There was no evidence to lead us to believe anything else. His tenant was in Wells, looking at a bull to improve the herd." He shrugged. "Not that anyone was surprised. Atkins had taken to drinking some years ago. That's why he couldn't afford more help. And there was a bottle in the barn, half empty. All in all he was a troubled and troublesome man. He bought that farm with money of his own, but he wasn't suited to it. His wife left him, he'd been involved in a number of schemes that never worked out the way he'd hoped, and that's when the drinking started. There were bruises on the body that weren't consistent with the fall, but Atkins was always resorting to his fists if he thought he'd been crossed. All right, I've told you what I know about Atkins. Now it's your turn to explain what this is about."

When Rutledge had finished, Holliston whistled.

"Are you certain about this?"

"As certain as I can be."

"But there was alcohol in Atkins's stomach. Not laudanum."

"In this case, perhaps laudanum was too gentle a weapon."

Holliston rubbed his face with both hands, then looked across at

Rutledge. "The inquest brought in its verdict. That will have to be changed to murder. Where is Dobson now?"

"We don't know. Possibly on his way to Portsmouth. I'll keep you informed."

"Thanks." They walked out together into the dusk. Holliston added, "I'll speak to the doctor again. About those bruises and abrasions. See what he can tell me in light of this information."

"A good idea." Rutledge turned to crank the motorcar. "I wish we knew where Dobson was tonight. I'd rest easier. And so would Fillmore Gilbert."

B y the time Rutledge reached Swan Walk, it was nearly dawn. He stopped by the closed gates. All was quiet. More bunches of flowers had replaced the wilted ones, and the huge crepe bows fluttered in the light wind, black splashes like great spiders in the web of the iron pattern.

He debated waking the household, decided against it, and drove on to Melinda's house where he knew he had a bed.

She was happy to see him, and his room, as always, was ready. She insisted that he must have a plate of sandwiches and something to drink, and he humored her while she filled him in on the news from Belgium.

"They are the bravest of the brave," she said, sadness and pride mingled in her voice. "They've stopped the advancing German Army at Liège. No one thought it was possible. But they can't hold forever, Ian. It's a question of when, not if, the Germans smash their way through. Meanwhile, London is flooded with refugees, those who can flee are leaving, for fear of retribution, once the Germans capture the country."

"And what are we doing?" Most of the British General Staff knew Melinda Crawford. Rutledge was reminded once more of Gilbert's comments about the Army as a family.

"Scrambling to put together an Expeditionary Force," she said. "We're spread thin, and I expect Kaiser Wilhelm knew this. I expect he believed he'd have France—Paris at least—before he could be stopped."

"And the French?"

"It's a long border. Colonel Crawford tells me the Germans intend to use the Marne Valley to lead them straight to Paris, while another force secures the Channel Coast so that the French can't be reinforced or resupplied from Britain. Effectively cutting France off."

If Colonel Crawford was worried, Rutledge thought, there was good reason for it. Melinda's cousin wouldn't alarm her unnecessarily. Rutledge had met him a number of times at Melinda's house, and he knew Crawford was an experienced and steady man, with a clear understanding of strategy and tactics.

"There's something else, Ian. Most of our generals are accustomed to a very different kind of war. What everyone took to calling 'Victoria's little wars.' The Indian Mutiny. South Africa. The Mahdi. Nasty enough, whatever you wish to call them, but nothing on the scale of what happened under Napoleon, when all of Europe was engaged. And in the end, of course, we were bound to win, however bloody it was. I'm not so sure, here. Napoleon was a superb general. We can only pray that the Kaiser isn't."

It was unlike her to be pessimistic.

Rutledge said, "Then this rush to enlist might well be a blessing after all."

She studied him for a moment. "You aren't planning to do anything rash?"

He smiled. "My hands are full with Yard business at the moment."

"See that they stay that way. I've lost a father and a husband to the Army. And I'm afraid Simon Brandon will be called back to active duty. You remember Simon. I should hate to lose that young man too. Or Ross. When last I saw him, he was talking about the Royal Navy.

And so many others I know. Even Ram was asking permission to go back to India and enlist. I ask you! At his age."

Ram kept her motorcar in perfect condition. Rutledge had had a look at the motor, and he'd told Melinda later that he'd nearly been blinded by the gleaming brass and copper.

Rutledge shook his head. "Temporary madness. It will pass."

But she wasn't convinced.

Later, he tried to call the Yard, using Melinda's telephone. But Gibson hadn't come in, and Cummins was in a meeting. Rutledge was told to call back later.

He went up to his room and slept.

18

It was late morning before Rutledge could reach Cummins at the Yard. And even then Cummins was brief.

"I'll ring you back at this number, shall I, in five minutes."

Rutledge agreed and waited, impatiently pacing the passage before finally walking out to the terrace.

Hearing the telephone bell at last, he raced back inside.

Cummins said, "Sorry. Everyone could hear me. Bowles is out for the morning, and I've commandeered his office so that we can both speak freely."

Rutledge asked, "Has Gibson traced either Chasten or Taylor?"

"Both, as a matter of fact. Taylor is in a Bristol hospital with pneumonia at the moment. Chasten on the other hand lives in Torquay. I've been trying to reach someone in the police force there."

"Damn! I was just in Portsmouth, speaking with Gilbert's daughter, Claudia Upchurch. I wish I'd known."

"Where are you now?"

"Back in Kent. I'm on my way to call on Mrs. Hadley." He gave the Chief Inspector a brief summary of what he'd done. "The younger Atkins, the greengrocer's son, is dead. There's no proof, but I'd guess that Dobson got to him early on."

"That just about rounds it out, doesn't it? I've sent word to the Chief Constable of Kent that we want to know if a man with a gunshot wound shows up anywhere for treatment. He'll see that the word is passed."

"We don't know how far he was able to travel."

"Still. Never hurts to be sure."

Rutledge said, "I needn't go on to Aylesbridge, then. Tell me more about Chasten. That's where I'll find Dobson. He can't reach Taylor until the man is out of hospital."

Cummins gave him the information, then said in a different tone of voice, "There's a problem here. For one thing, I've been talking to Bowles. The evidence is clear enough. Dobson's victims, save for Atkins of course, drank that milk of their own accord. It wasn't forced down their throats, they weren't under physical duress. If Henry Dobson was present, it's damned macabre, but I don't see how that will convict him of murder. Look at it from the Chief Superintendent's point of view, Ian. Even if you bring in Dobson, he can claim that he's not accountable for these deaths, that he'd come to ask about his father's trial and that guilt drove these men to suicide. There's a very good chance he can make a jury believe him. And laudanum is quieter than a revolver."

Rutledge could feel a surge of anger at Gilbert, lying in his bed, his face to the wall, refusing to help the police. Refusing to tell what he remembered about the night he nearly died.

"Go on," he said. The telephone had one advantage, he thought in another corner of his mind. Cummins couldn't see his face, read his eyes.

"And then there's the Hadley murder." Rutledge could hear Cummins take a deep breath before going on. "Watson, the man in Kent, is pressing for us to have another look at Peggy Goode, the housemaid who found the body. He's convinced that with Mrs. Hadley in Canterbury, Hadley could have made advances, and she tried to stop him by drugging him. Only, the dose was fatal."

"She would be more likely to scream the house down. What's more, she found the body."

"He thinks she came in to see if the drug had worn off, and if he was angry." Cummins cleared his throat. "She was terrified to find him dead. Simple answers are the best. That's the Chief Superintendent's motto. You know that."

Rutledge needed to pace, to think, but Melinda's telephone closet was too small. "What should I do? Let Kingston stand his trial and hope a jury will refuse to convict him? Let Gilbert die without speaking, as he wishes to do? And give up on Hadley? I can't do any of that. I'm going to Torquay to find Terrence Chasten before Dobson does. He may know something."

"For my part, I think you need a spot of leave. I have no way of knowing what my men do when they aren't on duty. Do you think Sergeant Gibson grows roses?"

Rutledge laughed, breaking the tension between the two men. Then he sobered. "Arrest will terrify Peggy Goode. And even if she's not convicted, she'll be marked for life. Mrs. Hadley might not want her back. How is she to earn her living? Try to convince Inspector Watson to hold off. Tell him—tell him we're evaluating new evidence."

"I don't know if I can persuade him. You'll have to give me something to use as an argument."

"God knows. Or—all right, tell Bowles and Inspector Watson that I'm waiting for a list of the hop workers, to interview them. And that will take some time. It's possible Hadley left those study windows open because he was expecting someone to come that way. Certainly not Peggy Goode."

"It might work. But hurry, Ian. We're dealing with Bowles."

Rutledge put up the receiver and went back to the terrace. Melinda was waiting for him, sitting in her favorite chair.

"It's Torquay. That's where our next victim is. And then possibly back to Bristol, when Taylor is well enough to go home."

She held out her hand to him, and he took it.

"Good luck, my dear. And somehow find the time to write to Jean. She'll be unhappy if she doesn't hear. To Frances too. She still hasn't agreed to a companion. At least your housekeeper is a sensible woman. That will help."

G ibson had discovered a good deal about one Terrence Chasten. Chasten had owned a Bristol foundry that specialized in toolmaking before broadening its trade as the city grew to include manufacturing scientific equipment. Some years later, he sold out to a competitor for a good price and moved to Torquay, where his brother lived. His brother owned a thriving bakery there, catering to the carriage trade. According to Gibson, the shop had moved to its present location five years ago, and Fred Chasten, the brother, had taken on more staff to keep up with demand.

Torquay, on Devon's southern coast, had been built to the north of the broad expanse of Tor Bay, once an anchorage for the Royal Navy. Now a popular seaside resort, it was still busy this late in the season.

Rutledge failed to find Chasten at his house, on a side street above a narrow wooded park, where modest villas had been put up before the turn of the century. A constable at the local police station gave him a description of the man, suggesting that he might be in the town at this time of day.

Rutledge finally ran him to earth just as Chasten was coming out of an afternoon musical concert in the domed confection of the Pavilion.

A tall, thin man with reddish hair and freckles that hadn't faded with age, he frowned at Rutledge and said, "Scotland Yard? What could you possibly want with me?"

"Is there somewhere we can talk privately?"

"I have a small room for business above the bakery. Will that do?"

The two men walked along the shaded streets to the heart of town, where the large baker's shop stood between a stationer's and a bookshop. The bakery was busy, and the women who came and went were prosperous and well dressed. Gibson had been right about the shop's popularity.

"We're thinking of adding a tea shop," Chasten said as they crossed the street toward it. "That's if we can convince the stationer to sell. We'll see."

Instead of entering through the main door, as Rutledge had expected, Chasten led him down a narrow service alley that ran between the bakery and the bookshop. A door toward the rear opened into a room piled with sacks of flour and sugar and tins of lard. A stairway to one side led up to the first floor. "The previous owner lived above the shop. My brother uses the space for storage and an office. This way."

They climbed the steps and came out into a passage with several doors opening off of it. Rutledge could smell spices, and Chasten, looking over his shoulder, smiled. "I'm used to it, but I'm told my clothes reek of cinnamon and nutmeg and cloves. That room over there is where they're stored. Ever since that business in Sarajevo, with the Archduke, I've doubled our orders of everything that has to come in by ship. The Germans have a sizable fleet of submarines. We'll find ourselves blockaded soon enough, mark my words."

The room he called his office was small, littered with bills and ledgers and even possessed a typewriter.

"I've taken over the bakery's accounts. The baking I leave to my brother and his staff. Fred doesn't have a good head for business, and retirement no longer suits me."

"You lived in Bristol before coming here?" Rutledge asked as he took the chair in front of the cluttered desk.

"I did. I was made a good offer for my firm there, and it seemed foolish not to take it."

"Are you married?"

"No. I never really had time to find myself a wife."

"While you were living in Bristol, did you serve on a jury?"

Chasten's face closed. "Why do you ask?"

"I'll take that as a yes. You needn't be concerned. It isn't the trial I'm interested in. However, it's the trial where all this began. Were you aware that Evan Dobson had a young son at the time he was charged with murder?"

"Dobson's wife was in the gallery. I didn't know that until when the verdict was read and she fainted. I wasn't aware of a son."

"His mother died in June of this year. Since then Henry Dobson has disappeared. And that's our problem. It appears that he's trying to right what he perceives to be a wrong—or he may view it as simple revenge. If that's true, you're very likely the next person on this man's list of victims. When he leaves your house, you'll probably be dead by your own hand."

"You are worrying me, Mr. Rutledge."

"And so you should be." Rutledge gave him a concise account of the other murders, holding very little back.

Chasten listened without expression, then shook his head.

"I have a difficult time believing that four able, intelligent men would calmly sit there and drink down a potion that they knew would kill them. There must have been something else to account for what they did. And you said yourself that in each case the Yard was prepared to accept another plausible explanation for what happened. Until, that is, you uncovered this connection to a trial."

Rutledge wondered then if Henry Dobson's other victims would have told him the same thing. That a warning would have done little or no good. He persevered. "It's an easier death than many choices a man might make. It's also quieter, which I think is one of the reasons it was chosen."

"If he doesn't believe his father was innocent, why does he want to kill the judge and jury? Besides, there was nothing about the trial that was unfair or questionable. The evidence, as I recall, was straightforward. We did question among ourselves what role the dead man's son might have played. But he wasn't the one who raised a fist to the older man."

"The son, Atkins, fell out of the loft of his barn directly onto a pitchfork. Coincidence? Or Dobson's doing? Remember, no one ever paid for that bridle. And there must have been very little money for Mrs. Dobson and her son to live on after his father's arrest. A child can grow up to hate when he watches his mother shunned and suffering."

"All right, he feels he must kill the greengrocer's son. That makes a little more sense. But the jury? We didn't ask to serve, after all."

"The logic of a man of business, who has never gone to bed hungry or done menial work to put food on his table or clothes on his back. That could be precisely what Dobson sees when he looks at the list of names. With the possible exception of the Alnwick schoolmaster, a good many of you went on to happy, uneventful lives."

"Well, I thank you for the warning, Mr. Rutledge. I will most certainly be on my guard."

"If I could find you so easily, Dobson will be able to do the same. He will come at night when he can be sure you're alone. I expect he watches, and bides his time."

"I understand."

But Rutledge didn't believe Chasten did. Chasten was arrogant. He'd built a company, sold it for a profit, and come to Torquay to lead a more leisurely life. Before very long he'd begun to take charge of his less successful brother's bakery, as he himself had said, leaving the baking to the staff. Even setting up an office for himself in the unused rooms above. How long before his brother found himself managed into a position of having very little say about his own shop?

There was nothing more he could do here. Rutledge rose, thanked Chasten for his time, and found his own way out.

Walking back to where he'd left the motorcar, he asked himself what more he could have said to convince Chasten to pay attention to his warning.

Exasperated with the man, Rutledge spent the next hour and a half driving the streets of Torquay. He'd seen Dobson walk, he'd seen him run. Broad shoulders, a slim build. Was he limping? Carrying his arm stiffly? Or already fully recovered from his gunshot wound?

He got nowhere. In the end, he sought out the police station and described for the sergeant on duty a man that the Yard considered a person of interest.

"If you find Dobson, he should be taken into custody at once, and Chief Inspector Cummins at the Yard should be notified. He'll send someone down to question the man."

"What's he done, then, that the Yard wants him?"

"He's a witness to murder," Rutledge said. "We want him badly."

The sergeant looked at his notes, and said bluntly, "This could describe any number of men. I don't hold out much hope."

"He has a Somerset accent. It's likely he uses a bicycle to travel. And he suffered a gunshot wound fairly recently. That should help."

The sergeant looked up at that. "I'll put out the word."

Rutledge went back to his motorcar and found a hotel where he could spend the night.

He slept for an hour or two, then dressed and walked to the tree-lined street where Chasten lived. Solidly middle-class and comfortable, number 21 sat at the top of a half dozen steps. There were hydrangeas and smaller plantings on either side of the short walk to the door.

Rutledge found a vantage point down the street from which he could watch the house, and settled himself as best he could. There was a sharp breeze off the sea that hadn't dropped with sunset, and before long he felt its bite.

He stayed there until an hour before sunrise, when it would soon be too light for someone to hide.

And there was no sign of Dobson.

It had been a long shot, he told himself as he headed back to the hotel. And yet all that previous afternoon he'd had a feeling that Dobson was here in Torquay.

Was it possible he hadn't found Chasten yet? Or was he still troubled by his wound? He couldn't afford to be noticeably injured. Any sign of weakness and he couldn't be sure his victim wouldn't put up a very good fight.

Rutledge slept for several hours, came down for a late breakfast, and saw the black headlines in the morning paper. They painted a dire picture of Belgium's plight.

The Army, pathetically small to begin with, still held out. But losses were heavy, and it was thought they would have to surrender soon or face utter annihilation.

And there were reports of atrocities as the frustrated German Army turned on civilians. Refugees reported witnessing many horrors, but there was no independent confirmation. Still, posters were appearing that showed Belgium's suffering, and this had increased enlistments. Meanwhile, a British Expeditionary Force was preparing to go to Belgium's aid.

Rutledge set the paper aside. He had visited Belgium and France a time or two while a student at Oxford. The place-names were familiar to him. He had been to Liège, to Bruges and Brussels. Had seen the fort where the worst of the fighting was taking place.

It made the war personal.

He waited two more days in Torquay, keeping watch at night, until he began to worry about Taylor, the policeman who had come with his men to take Evan Dobson into custody.

Was he still in hospital? Or sent home?

After some difficulty he found a telephone and put in a call to the Yard.

Sergeant Gibson reported that Taylor's pneumonia had begun to improve. But he was in hospital still, and very weak. There was talk of a convalescent home when he was finally released.

What's more, reports from the constable keeping watch on Fillmore Gilbert were not encouraging.

"He's eating, not with appetite, mind you. But eating. It's a start." Gibson's voice had an echo of doubt in it.

Rutledge remembered Gilbert pushing away even a glass of water.

"A start," he agreed. "But I want to know as soon as he is talking."

"There's a new inquiry on your desk," Gibson added.

"Pray God, nothing to do with laudanum."

"A shotgun," Gibson said. "Sir."

Rutledge thanked him and put up the receiver.

Where the hell was Dobson? If he wasn't in Torquay, and Taylor's illness in Bristol presented a temporary obstruction, where was he?

Rutledge wasn't completely convinced that being hunted himself had deterred Dobson. He wouldn't have come back to Swan Walk, if that were true. His wound, then? Or had he spotted Rutledge in Torquay and simply decided he could outwait Scotland Yard?

In the end, Rutledge spoke to the local police again, asking for a watch to be set on Chasten's house. The Torquay Inspector, whose wife bought her breads and cakes from the Chasten bakery, agreed to send a constable. "Or I'll have nothing for my tea," he said with a wry smile. "My wife has no time for baking. She's on a War Committee, God help us all."

T he plight of Belgium was the talk of the city when Rutledge reached London.

Jean and her mother had joined a charity to help Belgian refugees, many of whom had escaped from the fighting through Le Havre. Some had decided to remain in France because they were French-speaking, while others, already in a state of shock at what was happening to their country, were unconvinced that France herself could hold.

Rutledge had arrived just after six, and was dragooned into helping at one of the teas organized to raise money. And he listened to the speakers who had been invited to tell their stories.

They were harrowing. Families separated, husbands at the Front, children without parents—it was enough to open the pocketbooks of those present, and afterward, Rutledge spoke to one of the men. He'd been a policeman in Liège, wounded in the fighting even though he wasn't with the Army, and suspected of being a saboteur. And so he had left hastily, to avoid being taken by the Germans.

"It's an unfair fight," he said in perfectly good English. "We have no artillery. Only machine guns. But we know the countryside, we know each other, and we know how to defend ourselves. Learning to use a rifle is not difficult. Learning to kill a man with it is harder. But the time comes when we must decide. Let them kill me—or kill them first and worry about my soul later."

When the evening was over, Jean had asked what Rutledge and the middle-aged Belgian had found to talk about.

"Realities," he said, and changed the subject.

The next day when he went back to the Yard, he learned that Mrs. Hadley had given the policemen who had come to arrest Peggy Goode a very difficult time, and they had had to withdraw to lick their wounds.

"She told them in no uncertain terms," Cummins related to Rutledge, fighting to keep a straight face, "that if they took her maid into custody on such ridiculous charges, she would see to it that Inspector Watson was reduced to constable for his ineptness and his blind disregard of facts staring him in the face. As the Hadleys were on friendly terms with the Chief Constable and Mrs. Hadley has an uncle in the Home Office, Watson backed down, even apologized for disturbing her. He sent a telegram to the Chief Superintendent, but Mrs. Hadley's connections put Bowles off as well. I advised him to let everyone cool down."

It was galling for Rutledge to admit to Cummins that he hadn't brought in Dobson. Afterward he walked on to his own office and began to work his way through the files sitting on his desk before looking at his latest assignment.

Jean would be pleased, he thought, that he would be in London for the near future. The inquiry was in Hampstead, a dispute over a will that had escalated into violence.

"There's so much happening, Ian," she had told him just last night as he'd driven her home. "We've been working with the refugees as you know, and there's another tea coming up. And a dinner party tomorrow night. Papa had promised to be here, but we aren't quite sure where he is at the moment. He's been out of touch, and Mama feels he's already in France. There's a charity auction next week, and we've been assured that a member of the Royal Family will attend. Mama is going to ask you to escort us."

In fairness to her, he had agreed to help in any way he could.

That evening, after another charity event, she asked, when her mother had gone upstairs, giving them a few minutes alone, "Have you given any thought to being married in September? If Papa has leave, we could find a way to arrange it. I've had the last fitting for my gown. If we were married, surely the Yard would understand and not send you so far away."

He couldn't tell her that the Yard cared little for the happiness of its men. Murder didn't wait on the convenience of a policeman or the arrangements made by his wife. She would come to accept this, as most women did. Mrs. Cummins had a very active social life, a large group of friends. It occurred to him that he could ask Cummins for advice. He had met Mrs. Cummins, he thought she would be kind to Jean and help her.

But he still had qualms, and he said then, "Jean, are you sure you'll be happy as a policeman's wife?"

She laughed. "I've been a soldier's daughter. Why should it be any different? And I love you, Ian, more than you know. We'll be happy, I promise you."

Earlier, he'd found Frances at home, dressing to go out for the evening. She asked for his help doing up the buttons in the back of her gown, and reminded him that there was a cold chicken in the kitchen, if he had no other plans.

"Who is the lucky fellow tonight?" He stood back to admire her in the dark blue gown. "You'll break his heart."

"He hasn't a heart to break. But he's such fun, and I need to think about something other than the war. Those poor Belgians. We're so lucky, Ian." She shivered. "I want it to stay that way forever."

He kissed her cheek. "I'll be late myself. I must drive Mrs. Gordon and Jean back home when the event is over."

But the event was marred by the news from France.

Belgium had lost its fight with Germany. The German Army was now racing toward the French Frontier.

19

Through Cummins, Rutledge was able to stay in touch with Torquay, Tonbridge, and Bristol.

Taylor was now in the convalescent home, still surrounded by nurses and patients and doctors. That was very good news.

Chasten on the other hand had tired of the watch on his house and had asked that it be withdrawn. Torquay, also suffering from a shortage of men, was happy to agree. Rutledge swore in frustration when he heard the news.

Gilbert still refused to speak.

Rutledge tried to understand his silence. But there was nothing he could do about it.

In Kent, the inquest on the death of Jerome Hadley was to be recalled.

Henry Dobson, meanwhile, appeared to have vanished. Cummins was of the opinion that this was good news. Rutledge, who had tracked him for weeks now, was convinced he was simply waiting.

From Hampstead, Rutledge was sent to Carlisle and then on to Derby. He was grateful that all three inquiries had been straightforward, swiftly concluded. Each day that he was out of reach of London tested his patience.

He took Melinda Crawford's advice and wrote letters. To Jean, to Frances, and to Melinda, at one point asking a favor of her.

He was just about to leave Derby when the telegram came from Cummins.

Taylor was dead.

There had been a setback, and he was too frail from the pneumonia to survive.

That left Chasten. And Chasten had left himself vulnerable. But Dobson hadn't taken advantage of that fact. What was he waiting for?

I t was almost the end of August when Rutledge arrived in London from Derby. Just as the first salvoes of the Battle of Mons began. On the Belgian side of the border with France, the capital of Hainaut Province, and a city of heavy industry based on its coal, Mons was strategic. The British Expeditionary Force had reached it two days before, in an effort to close the coast road to the Germans. The French Army was poised to stop them wherever they crossed the Frontier.

At Mons the battle lasted two days, and then the outnumbered British were forced to retreat. But they managed to do it in an orderly fashion. They were professionals, and they knew what they were about, even against such odds.

It was the beginning of a long, slow withdrawal toward the coast and the city of Ypres. Still in Belgium, but for how much longer? How soon would it be a French town that was besieged?

London talked of nothing else. The call for volunteers had gone out afresh, and it was a race against time to train the new Army and get it into the field before the British Regulars had to be reinforced.

Jean, greeting Rutledge when he stopped by the Gordon house on his way home, asked if he had changed his mind about volunteering.

"There will be general conscription soon—it's almost certain. You won't wait for that, surely not. They are saying we need every man. That it's only a matter of time before the tide is turned. Don't you want to be a part of this brave undertaking?"

He'd seen the bands in the streets, stirring up enthusiasm as men marched behind them in growing numbers on their way to enlist. Firms urged their young men to go, and the poor and unemployed were pressed to sign their names.

"I have a duty, Jean. To a man facing trial in Moresby. To others whose lives have been cut short. To myself, as a sworn officer of the law." Yet he knew men who had left the Yard to fight. It had added immensely to the work those who remained had to deal with. There had been talk about calling men out of retirement, if the drain on resources went on.

"Yes, yes, I see that, of course I do. But you will consider it, won't you? As soon as you've finished what you must do?"

"Yes, all right, I promise."

When he reached the Yard, he sought out Cummins to ask for news.

Cummins shut his office door and lowered his voice. "Taylor died of natural causes. I made certain I was kept informed. That leaves Chasten. Why hasn't Dobson tried to reach him? Is it possible that Chasten sided with Evan Dobson?"

"He seemed to view the trial as a matter of duty. Unpleasant but necessary. Unlike Benjamin Clayton, who appeared to be disturbed by his part in it. Certainly not the sort of man Mrs. Dobson would have any reason to feel sympathetic toward." Rutledge took a deep breath. "Even if we've stopped the killing, there are the dead Dobson has left behind. It isn't over."

"I've wondered about that, Ian. He'd had everything his own way, until Swan Walk. He'd seemed invincible. You've shown him he wasn't."

"If I were Terrence Chasten, I wouldn't wager my life on it. Why won't Gilbert talk to me? I'm beginning to wonder if his mind has been damaged to the point that he can't tell us what happened that night. It's a bitter thought."

"Did you know the constable was recalled from Swan Walk? And from Mrs. Upchurch? The local constabularies are as shorthanded as we are."

"Where do we stand with the Hadleys' housemaid, Peggy Goode?"

Cummins smiled but he was watching Rutledge's face. "The inquest was reconvened, and the evidence against Miss Goode was presented. Mrs. Hadley was asked if she had gone to Canterbury because she was on bad terms with her husband and suspected him of straying. That was a mistake. Mrs. Hadley challenged everyone in that room to speak up at once if they possessed any knowledge of her husband's philandering. And when no one came forward, she went on to say a good bit more about the evidence in hand. She was quite knowledgeable about some matters, mentioning the fact that the police were refusing to look at other deaths too similar to her husband's to be ignored, and until they did, any verdict calling her husband's honor into question would result in dire consequences. What's more, the housekeeper and the rest of the staff backed up Mrs. Hadley, saying that they felt the police had leapt to conclusions without evidence to support them. I wonder how Mrs. Hadley came by such detailed information. You haven't been to see her, have you, Ian?"

"No, sir, I have not." The answer was firm, unequivocal.

"Did you write to her?"

"No, sir, I did not." But he had written to Melinda, whose slight acquaintance with the Hadleys provided the opportunity for a condolence call.

"Yes, well. However you managed it, Mrs. Hadley's speech left everyone stunned."

"What did the inquest say to that?"

"They're back to person or persons unknown."

Rutledge smiled for the first time. "Can we work a similar magic in Moresby? Although I'm afraid we have no Mrs. Hadley there to speak for Kingston. Just the opposite, in fact. What did the Chief Superintendent have to say when word got back to him about the outcome?"

"The worst of it was, the Home Office wanted to know what it was all about, and what this further evidence might be that was brought up in the inquest. Mrs. Hadley does indeed have friends in high places. An uncle, in fact." Cummins hesitated, then said what was on his mind. "Regarding Bowles. You do know that very likely you've made an enemy for life, there?"

"I didn't set out to do that."

"I'm quite sure you didn't. He always weighs the main chance, Ian. He doesn't want to bring a case to trial and have it fall apart in the Crown's face. Sadly, he doesn't possess the imagination that will let him judge the difference."

Rutledge said ruefully, "I shall have to learn a better way to deal with him."

"He holds the keys to the Yard, Ian. And so, yes, you will. You can run rings around him. But he must never know that. Or even guess it. On to other business, I've arranged for you to give testimony in the Moresby trial."

"That's very good news. Thank you. Inspector Farraday won't care for it, but I'll do my best to put a spoke in his wheel."

Cummins reached into his drawer and pulled out a sheet of paper. "I've been saving this for you. It came yesterday from Tonbridge. It might be worth looking into, although strictly speaking it isn't a Yard matter."

Rutledge took the sheet from him and scanned it, then looked up at Cummins. "It appears to be a missing person inquiry."

"Yes, Tonbridge forwarded it because it had to do with a wounded man. I happen to know there's nothing else on your desk at the moment. And you have a motorcar, which makes the distance to Tonbridge negligible."

Nodding, he said, "We asked for doctors and hospitals to report gunshot wounds—without any luck."

"Indeed."

Rutledge was on his feet, his mind already busy. "I'm on my way."

Rutledge stopped at home and encountered Frances on the stairs as he was going up them.

"There you are," he said. "I'm on my way to Kent. I'll take you as far as Melinda's, if you like."

"Thank you, Ian," she said, holding up her face for his kiss. "But I have engagements here. This new Army needs everything. And until the manufacturers catch up, there's much we can do. The weather is changing. Soldiers will soon be asking for warm stockings and sweaters and gloves. I'm working with a group of women who are willing to knit these things, but someone has to supply the patterns and the wool. And it must be khaki wool, not colors. I'm told the enemy would only be too glad to see our men decked out in blues and reds and greens. It makes sense."

She was so earnest. It was a new Frances, and he was surprised by her dedication and enthusiasm. What's more it suited her, and he told her so.

"By the way, there's a letter for you in Papa's study. It's from Ross Trevor. If your letter is like mine, he's telling us he's joining the Royal Navy. He always did like the sea."

"What a shock that must have been for his father."

"Yes, I think it must have been."

"I'll pick it up on my way out."

When he came downstairs again, he paused briefly to look at the post lying on the desk. And stopped, staring at the unfamiliar handwriting on another envelope bearing an address he knew.

Terrence Chasten. Torquay. Rutledge shoved it into his pocket along with Ross Trevor's letter, wondering briefly how Chasten had discovered this address rather than writing to him in care of the Yard. If it was a personal plea to withdraw police protection, it could wait.

I t was raining by the time he reached Kent, dark clouds foretelling heavier weather before nightfall.

The farm he sought was south of Tonbridge and well off the main road. Even with directions, he missed the turning he was after.

The house was set back from the road, Victorian and plain, but like the barn and the outbuildings, sturdy and in good order.

The woman who answered his knock looked up at the stranger on her doorstep and said hopefully, "Are you from Tonbridge? Have you found him then?" She was middle-aged, her fair hair already tending to gray, her face lined from work and the sun. Tall and strongly built, she looked like the farmer's wife he'd been told she was.

"I'm from the police, Mrs. Abbot. I've come about your missing farm worker."

"Step in, then. I'm just washing up from our dinner."

He followed her down the passage into the kitchen, ducking under the low lintel.

It was a bright room, four square but large enough to feed a family at the table at the center. Three girls, stair steps in age, were sitting at the table, and they stared up at him with curiosity bright in their faces.

"This is Mr. Rutledge, girls, and he's come to speak to your mama. Go and see to your chores, and then I'll read to you before bedtime."

They rose reluctantly and went out the kitchen door into the yard. Mrs. Abbot watched them for a moment and then turned back to Rutledge. "The kettle's on. Would you care for tea, then?"

"Yes. Thank you."

She busied herself with the tea things, her back to him. She said, as if it didn't matter, which told him it mattered a great deal, "Have you found Tommy, then?"

"Not yet. I'm afraid we don't have enough information to be going on with. Could you tell me more about Tommy?"

"Not really." She seemed wary, concentrating on measuring out tea into the pot. Then as if making up her mind, she turned to face him. "I found him on the road, bleeding from a gash in his leg, and his bicycle in the ditch. I'd been to market in Tonbridge, and I was too tired to take him back there. And so I loaded him and his bicycle into my cart and came home. I didn't know what else to do."

"Weren't you worried that you were taking a risk, that he was in trouble of some sort?"

"It was a nasty injury, going right through his calf. I hadn't noticed that on the road, not how bad it was, because he'd wrapped it in his shirt. He was on his way home, he told me, and someone had tried to steal his bicycle. There was a long scrape on the metal bit that holds the front wheel in place. I could see it for myself. And so I believed him."

Like so many others?

"Go on."

"He was feverish for days. I didn't have the money for the doctor and nor had he, but I'd doctored the livestock, I told myself it was no different. But it took a good bit of my time, what with the girls and the farm. I'm a widow, and I thought, when he was well again, he might repay me for what I did and help out here. And so he did. Not that he could do much at first, he couldn't hardly walk for days, but he made himself a crutch and he did what he could. I told him I'd pay him, if he'd stay on. He was good with the girls too. Judith is six and he taught her how to feed the hens. She'd been afraid of the cock before. That meant Nan, who is eight, could deal with the cows, and Bethy, who is ten, could help me with the mucking out. That left time to work in the vegetable garden of an evening, while the girls washed up after dinner. As he got stronger, he took on the milk cow, and he did the heavy work, said it helped his leg."

"What happened to him?"

"It's been a week now. One morning Tommy told me he thought he'd seen someone walking around outside and peering in the windows. He said he was afraid of this man, and didn't want him harming us. I wondered then if he owed money to this man, if taking the bicycle was just a means to collect. Before I got around to asking him, Tommy left in the night. He'd taken the clothes I'd given him and his bicycle, and a little food. That was all. He didn't touch the butter and eggs money."

"So it wasn't a question of theft?"

"I'm afraid something has happened to him. He hasn't come back, although I thought he might. Then, when I went in to market two days ago, I reported him to the police as missing. I told them about the leg, and how that man had worried him. And I said to tell him I wanted him back, if they found him. I can't help but wonder if he was afraid for us, and went home, out of that man's reach. Tommy was from Somerset. It's a long way to go on a bicycle. I wonder if his leg is up to it."

But Tommy would find it easy enough to beg a lift. He'd managed to find help even in this farmhouse.

Was it Dobson? If it was, then there was nothing for him in Somerset. He'd be heading for Torquay.

Rutledge asked Mrs. Abbot to tell him what Tommy looked like, and her description seemed to fit. As did the wound. It also could explain where Dobson had been hiding.

The youngest daughter, Judith, was peering in the kitchen window, her nose flattened again the glass. He smiled at her, and she grinned back at him, a gap where her two front teeth belonged.

"I'll do what I can," he promised Mrs. Abbot. "But I wouldn't hold out much hope. I expect Tommy needed to put space between himself and Kent. As for the man he saw outside, I wouldn't worry there. He could have been anxious enough to imagine him."

She brought him his cup of tea. "I wondered about that too. Except that he did watch the road. As if someone would come down it one day." She stirred her tea and said philosophically, "He did us no harm, but I'd like to have him back all the same."

"How strong was he, by the time he left?"

"Middling strong, I'd say." She looked squarely at Rutledge. "You're not telling me he tried to go after this man? To protect us. So he wouldn't come here?"

"I doubt it."

"Well, that's a relief, anyway. He used to listen as I read to the children of an evening. He said his mother had always been too tired to read to him. She was a widow too, poor woman. I've managed to keep the farm going, for the sake of the girls. But it's trying."

He'd finished his tea and asked to see Tommy's room. But when Mrs. Abbot had taken him upstairs to the small bedroom under the eaves, there was nothing to tell him who the occupant had been.

The trouble was, he wanted it to be Dobson in the worst possible way.

But the burning question now was, where had he gone from here?

Rutledge stopped in Tonbridge for a brief report to Inspector Williams, then drove on to Swan Walk. He didn't allow himself to hope. It was a formality only.

The rain had stopped, but not for long.

The crepe had been removed from the gates, and there were no longer any flowers there. He continued up to the house, to find that the crepe had also been removed from the door. The housekeeper's doing?

The constable was gone as well, but he knew that, although he was surprised to find the nurse had left too. What's more, Gilbert was now sitting downstairs in his usual chair overlooking the terrace.

He was thinner, if that were possible, and he looked a good ten years older, with deep lines in his face and haggard eyes. As Rutledge walked into the room and greeted him, he said, "Sit down."

Rutledge brought another chair to put next to Gilbert's, remembering how he'd sat here in this room himself, covered in shawls and blankets, while Dobson watched warily from the flower beds. He glanced out at the delphiniums, and saw that they were no longer blooming in profusion. It wouldn't be long before they would be faced with colder weather, even the first frost.

Gilbert said, "The French brandy is on the tray. Glasses, too."

"So they are." He went to pour the silky golden liquid into two of them, and brought one back to Gilbert, as he'd done once before. It seemed like years ago, not a matter of weeks.

"War's not going well," Gilbert said, taking his first sip and then setting the glass to one side.

As he did, Rutledge glimpsed the dark metal of Gilbert's revolver hidden in the shawls that kept him warm.

Gilbert saw his glance. "I won't be taken by surprise ever again," he said grimly.

"You can't shoot him. You know that."

"But I can. They won't hang me for it. Even if they try, I'll have had the satisfaction of it."

"You shouldn't be telling an Inspector at Scotland Yard such things."

"It doesn't matter. You want the bastard as much as I do. I heard the constable telling Greening that you'd shot at him yourself."

Rutledge couldn't think of a suitable reply.

Gilbert sipped his brandy for a time, and then he said, "I can talk about it now. I couldn't before. I thought it was the laudanum and nearly dying. Whatever, it left me confused, unable to be sure what was real and what was not. Do you know what it's like to doubt your own mind? To wonder if you've run mad? No, of course you don't. Not at your age. But I've sat here and pieced it together again. A bit at a time. It took me days. Weeks, for all I know."

Rutledge waited.

"He came through that window, Ian. Bold as brass, and wished me a good evening. I had no idea who he was. He was dressed neatly, but in work clothes. I thought perhaps he was about to ask me for money. Instead, he asked if he might sit down. He'd come a long way, he said. I'll admit, I was intrigued. I wondered just what it was he wanted. And after a while, he told me."

There was a long silence. Once more Rutledge waited. The afternoon was far gone. There would be no sunset, with the heavy clouds in the west. It would be dark soon.

"He was Evan Dobson's son. I had no idea who Evan Dobson was and told him so. He seemed surprised, as if he expected me to remember. Then he explained that I'd been the Crown prosecutor in his father's trial. His father was convicted, he said, and on the twenty-eighth of June, he was hanged. It had been scheduled at dawn, that hanging, but had been moved up to noon. His mother wasn't allowed to see him or even claim his body. And so she had sat in her cottage with her son by her side and watched the hands of the clock move inexorably to noon. She had cried out then, like someone in torment. He hadn't understood why. He knew his father had been taken away and couldn't come back. That's all. When he was older, his mother told him why."

Gilbert held out his glass, and Rutledge, without a word, got up and refilled it.

"He said he'd come to make me pay for what I'd done. I asked him if his father had been innocent, and that didn't seem to matter to him. It was the *loss* he had felt, and his mother's pain, and his father's inexplicable absence before he understood why this was so." Gilbert swirled the golden liquid in his glass and watched it catch the dying afternoon light.

"And then he asked where the kitchen was, that he'd come a long way and would like a glass of milk. I asked him if he were armed, and he said he wasn't. God help me, I told him where the kitchen was, and he left me sitting here and went out through the door there." Gilbert cleared his throat. "He came back soon enough, the glass of milk in his hand. I asked him if he'd helped himself to the silver while he was about it, but he assured me he was an honest man and didn't intend to steal a penny."

"Nor did he, from what I learned later," Rutledge agreed.

"I didn't know that. At any rate, he set the glass of milk there on the desk and took a vial from his pocket. He began counting the drops as they went in. I thought he was intending to drink it, that he intended to kill himself in front of me and leave me to take the blame. For the first time I began to feel a rising alarm. But he didn't touch the milk. After he'd put the vial away, he said to me in as quiet and sane a voice as my own, 'You have a daughter, I think. How much do you love her?'"

When Gilbert didn't go on, Rutledge felt his stomach churn, unable to stop himself from imagining the horror that was to come.

Gilbert drained his glass, and put it aside. "God forgive me. I told him that she was my only child and of course I loved her. 'Enough to die for her? Would you willingly give your life for hers?'"

And Rutledge remembered Mrs. Hadley's quiet, intense voice saying, *Ours was a love match. I'd have given my life for Jerry. And he for me.*

"He made a bargain with me," Gilbert went on, fighting to keep his voice steady. "If I would drink that glass of milk, right now, in front of him, he would swear on his mother's memory that he would not touch my daughter. But if I refused, he would leave, and at a time of his own choosing, he wouldn't offer her a glass of laudanum. He would hang her. Just as his father was hanged. And he reached under his coat and brought out a rope with a noose, which had been wrapped around his body. And he quietly recited her address and described her house to me, so that I would know he'd been there and he would do what he said he would do. That obscene noose was in his hands, moving a little, swinging a little. And I believed him. So help me God, I believed him."

His voice broke. It was several minutes before he could continue. "I'm an old man. My mind isn't what it used to be. I told you that myself, when you came asking questions about a trial I couldn't remember. I had to send you elsewhere to find the information you wanted. I asked him then what pleasure he got from threatening me if I didn't remember Evan Dobson. And he said it was no pleasure at all. But he and his mother had lived with loss and the torment of knowing that his father had been among strangers when the noose had been put around his neck and the hood dropped over his head. To spare the onlookers, he said. And so his father's last sight in this world were the men whose duty it was to take his life. Efficiently and coldly. There was no warmth or kindness or sorrow for his family. Even the priest brought for him hadn't cared, because he never came to tell Dobson's mother that his father's last thought was for her. He could have, you know. That was the sad thing."

Gilbert stared out into the growing darkness, then stirred, as if coming back from a long way.

"And so his son was about to inflict the same pain on me. I would die facing someone who had no warmth or kindness or pity for me. My daughter would live with the grief of losing her father, and wonder why I had chosen to take my own life, without a word of explanation or farewell. It was rather diabolical. He didn't seem angry, I think I'd have been less shocked if he had been. I could have understood it. He just sat there, waiting for me to make up my mind, that noose swinging before my eyes, and no mercy in his. And so in the end, I couldn't take the chance. I couldn't put Claudia at risk. So I asked for the glass and I drank it down quickly, bitter as it was. He sat there watching me until I had passed out. In no hurry. I remember at one point reminding him that I had his word that Claudia wouldn't be harmed. And he simply smiled at me. I didn't know then whether he would keep his promise or not, if he would find pleasure in killing her too. By that time it was too late. I didn't hear him leave. My last thought was that if I'd refused, I'd have had time to warn her. That I had failed her after all. It was terrifying to know that, as the darkness came down. I never expected to see the light again."

Rutledge sat there, stunned.

Benjamin Clayton had had a daughter, who had just left the house to stay the night with her brother and his wife.

Joel Tattersall had a sister who was sleeping upstairs.

Jerome Hadley loved his wife deeply, and she was in Canterbury with friends.

He didn't know how the headmaster Stoddard in Northumberland had felt about his wife. But there was the school he loved.

And of course Gilbert had had Claudia.

Rutledge didn't know if Terrence Chasten loved anyone. Would he drink a glass of laudanum to save his brother?

Gilbert put his head back against the pillow behind it. Spent, and silent.

Rutledge sat there with him, watching the night come down until it was dark enough to get up and light the lamp. He found himself thinking that if Dobson came again and Gilbert shot him, he himself would have no reservations about it. It would be justified, whatever the law felt about it.

After a while, he rose. "It's past time for your dinner. Let me fetch your housekeeper."

"I'm not particularly hungry tonight."

"You realize that I must go back to the Yard and tell them what you've told me."

"If you do," Gilbert said, rousing himself, "I will deny it. Every word of it. Do you think I want Claudia to know this? That I didn't have the courage to protect her? Why do you think I've refused to speak all this time?"

And there was Mrs. Hadley, who loved her husband deeply. She had spoken the words about dying for each other figuratively. As a measure of that love. How would she feel if she learned that he had quite literally died for her sake?

"Then why have you told me? You know I represent the Yard."

"Because you need to hear what manner of monster you're dealing with. And if you are very smart, you'll see that he never hurts anyone else again. Do I make myself clear?"

"I can't shoot him in cold blood."

"But you can keep the world from hearing what he did. Do you think Claudia and the others who survived his victims can bear to listen to what I've just told you? It's a final cruelty. He's better off dead, I tell you."

"I understand what you are asking. I don't know if it's possible to keep it all out of the record. I give you my word I will try."

He didn't offer to put Rutledge up that night. Gilbert bade him good night and went on sitting by the open window. Waiting.

20

The rain came back, harder this time, as Rutledge drove through the gates of Swan Walk and made his decision. Continue to London, or go to Melinda Crawford's house? It was nearer. And he didn't think he could face Frances, with Gilbert's voice still echoing in his ears. She would guess at once that something was wrong. And he couldn't tell her.

When Melinda came down the lovely staircase to greet him, her hair in a long plait behind her back, the lace at the throat of her dressing gown gleaming brightly in the lamplight, she took one look at his face and said sharply, "Ian. What has happened?"

"It's an inquiry. That's all. It—has turned rather nasty."

Relieved, she nodded. "I expect they sometimes do," she said, not pressing. "Are you hungry?" Over her shoulder she said to Shanta, "Tea, please. In the sitting room."

"I'd rather go up to bed. I'm not very good company."

"You'll be the better for a little food and some tea. Go along in, while I dress."

"No, don't worry—" he began, but she stopped him.

"I'm going to dress. Go and sit down before you fall down."

And so he walked on down the passage to her sitting room and sat there for a time staring into the empty hearth. He could hear the fast patter of the rain on the terrace outside. It was soothing in its own way.

It was then he remembered the letters he hadn't read. He took his friend Ross's out of his pocket, opened it, and scanned the brief message.

Ian,

I've decided to do my bit. My father isn't best pleased, but I don't feel I can look myself in the shaving mirror if I don't. I've chosen the Navy. You know how I feel about the sea. I'll be back soon enough. Look after my father for me if anything happens. Not that I expect it will, but if it should, he will need you.

It was signed, simply, *Ross*.

He sat there staring at the familiar handwriting. He and Ross had always been as close as brothers. He couldn't even contemplate something happening to him.

Folding the sheet and returning it to the envelope, he took out the second letter, the one from Terrence Chasten.

Only it wasn't from him.

An unformed hand had written, *You have a sister. If you go on trying to find me, I will know. And you will put her at risk.*

His fatigue fell away. He was on his feet and heading for the door when Melinda came down the stairs again, impeccably dressed as always. At the same moment, Shanta came through the door from the kitchen stairs, a tray in her hands.

He said, "I must go back to London. Now."

"I won't hear of it," Melinda said, stepping between him and the door. "What's this all about?"

"I can't tell you. It would take too long."

"Nonsense. There is nothing in London that can't wait ten minutes." She took his arm and drew him back toward the room he'd just left. "You will eat your sandwiches and drink your tea, and then you can go."

"Melinda—"

"It will do you no good nor London either if you find yourself in a ditch. Have you noticed how the rain is coming down?"

There was truth to that. The roads would be quagmires. He sat down at the tea table, and Shanta put the plate of sandwiches in front of him and set the teapot, two cups, the cream jug, and the sugar bowl in front of Melinda. She proceeded to pour the tea, and with a quick glance sent Shanta away.

"Now then. What's happened?"

"The man I've been searching for. He threatens Frances, if I go on hunting him."

"Do you believe him? Or is it an idle threat?"

"I believe him." He had to, he'd sat there listening to Fillmore Gilbert's agony, and he'd believed every word.

"Then you can stay the night here. Frances will be perfectly safe, and you won't frighten her to death rushing in to protect her."

It made good sense. But he found it hard to think of food as he pictured her as she had been on the stairs earlier, her mind full of wool and what could be done with it to help the troops. Alive with enthusiasm.

Melinda handed him his cup of tea, and added sugar to her own. Stirring vigorously, she said, "Now then. What's this about? Why can't you simply put in a call to the Yard and ask them to safeguard her?"

Rutledge tried to explain. To put into words how isolated he was.

"It has to do with a murderer I've been searching for. The one I didn't know existed when I went to Moresby. The Chief Superintendent refuses to listen. He can't see that sometimes we have a feeling about a case—about a person—even about the evidence. I've learned to listen to those feelings. It would be useless to go to Bowles with this letter. He'd tell me to ignore it and get on with what needed to be done."

"I'm not surprised that you do," she said. "You're your father's son. Those feelings were what made him such a good solicitor."

"I expect you know probably more about this man than anyone other than Chief Inspector Cummins. More, possibly, than is safe for you to know." But not what Gilbert had told him as the sun had dropped down in the black shadows of the western sky.

She said slowly, "I've told no one about the letter you sent from Derbyshire. Mrs. Hadley was very grateful, you know."

Ignoring his sandwiches and his tea, he went on as quietly, "The problem is, without the backing of the Yard, this threat to Frances can't be ignored. Cummins would do his best, but he would have to justify round-the-clock surveillance."

She sat there, trying to conceal her anger from him. Anger at his isolation and Bowles's stupidity. Rutledge reached into his pocket and took out the letter purportedly from Terrence Chasten. As she looked at the envelope, he said, "Dobson's next victim is this man Chasten. What Dobson is telling me is not to interfere while he goes after him. I called on him in Torquay, and while I think Chasten believed me when I told him he could be in grave danger, he seemed to feel he could deal with this man Dobson himself."

"And can he?"

"I don't know. In his shoes, I wouldn't take the risk. Still. I'm too close to catching him. That's why Dobson wants me out of the way. Why he's threatening Frances."

She opened the sheet of paper folded inside and read it. "Dear God, Ian," she said, looking quickly up at him. "Do you think Dobson has actually come to London?"

"I don't know. I have to take it for granted that he can do what he says. I can't guard Frances all the time. I'm here in Kent—or Derby—or wherever I'm sent. The question is, how rational is this man? What if next month I'm sent to Torquay or Somerset or Bristol on another case entirely. Will he give me the benefit of the doubt? Or will he make good on his promise then? If I go after him, she's in danger. If I do nothing, he will be out there forever. And I won't *know*." He hesitated, not wanting to tell her why he was so afraid for Frances. But Melinda had been a soldier's daughter, a soldier's wife. She had been one of the child heroines of the Great Indian Mutiny—the Sepoy Rebellion—carrying water to the wounded and to men fighting to save Lucknow from the mutineers bent on slaughtering the entire garrison. She had seen death in many guises.

"What is it?" she asked, with that uncanny ability to read him. He was never sure why she could. Whether it was love or only her deep knowledge of people. "What are you afraid to tell me?"

He smiled wryly. "I didn't want to upset you. It's rather ugly."

But in the end, she made him tell her.

After a long moment, she said, "Of course you have to take this threat as real. The question is, what will you do about it?"

"The best thing is to ask Chief Inspector Cummins to assign someone else to the case."

"I don't think that will answer," she told him. "Will you tell your sister? You must, you know. If only to allow her to be watchful. It could make all the difference."

Melinda Crawford was right, as she so often was.

"I don't want to. I don't want to drag her into my wretched world of crime and murder and fear."

"In my view, Frances will deal with it better than you think. Be grateful this man doesn't know about Jean."

Rutledge felt his heart lurch. "I was so worried about Frances, I didn't consider— If he's found where I live, he could just as easily find Jean."

"He could have discovered your identity easily enough. He saw you in Penshurst Place and Swan Walk. A question casually asked in a pub one night about the man from London? It's not that far from the village to London."

"I'd have seen him. I'd have recognized him. Besides, I usually drive to the Yard." But sometimes he didn't. Sometimes on a fine day, he walked. Dobson needed only to wait at the Yard to see where he went. And he needn't follow him all the way. He had already shown how easily he could discover a street and a number.

It was an appalling thought. It made the danger to Frances even more frightening.

"You've got to find him. This man Dobson. But not tonight, my dear. He won't touch Frances lightly. She's his hold over you. He knows you'll protect her at any price."

He wished he could believe her. He did, in his mind. He knew she was right. But he'd lost his parents, and he couldn't lose Frances. Not to this man. Not after what Gilbert had told him. And now that made him afraid to lose someone *he* loved. Just like the others.

"That letter was posted from Torquay," Rutledge said, willing himself to think clearly. "It means he's there. Looking for Chasten. I'll have to do something about that. But I shall have to see Frances safe first. I hesitate to ask, to put you at risk. But could I bring her here?"

"By all means. But tell her as little as possible, so as not to worry her. It's settled. Now go up to bed. A night's sleep won't make this go away. On the other hand, you'll be rested enough to plan properly."

He finished the sandwiches, if only to please her. Rising, he came around the table and took her hand. "I'm glad you don't live in the north of England."

"My dear, it's much too cold in the north." She walked with him as far as the stairs. Watching him go up them, her mouth tightened. If she could have put her hands on this man Dobson just then, she knew she wouldn't be responsible for her actions.

Back in London, Rutledge went first to the Yard and spoke to Cummins.

He said nothing to the Chief Inspector about the reasons Gilbert had willingly gone to his own death. But he did tell Cummins that the former Crown prosecutor had confirmed that it was Dobson who had invaded his home and nearly killed him.

Cummins said, "Why did he change his mind and speak to you? I didn't expect it."

"Nor did I," Rutledge said. "Sergeant Gibson needs to alert the police in Torquay. Dobson has a bicycle. I'll drive down straightaway. I can recognize him."

"You haven't said. Why was there no struggle, no attempt to call for help? Was Dobson armed?"

In his mind's eye, Rutledge could see again the glint of the revolver beneath the shawls that wrapped Gilbert's thin shoulders and body.

"We weren't there. I expect we'll never know the pressure Dobson brought to bear."

Cummins stared at him. "It's the difference," he said after a moment, "in whether it was suicide or murder. Legally."

"We weren't there," Rutledge said again. "We can't judge."

And he was gone before Cummins could frame his next question.

F rances was writing notes to contributors at the last fund-raiser, to thank them for their support.

He waited until she had finished, sealed the envelopes, and affixed stamps to them.

Turning to her brother, she said lightly, "If you had stood for Parliament instead of becoming a policeman, you could frank these for me. I'm spending a young fortune on stamps."

"Do MPs still have the right to sign a letter in lieu of stamping it?"

"How do I know? But it seems like such a good idea, don't you think?" She set the letters in a basket, ready to be posted, then said, "You've been sitting there very patiently. Am I to hear the lecture again on bringing in someone to live here and protect my good name? It won't do, Ian, you're wasting your breath."

"No. It's a case I've been working on. Somehow the man I believe to be a killer has found out where I live. I must leave for the south coast, and I would rather you went away for a few days. Just as a precaution. Would you mind terribly?"

Frances regarded him. "Are you quite serious? Are you really in danger?"

"I doubt it. Still. My hands are tied. I can't be in two places at once. I'd be happier knowing you weren't here. Melinda is always asking you to spend a little time with her. Why not go there? The Yard is looking for this man. We'll have him in custody soon enough."

It took a little persuasion. But in the end, she agreed. He thought she might even have been glad of an excuse to be away from the talk of war, at least for a bit.

"If he's found this house, whoever he is, there's Jean to think of. You're there nearly as often as you are at home."

"Yes, I know," he replied, trying to keep the worry out of his voice. "I'll deal with that later. Go and pack what you need. Do you think Toby MacBride would run you down to Kent?"

He was one of her numerous escorts, and at last word, he hadn't rushed off to enlist.

And so it was arranged. An hour later, Toby was at the door, and it was time to carry Frances's luggage out to the motorcar.

Rutledge left instructions with the household, then went up to pack. He wanted to call on Jean. He'd missed her, he wanted very much to see her. It felt as if their entire engagement had been at the mercy of the Yard and most especially Dobson. But he knew it would possibly mean putting her at risk.

And then he was on the road to Torquay.

With him he carried the letter Dobson had written using Terrence Chasten's name. He made the best time he could, driving through the night.

As it was, he was already too late.

21

Although it was barely seven in the morning, Rutledge went first to the house where Chasten lived. The housekeeper who opened the door told him that he was most likely at the shop at this hour. He drove on into the center of the town. The bay was a sparkling silver under the early sun, but he had no time to notice it.

A crowd had gathered in front of the baker's shop and he saw a number of blue uniforms moving slowly down the service alley, engaged in an arm's-length search. Another constable was posted at the door of the bakery.

It could mean only one thing. Dobson had got here first.

Rutledge had to show his identification twice to get through the throng of people. The constables who passed him through were tight-lipped.

The rear door was standing wide, and as he crossed the threshold, he could hear voices from above. He took the steps two at a time and came out in the passage where Chasten had his office.

The door to Chasten's office stood wide, and in the lamplight spilling out from it, he could see an overturned glass of milk, the contents spreading across the desk and pooling beneath an upended chair. A trail of trampled and torn papers led to another door that stood open. Here stairs went up to the attic storeroom above. He started up them, dreading what he would find there, and was just in time to see two constables lowering a rope that had been flung over the rafters.

A police Inspector wheeled about as he heard Rutledge on the stairs. He wasn't the man Rutledge had worked with earlier.

"Who are you, and who the hell let you through?" he snapped.

"Scotland Yard. I have an interest in this matter. Who found the victim?"

"His brother. He's downstairs." He turned his back on Rutledge and watched as the constables finished with the rope, leaving it snaked across the attic floor. Nodding to one of the men, he said, "All right, thank you. Go on down to the bakery and help with the statements."

He turned to Rutledge, saying only, "Sefton."

"Rutledge."

Sefton gestured to the remaining constable, and he switched on a torch.

In the dim light it had been hard to tell, but now Sefton pointed to one of the square oak girders that supported the rafters and the roof. "The rope was tied off over there."

Someone else was coming up the stairs behind Rutledge. As the constable switched off the torch, he turned to see a slender man carrying a doctor's bag. He nodded to Rutledge as he came into the attic and stared at the rope on the floor.

"Where is he, then?"

"Downstairs."

"The constable said he was badly knocked about."

"Yes. You'll see for yourself."

The doctor turned away, and Sefton, with a last look at the rope, its twisted, thick knot an obscene lump on the floor, made to follow him.

"You'll want a look at Chasten as well," he said over his shoulder to Rutledge. "You have an interest here, you say. What can you tell us about the man we're looking for?"

"His name is Dobson. Henry Dobson."

Sefton's eyebrows went up. "You seem damned sure of that. Is he likely to kill again? On my patch?"

"It's not likely. He was after Chasten."

Sefton nodded, and went on down the attic stairs. He turned to his right in the passage, where the doctor was already heading for a second flight farther along that must, Rutledge thought, lead to the bakery itself. "What's more, I'd like to hear how you arrived here in such a timely manner. Crystal ball gazing at the Yard now, are you? A pity you weren't in time to warn Chasten."

Rutledge smiled dutifully. He could smell burning bread, heavy on the air. He said, "I wish we had a crystal ball. I'd spoken earlier to one of your colleagues. A man named Reed. He put a watch on Chasten's house for a week. Unfortunately our quarry was recovering from an injury and we lost track of him. So, apparently, did Chasten. And the Yard sent a telegram to him yesterday, warning him that Dobson was likely to be here in Torquay. One also went to your station."

"John Reed has enlisted. So far I've only got through his current cases, not the backlog. As for any telegrams, only military traffic is getting through just now. There seems to be a twenty-four-to-thirty-six-hour delay on anything else. You're telling me this killer lives in Torquay?"

"Somerset, before he began killing people."

He had Sefton's full attention now. "So you'd come from London to find out why Chasten wasn't already a victim?" He had stopped at the foot of the stairs, twisting his head to look up at Rutledge, behind him. "How many more victims were there?"

"Four. Another survived. Barely."

"I'll want to know more," Sefton said, his eyes unfriendly. "But it will have to wait until I've dealt with Chasten."

He pushed open the door at the bottom of the stairs, and Rutledge found himself stepping into chaos, overlaid by heat, an even stronger smell of burning bread and heavy smoke from the ovens that irritated the eyes.

The room was a shambles. Ingredients strewn everywhere, pots and pans scattered around the floor, and the long table that held the great bowls of rising dough lying on its side. Like the office, the kitchen had seen a vicious struggle.

A man was sitting in a chair in the far corner of the room, his head in his hands. At the sound of the door opening, he lifted a battered, tear-streaked face as the policemen picked their way across the cluttered floor toward him.

As his gaze shifted from Sefton to Rutledge, there was instant recognition in his eyes.

Rutledge himself stopped short. "But *this* is Terrence Chasten."

"It is," Sefton replied over his shoulder. "The other one is in there. With the doctor." He gestured to a room just beyond where Chasten was sitting, then shouted to the constables in the front room of the bakery. "Someone get that damned bread out of the ovens."

"Gentle God," Rutledge said under his breath. He was still staring. It appeared that Chasten's nose was broken, and one eye was fast swelling closed. His hands, dangling on his knees now, were bloody, skinned, the knuckles swelling. One ear was torn and bleeding onto his coat. The man didn't seem to notice.

He knelt by the man's chair and said, "Tell me what happened?"

Sefton said brusquely, "There's no time for that. In here."

Rutledge rose, put a hand on Chasten's shoulder, and followed the Torquay Inspector into the next room, which had been an office and now was where employees kept their aprons and gear to clean the ovens and kitchen.

The doctor was working over another man lying on the floor, a tablecloth spread across his body.

"Severe concussion, but he'll live," he said, without stopping.

Rutledge moved around him to take a better look.

The unconscious man was so like Chasten that it was a shock. The same red hair and freckles, although the last stood out like flecks of blood against his pale face.

"Fred Chasten. Terrence's brother. Enough alike him to be his twin, but two years younger. Your man nearly hanged him."

"All right," Rutledge said, keeping his voice low. "It's my turn to ask the questions now. What happened? Do you have Dobson in custody?"

"I wish. The man who comes in at four was unwell, and Fred Chasten took his place this morning, to start the ovens, ready the first loaves of bread—the usual. He went upstairs for something, and there was your killer. I don't have all the story yet, but Fred fought him, lost, and was being dragged to the attic. Terrence Chasten came in to find his office a wreck, and he went looking for his brother. He prevented the hanging, but their attacker got away down the kitchen stairs, and Terrence went after him. You saw the state of the kitchen. But this man—your Dobson?—ran for it when a passing constable heard the fight and stopped to investigate. He got out through the rear door and disappeared before the constable had a clear look at him. We've no idea what state *he's* in. But Chasten saved his brother's life."

"It was Chasten who put his brother at risk," Rutledge said shortly. "I warned him, and he felt he could defend himself. Dobson didn't realize they were so alike. Neither did I. In the dark, he must have seen Fred leaving the house and went after him, taking him for Terrence."

The doctor stood up. "I think he's stable enough that he can be moved to the surgery now. I'll send someone for a stretcher. He'll need watching and a great deal of care. His brother got off lightly by comparison."

He went away to see to the stretcher. Standing there by the injured man, Rutledge gave Sefton a brief account of Dobson's past and his victims.

"There's more, but it can wait." He left the Inspector to watch over the bakery owner and went out to Terrence Chasten again. The scorched pans and charred loafs were out of the ovens, and the overturned table had been righted. Someone had opened the door to the street to clear away the smoke. Standing by the chair this time, Rutledge said, "You didn't believe me. Your brother paid for it."

"I thought he was looking for me. I thought I could deal with him."

"It never occurred to you that Dobson might mistake Fred for you?"

"No. God, no."

"Do you make a habit of holding your brother in such low esteem? You've come here, nearly taken over his business, and then you leave him to the mercy of a killer. Did you even tell him about the danger you were in?"

Chasten tried to shake his head, and stopped when it hurt. "He was after *me,* not Fred. I didn't think it was necessary."

Arrogance. Sheer, bloody *arrogance.*

"You're a fool, Chasten. You owe your brother more than you can repay."

"But I saved his life."

"It was probably the other way around. Because he'd already fought Dobson to a standstill, you found it easier to save your brother," Rutledge said, not hiding the contempt in his voice. "I saw what Dobson did with a heavy hammer, smashing a large marble monument to dust. If Dobson had found you in that office alone, you'd have been no match for him. And an hour ago, Sefton would have been cutting you down from that rope."

"Dear God." Chasten looked away then. After a moment, he said in a much more subdued voice, "Still, I must tell you. It was your warning that saved both of us. It gave me the advantage. I knew who that man must be. I knew why he was here. Before he could recover from the shock of seeing two of us, wondering which one he was about to hang, I hit him. That's when he dropped the rope and came after me."

"Count yourself lucky, then."

Rutledge turned away as the doctor returned with the stretcher and two constables. Chasten got to his feet and stumbled after them into the small room where his brother lay. Sefton came out, leaving the others to it.

"I must telephone the Yard directly. Where will I find a telephone I can use at this hour?"

Sefton gave him directions, adding, "I'll see you at the police station when I've finished here."

By late afternoon Rutledge was free to find a room in one of the hotels and threw himself down across the bed in exhaustion. He didn't sleep without dreams. Dobson was there, always just out of sight around a corner or walking out of a room filled with people while he dodged this way and that, trying to follow.

O n Rutledge's orders, Tonbridge in Kent sent men to the farm where Dobson recovered from his gunshot wound, but he failed to return there.

Half of England was on alert. Day after day, reports poured into the Yard. Mostly false alarms.

The manhunt went on. A guard was placed on Gilbert's house once more, and Chasten's. But there was still no sign of the man. He appeared to have vanished once more.

And Frances Rutledge stayed in Kent longer than she'd expected.

Meanwhile, the war news grew uglier with every passing day. The BEF had fallen back to Ypres, but they were still blocking the coast road.

There was a ridge above the town. Passchendaele. No one quite knew how to pronounce it or to spell it until men began dying there.

Rutledge was preparing to leave for Moresby when a Captain Devereaux from a Wiltshire regiment came in one afternoon. Bowles ordered everyone to listen to what the officer had to say.

He was eloquent as he described the need for men who had experience in the police to train as officers. Bowles looked around at his men and asked, "Right, then, who's for it?" His gaze rested on Rutledge for an instant longer than necessary and then moved on.

Afterward, when the men had been dismissed, Devereaux followed Rutledge into his office and sat down without waiting for an invitation.

"A hard business, convincing men to serve when the news from France is so bleak. The hotheads have already come forward. Finding officers is another matter." He paused. "A Major Gordon suggested you. Ideal officer material, he said. A natural leader. Any interest in soldiering, Inspector?"

"There's a case coming to trial in Moresby. I have to be there to give evidence."

"It's wartime. Surely a statement would do?"

"Not in this instance. This man isn't guilty. I know it. I've had the devil of a time proving it. And if I'm not there, he could very well hang for a murder he didn't commit."

"He's one man. Hundreds are dying in France."

"If he were your brother, would you feel that same way?"

Devereaux countered, "Is he your brother?"

"He's my responsibility."

Devereaux got to his feet. "Shall I tell Major Gordon that you'll think our offer over?"

"I don't make promises I can't keep."

The Captain nodded. "I understand. Good luck in Moresby. I can honestly say that I hope your man doesn't hang."

He walked out, shutting the door behind him.

Rutledge stared after him for a long time, then turned his attention to his preparations for Moresby.

They had never really made peace with each other over Dobson, he and Bowles. Sefton and the Torquay police had done everything in their power to find the man, even walking into darkened cinemas and crowded concerts. They kept a watch on the boats in Tor Bay. They took a dozen men into custody, only to be told by Chasten, rushed to the station each time to look at them, that they'd picked up the wrong person.

Bowles had quietly closed the still open inquiries—the blackened graves, the murders of Stoddard, Tattersall, and Hadley. He'd closed as well the attempted murder of Fillmore Gilbert. But he'd stubbornly drawn the line at Kingston.

When he reached the seaside town with its magnificent ruins high above on the cliff, Rutledge saw that the pleasure boats had vanished, and the fishing fleet was tied up in the harbor. War had come here too.

The trial was to be held in the tiny courthouse. The afternoon before it was to open, Rutledge walked up to the headland and spent an hour in the abbey ruins. He hadn't seen Inspector Farraday. He hadn't expected that he would.

In the morning, quite early, he'd dressed, then eaten his breakfast in the hotel dining room before walking up to the courthouse. There was a throng of people waiting to find seats. He moved through them to the doors and gave his name. Passed through to where witnesses waited, he found himself face-to-face with Mrs. Kingston, her expression smug. She recognized him, but he said nothing to her. He was waiting for Fred Chasten to appear. He hadn't been at the hotel last night, and Rutledge was not certain that he would keep his promise to come.

At the last minute, he walked in, his face pale, the freckles standing out starkly. The bruises had faded. "I didn't want to come," he said quietly to Rutledge. "I don't want to relive what happened. If it weren't for the need to keep the bakery going, I think I'd have gone mad. But Terrence told me it was my duty. He drove me here himself."

"It was good of you to do this," Rutledge said. And he meant it.

As it was, they spent the day waiting for the summons that never came. The prosecution was presenting its case, and Mrs. Kingston was one of the earliest to be called. Her husband, Tad, came in after she had gone. He saw Rutledge and walked over to sit down beside him.

"I couldn't stop her," he said. "But once this is over, I will not live with her any longer. I'd told the lawyers that I wouldn't sit in the same room with her. I've been cooling my heels in a back corridor." He twisted his hat around and around in his hands. "You believed in Mark. I know that. But public opinion has been against him. Benjamin Clayton and his family are well liked. If I hadn't taken my cousin to his father that day, he wouldn't have seen him at all."

"Was he forgiven?" Rutledge asked, finding he really wanted to know.

"He was. It was too late to change the will, but Mark told his father he'd begun a new life in Scarborough, and didn't think he'd make a good farmer. When—if—this is finished, I'll go with him myself to speak to his former employer. Hartle."

"Good man."

It was not until midmorning of the next day that the defense was given its turn. Tad Kingston was called first, and soon after that, Rutledge took the witness box.

Kingston looked haggard. He stood in the dock stoically, his gaze fixed straight ahead. Rutledge wondered if he had taken in any of the proceedings.

He gave his evidence clearly and objectively, explaining why he had gone to Bristol, and why it had taken so very long to find out the truth about Henry Dobson.

"Where is Dobson now?" he was asked.

"I wish I knew. He has much to answer for."

"And you are convinced that Benjamin Clayton was on his list of victims."

"You have been given a list of the jurors in that particular trial. Clayton's name is there." He went on, outlining the similarities in the deaths of the other victims. "It's difficult for me to believe, as a police officer, that Benjamin Clayton could have been killed by anyone else. If Mr. Kingston had broken into that house to steal money, he would have killed Clayton quickly and got himself out of there. And where did the rope come from in the first place? Hardly the tool of someone breaking and entering."

The prosecution tried to trip him up, but Rutledge was prepared for that and stated flatly that he'd warned Inspector Farraday that the inquiry was ongoing and that it would be premature to make an arrest at that early stage.

The neighbor who had met Dobson on the street gave her evidence in a quiet and steady voice.

"I didn't know," she said, "I didn't know who he was or why he was asking questions. I thought he was a nice young man."

She was asked if she had ever seen the defendant on the street where Clayton lived. She shook her head. "I'm afraid not."

It was Fred Chasten's evidence that stunned the court. He gave it in the husky voice of a man struggling not to let the memory overwhelm him. "Dobson meant what he said. His threat wasn't an idle one. As I know to my cost."

When the courtroom had quieted down, Rutledge slipped out. He had no doubt of the verdict now.

And he was right. The jury debated for fewer than two hours before finding Kingston not guilty of the murder of Benjamin Clayton.

It was Michael Clayton who came to speak to him on the street as Rutledge was putting his valise into the motorcar.

"I'll find him," he said earnestly. "If it takes the rest of my life."

"And then what? Will you hang for his murder?"

"I'll drag him to the nearest police station so that he can hang like his father before him."

Rutledge didn't see Fred Chasten again.

He stopped for the night in York, and spent most of it standing at the only window in his hotel room, looking down on the silent city, the Monk Bar Gate looming dark and massive just outside.

When he slept it was peacefully for the first time in weeks.

There were three other people now who could identify Dobson when he was found. Gilbert and the Chasten brothers. The sketch that appeared in newspapers across England wasn't a good likeness in Rutledge's opinion, and so far hadn't produced any trustworthy sightings. There wouldn't be another chance to find him: Dobson had done what he had set out to do, and while Gilbert and the Chastens were still alive, he seemed to feel no pressing need to finish what he'd started. And he was a master at disappearing, as he'd shown so many times before. It was possible the police would never find him. But he would stay on the list of wanted men. Even Bowles couldn't prevent that.

Rutledge slept in his own bed that night.

And the next morning, he went to the Yard, set all his files in order, finished his report on the Clayton trial, and then wrote to Mrs. Hadley, Miss Tattersall, and the vicars in the villages of Netherby and Beecham. He had promised them answers, but he had not taken anyone into custody. Still, he could set their minds at ease by telling them who had been behind these murders and the vandalism that preceded it.

That done, he shut his door behind him and walked down the passage to Cummins's office.

He wasn't at his desk, and Rutledge asked Sergeant Gibson if Cummins was expected back soon.

"Sorry, sir, I believe he's in meetings for the rest of the day. Is it anything urgent, sir?"

"Urgent? No. I'll leave him a note, I think."

He went back upstairs into Cummins's office, and after shutting the door, he sat down at the desk, found a sheet of paper and an envelope, only to sit there staring at nothing, the pen drying in his hand.

And then he began to write. Without rereading it, he folded the sheet, put it in the envelope, and wrote Cummins's name on the front before sealing it. He left it in the corner of the blotter, where it would be noticed as soon as Cummins walked through the door.

He had left his motorcar close by St. Margaret's Church. Just as he reached it, he saw Kate coming toward him from the direction of Westminster Abbey. She was dressed in black, and he realized that she must have just come from a memorial service for someone. There were more and more of those for the war dead buried in France.

She smiled and waved, hurrying to catch him up before he could turn the crank.

"You're not leaving London again, are you?" she called. "You've just come back."

"Not at the moment," he said. "Later, perhaps."

Something in his face must have given him away. Rutledge saw that at once, and cursed himself for waiting for her. She didn't need to say good-bye so soon to another friend on his way to the Front.

Then he realized that it went deeper than friendship.

"Ian?" she said, stricken. "Please, tell me Jean hasn't convinced you to do something rash. Have you seen the casualty lists in the newspapers? It's been dreadful, all that killing. I don't think I could bear it if— " She broke off, before she could say something she would forever regret. Turning away, she stared in the direction of the river, struggling to recover her self-possession. They could hear the river traffic from where they stood, and feel the cold wind off the water.

Neither one of them spoke.

Rutledge wanted to comfort her, but he knew he couldn't. Shouldn't. To try would only embarrass her more.

After a moment, she looked up at him, shielding her eyes with her hand, searching his face. And then she said, as if it was what she'd intended all along,

"I couldn't bear it if I had to break dreadful news to Jean."

"It will be all right," he responded, and reached out to touch her shoulder, a comradely gesture.

After a moment, she added brightly, "I'm sure it will be. I'm sure you'll come home safely to Jean and to Frances." She stood on tiptoe then and kissed his cheek.

"Godspeed." And then she was hurrying back the way she'd come, and he saw that several other young women dressed in black, one of them heavily veiled, were just coming out of the Abbey. Kate slowed her pace before reaching them, and he thought she must be giving herself time to recover.

He'd always been fond of Kate. He'd always enjoyed her company.

He had never meant to hurt her.

Cranking the motorcar, he got in and drove away.

It had been a sobering encounter. For an instant, waiting for Kate to come up to him, he'd had a fleeting glimpse of Jean in mourning. It had reinforced his resolve to ask her to wait until he came home again to marry him.

His first stop was the house his parents had left to his sister. Frances was out, busy with the charities and fund-raisers that had begun to transform the London social scene.

There was a message on the table in the hall. She was at a meeting of her knitting committee and would return well before dinner.

He was about to break his promise to her. He'd wanted a chance to explain. But perhaps it was better, perhaps it would be easier this way.

Rutledge left the house and went to find Captain Devereaux.

An hour later he went to tell Jean what he'd done.

She threw her arms around him and held him close for a moment. "An officer. Ian, I'm so proud of you. I can't wait to tell Mama—to write to Papa. And at Christmas, when we're married, we'll have sabers after all." Jean laughed, looking up at him. "You don't know how much I love you."

It could wait until tomorrow, he thought. Asking her to put off the wedding for a bit. She might even suggest it herself. Her father was a soldier. She would know the risks without being told, and understand that it wasn't death he feared. It was returning to England, to her, less a man, maimed and ugly in her eyes.

He was standing there, his arms around her, watching her face, watching happiness brightening her eyes and bringing a flush to her cheeks, when he remembered something Captain Devereaux had said.

"War is a bloody business, Rutledge. But you already know something about that. You'll hold steady when the time comes."

He learned later that Captain Devereaux had never been to France.

And the man was wrong. Dealing with murder victims, bad as it was, didn't hold a candle to war.

22

Boxing Day, December 26, 1914

Heavy gray clouds hung over London, promising more rain, and the Thames was an ugly pewter ribbon running through the city. Even the streets, gleaming in the uncertain morning light, were dreary, and passersby hurried about their business with heads down, as if burdened by their own thoughts.

At Victoria Station, the steam from the locomotive festooned the damp air, with nowhere to go because there was no breeze to move it along. The platform was crowded with families there to say good-bye to loved ones in uniform, trying to find the right words for men bound for Dover and Folkestone and the transports for France.

Fighting had been heavy throughout the autumn, and casualty lists in the newspapers made somber reading. The martial euphoria of

August, when the war had begun, promising to be an easy victory, had not survived for very long. The rush to enlist had become conscription. Like so many others, Rutledge had been glad he hadn't waited, that he had made his own decision to go.

Training was finished. He was a newly minted Lieutenant, with a company waiting for him in France. Highlanders, he'd been told. Good fighting men, so good it was said the Germans feared them. They went into battle in their regimental kilts, pipes skirling. He'd wondered what such men would make of an English officer. At least he'd spent some time in the Highlands, including summers with David Trevor and his son, Ross. He could understand the people who lived in such places.

Now as they made their way toward the carriages, Jean held tightly to Rutledge's hand. He could see that she was fighting back tears.

"Don't cry," he said, bracingly, smiling down at her, trying to sound reassuring. "You promised you wouldn't. I'll be home before you know it. This can't last much longer."

But he knew it could now. And very likely would.

The war was fast becoming a stalemate as each side dug in, unable to move forward, refusing to retreat. The lists of dead, wounded, and missing had cast a pall over the holidays, and here in the last few days of the old year, men heading for the Front were no longer expecting to cover themselves with glory and in a matter of weeks, march back into London to the cheers of a grateful nation.

He'd said good-bye to Frances and to Melinda Crawford at the house. They had discussed it and decided it was best that way. Melinda had told him how handsome he looked, and Frances had made him promise to come home safely. He'd read the worry in their eyes even as they tried to hide it.

Jean had been waiting for him outside the station when he got there.

Rutledge led her to a sheltered spot by the canteen door, his arm and his rank protecting her as the crowd grew larger the closer it came for time to board.

A company of Scots marched by, kilts swinging, and boarded the train. He knew they were new recruits. Their faces were apprehensive, not haunted.

"I'll miss you," he said quietly. "Don't worry if you don't hear from me straightaway or as often as you'd like. The post is regulated—censors—that sort of thing. It will mean delays. But I promise you I *will* write. Remember that."

She lifted her head and clutched at him, the finality of enlisting coming home to her at last. "I wish you hadn't volunteered. You needn't have. You were needed at Scotland Yard."

"You thought it was a splendid idea at the time," he reminded her, only half teasing.

"Yes, everyone was volunteering. It was exciting, exhilarating. The flags—the music. All the uniforms. I thought it would all be over before you saw any fighting. I thought it was all a lark. And now it's real." She began to cry. "You must come back to me, Ian. You must promise. I can't imagine life without you."

"Jean—my dear." It was he who had insisted that they postpone their Christmas wedding. He knew how much it had hurt her. But he'd seen the wounded coming back to England. He'd visited two hospitals where friends had been taken, and it was a sobering sight. He'd tried to explain, and she hadn't understood that he couldn't tie her to the wreckage he might so easily become. She had wanted to be his wife, and he was grateful, more grateful than he could say. But he also wanted her to have a choice. And if they were already married, that choice would be taken from her. He thought he could stand anything but pity. She deserved so much more.

A whistle blew, signaling that the remaining troops should board.

Rutledge took Jean's hands. "My love." He kissed her fingers and then her cheek. And suddenly she was in his arms, he wasn't quite sure how it had happened, and all the pent-up longing and loss swept him. And that kiss was very different.

Afterward, holding her at arm's length, he said huskily, "Good-bye."

And before she could say anything, or knew what he was about, he turned and walked swiftly toward the train without looking back.

He told himself that it was best for both of them.

T he landing in Calais went smoothly despite what appeared to be chaos in every direction, made worse by patches of mist that clung here and opened there, a hazard to men and machines, as well as the horses. Troops and stores were being off-loaded, wounded waiting to be carried on board, vehicles of every description clogging the streets near the port, refugees trying to find lodgings. It had been a rough crossing, many of the men seasick, including a few of the Scots who'd never been aboard a ship before.

He'd spent part of the voyage standing at the railing of the ship, watching England recede into the storm clouds obscuring the white cliffs. One of the Highlanders, a man nearly as tall as he was, had come to stand near him. They didn't speak. Not until France loomed ahead, a blur of coastline.

There had been a spot of trouble below, but neither of them referred to it now.

Above the sound of the sea, they could hear the guns. Artillery. He couldn't be sure whether it was British fire or German.

The Scot glanced at him. "Our turn, soon enough. Good luck to ye, sir."

"The same to you, Private MacLeod."

He'd just come down the gangway and was searching for his transport when he saw the man.

He was being helped out of an ambulance and onto a stretcher. He had a heavily bandaged foot and wasn't able to walk.

Rutledge recognized him straightaway.

Dobson must have felt his gaze, for he turned his head and their eyes met.

The man on the stretcher scowled but said nothing.

Just as Rutledge was turning away, a shot rang out, startlingly loud even in the chaos of the port, echoing against the cliffs above and sending the gulls into swirling flight. Rutledge whirled in time to see Dobson jerk, then fall back on the stretcher.

Soldiers were already hurrying to search the quay for whoever had fired the shot. In the mists he could be anywhere. Orderlies were still working feverishly over Dobson, but it was too late. There was nothing they could do for him. Even as Rutledge walked on, he saw one of them shake his head, then reach for the edge of a blanket, drawing it over Dobson's face.

Rutledge didn't stop. He was no longer an Inspector at Scotland Yard. He was a Lieutenant in the British Army.

Cummins would see Dobson's name in the listings of dead and wounded, and know it was finished. He had searched the lists since Dobson had disappeared the last time, without much hope of ever finding his name there.

He was just stepping into his transport when something made him turn and look back.

Michael Clayton, in the uniform of a medical orderly, was leaning against the side of a shed that had once been used by French customs and was now a staging area for the wounded. At his feet was a jumble of kits waiting to be taken down to the quays and loaded aboard. Not two yards from him was a soldier slumped against the same wall, head to one side in an exhausted sleep. His rifle lay across his knees.

It was a little backwater, no one else around, but it had an excellent view down to where a cluster of men stood, looking at the crumpled body lying at their feet.

How had he known—?

Then Rutledge realized that Clayton must have been among the orderlies who had just helped unload the train of wounded. There would have been a tag around the neck of every man, with his name, his rank, his regiment, and his wound. Easy enough to read. A word, a whispered question, and Clayton would have seen the reaction. Would have known he had the right man.

Scotland Yard had no authority here.

Rutledge got into the lorry, greeted his driver, and they began the long journey to the North and the waiting war.

About the author

About the book

Insights,
Interviews
& More . . .

Read on

Meet Charles Todd

CHARLES TODD is the *New York Times* bestselling author of the Inspector Ian Rutledge mysteries, the Bess Crawford mysteries, and two stand-alone novels. A mother-and-son writing team, they live in Delaware and North Carolina. ∾

Looking Back
An Essay from the Authors

WE BEGAN THE STORY of Inspector Ian Rutledge in June 1919, with his return to Scotland Yard at the end of the Great War. In *A Test of Wills*, we meet him as a shattered man striving with all his strength to pick up the pieces of a life that disappeared four years earlier, although everyone at the time was sure the war would change England very little, that what men were fighting and dying for would keep that world safe forever.

The war itself had ended on November 11, 1918. Rutledge had spent much of the time between November and June in the hospital, nearly mad from severe shell shock, what we know today as post-traumatic stress disorder. And for that reason, we'd decided to do something unusual—instead of letting a year pass with every book, as many series do, we wanted to tell the story more slowly, to see how this interesting man handled his healing. After all, he was not even thirty years old. And yet there was always the very real chance that he would take his service revolver out to the back garden and put an end to his suffering. Many men like him did just that.

Sixteen books into the series, when we thought we knew Rutledge pretty well, we found ourselves thinking, *Here we've been writing about him and how* ▶

the war had changed him—but we've never actually seen him as he must have been that fine summer's day in June 1914, when he was still unaware of the gunshots in Sarajevo, or that warm evening in August when war was declared, or that moment in the autumn when he had to make a choice: to hunt down killers for the Yard, or become one in the trenches.

What sort of person had he been then? Who were the people in his life, who loved him and who feared him, who cared about his career, who dreaded what they saw in his future? And who on the happiest day of Rutledge's life faced instead a crushing past that would drive him to murder?

Much to our surprise, *A Fine Summer's Day* showed us that we still had much to learn about Ian Rutledge, that policeman who had become such a force in our own lives. Every chapter was intriguing, exciting, absorbing. By the time we'd written "The End" on that very last page, it had become a bittersweet and yet very satisfying look back. We liked the man we'd discovered.

We return to 1920 with the next Rutledge, and it's going to be a great book to write. ∽

Reading Group Guide

1. What do you think of this younger Rutledge compared to the character in previous books?

2. Why don't Ian's friends approve of Jean as a wife for him? Why is he so drawn to her? Is she the sort of woman who attracts strong men? What do you think Rutledge's life would have been like if he'd never gone to war and had married Jean?

3. What do you think of Hamish in 1914? How does he compare to the voice that Rutledge hears in his head after the war? Does his cameo here make his death more tragic?

4. Why does Kingston's family treat him as an outcast? How does this affect Ian's opinion of him?

5. How does the perception of the war shift over the course of the novel? Does anyone anticipate the true toll it will take on individuals, England, and Europe as a whole?

6. Rutledge has some disagreements and tense relationships with his superiors at Scotland Yard. What does this reveal about the young Ian Rutledge? He's also given good advice about dealing with them in the future. Do you think that it will work?

7. Why is Rutledge reluctant to enlist in the army, despite Jean's urging? Do you think she is justified in ▶

calling him a coward? Why does he eventually change his mind?

8. What technique does Dobson use to gain access to his victims' houses? How does Rutledge discover his methods?

9. Why does Rutledge fake Mr. Gilbert's death?

10. How did Dobson force his victims to drink the laudanum? Do you think he would have followed through on his threats? Was that why he hanged his first victim?

11. Why does Rutledge feel responsible for proving Kingston's innocence? Even at the risk of his career?

12. Do you think Michael Clayton was justified in killing Dobson? Was it vengeance or justice? ∾

The History of Inspector Ian Rutledge

A Complete Timeline of Major Events

June 1919—*A Test of Wills*

Ian Rutledge, returning home from the trenches of the Great War, loses his fiancée, Jean, after long months in hospital with what is now called PTSD and faces a bleak future. Fighting back from the edge of madness, he returns to his career at Scotland Yard. But Chief Superintendent Bowles is determined to break him. And so Rutledge finds himself in Warwickshire, where the only witness to the murder of Colonel Harris is a drunken ex-soldier suffering from shell shock. Rutledge is fighting his own battles with the voice of Corporal Hamish MacLeod in his head, survivor's guilt after the bloody 1916 Battle of the Somme. The question is, will he win this test of wills with Hamish—or is the shell-shocked witness a mirror of what he'll become if he fails to keep his madness at bay?

July 1919—*Wings of Fire*

Rutledge is sent to Cornwall because the Home Office wants to be reassured that Nicholas Cheney wasn't murdered. But Nicholas committed suicide with his half sister, Olivia. And she's written a body of war poetry under the name of O. A. Manning. Rutledge, who had used her poetry in the trenches to keep his ▶

mind functioning, is shocked to discover she never saw France and may well be a cold-blooded killer. And yet even dead, she makes a lasting impression that he can't shake.

August 1919—*Search the Dark*

An out-of-work ex-soldier, sitting on a train in a Dorset station, suddenly sees his dead wife and two small children standing on the platform. He fights to get off the train, and soon thereafter the woman is found murdered and the children are missing. Rutledge is sent to coordinate a search and finds himself attracted to Aurore, a French war bride who will lie to protect her husband and may have killed because she was jealous of the murder victim's place in her husband's life.

September 1919—*Legacy of the Dead*

Just as Rutledge thinks he has come to terms—of a sort—with the voice that haunts him, he's sent to northern England to find the missing daughter of a woman who once slept with a king. Little does he know that his search will take him to Scotland, and to the woman Hamish would have married if he'd lived. But Fiona is certain to hang for murdering a mother to steal her child, and she doesn't know that Rutledge killed Hamish on the battlefield when she turns to him for help. He couldn't save Hamish—but Rutledge is honor bound to protect Fiona and the small child named for him.

October 1919—*Watchers of Time*

Still recovering from the nearly fatal wound he received in Scotland, Rutledge is sent to East Anglia to discover who murdered a priest and what the priest's death had to do with a dying man who knew secrets about the family that owns the village. But there's more to the murder than hearing a deathbed confession. And the key might well be a young woman as haunted as Rutledge is, because she survived the sinking of the *Titanic* and carries her own guilt for failure to save a companion.

November 1919—*A Fearsome Doubt*

A case from 1912 comes back to haunt Rutledge. Did he send an innocent man to the gallows? Meanwhile, he's trying to discover who has poisoned three ex-soldiers, all of them amputees in a small village in Kent. Mercy killings or murder? And he sees a face across the Guy Fawkes Day bonfire that is a terrifying reminder of what happened to him at the end of the war . . . something he is ashamed of, even though he can't remember why. What happened in the missing six months of his life?

December 1919—*A Cold Treachery*

Rutledge is already in the north and the closest man to Westmorland, where at the height of a blizzard, there has been a cold-blooded killing of an entire family, save one child, who is missing in the snow. But as the facts unfold, it's possible that the boy killed his own family. And where is he? Dead in the snow or hiding? And there are secrets in this isolated village of Urskdale that can lead to more deaths.

January 1920—*A Long Shadow*

A party that begins innocently enough ends with Rutledge finding machine gun casings engraved with death's-heads—a warning. But he's sent to Northamptonshire to discover why someone shot Constable Ward with an arrow in what the locals call a haunted wood. He discovers there are other deaths unaccounted for, and there's also a woman who knows too much about Rutledge for his own comfort. Then whoever has been stalking him comes north after him, and Rutledge knows if he doesn't find the man, he'll die. Hamish, pushing him hard, is all too aware that Rutledge's death will mean his own.

March 1920—*A False Mirror*

A man is nearly beaten to death, his wife is taken hostage by his assailant, and Rutledge is sent posthaste to Hampton Regis to find out who wanted Matthew Hamilton dead. But the man who may be guilty is someone Rutledge knew in the war, a reminder that some were lucky enough to be saved while ▶

Hamish was left to die. But this is a story of love gone wrong, and the next two deaths reek of madness. Are they? Or were the women mistaken for the intended victim?

April 1920—*A Pale Horse*

In the ruins of Yorkshire's Fountains Abbey lies the body of a man wrapped in a cloak, the face covered by a gas mask. Next to him is a book on alchemy, which belongs to the schoolmaster, a conscientious objector in the Great War. Who is this man, and is the investigation into his death being manipulated by a thirst for revenge? Meanwhile, the British War Office is searching for a missing man of their own, someone whose war work was so secret that even Rutledge isn't told his real name or what he did. Here is a puzzle requiring all of Rutledge's daring and skill, for there are layers of lies and deception, while a ruthless killer is determined to hold on to freedom at any cost.

May 1920—*A Matter of Justice*

At the turn of the century, in a war taking place far from England, two soldiers chance upon an opportunity that will change their lives forever. To take advantage of it, they will do the unthinkable and then put the past behind them. Twenty years later, a successful London businessman is found savagely and bizarrely murdered in a medieval tithe barn on his estate in Somerset. Called upon to investigate, Rutledge soon discovers that the victim was universally despised. Even the man's wife— who appears to be his wife in name only—and the town's police inspector are suspect. But who among the many hated enough to kill?

June 1920—*The Red Door*

In a house with a red door lies the body of a woman who has been bludgeoned to death. Rumor has it that two years earlier, she'd painted that door to welcome her husband back from the Front. Only he never came home. Meanwhile, in London, a man suffering from a mysterious illness goes missing and then just as suddenly reappears. Rutledge must solve two mysteries before he can bring a ruthless killer to justice: Who was the woman who lived and died behind the red door? Who was the man who never came home from the Great War, for the simple reason that he might never have gone? And what have they to do with a man who cannot break the seal of his own guilt without damning those he loves most?

July 1920—*A Lonely Death*

Three men have been murdered in a Sussex village, and Scotland Yard has been called in. The victims are soldiers, each surviving the nightmare of World War I only to meet a ghastly end in the quiet English countryside. Each man has been garroted, with a small ID disk left in his mouth, yet no other clue suggests a motive or a killer. Rutledge understands all too well the darkness that resides within men's souls. Yet his presence on the scene cannot deter a vicious and clever killer, and a fourth dead soldier is discovered shortly after Rutledge's arrival. Now a horror that strikes painfully close to home threatens to engulf the investigator, and he will have to risk his career, his good name, even his shattered life itself, to bring an elusive fiend to justice.

August 1920—*The Confession*

A man walks into Scotland Yard and confesses that he killed his cousin five years ago during the Great War. When Rutledge presses for details, the man evades his questions, revealing only that he hails from a village east of London. Less than two weeks later, the alleged killer's body is found floating in the Thames, a bullet in the back of his head. Rutledge discovers that the dead man was not who he claimed to be. The only clue is a gold locket, found around the victim's neck, that leads back to Essex and an insular village that will do anything to protect itself from notoriety.

Summer 1920—*Proof of Guilt*

An unidentified man appears to have been run down by a motorcar, and a clue leads Rutledge to a firm, built by two families, famous for producing and selling the world's best Madeira wine. There he discovers that the current head of the English enterprise is missing. But is he the dead man? And do either his fiancée or his jilted former lover have anything to do with his disappearance? ▶

The History of Inspector Ian Rutledge
(continued)

With a growing list of suspects, Rutledge knows that suspicion and circumstantial evidence are nothing without proof of guilt. But his new acting chief superintendent doesn't agree and wants Rutledge to stop digging and settle on the easy answer. Rutledge must tread very carefully, for it seems that someone has decided that he, too, must die so that justice can take its course.

August 1920—*Hunting Shadows*

A society wedding at Ely Cathedral becomes a crime scene when a guest is shot. After a fruitless search for clues, the local police call in Scotland Yard, but not before there is another shooting in a village close by. This second murder has a witness, but her description of the killer is so horrific it's unbelievable. Inspector Ian Rutledge can find no connection between the two deaths. One victim was an army officer, the other a solicitor standing for Parliament. Is there a link between these murders, or is it only in the mind of a clever killer? As the investigation presses on, Rutledge finds memories of the war beginning to surface. Struggling to contain the darkness that haunts him as he hunts for the missing link, he discovers the case turning in a most unexpected direction. Now he must put his trust in the devil in order to find the elusive and shocking answer. ◆

Discover great authors, exclusive offers, and more at hc.com.